ACCLAIM FOR *MY NAME IS WILL*

"A hilarious book."

—*New York Daily News*

"Cleverly structured . . . Winfield slings bucketfuls of double-entendres and wily puns . . . Chapter by chapter, Winfield fashions tantalizing, ironic parallels between the two Wills . . . Winfield's high-spirited tribute is a celebration of the power of language and story . . . He knows how to snare and enrapture an audience."

—*Los Angeles Times Book Review*

"Here is literary blasphemy full of raunch, cheek, and hilarity . . . larky, witty, punning outrage."

—*Buffalo News*

"To say that Jess Winfield knows his Shakespeare is laughable understatement. Upside down—boy, he knows him, inside out, and round and round . . . In MY NAME IS WILL, Winfield may be accused of treating his favorite literary lion unceremoniously. But, after all, no gentleman is a hero to his varlet . . . a lusty, pun-drunk first novel."

—*New York Times Book Review*

"The author pulls off a potentially clumsy conceit with nuance and panache."

—*Washington Post*

"Irreverence, humor, and literary gusto . . . Winfield uses his deep understanding of Shakespeare's work and times to great effect."

—*Publishers Weekly*

"There are those who turn out for the Shakespeare, and others who are more interested in the Sex and Drugs, all of which are brilliantly blended by the author."

—*Contra Costa Times*

more . . .

"From across the pond and across the centuries, the words of Stratford-upon-Avon's most famous resident have never rung with such screwball truthiness as in MY NAME IS WILL . . . [This book] deftly avoids the musty bouquet of the library stacks as Winfield's twin heroes vault off the page in 3-D, Technicolor, surround-sound exuberance. With Winfield, as with his muse, wordplay's the thing, and both of his Shakespeares live by their wit—sharp-thinking, sharp-tongued observers in a world that seems alternately obliging and oppressive."

—*BookPage*

"Lively, smart, and mature . . . William is utterly convincing as a character: callow and a bit lost, but witty and kind, and fully possessed of the ability to charm or flay with words . . . [In] the chapters on Shakespeare . . . the book comes to life with intelligence, humor, and high stakes."

—*New York Sun*

"The sex throughout is well done and not for the prim . . . Winfield delights in puns from low to high ("iamb what iamb"), and cleverly sprinkles conversations in the earlier age with lines that would later turn up in the plays . . . From the Renaissance Faire to the countless theses and Winfield's Reduced Shakespeare and every snippet, sonnet, or trope any one of us can toss off, the Bard abides."

—*Chicago Tribune*

"[Winfield] brings an intimate knowledge of the Bard as well as an infectious sense of humor to this witty first novel."

—*Booklist*

"A politically charged, irreverent, and humorous romp."

—*Folger Magazine*

"A hyperkinetic novel . . . We find several echoes here of the brilliant David Lodge, who also makes hay with academics' fumbling attempts at literary and sexual congress. But this particular brand of silly, filthy fun is Winfield's own . . . Is there another author today who would begin a tale of Shakespeare and self-discovery with two naughty references to the human anatomy and one use of a controlled substance? As earthy, snarky Winfield knows, while most authors reach for the brave o'erhanging firmament, sometimes it's better to just hit Bottom."

—Lizzie Skurnick, NPR.org, "Books We Like"

"MY NAME IS WILL is more than mere entertainment . . . Winfield has made Shakespeare an intimate of our day and age; but more, he has accomplished something the great playwright himself was master of— reworking his plays for new audiences."

—*Santa Cruz Sentinel*

"Witty . . . The narrative's ingenious achievement is to suggest how, by saturation in the past, a youthful rebel in Elizabethan Stratford and one in modern Berkeley can share comic misadventures, both paradoxically illuminating the historical Shakespeare family's inveterate Catholicism."

—Hugh Richmond, Shakespeare scholar and professor emeritus of English at UC Berkeley

"Winfield's tale is funny and interesting . . . Winfield's own love of Shakespeare, love of words, and love of theater shine through. He plays with words and captures the feeling of the times and places he is setting the action in, yet the themes remain timeless . . . This is a book that even Shakespeare may have enjoyed."

—BookReporter.com

MY NAME IS

A Novel of Sex,
Drugs, and
Shakespeare

WILL

JESS WINFIELD

TWELVE

New York   Boston

Copyright © 2008 by Jess Winfield
Reading Group Guide copyright © 2009 by Hachette Book Group, Inc.

Faire Opening Song ("Awake, Awake!") copyright © 1973, 1993 by Jon DeCles. Used by permission.

Twelve
Hachette Book Group
237 Park Avenue
New York, NY 10017

Visit our Web site at www.HachetteBookGroup.com.

Twelve is an imprint of Grand Central Publishing.
The Twelve name and logo are trademarks of Hachette Book Group, Inc.
Printed in the United States of America

Originally published in hardcover by Twelve.

First Trade Edition: July 2009
10 9 8 7 6 5 4 3 2 1

The Library of Congress has cataloged the hardcover edition as follows:
Winfield, Jess.
    My name is Will : a novel of sex, drugs, and Shakespeare / Jess Winfield. — 1st ed.
        p. cm.
    ISBN 978-0-446-50885-8
    1. Graduate students—Fiction. I. Title.
    PS3623.I64M9 2008
    813'.6—dc22

                                                                    2008000416

ISBN 978-0-446-50883-4 (pbk.)

Book design by Ralph Fowler/rlf design

In memory of my mother,

Lillian Borgeson,

who once told me I could write a novel.

MY NAME IS WILL

Part One

SEX AND DRUGS

Chapter One

Where is any author in the world
Teaches such beauty as a woman's eye?
Learning is but an adjunct to ourself
And where we are our learning likewise is:
Then when ourselves we see in ladies' eyes,
Do we not likewise see our learning there?
O, we have made a vow to study, lords,
And in that vow we have forsworn our books.

— Berowne, *Love's Labour's Lost*, IV.iii.308

Willie sat in the back row of a blocky white minibus, his hand cupped around the enormous psychedelic mushroom hidden under a denim jacket laid too casually across his lap. The *Psilocybe cubensis* was fresh, not dried; sweating slightly, it was smooth and moist to the touch. It possessed, he thought, a comforting fullness, an ancient, earthy quality. He felt a little high just touching it. Though he didn't know it, the mushroom's cap was exactly the size and shape of Queen Elizabeth I's left tit.

Willie also didn't know that the guy sitting up front, near the driver, was a narc.

And he also didn't know quite how he — a graduate student in literature, and according to his mother, the next William Shakespeare — had ended up as a drug runner.

But he did know that the woman sitting next to him was giving him a boner.

Just two days earlier, he'd been in the office of Clarence Welsh, professor of literature at the University of California, Santa Cruz. Welsh's office, in a third-floor crow's nest perched atop the jumbled modernist slabs of Kresge College, had a window with a bucolic view of the surrounding redwood forest and a glimpse of Monterey Bay in the distance; a view now entirely obscured, alas, by a stack of bound periodicals labeled *Journal of Shakespearean Studies* on their spines, with dates ranging from "1961–65" all the way to "1983–"

Willie heard the title of his proposed master's thesis read back to him aloud: "Shakespeare and the Crucifix: Catholic Persecution in Sixteenth-Century England and Its Effect on Elizabethan Theater."

Clarence Welsh was a smallish, rotund man. His greasy, dandruff-flecked hair looked as though it had been cut by a drunken gardener with a rusty hedge trimmer. His face was red with English jollity and suppressed perversion.

Willie liked Clarence Welsh.

But the voice speaking in Professor Welsh's office was not that of Clarence Welsh. At this precise moment, Welsh was spilling his fifth glass of wine at a luncheon in San Francisco celebrating the publication of his latest book, *Getting Bottom: Bestiality in* A Midsummer Night's Dream.

No, the voice speaking in Welsh's office belonged to his top-gun doctoral candidate, Dashka Demitra. She was covering for Welsh during his book tour, and her duties included vetting the topic for Willie's long-overdue master's thesis. She handed back the one-page proposal without finishing it.

"What have you been smoking?"

Willie opened his mouth, then thought better and closed it again. The answer was "Lebanese hashish." He'd smoked a little—just one hit, to clear his head—before the meeting.

Dashka leaned back in Clarence Welsh's chair—it went *squeeeeeeeeeee*—and crossed her legs, exposing a flash of inner thigh in the process. She rocked back and forth a little in the chair—*squee squee squee squee*—"Look...sorry, what's your last name?" she asked as she picked up a dog-eared list off the desk and flipped through it.

"Greenberg."

She scanned quickly until she found his name on the list, then stopped and looked up at him. She said it deliberately, wrapping her lips around the words:

"William . . . *Shakespeare* . . . Greenberg?" Dashka blinked. "That's quite a name. Your —"

"I know," Willie interrupted. "I'm Shakespeare, my thesis had better be good."

"Actually, I was going to ask what your parents were thinking."

"They're Jewish. Mom was an Anglophile." Willie shifted in his chair. "My friends call me Willie."

"Willie," Dashka repeated, with an almost imperceptible raise of her eyebrow, letting the name hang in the air for a moment.

Squee. Squee.

Then, referring to the paper: "I'm sure it's an interesting area — your thesis, that is —"

"I think it's valid," Willie interrupted. "Shakespeare was a Catholic, and there's a level where his writing is all about —"

Dashka interrupted him back. "Every bio I've ever read suggests he was Church of England. All his scriptural quotations are from a Protestant Bible."

"Right, right . . ." said Willie, trying to collect fuzzy thoughts. It hadn't even occurred to him that there were "Catholic" and "Protestant" Bibles. He could feel the go-ahead slipping away, and his degree and career along with it. He had put off getting the approval until the last possible week. If this pitch didn't fly . . .

"Right, but I think that was just a cover," he continued, his voice heavy in the cramped, musty room. "His mother's family at least — the Ardens — they were Catholic, right? But he couldn't just go around spewing quotes from the . . . the Catholic Bible, right? Because they were *executing* Catholics. Historically . . ."

"No-no-no-no," Dashka said, and waved her hands to interrupt him, partly to Willie's relief, as he had no idea what was going to come out of his mouth after "Historically," but much to his dread, that she would kill the proposal.

"Listen," began Dashka. She leaned forward again in the chair — *squeeeee* — and as she did so she dropped the list in her hand. When she bent to pick it up the top of her blouse fell away from her collarbone. It was unbuttoned to her sternum. Caught with his eyes deep in the cookie jar, Willie's gaze leaped up so quickly that he barely had time to register a black lace bra, a breast — evenly tanned to a golden brown, small yet not so small that it wasn't straining against the bra — and a cappuccino aureole peeking out from the lace like the muted disk of the sun on a foggy day.

She was still speaking, but Willie had forgotten to listen. He was thinking that UCSC women, while generally smart, funny, and talented, also tended toward the overweight, the frumpy, the geeky, the gawky, the Coke bottle–lensed, the makeup-challenged, the awkward, the mousy, the unshaven. But Dashka...he was hooked from the day she walked into one of Welsh's classes, silently left a stack of papers on his lectern, and swept out. Every eye in the room — straight, gay, and lesbian alike — followed her out the door. Even Welsh stole a glance.

Now, Willie took in the shining, raven-black hair, dyed with streaks of purple and green: a rocker's hair, somewhere on the Jett end of a Siouxsie Sioux/Kate Bush/Joan Jett axis. In fact, thought Willie, she looked just like the brunette from the Bangles. Blue eyes; not a pale blue but the unfathomable, dark, indigo blue of an alpine lake at twilight. Sparkle-green eye shadow. Bright red lipstick. And — right here at UC Santa Cruz, last bastion of Birkenstocks — green Doc Martens, hand painted with a black Maori tribal design. Add the palpable intellect of a fast-track doctoral student from a tony East Coast liberal arts college, and *Jesus*. In the time between two *squee*s of the chair, he'd thought of five different possible positions.

"Maybe they don't tell you this in the *master's* program," she said, "but since Wimsatt and Beardly and the ascendance of New Criticism, authorial intent and historical context carry very little weight in literary analysis." She took the cap off of her red pen, and shook her head. "I think maybe you should—"

In the instant before she could finish her sentence, her pen poised over the desk, Willie saw the life he hadn't yet lived flash before his eyes. The master's degree; the creative writing program; the grants and fellowships; the burgeoning life as scholar, playwright, poet, actor, modern day Renaissance man, truly the second coming of Shakespeare...gone in a puff of New Critical smoke.

"I've already done most of the research," he blurted.

A lie. He'd done no significant master's research for a year. He spent an hour or two a day buried in his *Riverside Shakespeare*, reading the plays, but mostly he smoked hash in his room and listened to music, living off his father's increasingly reluctant benefaction. The only thing he'd truly mastered was the Rubik's Cube. He did *think* about Shakespeare a lot while endlessly spinning rows of green squares and blue squares, yellow squares and white squares, trying to get them to line up—trying to get a grip on it, to figure it out: what was it that made Shakespeare great? What made him Shakespeare? That would be the key that would unlock the doors of Shakespeare's past, and his own future.

Dashka rocked back and forth slowly on the chair. *Squee... Squee...* considering.

"It'll be a whole new approach to literary evaluation. New Historic... al... ism," Willie said, piling layer of bs on layer of bs. Then the quote sprang unbidden to Willie's mind and from his lips: "The trust I have is in my innocence, and therefore am I bold and resolute."

Trying to hold Dashka's fathomless blue gaze in the pause that followed, he felt neither innocent nor bold nor resolute.

She finally asked, *"Henry VI, Part Three?"*

"Part Two," Willie replied.

Quoting Shakespeare seemed to have done the trick. As Dashka turned back to the desk he could have sworn she stole a quick glance down his body. He suddenly felt underdressed—green drawstring pants and inky denim jacket over a shredded Ramones tank top.

She shrugged. "Okay. It's your thesis. Who knows, maybe it'll be a masterpiece. I'll discuss it with the professor. He'll still have to give the final approval, so I suggest you talk to him the instant he gets back. If you want my advice, keep it focused on the text. Don't get caught up in the history. Text, text, text, right?"

Dashka set down her red pen, picked up one that matched her green Docs, and made a check mark on the list.

"I will," said Willie, relief flooding through his body like a drug rush. "Thanks." He gathered up his notebook, slipped the proposal inside, and shuffled it into his green nylon backpack. "I'll see you in section next week."

Willie wanted to get out before she changed her mind. As he stood, he zipped open the front pouch of his pack to slip his pen inside. But the main part of the backpack was still unzipped. The whole pack fell open, spilling out his notebook and the November issue of a hard-core porn rag. The magazine fluttered to the floor, open to a layout of two female Santa's elves in fur-trimmed, red-sequined spandex miniskirts, topless and flashing beaver, about to go down on a fully erect black shopping mall Santa. As Willie lurched forward to snatch up the magazine, something silvery flashed out of the backpack's open front pouch. He instinctively lunged to grab it out of midair.

Willie had quick hands. Four times out of five if he dropped a small item he could catch it before it hit the floor. But he had recently caught a dropped toothbrush, a pizza-parlor pepper shaker, a lighter, and a diaphragm case. This was the fifth time, and he only succeeded in knocking the item out of the air. He had a sinking, exhilarating feeling as it clattered across Clarence Welsh's desk and spun to a stop directly under Dashka Demitra's pen.

The item was Willie Shakespeare Greenberg's hash pipe.

Dashka looked at the pipe; then at the magazine; then at Willie.

"Sorry..." Willie said, reaching for the magazine.

But Dashka quickly leaned over and scooped it up first. She glanced at the cover. "They start in with the holiday porn earlier and earlier every year, don't they?" she said. She flipped to the Santa's elves spread. "Damn, I wonder how Santa gets *that* down the chimney." Then she closed the magazine and held it out for Willie with an inscrutable look.

As he put the magazine back in his pack, he weighed two options: he could walk out, utterly humiliated; or he could take one desperate stab at redemption.

Willie nodded toward the pipe still sitting on the desk. "So can I have my pipe back? Or did you want to sample that as well?"

Willie saw a spark in the depths of Dashka's eyes. She rocked back in her chair with a mischievous smile.

Squee.

Chapter Two

I will argue that 1582 was the year Shakespeare became Shakespeare. His coming of age didn't take place in a vacuum, nor in some idealized, pastoral-watercolor vision of Merry Olde England. The Stratford-upon-Avon of the Bard's youth was one of social turmoil and religious oppression. King Henry VIII had split with the Roman Catholic Church so that he might divorce his first wife and leave a male heir. He failed, and his daughter "Bloody" Mary I forced England back to Catholicism by burning hundreds of Protestants at the stake. On Mary's death, Henry's second daughter took the throne as Elizabeth I, returned the country to Protestantism, and established a network of spies and informants to enforce the state religion.

Eighteen-year-old William Shakespeare had a love/hate relationship with Latin.

He loved the language. Even the repetitive declension of demonstratives — *hic haec hoc, huius huius huius* — brought vague memories to his mind of the sweet smell of incense, wise men bearing strange Eastern unguents, and the taste of wine. But he hated teaching the lessons. As a student, he had always struggled with the tongue, and now keeping one step ahead of the older boys was a tail-chasing proposition. He still felt, in only his second term, more like one of the pupils than an assistant schoolmaster, or "usher," which was what he was.

William's students sat along the walls of the King's New School of Stratford-upon-Avon. It was the third day of the Michaelmas term — a nominal distinction, as the pale, bug-eyed little moppets attended school nearly year-round, six days a week from six a.m. to six p.m., less a half day on Thursday. On their "day off" they were expected to go to church and Sunday school.

The class was diving into Lyly's *A Short Introduction to Grammar*, the sine qua non of Elizabethan secular education. The three oldest boys held the school's three precious copies and read together aloud in the singsongy voice that afflicts all readers-together-aloud:

"An Introduction to the Numbers of Nouns. In nouns be two numbers; the singular, and the plural. The singular number speaketh of but one: as, *lapis*, a stone. The plural number speaketh of more than one: as, *lapides*, stones."

"Close the books," William Shakespeare commanded. A *thwap* as the students obliged. "Now how many numbers be there in nouns?"

There was an absolutely still silence. No one raised a hand. A few stole glances at their hornbooks. No help there; just a cheat sheet for the English alphabet, the Lord's Prayer, and the Roman numerals.

"Taught your masters naught in petty school? To read and retain? How many numbers be there in nouns!?"

"Two," said three or four voices—the older boys.

"Better. Ay. And what is *lapis*?"

"Stones," offered an especially pale boy.

"Nay," said William, "'tis but the singular, stone."

A wicked laugh from young Richard Wheeler, class ass. "Forgive him, for he is breechless, and knows not the stones of which you speak."

The reference, to the fact that the pale lad was still wearing a dress, as was the custom for very young boys, and therefore by extension had no "stones"—testicles—was technically an "oath" under the new rules of the King's School and subject to punishment. But William Shakespeare didn't countenance giving young boys the whip when he had a sharper tool at his disposal.

"Richard," William said, "I should strip thee and whip thee for thy *stones*, wert thou not already naked."

The other boys laughed with nervous confusion; young Richard was obviously fully clothed.

After a tense pause, William raised an eyebrow high on his high brow.

"I see on you no breeches, yet despite thy dick of a name, I suspect a breach—a vertical one—in thy lap. Gloves, I note thou hast none, but that of Venus. No ruff, but that which circles thy perfect maidenhead. Ay, I should whip thee, but the gentle whipping of maids is, sadly, frowned upon amongst the better classes. So will I let thy *case* rest."

William looked stern as he sat back down on his desk, but he smiled to himself. Only half the boys, he knew, got only half the puns, but they all got the gist: their teacher had just told the class wit that he was a pussy in five different ways.

William moved on. "Continue reading aloud, after 'Cases of Nouns.'"

"Nouns be declined," went the singsong, "with six cases, singularly and plurally. The nominative, the genitive, the dative, the accusative, the vocative, and the ablative."

"Richard, what be the cases of nouns?"

"Nouns be declined with six cases, the nominative, the dative, the accusative, and the ablative," Richard responded.

"Two hast thou forgotten."

"Nay, I forget not, but speak not for fear of whipping, magister."

"Why should I whip thee for naming the cases?" asked William, puzzled.

"Two be oaths, magister."

"Oaths?"

"Ay. The genital and the vocative." He pronounced the *v* in "vocative" like an *f*.

All the boys got that one. The laughter cascaded through the open timbers of the roof like angels in flight.

William looked angry for a moment, then broke his mask and laughed along. "*Veritas!* The master teaches and the pupil learns, all too well."

"WILLIAM SHAKESPEARE!"

The booming voice from the doorway stopped the laughter midpeal. All heads in the room turned as one to see a black-robed figure in the doorway, holding a Bible under his arm, his face reddening.

"Did I hear thee professing profanity and vulgarity to my charges?"

William leapt up from the desk with the instinctive fear of a schoolboy for his master. He gave a deep reverence. "Merely teaching Lyly as writ, magister."

"I do not recall Lyly teaching declensions thus. I would speak with thee. Outside, sirrah. *Nunc.*"

Snickers from the class; a barely audible fart.

William followed the schoolmaster of the King's New School out of the class and into the street.

He'd been dreading this.

When William was himself a breechless little moppet, Stratford was an openly Catholic town, and so were the New School's headmasters. But in the year when William was eleven, public officials were forced to take the Oath of Supremacy, acknowledging the Protestant Church of England as their religion and Elizabeth as its head. Rather than take the oath, William's schoolmaster, Simon Hunt, left to study for the priesthood at Rheims, a Catholic seminary on the Continent. More than one of his Stratford students went with him.

But Stratford was still a Catholic town, so it hired yet another Catholic schoolmaster, John Cottom. He was William's teacher for three years, and allowed William to stay in school even when the Shakespeare family could no longer pay his tuition. And when William, despite all aptitude, couldn't afford to go to Oxford or Cambridge, John Cottom had given William a position as his assistant, teaching Latin to the younger students.

But during the past summer, word arrived in Stratford that John's brother, Thomas Cottom—yet another who had gone to Rheims to study for the priesthood, and had returned to preach in secret amongst faithful English Catholics—had been arrested and taken to the Tower of London for imprisonment and torture. Then, in the short break before the current term, William heard that John Cottom had vanished from Stratford in the middle of the night. Rumors flew through Stratford like spooked ravens. Some said Cottom had gone to London to plead for his brother's life; some that he had gone to Rheims; some that he had fled to his family's lands in Lancashire; some that he himself had been taken to the Tower; some that he was already dead.

Three days before classes resumed, William received a brief letter from the new schoolmaster, Alexander Aspinall: William was to return for the new term as expected. It was the second day of class, and Aspinall had yet to make an appearance ... until now.

The smell of roasting meat, fresh-cut hay, and human waste walloped

William in the face as he emerged into the late morning air. It was coolish for autumn in Stratford—which is to say, bitterly cold. The puddles in the muddy street were turning toward slush. Fog hung nearly as low as the top of the Guild Hall Chapel next door, where the school had begun its day in the dark, with morning services. A fishmonger walked past missing all but one visible tooth, proffering "eelsh, bash, and shalmon." William couldn't help but note that the fishmonger—twenty-one or twenty-two, Irish, he guessed, with large pale green eyes and black hair—aside from being near toothless, was exceedingly attractive. In fact, he ruminated, there must be certain advantages—

"So: you are Will," rasped an impatient, rheumy voice.

William turned to face Alexander Aspinall.

"No Will I, magister. I am small of purse and stature, and therefore make amends with a rich and lofty name. So: my name is William."

Aspinall closed his black cassock over a staid white shirt, sheltering from an icy blade of cold wind from the north. He looked William over.

"William, then," he said at last. "John Cottom spoke well of you."

"I knew not that you were acquainted," William replied.

"He left a letter to his replacement. Most eloquent."

"He was an excellent schoolmaster," William said warily, but with some relief. If John had found the time to leave such a letter, he at least hadn't been suddenly snatched away to the Tower.

"But he was a papist, they say," Aspinall ventured.

"I know not."

"Do you not?" asked Aspinall with a flash in his eyes. "His brother was, 'tis certain, along with many students and masters of the King's School past." Aspinall opened the cover of his Bible and referred to papers tucked inside. "Simon Hunt, Thomas Jenkins, Robert Debdale..."

William was beginning to calm down. He answered coolly, "A man may be many things that his brother—or his schoolmaster—is not."

"Yet Thomas's faith was wicked. And his brother John, 'twould seem by his sudden absence, shares in his guilt."

"Of the righteousness of Thomas Cottom's faith, or John's, or indeed the faith of any man, only God might know of a certainty."

Aspinall frowned. His gaze bored into William like a thumbscrew. Then he drew in a breath, still regarding William curiously. "Indeed. Well spoken, William. The soul of a man finds purchase with God only by private piety, not by the baubles of priests, nor by the gold of St. Peter's coffers, nor by the display of the bloody Roman crucifix. So the new faith teaches our princes; so our sovereign Queen teaches us; and so shall we teach our pupils. I neither know nor care what philosophy my predecessors loosed in this our school that brought the Crown's displeasure upon Stratford, but no lasciviousness nor other popery will abide here while I am master. Neither would I have even the suspicion of recusancy fall upon my new usher, lest it fall thence on me."

William fought back his rising spleen and said, "Ay, magister."

"Therefore, thou shalt cease thy instruction in stones and cases, the genital, the fuckative, and all other such privy parts of speech in my school; or thou shalt find thyself pondering, at thy soon-arrived last, how best to distribute the four parts of thy personal estate unto the dismembers of thy family. *Comprehendisne?*"

"Ay, magister."

Alexander Aspinall harrumphed, then opened the door leading back into the schoolhouse. William entered and Aspinall followed. Clothing rustled as pupils turned to watch William return from his censure. As he strode to the master's desk, he felt the eyes of both students and master heating his back from the inside like peat fire. From the desk, he picked up the open copy of Lyly's grammar. With a glance at Aspinall, who stood watching from the doorway, William closed the book and set it gingerly on the desk.

"*Satis Linguae Latinae hodie.* Enough of that. Let us move on to matters of less controversy." He quickly took up another, much larger book from the desk, and opened it to the marked page.

"Where stood we in the Gospels yesterday? Ah, Matthew, chapter one, verse eighteen." He cleared his throat and read in Latin: "*Christi autem generatio sic erat cum esset desponsata mater eius Maria Ioseph antequam convenirent inventa est in utero habens de Spiritu Sancto.*" (Which two decades later would be translated for the King James version thus: "Now the birth of Jesus Christ was on this wise: when as his mother Mary was espoused to Joseph, before they came together, she was found with child of the Holy Ghost.")

He dropped the book onto the desk; it landed with a thump like Anne Boleyn's head into the basket.

"*Disputate*," William barked. "Discuss."

Several hands shot up. William acknowledged one.

"How came Mary with the child of the Holy Ghost?" asked an older boy who understood the Latin well.

"And what means *convenirent*, 'they came together'?" asked a younger boy who did not.

William cast a studiously blank look toward the door, but it was already closing with a slam; Alexander Aspinall was gone.

Chapter Three

This is the excellent foppery of the world, that, when we are sick in fortune—often the surfeit of our own behavior—we make guilty of our disasters the sun, the moon, and the stars: as if we were villains by necessity; fools by heavenly compulsion; knaves, thieves, and treachers, by spherical predominance; drunkards, liars, and adulterers, by an enforc'd obedience of planetary influence; and all that we are evil in, by a divine thrusting on. An admirable evasion of whoremaster man, to lay his goatish disposition on the charge of a star!

—Edmund, *King Lear*, I.ii.118

Todd Deuter knelt on all fours, his face glowing in the moonlight, his nose two inches from a large cow pie. Springing forth from the mound of bovine poop was a mushroom. Todd plucked it from the patty to examine it more closely.

"*Panaeolus sphinctrinus*," Todd called to Willie. "Shakespeare, you're the Latin scholar, you know what it means?"

"Something about a sphincter," Willie responded.

"Correct!" said Todd, holding up the toadstool like a puppet. "It means, *I no get you high, but I maybe kill you, ASSHOLE!*" He laughed and tossed it aside.

The University of California at Santa Cruz is nestled in the treeline where the foothills of the Santa Cruz Mountains rise up to meet the ancient redwood forest. The school's small residential colleges are scattered among clearings in the trees, connected by long wooden footbridges that span the forest ravines. The urban legend is that the school, built in the 1960s, was decentralized by design, with no focal point for Berkeley-style student protests. As a result, the campus itself is shady, moody, mysterious, solitary. But between the campus on the hill and the sleepy town of Santa Cruz below lay the rolling pastures of the Cowell Ranch. At night, the pastures are wide open to the sky, quiet, starlit, and empty but for the occasional group of drunk, stoned, or tripping students and the cow patties and confused cows that are their prey.

Ultraprogressive UCSC had no fraternities, no sororities, no athletic programs, no grades, for that matter. Students took classes exclusively on a pass/no pass basis. With so few attractions for jarheads and jocks, it was therefore a tiny—though not null—subset of UCSC students who engaged in the rural-campus, drunken-frat-boy pastime of cow tipping. The activity, for those not familiar, involves sneaking up on a sleeping, standing cow, running at it full speed, and knocking it over onto its side before it wakes up. Good times.

The cow pastures of UCSC were more popular for activity of another sort. "Cow tripping," Todd called it. Go out under the moonlight, hunt for magic mushrooms, and if found, consume immediately. Guitars, dumbeks, and Hacky Sacks optional, female companionship preferred.

That had been Willie's plan for the night, cow tripping with Todd and a few other friends. Willie had invited Dashka to come along, and to his shock, she'd agreed. Dashka had studying to do, so they had gotten a late start; Willie guessed it was already two a.m.

Todd moved away down the hill, scanning the ground for mushrooms, while Willie and Dashka sprawled on a Mexican blanket in the grass. No one had brought a flashlight, but even on this moonless night it wasn't necessary. There were stars galore glimmering in a cloudless sky and illuminating the small depression where they sat. The light from the town below and from the occasional car coming to or from the campus was blocked out by rises in the rolling pastures.

Willie pulled his green backpack toward him and took out his pipe and a small bundle of tinfoil, which he opened carefully to reveal a small cube of hashish the size of the tip of his little finger and the color of raw honey.

Dashka watched silently as Willie took the cube and waved a lighter under it to soften it, then broke off a small corner and crumbled it into the pipe. Dashka took the pipe and lighter, and smoked; then coughed as she tried to hold in the hit.

"Shit," she said in the comically held-breath voice of all practicing stoners, "that's strong shit."

"Nice vocabulary. They don't teach us that in the lowly master's program."

"'Shit,'" Dashka said, blowing out a cloud of smoke, "is one of the oldest words in the English language. Along with 'dick,' 'fuck,' and 'cunt,' by the way. All perfectly good, concise, four-letter Anglo-Saxon words. If you were doctoral material you'd know that."

As she passed the pipe back to Willie, his eyes lingered on her lips in the starlight. Full. Sensuous. Willie took the pipe, and took a hit.

"So do some Shakespeare for me, Shakespeare," Dashka said, rolling onto her stomach, her chin in her hand.

"Like what?"

"What do you know?"

Willie knew a lot. In addition to his daily forays into the *Riverside Shakespeare*, he'd been a theater major as an undergrad; he'd played Lysimachus in a student production of *Pericles*, and Rosencrantz in *Hamlet* at Berkeley's Greek Theater. He was quick at memorization. Words tended to fall into his mind and stay there in bunches, like strands of DNA, whole double helixes of poetry, prose, scraps of movie and TV dialogue. He sometimes wondered if he would eventually run out of brain cells to store it all.

Several passages sprang to mind. He ran a quick calculation: which one would be most likely to get him laid? "I know a bit about a lovers' kiss," he said.

> "'Now let me say "Good night," and so say you;
> If you will say so, you shall have a kiss.'
> 'Good night,' quoth she, and, ere he says 'Adieu,'
> The honey fee of parting tender'd is:
> Her arms do lend his neck a sweet embrace;
> Incorporate then they seem; face grows to face.
> Till, breathless, he disjoin'd, and backward drew
> The heavenly moisture, that sweet coral mouth,
> Whose precious taste her thirsty lips well knew,
> Whereon they surfeit, yet complain on drouth:
> He with her plenty press'd, she faint with dearth
> Their lips together glued, fall to the earth."

He stopped.

He wasn't sure whether he had bored her or not. She hadn't moved. Her chin was still in her hand.

"*The Rape of Lucrece?*" she asked.

"*Venus and Adonis.*"

Dashka looked at him intently. "Nobody studies the long poems, much less memorizes them. I read it once, but...how does it end?"

"For Adonis? Not well. It's actually very female-empowering. She comes on to him pretty hard."

She shifted position just a little bit. "Really?" Looked at him a certain way. Open.

Willie leaned over and kissed her. From the first millisecond, it was a great kiss. He could taste the sweetness of the hashish on her tongue as she ran it lightly across his. Her lower lip melted under gentle pressure from his teeth, like a ripe apricot just before it bursts forth with juice. The kiss didn't last long. She leaned away and said, "Mmm." Then, "How old are you?"

"Twenty-five. You?"

"Twenty-six."

They were nearly the same age, yet Dashka was probably four years ahead of him academically.

"Did you take time off between undergrad and grad school?" she asked.

"No." Willie shifted. "No. I finished my coursework fall of eighty-four. I've just been, you know, working on that thesis topic, researching—"

"For two *years*? And you're only now submitting a topic? You should either be done or kicked out of the program by now. Welsh must like you. What's holding you back?"

Willie felt himself tense, and wondered if she noticed. He took a hit and felt the smoke course straight through him, making his limbs go simultaneously light and heavy. He closed his eyes, and as the chemical hit his brain, a series of pulsing, abstract shapes flashed across his retinas. Abstract, yet almost recognizable, like last night's first dream. That shape...in blue and green, like the shape of a footprint in the sand...or was it the handle of the refrigerator door from his childhood? And that one, a blazing gold swirl of concentric rings against the blackness...what was it? Something to do with his mother. Her hair...

He opened his eyes as Todd hollered from the darkness below, "Dude! Eureka!"

Dashka and Willie found Todd standing over a cow patty from which sprang a small cluster of brownish-white mushrooms. *"Psilocybe cubensis,"* he announced. He plucked out the four small mushrooms, handed one each to Willie and Dashka, and immediately popped the other two into his mouth. "Straight from the cowshit to your mouth! C'mon, chow down!"

An hour later, Willie still had the taste on his tongue, but he was beginning not to care. The high had started in his stomach, some rumbling and bloating in mild reaction to the fungus. He briefly had the thought, heightened by pot paranoia, that Todd just *could* be wrong with his mushroom identification.

Maybe I'm dying.

But then he and Dashka took another toke of the mellow Lebanese hash. Almost immediately his stomach relaxed (one of the well-known medical effects of tetrahydrocannabinol, the active ingredient in both marijuana and hashish) and his tension eased. It was a good combination, hash and mushrooms. The mushroom high could be a little edgy, a little speedy when it came on, but the gently dulling hashish glow took the edge off, smoothing it all out like the Teflon strip on a razor blade.

Willie's housemate, Jojo, and Todd's housemate, André, had shown up and gone shroom-foraging with Todd, leaving Willie and Dashka alone. Dashka shivered and snuggled up next to him, sheltering from the chilly bay breeze now blowing over the pastures.

"The sky is fucking amazing," she said, looking up.

"You can see the nebula in Orion's sword," said Willie.

Funny, Willie thought, *why did the Greeks, who were into anything priapic, call it Orion's Sword rather than Orion's Wang? It's so there. No sword ever hung so directly between the legs. True, the girth would, if it were a phallus, make Orion exceedingly well hung, but what the hell, he was a giant, right? You'd expect him to have a giant cock, too, maybe even well out of proportion, the better for terrifying the local maidenry. Maybe the ancients were thinking that Orion must be wearing a tunic, since he's wearing a "belt." But why did it have to be a belt? Why not just his waist? The Greeks were mostly naked anyway, especially their heroes. No, the banana-shaped object must surely, to the ancient Greeks, have been Orion's Tool. There must have been some intervening, repressive regime—no doubt Northern European—who decided that the constellation of Orion's Johnson would somehow offend Jesus and so, for the sake of public morality and entrance to the Kingdom of Heaven, covered up the Great Hunter's loins with a tunic and turned his wiener into his sword...or worse, his "hunting knife." Hunh. His naked blade, more like. Beaver-hunting knife. Ha! First thing tomorrow, I'm going to start a public campaign to have the constellation referred to by its full and proper name, Orion the Hunter, He of the Shining Waist and Massive Schlong.*

Willie was stoned.

He was just embarking on a tributary stream of consciousness about whether any planets in the constellation of Orion's Schlong might be inhabited, and what they would think if they knew they lived on a big interstellar dick, when his reverie was interrupted.

"What is that?" Dashka asked.

"What?"

"That...galaxy...or supernova. That!"

Willie was always amazed when otherwise intelligent people didn't know the difference between a galaxy, a supernova, and the Pleiades—which, he informed Dashka, was the cluster of newborn stars she was pointing at.

"It looks like it's waving. Shimmering. Like a fairy cobweb." They sat in silence for a few moments, just looking at the stars. "Do you believe in astrology?" she asked.

"No. Why, do you?"

"Scientifically? Not really. Although as a faith, I find it more credible than Christianity. I've never seen an angel, but I certainly know a Libra when I kiss one."

Willie stared at her for a moment. It had been a one-in-twelve chance, he told himself. "Maybe that has less to do with the planets than with the malleability of the young mind," he said. "I was probably seven when a reputable newspaper told me that because my birthday is October seventeenth, I'm 'charming, but fickle and indecisive, with a tendency to let the approval or disapproval of others, especially parents, weigh heavily' on me. That stuff stays with you."

"So why Catholicism?" Dashka suddenly asked. "Why is Shakespeare's religion important? Why should we care? Why do *you* care?"

Willie couldn't tell her the truth, that he didn't really care, at least not about Catholicism. He couldn't tell her that the "research" for his thesis consisted of the last hour of a movie about Sir Thomas More and one line from a sonnet that he'd stumbled across while frantically trying to pull together a thesis—any thesis—for his already scheduled approval meeting.

Willie smoked a little more to cover the fact that he didn't have an answer, and found himself asking why, aside from the compelling oddity of his name, he cared about a dead playwright.

Why do I care? What's the Bard to me, or me to the Bard, to paraphrase Hamlet, *Act Two, Scene Two, yet here I am quoting Shakespeare, even to myself, like verses from the Bible or something. Why?*

Finally he said, grasping to tie it all together, "I guess Shakespeare's the closest thing I have to a religion. Maybe if I figure out *his* faith—his God, his passion, whatever it was that moved him—"

"Then you figure out yourself?" She whistled. "Heavy, man. Self-realization via Shakespeare."

"Catholicism and astrology aren't options for me. So maybe I'll find the meaning of life in a sonnet." He crumbled a little more Lebanese into the bowl. "Or maybe in a cow patty. Or a hash pipe," he said, reaching for the lighter next to Dashka.

She snatched it up and held it away from him teasingly. "Or maybe you'll find it somewhere else." She took his right hand and put the tips of his fore- and middle finger in her mouth and sucked them where they were dusted with the sticky residue of the hash. "Mmm. Sweet."

"Sex, drugs, and Shakespeare," Willie said. "A sure path to Nirvana."

"Who said anything about sex?" Dashka said, and began giggling. Soon they were both laughing, Willie grinding his teeth together as the endorphins released by laughter and arousal raised his heart rate, and the blood pumped psilocybin faster and faster into his brain, and suddenly he was peaking, his face feeling like chilled alabaster, his breathing like silk, his torso...where was his torso, anyway? He suddenly felt impossibly skinny, as if he could put his hands on either side of his waist and pinch them together. He was giggling uncontrollably, his nose running, his eyes streaming with tears of laughter, his tear ducts feeling raw and swollen to the size of chestnuts. Next thing he knew, he and Dashka were kissing and dry humping, the short, dry, cattle-mown grass from the summer crunching beneath them and a few green blades born of an early fall rain releasing a freshly scented hint of spring yet to come.

Dashka had her knee between Willie's legs, rubbing his hard-on with her thigh, and he could feel a sticky stain developing on his boxers. He wedged a hand in between his own leg and her crotch and rubbed, getting a suggestion of labia but mostly just hard blue-jean seam. He was wondering if he should try to unbutton her jeans or maybe get to her bra when she rolled him over twice, laughing, ending up with her on top and Willie with his temple one inch away from a huge cow patty.

He did a take, and then a double take.

Crowning the patty was the largest mushroom he'd ever seen.

Psychedelic mushrooms, when one is tripping on mushrooms, have an eerie blue glow about them, like Frodo's sword when Orcs are near. This one was haloed like the aurora borealis, shimmering blue with a secondary corona of shifting green and white.

"Holy...fucking...shit," Willie said, and he meant every word.

Chapter Four

If the Protestant orthodoxy was the tyrant in Reformation England, then the English Jesuit priests of the Counter-Reformation were its dissidents. Educated in exile, they began returning to England around 1580 to preach the "Old Faith" to their hidden flock. Their movements were conducted in cloak-and-dagger secrecy, for they were officially heretics, traitors, and outlaws. Several were also neighbors and acquaintances of William Shakespeare.

The rest of William's day at the New School had been uneventful, with the exception of Oliver Gasper's sudden gusher of a bloody nose, the treatment of which left a deep, scarlet stain on William's white sleeve. He was closing the schoolhouse door, preoccupied with libidinous thoughts of the girl he was rushing off to meet, when a horse splattered up the muddy, straw-strewn street and checked up next to him, steaming and huffing.

"Good den, sir," its rider said, and dismounted. "I seek the schoolmaster of Edward the Sixth's New School." His clothes were stained and torn, his horse muddied. He had long black hair and a wispy black mustache, but no beard. His eyes, too, were dark, black on black, and there was an intensity to them that put William on edge.

"You've found it, at the end of the day," said William warily.

"I bear a gift for schoolmaster John Cottom."

William thought quickly. Alexander Aspinall was attending to administrative duties inside. "Whence comes it, and who bears it?"

"I am Simon Pray, clerk to a lawyer, Master Humphrey Ely of London. He got it of John Cottom's brother, Thomas."

"Master Cottom is master here no longer," William replied. "He vanished some weeks past."

"Vanished?" said the horseman, and his face fell. "Has he no relations here?"

"None in Stratford. He was of Lancashire."

"Lancashire..."

William could see him calculating: another two days' ride. The horseman looked to the east. His horse stamped impatiently.

"I have urgent business in Shottery..." he said, half to himself, then turned to William. "And my Master Ely would have me whipped upon returning so tardy to London." The horseman's cutpurse eyes appraised William, up and down. His glance lingered at the bloodstain on William's sleeve, and then again at his throat.

Finally the horseman looked William deep in the eyes, and said deliberately, "I would ask thee, young sir, if there be an inn of Stratford where a man might—in the blessed embrace of Father, Son, and Holy Ghost, three Persons and one God, and of the Blessed Virgin Mary—rest secure?"

William understood the code.

"The Bear," said William. "Not the Swan."

The horseman nodded as though he already knew the answer. "I give you gramercies, good sir." Then he hesitated for another beat. "Know you John Cottom?"

"Ay," William answered. "In sooth, I love him as a father, and am greatly discomfited by his sudden absence."

"Then I would ask a further boon of you, and a greater." The rider took a parcel wrapped in a rough cloth from the horse's saddlebag. "I am charged to deliver this to Master Cottom, yet I have other cares which crave my attendance. As one who loves John Cottom, who knows his family and their whereabouts, might I prevail upon you to complete the delivery? It is a precious lading."

The horseman looked up and down High Street, and as no one was paying them any mind, he unwrapped the parcel to reveal a fine mahogany box. Bigger than a tinderbox but smaller than a hurdy-gurdy, it was inlaid with ivory delicately fashioned in the shape of a St. George's cross—a symbol of the Old Faith on the Continent.

"What does it contain?" William asked.

The horseman hesitated for a moment, then replied, "It is locked."

"Is there no key?"

"None. Nor was there any when Thomas Cottom gave it unto Master Ely."

William took a deep breath, and looked at the inlaid cross glittering in the late afternoon sun. He couldn't have explained why, but somehow its very brightness frightened him.

"Will you take it to John Cottom?" the rider asked quietly.

"Nay," said William, shaking his head. "I cannot. My teaching here is my family's sole support, and the term has just begun."

The horseman dropped his voice even lower. "It would aid the cause," he said, dark eyes aflame.

William hesitated. Between the shining cross and the horseman's unnerving stare, he felt nearly bewitched. But suddenly the schoolhouse door slammed open. The horseman covered the box again as Aspinall emerged and looked at them suspiciously.

"What, William, hast thou lingered to practice thy declensions?" Aspinall stepped around the corner of the building, opened his breeches, and began to piss. "Master Cottom also warned me of thy difficulties in Latin. And who is this, thy tutor?"

"Merely recommending, magister, a reputable inn to this weary traveler," William responded with a slight bow.

Aspinall looked back and forth between them as he piddled against the wall, steam hissing and rising. "The Swan," he said to the rider. "Not the Bear. The Swan's the only tavern for a virtuous man." He gave his prick a lusty shake. "If you be not virtuous, then you may drown yourself at the Bear, though in recompense you will hang in this life, and burn in the next!" Aspinall laughed at his own wordplay as he tucked his tool away and hiked his trousers.

"I thank you for your words of caution," the horseman replied with a twitchy smile to Aspinall, who was headed back for the door. "One must indeed exercise care in one's faith," he added with a glance to William.

Aspinall grunted and, with a last dark look at the rider and the bundle in his arms, returned to the schoolhouse.

The horseman waited a moment, then addressed William. "If you are of the true faith," he said quietly, "to perform this office may be your family's salvation."

William took a step back as though he were being hounded by a beggar. "Nay. I and my family care little for faith and not at all for causes. I prithee go to."

"See, then, how I go," the rider said, replacing the box and mounting his horse. "Fare thee well, boy."

He splattered away down the street toward the town's two largest inns, leaving William standing in the cold fall air with Alexander Aspinall's urine trickling past his feet.

... my mind misgives
Some consequence yet hanging in the stars
Shall bitterly begin his fearful date
With this night's revels...

—Romeo, *Romeo and Juliet*, I.iv.106

Willie and Todd sat cross-legged like monks before an image of the Buddha, meditating on the mushroom.

"*Cubensis*," Todd said. "Biggest I've ever seen. Probably thirty grams. One shroom, dude, thirty g's!"

"Should we dry it, or...?"

"No need. We could just eat it, if we had a party. It's enough to get ten people ridiculously high."

Willie considered the group. Another couple of Todd's friends had arrived. One, an older-looking guy with a mustache and long black hair, knew Dashka from high school, and they were making small talk about mutual friends. Willie's roommate Jojo was lying on the blanket with André, giggling; they had found some mushrooms of their own.

"I'm already plenty high," Willie said.

"We could sell it," Todd said. "Piece this big, fresh...it'd bring top dollar, man. It's like a collector's item. Bragging rights. Tell you what, I could set up a deal, and we could split the dough."

Todd lived in the student apartment above Willie's. He was the drug dealer for most of the east side of the campus. He had fine, angelic blond hair that almost glowed on the rare occasions it was clean, and glistened when it was greasy. He had pale, almost translucent skin that turned a little ruddy around the cheeks in cool weather. He claimed to be a grad student in philosophy, though Willie had never seen him with a book. He had a huge record collection, and mostly stayed in his room blaring prog rock and Grateful Dead at weapons-grade volume and making a nearly incessant thumping sound on Willie's ceiling as if he were rolling a sofa back and forth across the floor. Willie had finally asked him what that sound was, and Todd had answered, "Rolling the sofa, man."

Every few days Todd would emerge from his room and go around the graduate student residences and Kresge College, knocking on doors, *bam-bam-bam-bam*, "Gotta pay my tuition!" or *bam-bam-bam-bam*, "Gotta buy books!" or *bam-bam-bam-bam*, "Gotta date tonight, who's paying?!" He'd dole out bags of crappy shake, an ounce for ten bucks. It was nasty, guaranteed-headache stuff, but at ten bucks a lid you could smoke it all night—and pretty much had to if you wanted to get high. Occasionally he'd have more exotic stuff. Blond Lebanese hash was common; mild and sweet-smelling, it crumbled easily in your fingers and left a flowery mist behind in the air. You could smoke a half a gram and still translate Latin, probably better than if you were straight. Black Afghani hash, sticky and oily like an extra-rich truffle, was less desirable: smoke that shit and don't plan on moving for at least two hours. And then he could sometimes get his hands on higher quality sinsemilla buds from Mendocino, and upon request, Ecstasy or Quaaludes. Once or twice a quarter he had blotter acid, the best being Mickey Mouse brand, each sheet comprising a hundred perforated tabs on which were replicated the classic image of Mickey as the Sorcerer's Apprentice from *Fantasia*, a stream of stars doing Mickey's magical bidding between his fingertips.

Willie had never sold drugs before, but now he considered it. He was almost broke, and there would be no support check from his dad for another week or so. He had exactly nine dollars in his pocket. "How much can we get?"

"I know this guy. He'll be perfect, man. I bet he pays two hundred for it. He's outta town, though. You'll have to run it up to the Renaissance Faire."

"The Renaissance Faire?! That's in Marin County, isn't it? Why don't you go?"

"I got other biz. You're going up to Berkeley anyway, right?"

"Well, yeah, but—"

"So you're halfway there. I can get you on the pass list. You'll get in for free. Come *on*, dude, it's free money."

Willie tried to get his thoughts together. It seemed like easy cash, but even high on shrooms, he suspected it was a bad idea. He should probably, to quote Nancy Reagan, just say no. "I don't need the money."

"Everybody needs money. Plus you'll be at the *Ren Faire*, dude. You'll probably get laid."

Willie felt a little jump in his pants. His heartbeat quickened again, and as it did he felt another wave of the mushroom high. Todd was looking at him with a devilish grin, the cold starlight giving his face a ghastly cast. Todd was right. He probably *would* get laid at the Faire. He'd been to a Renaissance Faire once before, near L.A., a few months ago—May, was it?—and he'd gotten lucky, way lucky. Jesus, he'd fantasized about it dozens of times since. There was this game, Drench-a-Wench, that involved sling-shooting a wet sponge at an array of wanton maids sitting on a little bleacher of hay bales. If you hit one, you got a kiss. He'd wondered how long that game could possibly last with a new STD being discovered every day. Just for fun, he'd played. He'd hit a buxom bleach-blonde, and she'd given him a good if too-professional kiss. He'd turned around to go, and there had been another girl watching him—was her name Joan? Juliet?—something Renaissancey that was at odds with her exotic looks. Some sort of Asian or maybe island blend: tall; long wavy black hair; slim hips.

"Truly, I am shocked, sir. Paying for thy kisses when thou couldst surely get them free." He'd suspected she was just a paid Faire shill playing street theater with him, but when he'd moved toward her ever so slightly, smiled, and said, "Verily a fool and peasant knave am I," she'd swooped right into his arms and taken his lips into hers in a passionate yet light-touched French kiss, running her hands through the thick curls of hair around his shoulders.

"Mmm," she'd said dreamily, "I *never* do that."

"What, kiss a man?"

"No, kiss a stranger."

Half an hour and a couple of cold pints of ale later, he was on a blanket in the woods behind the jewelry booth where she worked, deep inside what was surely the *caelestissime strictus cunnus caelorum*. She was still wearing her Faire costume, skirts hiked up around her waist, one small breast peeking from her bodice, almond eyes closed, murmuring things that weren't quite audible but, Willie was certain, were not G-rated.

Now, as Willie sat cross-legged on the foothills of the Santa Cruz mountains, tripping on mushrooms and reliving that searing sweetness in his loins, a strange thing happened. To say he thought deeply about Shakespeare, or felt a sudden empathy with the Bard, doesn't describe it. It was more than that: a synapse somewhere fired across a virginal neuron, and for a brief instant, he could feel a coolness on the back of his already-thinning pate, his black locks brushing against his face as he thrust in and out of that heavenly, glovelike cunt, zounds and marry, a triumph of a cunt—

And then, in a flash, as quickly as the vision came it went.

"Jesus!" Willie said with a sudden shudder that came, not from the cold, but from somewhere inside.

He still sat cross-legged, looking at the glowing blue mushroom atop its excremental altar. It looked entirely alien to him, and a little scary. The hallucination, if that's what it was, freaked him out. He felt sudden tension in his shoulders and his back, the feeling of a good trip about to turn bad.

"So what do you say?" Todd asked.

"No," Willie said vaguely. "No, I've really got to work on my thesis this weekend. I'm not a dealer. I'm not into breaking the law."

"Dude," said Todd. "You're already breaking the law. Sometimes the law sucks. You gotta stand up for your right."

Willie stood up, but it was only to walk away.

Chapter Six

As the social and religious climate in England changed, so did its theater. For centuries, "mystery plays" based on scenes from the Bible were acted at holiday festivals throughout the year, and were also favorites in the inn yards. But Protestant doctrine banned these plays as superstitious and idolatrous, and that left a void needing to be filled. Enter William Shakespeare, with his towering intellect, vigorous style, masterful technique, and his love of classical forms.

"Jesus!" William Shakespeare cried, his hose around his ankles, as he spent himself in the heaven that lay twixt the thighs of Isabella Burns.

"And Sweet Mary, and the Holy Ghost," Isabella gasped.

William heard a "Ho! William!" from the distance.

"Anon, anon!" he called. "I come!" Isabella, the middle daughter of Anthony Burns of High Street, giggled and grabbed at his ass as he leapt up. He hesitated for a moment at leaving behind her dark, exotic eyes, her olive skin, and...what lay below. But then he kissed her quickly and, still pulling up his hose, ran out of the shadows of a small clearing in the forest of Arden and through the brush to a much larger clearing nearby.

William emerged to find five men waiting for him next to a rough-hewn platform that had been erected as a rehearsal stage. A small pine tree hung over the back corner of the platform, and there were several fallen logs arranged as primitive seating. Lanterns fought the early arriving gloom of autumn in Stratford; although William had rushed to the wood after his encounter with the horseman to meet Isabella, it was already nearly dark.

Davy Jones, wearing the traditional green hose and leather jerkin of Robin Hood, stood surrounded by his own merry band of brothers. William's friend Arthur Cawdrey gestured apologetically toward William. "Ah, see? He comes."

"Indeed he did," snickered Richard Tyler, two years younger than William. "In the bush, I'll warrant."

Isabella Burns emerged flush from the wood, giggling. "Go thy ways, boys, with thy play!" she said, clearly enjoying their shock, and went laughing and skipping back toward Stratford.

The other men looked at William, who shrugged. "Whatever wisdom may say, I deem one in the bush worth more than two in the hand."

William picked up his cup amidst the ensuing laughter, and held it forth to Arthur Cawdrey, vintner of the Angel, the fifth-best tavern in Stratford and one of the worst in Warwickshire, who filled it for him.

As Arthur poured, he quietly lectured. "You'd best temper your husbandry, William, lest you nip the bud ere the bush is full grown." Isabella Burns, at sixteen, was two years younger than William.

William responded, "Do we not, at harvesttime, pluck the fruit before the rude jaybird pierces it? A young bush grows to fullness only by regular husbandry. In fact, this bush, as I gleaned by a noted lack of bud, has been tended by other gardeners. She was deflowered ere I nipped her."

"What a university of wits I have about me," interrupted Davy Jones. "A witty libertine Latin tutor, a half-witty ill-dressed tailor, a drunken vintner, a one-eared Jesuit, and an addlepated apothecary. An unlikelier band of Merry Men never was."

Davy Jones leapt up onto the rustic platform. "May we continue?"

"How may we continue when we've not yet begun?" asked William.

"Ay, Davy. What parts are we to play?" asked Richard Tyler, who wore a dress. At sixteen he was the youngest of the troupe, and had no beard. He was apprenticed to a tailor and had joined the troupe with the promise that he could play the ingenue and make all the costumes.

"And in what play?" asked George Cawdry. George was Arthur's younger brother; he had just returned from the seminary at Rheims, though he hadn't completed his studies due to ill health. He had a mangled ear from a childhood riding accident, and several other ailments besides.

"'Tis a tale of Robin Hood," replied Davy Jones.

"Ay, but which?" asked Arthur Cawdry. "There be as many tales of Robin Hood as there be tails in a bawdy house."

Thereupon with a great flourish Davy Jones produced a manuscript.

"'Tis a new text of an old story, procured from the author himself and as fit for Whitsuntide performance as fit might be. We shall enact the Stratford premiere of *The Death of Robin Hood*."

There was a long, stunned silence; shifting of feet.

"'Tis a comedy, then?" asked Arthur Cawdrey.

"No, of course not a comedy," said Davy, annoyed. "Tragedy rather, and in the high style. Robin Hood, having fallen ill, seeks to be bled by the prioress of an abbey. She performs her office too well and bleeds him even unto death."

There was another uncomfortable silence.

"'Tis surely an allegory of the supposed rape of England by the Church of Rome," said George Cawdrey.

"'Tis but a tale of Robin Hood," replied Davy Jones.

"Wherein an emissary of the Pope bleeds the very image of England to death," replied George.

William reached out and quietly took the manuscript from Davy Jones's hand. Upon the front page was written in a jagged, weak hand: *The Death of Robin Hood, by Anthony Munday.*

William had heard of Anthony Munday.

A few years older than William, he was a player, poet, and playwright of some renown. A real *Johannes fac totum*. Apprenticed as a draper, he had gone to the English College in Rome and published a tract, *English Roman Life*, that described the life of Catholic expatriates in the seminaries. He was now back in England where he published mediocre plays and worse poetry. There were only two reasons why London writers would go to Rome: either to be a Catholic, or to spy on Catholics. Given his success in the arts with such meager talent, it was likely the latter.

William handed the manuscript back to Davy Jones. "I for one shall not murder Robin Hood as our priests are murdered, for the people's delight in the public square. I'll see myself hanged first."

Davy Jones snatched back the tract, perturbed. "As well you might! The trees this season are abloom with papists; even some hidden papists who remained silent and professed no faith." He looked around the group; several dropped their eyes. "We would all be wise to embrace the new religion in public fashion. With this tale of Robin Hood, we may honor England, our Queen, her court, and her church at one blow."

"Honor England by killing Robin Hood?" said William. "Do you also honor your sister by taking her maidenhead?"

The tension between them was palpable; young Richard Tyler didn't like palpable, and strove to diffuse it. "Faith aside, Robin Hood is so exceeding...so exceeding *done*, is it not?"

Arthur Cawdrey, who had the biggest belly in the group, chimed in, "My brother sees in it an allegory against the Pope; yet I'd hate to be hanged as a traitor for wearing the crucifix of a Friar Tuck!"

There was some murmured assent at this.

William was suddenly bored of the discussion, and turned to see Philip Rogers, apothecary, crouched, examining something in the dirt next to the rough-hewn platform. William went over and sat on the stage next to him as the debate raged on. Philip Rogers was bent close to what looked like a pile of dung. He reached out and pulled three small mushrooms from the pile, examined them, and put them in a pouch on his belt.

"Are they edible?" William asked idly.

Rogers cocked his head. "In a way."

William nodded noncommittally. Philip Rogers was a bit eccentric; it was generally blamed on his diligence in personally testing the various herbs, potions, and decoctions for sale in his shop.

William looked up, and for the first time he noticed a young woman, with red hair and green eyes, sitting on a fallen tree under a lantern at the edge of the clearing, watching the escalating argument about the politics of Robin Hood. William nudged Philip, who knew everyone in and around Stratford.

"Who is yon bonny maid?"

Rogers glanced up, squinted, then pulled a pair of spectacles from beneath his shirt and peered through them.

"Ah. That would be young Rosaline. A kinswoman of Davy Jones's. Up from Abbot's Lench."

"She is wondrous fair," said William.

"Ay, and accomplished by all accounts," said Rogers. "She works the loom, has her letters, even some small Latin, I'm told. She is enamored of the stage, and wished to come and watch our rehearsal."

Then Philip Rogers lowered his voice. "They also say that she has a way with all things that grow. Bud and root...stalk and bulb. And though I would not speak of it if I knew you not to be of uncommon discretion..."

And now Rogers leaned in close to William's ear, and said softly, "Her own lap's garden is exceeding well tended: hedged and trimmed like unto the fancy of a fairy's lawn."

"In sooth?" William asked, looking at the girl with rising interest.

Now the voice of Philip Rogers, apothecary, dropped to a barely audible whisper. "And further: though the most precious flower at the heart of that garden be ever so dainty, when ministered to just so, it sprays forth a very fountain of Venus's sweetest nectar."

William felt a leap in his loins. He whispered back, "A fountain...? How know you this? Wanton news spreads like the pox, they say; or is this the report of your own dalliance?"

"Nay, 'twas a strictly professional encounter. She came to me as apothecary, seeking a cure for the curious affliction."

She noticed them talking about her, smiled and waved.

William raised his cup toward her, then drained it.

The conversation about Robin Hood had degenerated to a yelling match about the desecration of Holy Trinity Church some twenty years ago—the tearing down of its papist icons, its crucifixes, its jeweled altar—fingers were being pointed.

William rejoined the group, interrupting. "Arthur Cawdrey, I see these cups are but half full. And yet a vintner and an alemonger you call yourself. Why have we you in the troupe, if not to keep filled our cups with the juice of our invention?"

Cawdrey obliged, taking up a large skin and pouring wine into the five extended cups.

"God Save the Queen!" William toasted, and "God Save the Queen!" came the chorused reply.

William moved casually to the front of the stage.

"*The Death of Robin Hood*," he mused aloud. "Would it not be best, in these circumspect times, to choose our plays more circumspectly? A literary pistol less loaded, mayhap, would be more suitable and as well-approved, and less like to lead to inadvertent hangings. What of the classics?"

"You would ask a greater classic than Robin Hood?" said Davy Jones, still angry.

"A classic of ancient Greece or Rome, methinks he means," said Richard Tyler, drinking deeply from his cup of wine.

Davy Jones laughed. "What would you have us play, *magister*? Lyly's *Latin Grammar*?"

"What of Ovid?" asked William innocently. "Many merry jests there are in his works, and yet somewhat of romance, of gods and goddesses both righteous and lusty. Also huntsmanship and swordplay aplenty. And we have in England no Church of Jove to take offense one way or another."

"You'd best leave the dramaturgy to those with experience of the stage," Davy Jones huffed. William was a neophyte player, and had only just joined the fledgling troupe at the Cawdreys' suggestion.

George Cawdrey came to his defense. "Let him speak, Davy. This Ofydd sounds well."

"Tell us one of his tales, in brief," said Arthur.

William pretended to think for a moment. "There is a tale," he said, and here he looked at Rosaline, "with a fountain—that I have oft wished to wrap my lips around." Then he turned to the company. "Yea, i'faith, the most lamentable tragedy of Salmacis and Hermaphroditus might serve our present need."

"Salacious and hermaphroditic?" said Arthur Cawdrey, looking uncertain. "Is it an apt tale for a Whitsunday fair?"

"It matters not; we have no lines composed, and of a certain cannot by Whitsunday," answered Davy Jones, although Whitsunday was months away.

"Nonsense. We may act it extempore," said William, and leapt—for the very first time—up onto the stage. "But fill our cups once more, Arthur Cawdrey. The emptier your wineskin, the fairer my tale." He looked out over his expectant audience as Arthur Cawdrey dutifully poured.

"But it cannot be played *solus*. Mayhap yon fair Rosaline will assist, and act the part of Salmacis?"

Rosaline jumped up from her seat. "Ay, good sir!"

Davy Jones stepped in front of her. "It is not meet that a woman ascend the stage," he said angrily. "And less so my cousin."

"'Tis but rehearsal, not performance, and thus outside the scope of our Master of Revels or even of custom," said William.

"But," said young Richard Tyler, looking disappointed, "if I am to play the maiden's part, surely I should extemporize with you?"

Topping the rising grumbling, William continued. "Our play shall surely not be marred from having the woman's part devised by woman, will it? And as she plays, you, Richard, may note her voice, her lips, her hair, how she gestures thus and sighs thus or thus, and raises her skirts so, with lips pouting so, and by close examination capture the very quintessence of the feminine art. What say you?"

No man present knew quite how to respond to William Shakespeare, as no man in England had ever said anything quite like this before.

Rosaline took her cue from the stunned silence of the men, hiked her skirts, and rushed toward the stage. William extended a hand and lifted her up to the platform.

William raised his tankard once more. "Arthur, refill the cups and we shall begin." Arthur Cawdrey dutifully obliged.

William took a breath, strode forward one step, and began:

"Behold, good gentles all, the Grecian scene wherein, beneath the creeping shade Olympus casts, fauns, satyrs, and centaurs roam, and where the crocus blooms at Whitsuntide."

Arthur Cawdrey nodded approvingly, and nudged Davy Jones.

William continued, gesturing toward Rosaline. "There a nymph divine, which yon bonny English maid presents, was wont to bathe at leisure in her pool. Now follows, if you will, the tale of Hermaphroditus, from blood immortal born, who stumbled lost upon Salmacis' grotto fair, and sealed thus his doom...and mayhap yours and mine."

He bowed with a flourish, and everyone applauded and hooted except for Davy Jones. George Cawdrey cried aloud, "Behold, our mild-mannered tutor bursts forth his shell. Have you been penning lines in secret twixt conjugations, William?"

William smiled. He felt like a god.

"See the nymph," said William, "bathing naked in her pool." He gestured to Rosaline, and kicked toward her the one small stool that stood upon the stage. It slid neatly across and stopped inches from her shapely derriere. She sat.

"Bathing *naked*, he said!" heckled Arthur Cawdrey, and all the other men laughed.

Rosaline replied with mock offense. "Let thy imagination reveal what my modesty may hide," she said. The merry band of brothers laughed. She turned upstage, and cast a longing glance into the distance.

William continued, "Salmacis hunts not, nor toils at loom nor well, but all day combs her hair, bathing lissome limbs in waters clear and fine." Rosaline took a comb from her hair, letting it cascade around her shoulders. Languidly she began to pull the comb through long tresses.

William stepped back to the rear of the stage. "Comes a youth, of features fair in which his father and mother might both be seen, of whom he also took his name..."

William, enacting the weary traveler, strode forward.

"Hermaphroditus is he, of Mercury and Venus born, and fifteen be his age. Adventuring from his country far to see the world, into fair Cyrie he roams. By a chance, the nymph divine has left the pool to gather flowers for her hair, and strayed amongst the woods nearby."

Rosaline, taking William's cue, danced lightly to the edge of the stage, and mimed plucking flowers from the grass.

"When from behind a tree," William continued, "the beauteous youth does she espy."

Rosaline ducked behind the branch of the tree that overhung the back corner of the stage and gazed at William as he enacted the youth. Rosaline swooned with instant love.

"What god is this?" she asided to the audience, which was by now rapt—even Davy Jones held his half-full cup dangling unattended between his legs.

"Fair is he beyond any mortal I e'er have seen," Rosaline continued with rising passion. "His face, his hair, his chest, his limbs bespeak of blood divine. Have him I must. Have him, I will. Will I not? Say 'Ay!'"

The audience answered heartily, "Ay!!"

Rosaline, as though looking in a mirror, took a moment to scrunch her hair. She curled a curl. She took a little finger to each corner of her lips. She hoisted her breasts up in her bodice, showing them to their best advantage.

Young Richard Tyler leaned over to Philip Rogers. "Is a maid so cunning when she woos, so forward?" he whispered.

"The stage is but a mirror and a shadow of nature, my boy," Rogers replied. "You have no idea."

Rosaline turned to William. "O most stately boy—or are you a god? If a god, then surely the god of love—if mortal, how blessed are your father and mother? How happy your brother? But"—and now she stalked toward William, predatory, like a fox toward the hare—"so much more blessed and happy was whoever had the good fortune to be your *sister*."

Here the audience exchanged uncomfortable glances. Davy Jones bristled and drained his cup with eyes still fixed on the stage.

"And even more…" teased Rosaline, and she reached out and slowly circled a fingertip lightly around William's left nipple.

"And even more blessed, she who nursed you…"

She let her finger trail down William's trunk toward his belt.

"…she who gave you suck. But how much *more* blessed she who becomes thy wife? Thy bedfellow?"

The last word hung in the air for a perfect moment before William turned to the audience.

"She knows her Ovid well."

A huge laugh.

Sensing a climax, William took a step toward the edge of the stage.

"We may gallop apace through the rest, as I think you apprehend the particular tone. She woos the youth, but he, knowing aught of love and much afear'd, the nymph denies."

Rosaline, as William tried to speak, was caressing him from behind, pawing him like a maenad in heat. Distracted, he continued. "Her suit she presses with kisses and caresses, until 'LEAVE OFF!' he shouts, 'or I must quit this place, and leave thee to thy tears!' She demurs, entreats him stay, and into the forest slips away." Rosaline mimed all this as William spoke it, and hid behind the branches of the tree overhanging the stage.

"About the wood he roams, as she, behind a bush, hides as only nymphs can hide. The youth, unknowing, espies her pool. Clear as crystal. No sign of weed or reed, of fen or bog. Ay, the very pebbles of the pool, a fathom deep, glitter through the shimmering waves and beckon him to dive. At first he dips a toe, and then a foot into the lapping water. At last, thinking himself alone..."

And here William paused a moment for effect.

"...the fair youth puts off his robes, and naked doth his body shine. His beauty strikes Salmacis in her ardent eye, inflaming her with sudden passion. Barely can she restrain her desire to run and take him there"—behind William, Rosaline writhed lasciviously—"ere he claps his hollow hands against his naked flesh, raises arms, and into the water glides."

And with that he mimed Hermaphroditus's fateful dive into the pool of Salmacis.

"Imagine, if you will, our stagecraft here: a simple trick, of azure water made of fabric from young Tyler's shop, flowing by. Hermaphroditus swims before it, his arms flashing white. Salmacis cries aloud..."

"Ohhhh!!!" Rosaline moaned.

"...and spraying clothes aside, naked casts herself into the pool."

As Rosaline mimed diving into the pool, Arthur Cawdrey heckled, again: "*Naked*, he said!"

"She envelops him, holds him, and struggle though he might, escape he is denied. Beneath the waves their bodies entwine, flesh pressing into flesh, and Salmacis cries unto the gods..."

Rosaline, now wrapped around William, standing on one toe, one leg about his waist, cried to the heavens, "Gods hear me, grant my prayer that this unholy willful boy shall never from me sundered be!"

William, still in Rosaline's arms, turned his face out to the audience.

"And the gods, good gentles, did grant indeed her prayer, joining their bodies in one, yet leaving privy members twain. And Hermaphroditus, once a manly youth, beholding what he had become, soft and yielding, cursed all else who bathed in those waters clear to share his fate. And so it is, my friends, that if you bathe, beware toward what ends!"

And with that, still entwined, William and Rosaline kissed. Their audience stood, cheered, lifted their cups, clanked them together, and drained them.

All except the fuming Davy Jones, who felt Arthur Cawdrey nudge him again in the ribs. "William's play even managed to end with a couplet," Cawdrey said.

Anthony Munday's play did not.

On the stage, Rosaline leaned close into William's ear. "You, William Shakespeare," she whispered under the applause, "ought not enact the minor role of a country schoolmaster, but rather a player, poet, and—by God's very prick I prithee—a lover, be."

Chapter Seven

Could such inordinate and low desires,
Such poor, such bare, such lewd, such mean attempts,
Such barren pleasures, rude society,
As thou art match'd withal and grafted to,
Accompany the greatness of thy blood
And hold their level with thy princely heart?

—King Henry IV to Prince Hal, *1 Henry IV*, III.ii.12

It was past dawn by the time Willie came down from the mushrooms. He and his fellow night-trippers returned from the cow pastures to the South Remote parking lot near Cowell College via a tiny, rickety redwood set of steps between two sentinel oaks that allowed humans, but not cows, to pass over the barbed wire fence and move back and forth between the humdrum life of classes and the spirit world of the cow pastures at night. He walked Dashka back to her car, but she'd been strangely quiet since the discovery of the giant mushroom. She gave him a distracted good-bye kiss, then turned back to him suddenly after she opened the door to her faded red Honda Civic.

"Do you want to get together sometime?"

"Um, yeah..." Willie said. "Maybe next week. I don't know... I'm taking the library jitney to Berkeley tomorrow."

Dashka cocked her head oddly.

"To work on my thesis," Willie added, convincing himself that he wasn't lying.

"Really?" Dashka replied, nodding. She seemed to be making a decision. Finally she said the last thing Willie expected to hear: "Me, too."

With a last spark of energy, she managed a mischievous smile. "I guess I'll see you in the back seat." Then she got in the car and drove away down the hill.

.   .   .

The Graduate Student Residences at UCSC consisted not of traditional dorms, but coed apartments of four small single bedrooms with a common kitchen, dining room, and living room. Willie awoke at noon to the sound of the sofa rolling upstairs. No one else was home. He had a meager breakfast—a slice of leftover pizza from the fridge—and read the third act of *Hamlet* for the zillionth time, spinning his Rubik's Cube and wondering why Hamlet didn't kill his usurping uncle when he had the chance. Then he went to his afternoon fencing class, the only one he'd registered for this quarter. He came back in time for dinner, and found a note tacked to his bedroom door with a pushpin: *Dood…some chick called.* He plucked off the note and turned to the common area, holding it aloft.

"Hey, who took this note?"

Jill, standing at the kitchen counter grating a huge, bright orange brick of cheddar cheese, shrugged.

Jojo, a mess of dyed-black hair and black nail polish, sat at the dining room table, hunched over a new Macintosh SE, an early Christmas gift from her parents, clicking away on a mouse. "Dunno," she said without looking up. "Josh and those guys were here earlier. Probably one of them."

Now he looked again at the note. "Some chick…" *Dashka, or someone else?* He crumpled it up and tossed it toward the kitchen garbage can, missing. He peeked over Jojo's shoulder at the Macintosh.

"What are you working on?"

"A fucking 'no pass' in *Gender and Globalization*, you oppressive pig." She was playing Dark Castle, maneuvering a little warrior man with a pageboy haircut through a medieval dungeon, throwing rocks at bats. Every time a bat took a hit, it plummeted to the floor with a dying *squeak. Squeak, squeak. Squeak.* "Wanna play?"

"No, I'm good. Oh, hey," Willie said too innocently to Jill, "you cooking?"

"Of course I am," responded Jill, leaning into the grater with a vengeance. "It's my night. Not that that means anything to anybody *else* around here." There was a calendar on the side of the refrigerator with nothing on it except, in Jill's fussy backward-slanted script, a schedule for the three nights each week when one of the apartment mates was responsible for cooking dinner. In theory, it saved on groceries and kept everyone from eating in the cafeteria or coffee shop every meal. In practice, it meant Jill cooked them all dinner once a week or so, and then bitched about it. "I don't understand why no one else will cook. What's the point of being *independent* and living in an apartment if you don't take advantage of the kitchen and cook sometimes? It's not even like everyone has to cook *every* week. There's a *rotation*." No one answered. "Hello, is anyone even *listening* to me?"

Jill was working on a Ph.D. in sociology.

The phone rang. Willie, glad to get away from Jill, picked it up.

"Hello?"

"Hello, Willie."

Willie immediately wished he'd responded to Jill instead.

"Oh...hi."

"Did I catch you at a good time?"

"Actually, I'm tired, just back from a class."

"How's the thesis?"

"Good, good, I'm rolling on it."

A pause.

"Really?"

"Yeah, I got the topic approved yesterday."

He waited for what he was certain would be an outpouring of approval—or at least relief—from his father. Instead there was a longer pause. And then:

"Well...then either you're a liar or the provost is."

"The provost?"

"I just got off the phone with him."

"What? Why?"

"Last week I asked him to find out how the academic career of my only child is going. I called today to follow up, and he told me that he talked to your advisor, Professor Walsh."

"Welsh. And he's—"

"He told the provost that he hadn't seen you academically in months, that you hadn't given him the abstract for your thesis—"

"That's because—"

"Let me finish, please. The provost also said that he personally is concerned about you and marijuana, that you looked stoned the last couple of times he saw you around the college. So, I just wanted to ask you if, for the past year, when I thought I was investing in your education, you've been merely sponging off of me and buying drugs?"

Willie's hands were shaking with anger, but he tried to control his voice. "Are you finished now?"

"Yes."

"I'm not sponging off you, I'm working on the thesis. I was just researching the influence of religion on psychological development in *Hamlet* this afternoon. And I'm not lying to you, either. Professor Welsh is on a book tour, but his TA approved the topic. Yesterday." This news, Willie thought, would surely change the tone of the conversation.

There was a longish pause.

"Well, that means nothing. TAs mean nothing. You need to get approval from *him*."

"Oh, for fuck's sake! I'm doing the best—"

"Don't curse at me, it's extremely rude."

"*I'm* rude? You just called me a sponge."

"I know I don't have to tell you that you can't get anywhere in academia without a master's. But the pace of your career matters, too. By the time I was your age I'd worked my own way through grad school and was starting on my dissertation."

"Right, well..." Willie took a deep breath, but the anger he held back had turned into a snake in his mouth, and he couldn't keep it from striking. "I guess I'm just not finding my inner Shakespeare as fast or as completely as you found your inner Woody Allen. How's the *Manhattan* lecture going over this year?"

There was a very, very long silence. Willie knew he'd gone too far, but it was already said.

On the other end of the line, he thought he heard the sound of ice clinking into a glass, followed by another long pause. "Perhaps it would be best for both of us if I simply stopped paying your way. Your tuition for the quarter is paid. Your thesis is approved, you say. So write the damn thing. If you need extra money, you could get a job."

Now the pause came from Willie's end. What could he possibly say? He'd painted himself into this corner; he might as well grab a stool and a dunce cap and face the wall.

"Fine. I don't need your money."

Another eternal pause.

"My point is—"

"Okay, well, I gotta go. Bye."

"Willie, wait—"

Willie hung up.

There was a studious hush in the room, broken only by the rhythm of Jill, still grating, and the occasional death of a bat in the Dark Castle. *Squeak...squeak.*

After a few seconds, Jojo broke the silence without looking away from her game. "Fuckin' parents."

Willie was cut off.

Chapter Eight

One of the most well-known stories of Shakespeare's youth involves his running afoul of a local justice of the peace, Sir Thomas Lucy. This paints a quaint image of Shakespeare as a boisterous youth, mildly rebellious in the face of blustering, provincial authority. But Sir Thomas Lucy was a heavy character: a "pursuivant," a local officer of the Crown charged with ferreting out Catholic "recusants" who refused to attend reformed church services — and making their lives as miserable as possible.

On Thursday, as William walked home through the crisp fall air toward his midday meal and a free afternoon, he thought of Rosaline and of the improvised triumph of *Salmacis and Hermaphroditus*. Then he thought of Isabella Burns; and then again, happily, of Rosaline. The incessant fog of the past few days had broken, and sunlight gleamed on the walls and windows of New Place and the bustling shops of High Street. William thought that Stratford, today, looked uncommonly beautiful.

It did not smell nearly so pretty.

As he turned the corner into Henley Street and crossed the Meer Stream that ran through it, he heard a female voice overhead. "Ho, there!" Instinctively he jumped back as a rain of shit and piss splattered into the brook beside him. "Mark thy ways, boy!" He looked up to see a housewife leaning out a second-story window, shaking the dregs out of her emptied chamber pot. This was a fairly common occurrence.

The Shakespeare house in Henley Street looked like crap; or more accurately, like a dunghill. That was the first thing one noticed on approaching the property. A ten-foot-high pile of table scraps, dead cats, festering turds of cow, sheep, goat, and dog, and last night's chamber-pot contents greeted the potential customer or visitor who approached the humble shoppe and attached home of John Shakespeare, Whittawer & Glover.

William shook his head at the dung heap and grumbled past it. Its mere presence here—the farmishness and ugliness of its blight on the fairest street of the fairest town in Warwickshire, where a young man might daydream of the fairest women in England—annoyed him with that peculiar annoyance that comes only from daily reminders of parents' shortcomings. Behind the dunghill, the house teetered over Henley Street. It was badly in need of attention, the whitewash peeling and the timbers splintering. Two shutters wanted repairing. The windows had no glass; such extravagances were strictly for the wealthy. Instead they were stretched across with linen that was stained and torn. The wide, horizontally hinged window that swung open as the storefront for the family business was closed, though it was midday. The thatch roof was threadbare in places; it perched slightly askew atop the house, like a drunk's hat.

William ducked into the carriageway that passed through from Henley Street to the Shakespeares' backyard and separated the structure into business and residence. On the right was the entrance to the workshop, on the left the entrance to the house. William peeked in at the workshop door. Inside was, of all things, a black-clad nobleman, poking idly and impatiently at the littered array of purses, bags, laces, gloves, mittens, satchels, and various scraps and whole skins of kid, lamb, calf, and dog.

"God ye good den, noble sir," William offered from the hallway. The noble figure turned and William, seeing the face, started and bowed immediately. Despite the protection it offered from chamber-pot bombardment, William never wore a hat. But if he had, he'd have doffed it. "My Lord Lucy. You honor our humble shop by your presence. I cry you mercy, sir, at finding the shop thus closed before its time. If you would withdraw—"

"Pray hold thy obsequious prattling tongue," Sir Thomas Lucy snapped. William could never remember that in the presence of nobility, he should never speak first. "What is thy name, boy?" Lucy said, and threw down the small, empty coin purse he had been examining onto a pile of similar items heaped in a cobwebby corner.

"William Shakespeare, my lord," William responded with another reverence.

"Where is thy father?"

"I know not, my lord. I'the tanning yard most like, tending to his trade."

Lucy looked about distractedly, as though not quite certain where he was or what he was doing there. "I am in need of"—he put a hand to his arrowhead-pointed, razor-sharp red beard, and the touch seemed to inspire him—"gloves," he continued. "*Master* Shakespeare is a glover, 'struth?"

William glanced quickly down the hall to the yard and then over a shoulder into the house's main hall, looking hopefully for Gilbert or his father. Inside the house, he heard his baby brother, Edmund, screaming bloody murder as usual and his younger sister, Joan, trying desperately to shush him. Gilbert and his father were nowhere to be seen.

"Ay, my lord," William said. He entered the shop and put on his business face. Only then did he see the large and hairy man standing, arms crossed and feet apart, in the shadows behind the door.

William cast a glance at him, and bowed tentatively. The henchman did not move.

William went to the shop chest, turning his attention back to Lucy. "Gloves for work or leisure?"

Sir Thomas Lucy didn't reply.

William held up a pair. "I know the park at Charlecote is fine for falconry." He passed Lucy the gloves. "These are made for such sport. Buck's leather, rabbit lined—"

"What knowest thou of my park, boy? Dost thou come at times unawares to thieve and sport at mine expense? Mayhap to poach my deer?" Lucy snatched the gloves away. "Wouldst thou, like a Jew of the Orient, sell me at a profit that which thou hast stolen from me?" He threw the deerskin gloves like a discarded noserag at William's feet. "No, I want none of thy buckskin for falconry."

William held Lucy's gaze for a moment. Then he stooped, picked up the gloves, and tossed them back on the table. "Swordplay, then?" William offered brightly. "A most sharp-edged blade you wield, my lord. These are made for playing at fencing." He held out a pair of fine chamois gloves.

Lucy screwed up his nose. "Fie! They reek of piss. A foul wind blows from this shop, and infects this house, this street, nay this very county."

William Shakespeare bowed. "An' it please your lord, it is, after all, a glover's shop, which are rarely known for sweetness of scent."

Lucy gave Shakespeare a sour stare, then turned away. Rummaging amongst the goods in the shop, his gaze landed on a large leather triangle with a hardened leather peak.

Lucy picked it up by one corner as though it might carry the plague. "A codpiece! Tell me not thou sellest this as an item of *fashion*?" He laughed, and looked to his colleague in the corner, who snorted once, derisively. "'Tis a popish affectation," Lucy continued, "a devilish idolatry of the privy parts. Yet, as a collector's piece...what is thy price?"

"Two crowns, my lord?"

"Two crowns?! Surely 'tis worth less than half that." Sir Thomas Lucy paused a moment. "Thou hadst best ask thy father the price."

William knew his father would want simply to unload the thing, but he also knew he should ask first—John Shakespeare didn't like others making his deals for him. "An't please my lord, take your ease but a moment and I shall enquire." He slipped back out the door with a bow and a glance at the muscle who hadn't yet moved from his henchman's pose.

As William stepped out of the carriageway and into the backyard of the house, a decapitated chicken went flailing and scrabbling across his path. A second later it was followed by a rooster who pecked and poked hungrily at the gore trailing and drizzling from the hen's neck.

Another second later, the cock was followed by a man. He wore a filthy apron over a filthier chemise and greasy leather hose, and ran bent forward at the waist, his cheeks flaming red, his nose a bouquet of booze blossoms, hair wild and matted, with both arms extended toward the headless running fowl. "It's the stew pot or foul hell for thee, Mary!" Mary was the name of the bifurcated hen.

William observed: "You speak, Father, to the bird's nether, senseless part. Address rather the gory chopping block where lie our supper's ears." The bottom portion of Mary (the hen) was still running full speed. "Or but wait a moment," William said.

And indeed, Mary (the hen) ran into the side of a barrel with a wet, feathery *fwap*, bounced backward, twitched three times, and finally died.

"And there 'tis," said William.

John shooed away the snacking rooster, picked up Mary (the hen's) carcass, and handed it to William's younger brother Gilbert, who stood next to the chopping block still holding a bloodied axe. "Take that to thy mother, Gil."

"Ay, Father," said Gilbert, and ran inside.

"There's an enquiry about the codpiece," William continued after Gilbert scurried into the house. He gestured back over his shoulder and widened his eyes significantly, a cue that his father missed.

"To buy it?" John asked.

"Ay. I priced it at two crowns," William said, and nodded urgently toward the shop behind him while mouthing "Sir Thomas Lucy." Again his father didn't notice.

"Od's teeth!" said John, "'tis but a scrap Adrian Quiney bade me remove from his hose, for he is e'er the fop and the codpiece is no longer in the courtly fashion. Sell it for a penny if they'll have it. What fool—"

A voice from behind William mocked, "What fool, nay knave, nay, I prithee pardon...what *alderman* lives in such squalor as this?" Sir Thomas Lucy had appeared in the yard.

John Shakespeare swept back his matted, sweaty hair streaked with flour and egg yolk, and did his reverence. "Sir Thomas."

To say Thomas Lucy looked with distaste at John Shakespeare would understate the matter; his look positively puked at him. "*Master* Shakespeare," he said. "I have not seen thee of late, neither at meetings, nor parades, nor any public affair nigh these—how long is it, Master Rogers?" He turned to his muscle, who uncrossed his arms long enough to hold up six knobby fingers—one of which was gnarled and cut off at the second knuckle—and then return to his pose.

"Five and a half years?" said Lucy. "A long time, thus to neglect thy civic duty."

"I beg your pardon, my lord," replied John. "But you know my office is discharged as charity. I have been much engaged with private toil in this my humble trade."

Lucy looked around at the yard. "Which indeed looks...and smells...like discharge."

Following Lucy's surveying gaze, William had to agree. In addition to the chicken head still on the block, there were three goats, two sheep, two dogs, a rooster, eight hens, a pig, and a half-dead ass named, not coincidentally, Lucy. The rooster and chickens were still in a clucking tizzy about the recent offing of one of their kin. The family cart listed on one side, its broken left wheel lying nearby awaiting repair. Skins in various stages of the process from animal part to clothing were strewn everywhere. There were three large vats, one filled with sulphuric alum and oil, one with bubbling lactic acid made of fermenting bran and water, and another boiling a twenty percent solution of dog manure and urine. A smaller vat, which John had been stirring just prior to Mary (the hen's) demise, was filled with a viscous bushel of flour and fresh egg yolks for softening leather. The discarded eggshells and -whites oozed and congealed in a crate nearby. The whole place smelled like a particularly nasty breakfast fart.

"Since you have removed yourself from public discourse for some time," said Lucy with mock ceremony, "perhaps you have yet to meet your new magistrate? Allow me to introduce you to Henry Rogers, until recently apprenticed to Richard Topcliffe of London." Richard Topcliffe was a well-known name, a name of fear: he was an expert torturer in the employ of Elizabeth's spymaster, Sir Francis Walsingham.

"Master Rogers," said Lucy, "this proud citizen is Master John Shakespeare, alderman, onetime bailiff, ale-taster, and husband to Mary Arden of the Ardens of Park Hall. A very, very honorable and important man." Lucy smiled with mock sympathy. "Now seemingly fallen on hard times."

Henry Rogers stepped forward to examine John Shakespeare's bulbous nose. "Still an ale-taster, by the looks of it."

"Strictly amateur," John joked nervously. "Of my days of public service in that regard I have fond remembrance; but they were long ago."

"I have not seen thee i'the church, Master Shakespeare," said Rogers.

"They say," said Lucy, turning to Henry Rogers, "it has been some three years since Master John graced God's house in his alderman's robes. There are rumors of recusancy."

Henry Rogers looked hard at John Shakespeare, awaiting an answer.

"I go not to the church not for lack of devotion to the new rites, my lord, but for fear of being served for process of debt," John Shakespeare replied, looking at the ground. "My affairs are much disordered, and I am debtor to many, creditor to none. Some there are who have threatened violence upon my person for debts outstanding, which I intend full well someday to honor, but cannot now redeem with aught but blood or limb."

Lucy exchanged a look with Henry Rogers.

"I suggest, Master Shakespeare, that if thy limbs are threatened, you take a surety against those that would harm you, rather than skulk in your barnyard at the peril of your eternal soul. It is given to Henry Rogers to enforce the Queen's law in this as in all things. See you look to't."

John Shakespeare bowed. "Ay, my lord."

"Then all is well. We will take our leave and see thee i'the church." Lucy tossed a small coin purse to John. "Here is two crowns for thy codpiece. It would be well spent on removing the dung heap from thy doorstep — which, I believe, is it not, Master Rogers, against the town charter?"

Henry Rogers nodded silently.

Sir Thomas Lucy gave a last withering look to John, then to William, and then to the tanning yard. Without a farewell he spun and swept out through the hallway in a flurry of black velvet. Henry Rogers gave one last, hard look at William, a longer, harder look at John, and left.

When they were gone, John's forced smile turned to a frown. "Puritan scum," he muttered under his breath to William, and cocked his arm as if to throw the coin purse after them. But then he seemed to think better of it, and tucked it into his belt.

"Shall we move the dunghill?" asked William.

Before his father could answer, there came the clanging of a spoon on a pot from the house.

"Not now, William," said John. "Come, let's to table. Your mother awaits."

Chapter Nine

... O thou weed,
Who art so lovely fair and smell'st so sweet
That the sense aches at thee, would thou hadst
Ne'er been born!

—*Othello*, IV.ii.67

Willie walked through the open front door of Todd's apartment. The communal areas of Todd's place were a riot of bicycle parts, musical equipment, art supplies, textbooks, and newspapers. André was sprawled on the couch listening to a cassette tape on his Walkman and scribbling on a sketch pad. Tinny bass escaped from his earphones. Sounded like Dead Kennedys. André nodded to Willie and said, way too loud for the room, "WANT SOME?!!" He gestured to the white laminate coffee table. It was covered with magazines, flyers for bands, André's caricatures of Ronald Reagan, unopened mail, a class catalog, and balanced on top of it all, a U2 album cover on which lay a baggie filled with purple, sticky-sweet sinsemilla bud—Willie could smell it from ten feet away. A bong plastered with stickers from Amsterdam's famously legal hashish bars leaked a little bit of water onto a history text.

Willie's heart was still pounding from the conversation with his dad; he nodded thanks and loaded himself a bowl. As Willie picked up the lighter, André shouted at him, "JUST BE CAREFUL, MAN, THEY'RE LOOKING FOR YOU!" and held up the cartoon he was working on: an armored helicopter with a strap-on pig snout and tail and labeled DEA, firing two huge heat-seeking rockets at an oblivious teenager listening to a Walkman and smoking a joint. The caption read: WHEN PIGS FLY.

Willie smiled and gave André a thumbs-up. He smoked, the reassuring cherry of flame blazing then guttering in the bowl. He sucked the ash through into the water with a pop, then released the carburetor to add a fresh dose of air into the column and *bubblebubblewhooosh*, the smoke entered his lungs. He felt the tension drain from his shoulders and the knot in his stomach loosen.

He nodded again to André, then followed the sound of *Terrapin Station* to Todd's bedroom door and knocked: *bam bam bam bam...bam bam*. A code knock, the bassline from "And You And I." Todd opened, his alabaster face flushed. "Hey. Whassup?"

"Can I come in?"

"Yeah, sit, dude, sit!"

Willie looked around for a place to sit. Todd's bed was covered with dirty clothes and album covers. Todd closed the door and plunked down on top of the pile of crap on the bed. Willie winced; he thought he heard a vinyl album crunch.

Willie sat on the edge of Todd's desk chair, the only sliver of it that wasn't covered with flannel shirts, pajamas, and boxer shorts. Todd looked at Willie expectantly.

"So...I was wondering if it's too late for me to get in on that transaction."

Willie wasn't sure how Todd would take this, but he actually leaped off the bed with joy. "Oh, yes. YES!! I got the deal all set up and have been trying *all fucking day* to get someone to deliver it. I was seriously considering selling my Dead tix for this weekend to do it myself."

Todd pulled an army-surplus duffel bag from under the bed, zipped it open, and took out a large Yuban coffee can. Opening it carefully, he gingerly reached in and coaxed out the giant mushroom. Here, in the light of day, it didn't seem to glow. In fact, it looked kind of gross: like a big fungus that had grown in some cowshit.

"There you go, all packed up and ready for sale. Thirty-two grams, dude! I talked to my guy. He's gonna pay two bills for it, but *don't* let it break. He's only interested in it as an unusual specimen. Ounce-wise it's only worth like thirty bucks."

Willie nodded. "Okay. How do I find him?"

As Todd carefully replaced the mushroom in the coffee can, he gave Willie his instructions.

"Go to the Renaissance Faire site. You know where it is, right? You can get there anytime Friday night through Sunday. Go to the gatehouse. Tell 'em you're in the Fools Guild. They'll have passes for you. Once you're in, ask anyone who works there for Friar Lawrence. Everybody knows him. He's your dude."

"Friar Lawrence is from *Romeo and Juliet*. Do I get to know his real name?"

"Sorry, strictly a need-to-know basis. No one there knows his real name, anyway."

"Very James Bond."

"I was wondering if you could do me one more favor."

"Now what?" Willie asked warily.

Todd reached into the duffel again and pulled out a large baggie stuffed with sixteen smaller baggies of marijuana buds.

Willie winced. "Is that a *pound*?"

"Another hundred in it for you just to deliver it to a second buyer."

Willie looked at the baggie. It was more pot than he was comfortable with. About sixteen hundred dollars' worth, retail: more money than he had ever seen in one place at one time, ever.

"I'm not a drug runner."

"I know, but this guy's totally cool. Plus he's the one getting you into the Faire for free. It's strictly for his personal consumption."

"Then why's it divided into ounces?"

"Come on. More free money."

Willie really did need the money. His dad paid for his tuition, a meal plan of three inedible cafeteria meals a day, and a monthly pittance. Anything else — movies, drugs, real food, the occasional concert — was strictly his responsibility. He'd worked waiting tables over the past two summers, but that money was gone. He'd timed the breakoff poorly. His dad always paid bills on the seventh, just a couple of days away. Willie had already kited a check at the student store on Tuesday for twenty-five dollars cash, and even that was nearly gone. Without money, and fast, he'd be caged in a prison of higher learning, with three squares a day and a shared cell.

He calculated. A hundred for the shroom, another hundred for delivering the other stuff…that would pay the overdraft fee and cover him for a few weeks until he could get a job.

"Okay. This guy's cash better be as green as his lungs."

Todd grinned. "Excellent. His cash is totally green. His name's Jacob. Just ask for the King of the Fools. He has a flag with a joker on it over his tent in the actors' camp. All you gotta do is deliver this"—he set the baggie down on the bed—"oh, and this," he added casually, dropping another small baggie filled with much smaller mushrooms on top of it—an ounce, divided into four seven-gram, quarter-ounce bags.

Willie shook his head, both at Todd and at himself for what he was certain was about to be a big mistake.

"Collect seventeen fifty, and you keep two hundred," said Todd.

"Three hundred."

"Two fifty, and we're done."

Willie shrugged agreement.

Todd picked up the entire duffel once more. It jingled. "And I'll throw in the rental of this fine ensemble of period costume absolutely free of charge."

He turned the pack upside down over the bed. Onto the array of dirty clothes, porn, scribbled notebooks, and a now-shattered recording of Talking Heads' *Fear of Music* spilled a blindingly colorful bundle of cotton: bright blues and yellows accentuated with red, purple, white, and green silk ribbons. Todd sorted it out, and it resolved itself into a fool's costume: baggy, tricolored trousers; tights with one red and one yellow leg; a green billowy shirt; a jerkin festooned with knotted strips of colored fabric, on the ends of which dangled small bells; and an elaborate coxcomb, complete with cuckold's horns.

"Oh, Jesus," Willie said. "I don't think so."

"You need a costume to get in for free," Todd replied. "But wait, here's the best part." He dug into the pack for something seemingly stuck inside, then pulled out a battered hunk of leather, fitted with straps and some tacked-on elastic. The piece itself looked not unlike one of the devices featured on the currently open ad pages of the magazine on the bed.

"A codpiece?" asked Willie.

"Wicked, huh? Found it at a garage sale. Two bucks. I think it might be an actual antique."

Willie took it from Todd and held it up, experimentally, to his crotch. He had to admit, it looked pretty cool. He shrugged.

"Well...if the cock fits..."

With the duffel bag repacked and slung over his shoulder, Willie went downstairs to his own apartment. To his amazement, Jill was still grating cheese, a mound now the size of a basketball on the cutting board in front of her. Willie went into his room and tucked the duffel bag under his own bed. He wanted nothing more than to lie down. The bed had other ideas. It was unmade and covered in nearly as much crap as Todd's. It would take five minutes just to clear enough space.

He went back out to the living room, moved a couple of pieces of mail off the couch, and fell heavily into its cushions. He figured he could catch a nap before Jill's cheese bomb went off.

Then he opened his eyes with a start: his mind's eye belatedly recognized the handwriting on one of the pieces of unopened mail. He snatched it up. Opened it.

Dear Willie, Just a note to see how your doing. Your dad and I are good, just hanging out. We went to see a Shakespeare play last night and I thought of you ☺. *It was Twelvth Night, it had some funny parts but I got confused with all the cross-dressing ha-ha. Well I hope that you are happy and you're school is going good and your getting lots of GIRLS (I know you are!). Are you coming for Thanksgiving? Call sometime soon. Love, M.*

Squeezed in at the bottom of the page was a single line, in a different hand.

What ho, Son, how's the thesis coming? Hope you're well. Dad.

He put the letter into its envelope and tossed it back onto the table. He was too tired to think about his fucked-up family. Once he wrote the paper, he wouldn't need them. He had friends here. Maybe young, irresponsible friends, maybe a little eccentric. But good friends. He curled up to try to sleep. Immediately there came a loud bumping from upstairs. *Rolling the sofa.*

He grabbed a pillow, put it over his head, and fell asleep.

And he dreamed.

I'm backstage during *Hamlet* at the Greek Theater in Berkeley, about to go on as Rosencrantz. It's the scene with Claudius, discussing the source of Hamlet's madness: "He does confess he feels himself distracted; but from what cause he will by no means speak...."

A light comes up on stage. I take a breath and move forward—but the stage manager stops me.

"What are you doing?" she says, "you're not Rosencrantz, you're Hamlet. You're the lead. It's your play!" I look down—I'm wearing the black doublet and disheveled shirt of the melancholy Dane.

There's a crowd. Hundreds. All waiting for me—the classic actor's nightmare. Only it's real.

"I can't," I say, "I don't know the part!" But the stage manager's gone.

It's Act Three, I think. To be or not to be. Get thee to a nunnery. Speak the speech, I pray you....I know the big monologues, but the other lines...the closet scene...I have no idea how that goes!

Polonius throws me my entrance cue: "I hear him coming: let's withdraw, my lord."

I walk on stage. But it's not the Greek Theater, it's not Berkeley, it's...UCSC. The Quarry Amphitheater. The only light on stage is a searingly bright full moon. It's blinding me, but the audience is there, I can hear them rustling and waiting in the dark, like trees in the forest.

I open my mouth. "To be or not to be..."

But I'm not speaking, I'm singing...holy fuck, I'm singing the scene from *Gilligan's Island* where the castaways perform *Hamlet* as a musical. Fuck! I can't SING!!!

The unseen audience is laughing now, and there's no escape—

"Good my lord, how does your honour for this many a day?"

Saved. It's Ophelia. This scene I know.

"Are you honest?" I ask.

"My lord?"

"Are you fair?"

"What means your lordship?"

"That if you be honest and fair, your honesty should admit no discourse to your beauty."

"Could beauty, my lord, have better commerce than with honesty?"

She's playing this seductively, almost wantonly. I like it.

"I did love you once," I tease.

"Nay, you have not, my lord. Not yet."

That's not the right line. Ophelia smiles mischievously, looks at me with deep blue eyes as she unlaces her bodice...And I realize...it's Dashka. Dashka, playing Ophelia...how did I not notice that before? Jesus, I think, I'm going to see her naked, and I get a hard-on. But just then the moon goes out. It's dark. The audience murmurs expectantly.

A light comes on...from where? I look up...it's coming, impossibly, from a star in Orion's sword. It forms a pin spotlight, center stage, illuminating a bed in nebulous light. There's a woman on it. I'm hoping it's Dashka, naked, but I feel a cold dread and I know it's not her.

A tap on my shoulder: Polonius. He whispers, "The Queen would speak with you, and presently," and slips away.

I back away from the bed, toward the wings.

I feel a hand on my arm...it's the stage manager, pushing me. "You have to finish the scene!" I want to tell her no, I quit, I don't want to be an actor anymore. I open my mouth, but no words come out, and she keeps saying "Willie, you have to go on, Willie. Willie!"

He awoke to Jojo shaking his arm gently. "Willie! Wake up." He sat up, disoriented. The bumping upstairs had stopped.

"What is it?"

Jojo's face was white.

"The feds just raided Todd's apartment. Narcs. They arrested Todd and André. If you have anything, you'd better flush it, fast."

Willie was still in dream world for a moment. He was in Berkeley, an undergrad...his mother was alive. No...she was dead, and he was broke, and running drugs—

With sudden panic and realization, he jumped up, ran to his room, and yanked the duffel bag out from under the bed with trembling hands. He zipped it open to assess the danger. A pound of pot, thirty-two grams of mushroom, plus a little more. He could flush it. But it was quiet upstairs. Why should the feds who had raided Todd's apartment come down here? There were no drug dealers in Willie's apartment.

Then Willie had a brief image of Todd in a bare room at a metal desk lit by a single bare bulb. *"I don't have any drugs...I gave them all to Willie, man."*

Todd wouldn't do that. Nor would André. Would they?

He could flush the evidence. But what if the narcs busted in while he was flushing? Caught red-handed. But if he got out now, delivered it—

Seventeen hundred fifty dollars. Most of it Todd's, and he'd be needing it. For bail. For legal fees. The rest of it Willie's, and he'd be needing it, too.

Willie zipped up the duffel, shoved a change of clothes into his backpack, put on his denim jacket. Jojo watched silently as Willie walked, as casually as possible, toward the sliding glass door in the living room that opened out onto the balcony. "See you later," he muttered to Jill, who was still grating cheese, a vast Devil's Tower of dairy teetering over the sink.

Jill peered out from behind the orange monolith. "What? Where are you going? Aren't you staying for dinner? I'm making ch—" was all Willie heard before he slid the door closed behind him. He plowed through a jumble of cheap plastic patio furniture and haggard spider plants to clamber over the balcony's railing. They were on the second story; carrying the duffel on his shoulder, he awkwardly shimmied down to the balcony below, caught a pant leg on the brake handle of someone's bike, and plummeted to the ground. He recovered, started down the steep bank of the ravine, tripped, then rolled and tumbled as quietly as possible all the way to the bottom.

Chapter Ten

Shakespeare's greatest tragedies are nearly all driven by family dynamics: dysfunctional families, as in King Lear; *families overwhelmed by external circumstances, as in* Titus Andronicus; *families fighting against each other, in the case of* Romeo and Juliet; *and families fighting themselves, as in* Othello *and* Macbeth. *It should come as no surprise that in arguably his greatest tragedy,* Hamlet, *ALL of these dynamics are present. Shakespeare was the first English playwright to capture the essence of what makes families so frustrating, so frail, and, ultimately, so beautiful.*

For a Shakespeare of Stratford-upon-Avon, the call to dinner was one 'twere well to heed, and heed quickly.

In a pot in the Henley house kitchen, over a low fire, bubbled a watery stew of onions, turnips, and leeks. There was a two-day-old quarter loaf of bread and a pitcher of ale on the long oak dining table. William's mother, Mary Arden Shakespeare, took Mary (the hen) from the spit upon which she slowly roasted and, with six sure strokes of a cleaver, dismembered her. Dishes and mugs clattered noisily as the family passed their pewter plates to Mary one at a time to be filled.

There were six mouths to feed in the house: John, Mary, William, William's younger brother Gilbert, his younger sister, Joan, and two-year-old Edmund. When the dinner was chicken, there were nine pieces of meat to be parceled out: two breasts, two thighs, two legs, two wings, and the back. John always got a breast and a thigh. Mary insisted on taking just the back; she was a light eater. Gilbert and Joan each got a leg and a wing. Mary picked apart the other wing and fed it to baby Edmund. William, the eldest, got the other breast.

That left a thigh.

It would sit there on the cutting board, oozing its sweet thigh juices as John, secure in his guaranteed, head-of-household second piece, boomed on at the head of the table about the day's events, local politics, gossip of Queen Elizabeth's court. The rest of the table ate silently, quickly, with furtive glances up, down, and across the table. Whoever finished their portion first, without appearing to be greedy, got the second thigh. William and Gilbert had the edge in size and reach, but Joan was always a dangerous outside threat.

William received his bowl of broth and his plate, and casually placed a finger atop the plumpest bit of Mary's (the hen's) breast.

"What men were those today, William?" asked Joan. It was a ploy. William would sometimes slip in a large bite before grace, but he couldn't eat while he answered a question: and now the focus of the table was on him. Joan never liked to fall behind waiting for her plate.

"Men? What men? I know not—"

Joan rolled her eyes and let out a short, sharp breath of impatience. "The *men*! Think you I know not a man by his beard when I see one? Though I be only thirteen, I know a man—"

"I hope you know not a man yet," sniggered Gilbert under his breath.

Everyone now had their plates, so William gave up and removed his hand from Mary's (the hen's) breast. John led grace before the meal.

"Benedic, Domine, nos et haec tua dona quae de tua largitate sumus sumpturi. Per Christum Dominum nostrum. Amen."

"So who was it?" Joan asked as she tucked into her chicken.

Around his first bite, William replied, "Sir Thomas Lucy, no less. He was—"

"Shopping for gloves, methinks, wasn't it, William?" interrupted his father. "Falconing?"

"I'm not sure what he was after," responded William. "He bought a codpiece."

"Why be it called a codpiece, Mum?" asked Joan. "The piece covers not a cod."

The entire table laughed.

"Nay, though the piece it covers may smell like one," Mary answered quietly. "Especially as it ages," she added with a smile to John. There was a collective groan from the table.

John replied, "As may the pond in which it swims, as it withers, dries, and becomes choked with weeds, my love."

Mary laughed and kissed him on the head.

"A rare touch for Dad," whispered Gilbert to William.

William thought the topic had been successfully deflected from Sir Thomas Lucy, whom his father was clearly loath to discuss.

But Joan was young and persistent. "I see not why the family Lucy has such a black name in this house. Methinks Spencer a bonny boy, and my age, too."

"Four years your senior he is, and his face as spotted as his name," said Gilbert as he sucked the marrow from Mary's (the hen's) right thigh.

"'Tisn't!" said Joan. "And what's in a name, anyway?"

"Everything," Gilbert replied. "Lucy is lousy, and lousy is Lucy. The word is one and the same." In the Warwickshire dialect, the pronunciation was similar.

"Then am I the same as my sister Joan: dead and buried, with a mean headstone marking two years of life and a lifetime of death, and worms wriggling in and out my eye sockets."

Joan was named after her own sister. John and Mary's first child had died at six months. William saw in the pain that passed across his mother's face the regret—which came whenever Joan mentioned Joan—that she had given her the same name. This Joan seemed to have an unhealthy obsession with mortality: crypts and poisons, suicides and stabbings, skeletons and skulls, fascinated her. She preferred to wear black clothing that contrasted with her notably pale skin and dark eyes.

"Methinks you find Spencer Lucy's fine clothes and plumed hats more bonny than his face, Joan," said Mary Shakespeare as she dug with delicate, crafty hands between two of Mary's (the hen's) back ribs for a bit of tender meat.

"And what harm in bonny clothes?" Joan said. "I should be happy to be Lady Lucy, and live at Charlecote with waiting maids and parks full of deer and rabbits, and attend the Queen. *Yes, Your Highness! How fares Your Grace?*"

John, who had been eating and swilling his ale in silence, slammed his mug down on the table. "No more!"

His family turned to him in surprise. It was not often, in recent years, that he got so worked up. "We'll have no talk of a union of Shakespeares and Lucys at my table. A plague on their house." He paused a moment, seemingly taken aback by his own outburst, then took his second piece of chicken.

As he chewed a crust of bread, William glanced furtively at his father. John used to be quick to anger, when he was bailiff and carried all the cares of the Corporation of Stratford-upon-Avon on his shoulders, but he was just as quick to laugh.

Those were days that now seemed like a dream. William drifted out of the conversation as it turned to Joan's sewing and Edmund's appetite and other family matters. He tried to remember his father in his prime. William would have been nine — no, eight — at the peak of John Shakespeare's wealth and standing in the community. William had fine clothes, and was learning letters and Latin from Simon Hunt, the schoolmaster at the New School before he left scandalously to study in Rheims. The other boys would stare at William in awe as he and his family went in formal procession from their home to Holy Trinity on Sundays, John carrying the ceremonial staff of his office, wearing his bailiff's scarlet robes, and escorted by two sergeants at arms carrying deadly maces, to the family's favored place at the front of the church.

John Shakespeare the glover was the most important man in town, and William his eldest son and heir. Laden wagons would roll in and out of the yard at Henley Street all day long, and John would retreat to the parlor with their drivers, talking tods of wool, the Queen's monopoly, and the intransigence and corruption of the Guild of Glovers. John, as many glovers did, sold the wool from the sheep they kept for lambskin on a large and profitable black market. Soon he stopped making gloves altogether, and merely bought and sold wool. He grew wealthy quickly, and bought two fair houses in Stratford as investments, and leased them. He had two apprentices who lived amongst the bales of wool in the house's voluminous attic. There was lamb for dinner more often than not, also beef, venison, veal, rich cheeses, pheasant, rabbit, whole stewed fish, cooked by a cook and served by a serving maid. Sometimes in the winter months a merchant from Plymouth or Lancashire would bring an offering of oysters and they would eat them by the hundred. William loved the oysters with their hint of the far-off sea and something else ineffable and irresistible.

John reveled in his role as bailiff. He ate, he drank, he held forth, he pomped and he circumstanced. These had always been his favorite things, and now he did them on the town's penny. Ever a fixture at the Bear (the Catholic-leaning of the town's two inns), John would now spend public money on his favorite private entertainments. He brought the first professional theater company to Stratford, hiring the Queen's Men to perform a bit of Italian comedy about a servant trying simultaneously to serve two masters. Sitting in the bailiff's reserved space in the front row of the Bear's inn yard, John must have spilled a quart of ale during the performance, nearly choking as he sucked in a bit of cheese pie while laughing during an extended bit of business involving a lute teacher, his young female student, and an amorous salami. The performance was a smashing success, and Master Bailiff Shakespeare leapt on the stage and, with great theatricality of his own and after much bowing, laughing, and clapping on the back, lavished a generous prize of seventeen shillings on the appreciative troupe.

Then there had been—was it the very next summer?—the dreamlike day when William, a wide-eyed child, sat on the great lawn amongst dukes and earls, barons, viscounts, knights, and ladies—sitting not in the front, but not in the back, either—at Kenilworth Castle as the Earl of Leicester's Men performed a watery pageant of *Cupid and Aphrodite* on the wide lake at the castle's south side.

His mother sat next to him on one side, poised and dignified, and next to her were distant relatives: Ardens he had never met, including the best-dressed man he had ever seen. "Your cousin and the patriarch of your mother's family, the master of Park Hall, Edward Arden," John had whispered to William at their introduction. Next to him, his cold and beautiful wife, Mary Arden. And next to her, a proud and statuesque woman, dressed all in black. She wore openly a crucifix, and held in her hand a forbidden rosary, which she flipped quickly between her fingers.

"And who is the tall lady?" William had asked his father.

"Lady Magdalen, Viscountess Montague," John whispered. "Once a lady of honor to Queen Mary, and even now, 'tis said, friendly with Her Majesty the Queen. A great woman, William, and great indeed in the Queen's favor to practice so openly and without rebuke the Old Faith."

The pageant began, and the splendors of it were too many for William later to recall. But the end he remembered. As if by magic, Aphrodite had risen on a bark from the waves. Cupid, at her side, had aimed his bow strung with love's shaft at the Queen herself, sitting upon a gilded chair by the lake's shore. The crowd had gasped, and the Queen's guard drew around her, spears leveled. But Aphrodite raised Cupid's arm as he fired, and the arrow went far astray, out over the lake, where it burst into a firework that lit up the water and ended the pageant to cheers of delight.

The Earl of Leicester, Sir Robert Dudley himself, had risen and smiled and bowed, and the Queen had risen and smiled with him and said in a voice loud enough for all to hear that she would never be wounded by such an errant, false shaft of love, that she would remain her people's chaste Queen, and John Shakespeare and the crowd had roared, though Leicester's hostly smile was a tight one.

As she passed out through the crowd on her sedan chair, the Queen had come within ten yards of the place where William and his father bowed in obeisance, and William had looked up. Her face was at the heart of a constellation of rich jewels and fabric, at the center of which her eyes blazed like the sun reflected off of polished onyx. Her skin he remembered only as a drift of white, like a frozen lake, for so it was painted, to hide the scars of age and smallpox. And as she waved her queenly gloved hand—the finest cheveril, the glover's son William had noted, with fourchette and stitching extending almost to the second knuckle, fingers extra long and padded at the tips to accentuate her feminine hands, embroidered with white silk thread and pearls and golden beads—as she waved her hand to her subjects, her eyes and William's had met. When she saw the eager, awed little boy next to the fat, ruddy-cheeked man in fading scarlet robes, the smallest hint of a smile had crossed the Queen's lips. And then she was gone amidst a cheering and a ringing of bells.

Immediately following her had come the Earl of Leicester and his household. Leicester smiled proudly and nodded to the various nobility who bowed as he passed. He thanked them vociferously "For gazing upon this pageant, which is but a pale reflection of my true love and worship for Her Majesty." His smile faded faintly as he glanced at Edward Arden, and Lady Magdalen with her rosary. He passed on, but the Earl of Warwick, behind him, stopped and glared at Arden.

"Master Arden! You do my Lord of Leicester wrong, sir!"

The cheering faded around them.

"I humbly beseech your pardon, my lord," Arden replied to Warwick. "How have I offended mine host Leicester?"

"Play not the fool with me, sir," Warwick replied. "All other of our rank and station wear Leicester's livery this day, in honor of his beneficence in providing the day's pageantry. Surely the rite and fashion is known to you?"

Young William looked around him, and noted that all the noblemen wore emblems of Leicester's livery: tunics or sashes of blue and gold with devices of fleur-de-lis, or a bear leaning on a rough staff, or a lion, rampant, with two tails—all, that is, except Edward Arden.

There was uncomfortable shifting of feet. Leicester himself had stopped and turned to stare at Edward Arden, and was now awaiting his reply.

Arden glanced disdainfully at Leicester, then turned to Warwick. "I'faith, my lord, my livery is by its absence meant to honor the Earl of Essex."

The hush quietened beyond silence.

It was rumored that Leicester was bedding Essex's wife while he was making war in Ireland. Amidst the collective held breath, Arden continued, "To wear the livery of one who would take advantage of the distant commission of a Queen's officer to gain private access to the officer's lady, would be to honor a whoremaster."

Leicester drew his sword and leapt forward, enraged. "God's teeth, will you speak thus to me, even here?!" Arden also drew, and it might have turned into an ugly pageant indeed.

It was Viscountess Montague who stepped in between them. "Good my lords, I pray you put your weapons by. Let not the majesty and pageantry of the day be marred by such intemperance. It is not meet, to try so private a grievance in so public a court. Forbear, forbear."

Leicester looked around at the festivities still going on outside their little circle, and, trembling in anger, sheathed his sword. "For that I would not stain the honor of the Queen, and as my Lady Magdalen is ever a voice of conscience, I shall stand down. But this slight, sir, is not slight, and will not unpunish'd go. Mark you."

Without another word, Leicester had passed on, and Mary had hustled John and William straight back to Stratford.

After that extraordinary day, John's mood seemed slowly to turn. His gifts and entertainments became less lavish day by day. He drank more and laughed less. The apprentices left one by one, and were not replaced. The cook was let go, and their sole help now was a string of increasingly poorly remunerated local girls, who came in a few hours daily — and later, weekly — to clean. Once, when William was home during his midday break from school and eating bread, John burst in the door, drunk at noon and raging at Mary because she was there.

"Blast and damn to hell guilds and the Queen, Leicesters and Lucys, and Luther and Lucifer alike! Fifty pounds, fifty pounds he owes me, doth John Luther, aptly named, the little Puritan flea, and now he hides himself behind 'his' Queen and accuses me of usury to my face, and of popery! And if he will accuse, Sir Thomas Lucy will prosecute, Leicester's mangy hunting dog, rabid and drooling and willing to rend flesh for a scrap of meat tossed by the Earl. Marry, may not a man pursue his faith and his business with — OW! God's WOUNDS!!!" he yelled, for he had walked shin-first into a corner of the best bed (which was set in the parlor, both for easy availability to drunken guests and to show off the family's lustrous mahogany wealth). He sat on the bed, groaned, and continued, "The whoresons shall find the Queen looks kindly on her loyal subjects and appointed officers who serve the crown, not these worms who would eat the heart of her realm, marry! Fifty pounds!" He continued muttering as he limped heavily up the stairs into the second-best bed and fell asleep.

Fifty pounds. William, at the time, could barely conceive such a sum. In his mind, it would buy the finest house in Stratford, and he was not far from wrong. The next year, John rode in an "official capacity" to London as deputy to the next bailiff, his friend John Quiney, ostensibly to represent "the affairs of the borough according to their discretions." In fact, it was a personal junket he had rammed through the town council. While in London on Stratford's tab he sued John Luther for the fifty pounds and won.

But it was one of his last victories. The Guild of Glovers, run by Protestants and influenced by Leicester, got wind of John's extracurricular activities in wool brokering, and he was fined twenty pounds. Twice. A house's-worth of his fortune, equal to his entire inheritance from his own father, gone. Overextended, John mortgaged part of his wife's family's ancestral home, then defaulted on the loan. He was fined another twenty pounds for usury after charging a local wooler — a Protestant — twenty pounds for a short-term hundred-pound loan. Another house's-worth, fare thee well. Recourse to the local authorities? None. He was a suspected Catholic with marriage ties to the powerful Ardens; the "authorities" were Protestant reformers happy to see Catholics on the ropes. He finally stopped leaving the house entirely unless it were to sneak down to the Bear at off-hours, preferring to simply stay at home and pretend to make gloves and drink and eat and hold forth. Yet he was still amiable and quick of wit. His fellow aldermen on the council were too kind to take his office away from him, and forgave him the taxes expected to help the poor. They simply noted him as missing from meetings, every fortnight, for ten years.

Thus had John Shakespeare gone from middle-class success story — a yeoman shaking his spear in upwardly mobile civic triumph — to holding the staff of his office in shadow and disgrace: a John False-staff, indeed.

William drifted back into the dinner table scene to see Joan holding out her empty plate to Mary. Gilbert thrust his forward a second too late. Mary reached out and speared the last bit of Mary (the hen) — the succulent thigh — and dropped it onto Joan's plate. Joan discreetly stuck out her tongue at William and Gilbert across the table. Gilbert wrinkled his nose back.

William smiled; he always let Joan win.

Her victory secure, Joan took up her complaint again. "Still I know not why the house of Shakespeare, whose master was bailiff, must be held lower in esteem than the house of Lucy."

Suddenly William felt Joan's incomprehension as his own, and also anger rising from somewhere deep in the pit of his stomach. "Why? my sister asks, and rightly so. Why must the Shakespeares grunt and sweat under a weary life of gloves for the lily-white hands of Thomas Lucy, who feasts at Charlecote while we are left to gnaw at the bones of a single shriveled hen? Because of a matter of doctrine?! The wheezes and mutterings of aged bishops and choleric Puritan scholars?"

"William, not in front of Gil and Joan—"

"I speak on their behalf, Mum," William said without slowing down. "Are we not Catholic? We say a Catholic blessing before each meal, but what means it? We eat meat of a Friday, when the faithful eat fish. Our mother drags us to the church of a Sunday and we feign to honor the new rites, but then we slink back home and, behind closed doors, pray and beg forgiveness for the selfsame worship as a mortal sin! Why must we skulk so under these oppressors' wrongs? Are we to hide here until at last they come to cut up the laymen as they cut up the priests?"

Mary and John had listened quietly. When William finished, John said haltingly, "William…we all do what we may, at what time we may. Elizabeth and her Puritan counselors will not live forever—"

"Nor will I. Nor will Joan and Gilbert," William interrupted.

His mother said calmly, "Mary, Queen of Scots, if she is restored to the throne, will restore the faith. We must wait and hope."

"Elizabeth will never let her cousin accede to the throne. Mary will no more be Queen than Mary Arden Shakespeare, or Mary the hen," William said, tossing his gnawed breastbone into the center of the table, and standing to pace restlessly. "Mayhap I should follow Thomas Cottom, and Robert Debdale of Shottery, and go to Rheims, and study the priesthood."

Mary fell grey at the mention. "If you would serve the true church, your God, and your family, you would not do such a thing. Your family has need of you here, William. Gilbert, Joan, and Edmund need you here."

Joan looked at her brother, terrified at the mention that he might leave. She held out what was left of Mary (the hen's) last quarter. "Don't go, Will. You can have the rest."

William took a deep breath, and smiled at Joan. "Nay, Joanie," he said, "nay. Fear not. I spoke but in jest. I'll take neither a ship to Rheims nor your well-deserved bit of meat."

He mussed Joan's hair playfully, but as he did he spoke darkly to Mary and John.

"Yet if I must needs stay, then shall I do what little I may here."

Without looking back at his parents, William walked out the front door and turned left. The air was heavy. Even as he strode down Henley Street, rain began to patter into the Meer Stream. He crossed into Bridge Street and finally through the open door of the Bear. He stood steaming in the doorway for a moment as his eyes adjusted to the darkness. There was a boisterous midday crowd.

William saw the figure he was looking for at a corner table in the shadows, washing down a meat pie with a cup of wine. William walked over and sat without being invited.

"I beg your mercy, good sir. I wonder if the office which late you offered remains unfulfilled?"

The horseman looked at him steadily.

"Ay, good lad. Indeed, I've spent a fruitless morning in search of another to do the errand."

"Good sir, John Cottom was my teacher, my mentor, and my friend. I swear to you upon his family name, and upon mine, that if he be alive and to be found, I will deliver it unto him. Mayhap not today nor this week nor even by this year's end, for I yet must school my class and bring my family bread. But if John Cottom yet lives I promise you this charge will be dispatched by me with the same diligence you have essayed to bring it thus far."

The horseman nodded slowly. "Excellent well." He rose and beckoned William to follow him. They went upstairs and into a cramped room.

Taking down the wrapped box from a high shelf, the horseman said, "God willing, this remembrance of Thomas Cottom will be delivered...as its owner was not."

"Remembrance? What mean you?" William asked, going numb.

"Do you not know?" the horseman replied. "Forsooth, news travels from London to Stratford like unto a wounded snail! Thomas Cottom was martyred some weeks past."

"Thomas Cottom is hanged?"

"Ay...and drawn and quartered, too, as a traitor to Her Majesty. My master Ely was the last to see him alive. Cottom's last wish, cried most piteously, was that this box should find his brother." He handed the box to a dumbfounded William.

"The head of the last to bear this burden stands skewered atop the gates of London. May you meet a better fate."

The horseman then solemnly made the sign of the cross over William.

"Benedicite."

Chapter Eleven

Herein will I imitate the sun,
Who doth permit the base contagious clouds
To smother up his beauty from the world,
That, when he please again to be himself,
Being wanted, he may be more wonder'd at,
By breaking through the foul and ugly mists
Of vapours that did seem to strangle him.

—Prince Hal, *1 Henry IV*, I.ii.197

Willie awoke to the sound of a banana slug rustling along the forest floor a few inches from his right ear. He sat up with a start and checked to make sure the duffel bag next to him was undisturbed. After his fall, he had limped a few hundred yards up the ravine until he found a closely circled stand of redwoods, crawled into the depression between them, and spent a cold and fitful night listening for the sounds of approaching dogs and jackboots before finally falling asleep.

He rubbed the sleep from his eyes and looked around.

It was a foggy morning, and still gloomy in the misty ravine. The forest floor was punctuated by bright yellow exclamation points: more banana slugs.

Fascinating creatures, banana slugs. Peculiar to the redwood forests of the Pacific Coast, they are plentiful in the Santa Cruz Mountains. Though they can change color over time to adapt to the amount of light and moisture in their environment, the ones in Santa Cruz are a bright yellow: fireman's-coat yellow, bomb shelter sign yellow, *Yellow Submarine* yellow. After a rain, they would litter the forest floor like banana-flavored condoms after Mardi Gras. On damp days like today they would come out to suck what moisture they could from the air. They are hermaphroditic.

And though they will eat anything—living or decaying vegetation, droppings, animal carcasses—they are particularly fond of mushrooms. Willie watched them for a few minutes, crossing with infinite patience from one side of the ravine to the other, inserting themselves into cracks in fetid logs, soaking up the mud under the occasional rock, and busily digesting bits of local mushroom, which caused who knows what joyous waves of banana slug psychotropia.

Willie tended to look kindly on the banana slug. He was not alone: the shining mollusk was the unofficial mascot of the university.

Willie stretched, gathered up his bags, and walked warily back down the ravine among the redwoods and the slugs. After he had passed his own apartment atop the bank, he scrambled back up the slope beneath the wide span of a footbridge. He crossed Heller Avenue and passed out onto the expanse of a second redwood bridge, which disappeared into the fog long before its far end. Mist wafted up the ravine, though there wasn't enough wind to disturb the redwoods. It was silent but for the sound of a few birds, and, perhaps, the rustle of banana slugs inching along below.

He was halfway across the bridge when he heard footsteps running toward him, audible long before the runner became visible—*just like Hitchcock would do it*, Willie thought. His heart raced as he flashed on the image of Cary Grant pursued by a crop duster.

But then the footsteps became sneakered feet, and a pale, haggard face—*computer programmer*—sprinted past, looking pissed off. "Fuck!" he blurted as he passed Willie, and Willie realized that the bus engine he now heard rumbling down Heller toward the town must have been the programmer's, and he'd missed it.

Willie glanced at his cheap digital watch, and broke into a run. The library shuttle was scheduled to leave at seven thirty...now.

He took a quick shortcut across Steinhart Way and down a well-trodden embankment, around the dismal gray modern cement of Kerr Hall, and arrived at the library. He fast-walked through the foyer and atrium and toward the driveway at its rear entrance.

Crap, I hope I didn't miss it....

But no, there it sat, steam chugging from its exhaust. There was no one waiting to board, and the driver was in his seat. Willie rushed up the steps.

"Thanks. Just made it, huh?" Willie said to the driver, an older man with smoker's wrinkles and gray, stubbled hair peeking out from a motor oil cap.

"Only because your friend said to wait," he growled with a twitch of a nod toward the rear.

Willie glanced down the aisle. There, sitting in the back row, looking over the top of a book, was Dashka. He had really, truly forgotten she would be there. "Thanks," he murmured to the driver, and started down the aisle. There were only two other passengers on the bus: one mousy, bespectacled girl who looked as though she was actually going to Berkeley to use the library for the day; and an older student, thirtyish maybe, probably a grad student, with a black mustache and long hair pulled into a ponytail. Willie nodded at him instinctively; he had the vague impression he knew him from somewhere. The word "clerk" and an image of Dashka came to mind; was he the guy at the adult bookstore where he'd bought the porn rag? But the mustachioed man showed no sign of recognizing Willie and didn't nod back, so Willie sidestepped with his backpack and duffel all the way to the rear of the jitney bus.

Dashka lowered her book and gave the disheveled Willie a once-over. "Hey, morning glory. Take the window," she said, and slid slightly toward the center aisle. She moved her knees aside to allow Willie access. As she did, he noticed that her cotton skirt was sheer.

He complied.

The idea of the library jitney was that students with more serious research needs than UCSC's modest McHenry Library might accommodate could go to Berkeley for the day on the university's dime. There they could run free in an orgy of academic delights, of chemistry libraries, antiquities libraries, botany, chemistry, theater, arts, theology, and nuclear engineering libraries: all the musty edifices of higher learning.

The drive from Santa Cruz to Berkeley takes ninety minutes. The first half hour is over a sinuous four-lane mountain freeway through Pitchen Pass, from Santa Cruz on the coast to Silicon Valley inland, a beautiful drive but one of the most dangerous in the country: it's narrow, the curves are treacherous, and people drive it fast.

It didn't seem to bother the jitney driver. He had turned on the radio to a local AOR station, which was playing "Synchronicity" by the Police. The driver slowed once, suddenly, as a black BMW tailgated him, passed him on the right, then cut him off at eighty mph on a wicked turn and sped ahead, its smug REAGAN/BUSH '84 bumper sticker glinting in the sun. "Goddamn Reaganites!" the crusty bus driver muttered to no one in particular. "Think they own the damn world."

"Maybe they do," replied the mustachioed man.

Dashka had nudged her glasses up onto her nose and returned to her book. Willie, seated next to her in an awkward silence, had a sudden urge to check on the mushroom. Taking off his jacket — it was warm in the jitney, and he was sweating from his run to the library — he laid it across his lap. Dashka glanced over at the movement, then returned to her book and turned a page. After she turned the next page, Willie bent down, quietly opened his backpack, removed the mushroom gently from its coffee can, and held it in his lap, under his jacket.

As he fondled the mushroom and thought his thoughts, he found himself thinking less and less about the mushroom and any sense of danger and more and more about Dashka and what she would look like naked.

As they descended the winding mountain road toward Los Gatos, Dashka suddenly marked her place in her book, set it aside, and took off her glasses.

"I'm feeling a little queasy. Mind if I lie down?"

"No, of course, go ahead," Willie said.

She went to put her head in Willie's lap.

Don't let it break, he heard Todd saying. "Let me move my jacket." Willie managed to slip the mushroom back into its can and drape the jacket over it in one relatively smooth motion. "Okay."

"What were you doing under there?" Dashka asked with a wry smile. Willie just smiled back, thinking he might let her guess wrong.

Dashka laid her head in his lap and then lay there, perfectly still. She did look a bit pale; if there was any color in her face it was a faint shade of the deep blue of her eyes. Willie put a hand on her arm and stared straight ahead.

From the front of the van came political discourse. "Say what you want,

Ronald Reagan's a great American, a great politician, a real patriot. He's turned this country around." It was the mustachioed man speaking.

"Turned it into a shit pile, I'd say," replied the driver. "Rich getting richer, poor getting poorer. We're spending all this money on Star Wars while people in mental institutions are getting thrown out into the streets. Then there's the whole 'trickle down' theory. Well, it ain't trickled down to me."

Willie noted absently the incongruity of the mustachioed graduate student taking Reagan's side against the crusty old liberal bus driver, but mostly he was trying not to think about the weight of Dashka's head in his lap, the smell of her hair.

The radio had moved on to a new tune. Phil Collins could feel something coming in the air tonight.

Willie tried to distract himself.

Phil Collins should have stuck to drums and singing backup for Peter Gabriel. Still...pretty catchy tune.

"Then there's the whole war on drugs," the driver continued. "I lived through Prohibition, and I can tell you now it ain't gonna work. People get high. It's part of life. I mean, you get high somehow, right?"

The grad student, or clerk, or whatever he was, checked his watch and changed the subject. "What time do we get to Berkeley?" They chatted on, about the traffic and the weather.

After about twenty minutes, Dashka finally stirred in Willie's lap. "Mmmm...much better."

Rather than sitting up, she left her head in his lap. In fact, she nuzzled in a little bit farther, and brought her hand up onto his thigh next to her cheek. "So..." she said, "tell me more about your paper."

"Really? Now?"

After a beat, Dashka shifted her head, ever so slightly. "Why not now?"

Willie felt a stirring in his jeans, like he might have to change position a little bit.

Dashka continued. "I mean, your thesis...it's a big proposition, isn't it? I'm thinking the premise could use a little massaging."

Dashka caressed his thigh.

"Well," Willie responded carefully, "it's definitely already a hard topic, and I know it's only going to get harder. I'm sure the more I research it, the more it'll expand."

"Mm-hm," Dashka hummed, and the vibrations went right through his lap into the seat cushion beneath him. "What makes you so sure Shakespeare was a closet Catholic, anyway?"

Willie's dick was trying to get erect, but it was pinned between his thigh and the seat. He shifted position. "I was reading Sonnet Twenty-three. You know it?" The shift in position did the trick.

"Not offhand," she said, and began to move her hand up his thigh.

Willie said,

> *"As an unperfect actor on the stage*
> *Who with his fear is put besides his part,*
> *Or some fierce thing replete with too much rage,*
> *Whose strength's abundance weakens his own heart.*
> *So I, for fear of trust, forget to say*
> *The perfect ceremony of love's rite,*
> *And in mine own love's strength seem to decay,*
> *O'ercharged with burden of mine own love's might."*

As Willie spoke, Dashka began to rub her cheek against Willie's lap. Clever cheek that it was, it found the swelling bulge along his left thigh. She began to move her cheek slowly up and down its length. Her caresses on his thigh moved slowly upward, until she brushed a hand lightly against his balls. "Don't stop," she said.

> *"O, let my books be then the eloquence*
> *And dumb presagers of my speaking breast,*
> *Who plead for love and look for recompense*
> *More than that tongue that more hath more express'd."*

In the space of four lines, Dashka had deftly and silently unbuckled Willie's belt, unbuttoned and unzipped his trousers, extricated his dick from his boxers, and taken two deep, silent sucks. Now she ran her tongue lightly up its length twice, and flicked quickly across its tip. Two more deep movements and he was fully erect. She pulled her mouth away, and stroked him with one hand.

"More than that tongue that more hath more express'd," Willie said, reiterating the last line of the sonnet.

"More tongue?" repeated Dashka, and obliged.

"That's the key line. Notice anything?"

"It's hard to say," she said, and as she spoke she stood up and straddled him, facing toward the front of the bus. He reached under her skirt, unsure how he would deal with her underwear, and was thrilled to find none.

"You never really know what a sonnet's like until you reach the end, do you?" she said. "That's what really allows you inside the poet, don't you think?"

He stroked her utterly smooth and firm ass, then reached two fingers around between her legs to find her already wet. *Oh my god.*

She said, in an utterly conversational tone that belied the fact that she had reached down and placed the head of his cock on her clitoris and was circling it there, "How does the final couplet go?"

"O, learn to read what silent love hath writ:
To hear with eyes belongs to love's fine wit."

Dashka lowered herself down on him, gasped almost imperceptibly, closed her eyes for just a moment, and as she began rocking slowly back and forth said, "It's a good sonnet, very good. But what does it mean to you?"

"It's that...ah...final line...before the couplet. That's the, ahm...crucial point," Willie said, and reached around her waist to finger her as she moved gently on top of him.

Willie brushed Dashka's hair aside from her left ear to look past her, up toward the front of the van. The mousy girl was asleep; the driver had reengaged the grad student–clerk in political discussion. "Hell, did you read that thing in the paper today where Reagan was selling arms to Iran and giving the profits to the Contras? It's against the goddamn law, but ol' Ronnie'll just smile and shake his head and get away with it. Could be worse, I guess, we could have Pat Robertson or one of those other born-again nut jobs as President."

"Or George Bush," said the grad student, and they both laughed.

"Tell me," Dashka said as she bit her lip, "tell me...more...about the crucial point. What's the line again?"

"It says to let the poet's books 'plead for love and look for recompense/More than that tongue that more hath more express'd.'"

"His poet's pen speaks of love more eloquently than his tongue," Dashka said.

"Only on one level," Willie replied. He reached up with his other hand inside her shirt, and unhooked her bra. "But I think there is another, hidden level." He slid his hand under her loosened bra. Smallish breast, soft. Small nipple, hard. "'More than that tongue that more hath more express'd.' You're a grad student. What does it mean?" He nibbled her ear, and flicked his tongue lightly into it.

"More...more," she breathed. "It's an unusual locution. His tongue has expressed more things than...more...No, it doesn't make sense. There's an extra...'more'...in there..."

He quickened the pace of his middle finger, circling faster now, but lighter. "You're right. It doesn't make sense. Unless," Willie said, "unless the second 'more' is capitalized." And with that he began to write an imaginary "M-o-r-e" on her with his middle finger, trying to replicate the most florid script he could picture in his head.

Almost immediately Dashka began to breathe audibly harder, rocking more quickly now. Willie watched a beaded earring with a feather on the end that hung halfway down her neck. It was beating silently with her motion, like a sparrow's wing, as though there was an invisible breeze causing it slowly to wave back and forth, back and forth.

"More...than that tongue that More...hath more...express'd." She was breathing hard now, and he began to move also, writing with the right, kneading gently with the left, and thrusting quietly in the middle.

"Sir...Thomas...MORE!?" she whispered urgently, and then she tightened, wrapping each of her legs around each of his, as if climbing a rope. He felt her spasm once, twice, three times, and that made him come too, shuddering silently and trying not to cry out into the rushing void of oneness the words that again came to him inexplicably, "O true apothecary!"

After a few moments of ragged breathing together, Dashka slid off of Willie and onto the seat next to him.

Dashka leaned back, with her eyes closed. After a minute, she finally said, "Sir Thomas More."

"*Saint* Thomas More, if you're Catholic," Willie replied, putting himself away. "Henry the Eighth's Lord Chancellor. He refused to honor Henry's divorce from his first wife, and from the Catholic Church, and was beheaded. The first great Catholic martyr in England. A hero."

"You're telling me Shakespeare's writing coded, dissident Catholic messages?"

"Yeah," Willie said, "I think so. 'Learn to read what silent love hath writ.' He's telling his reader to look for the code in his poetry that reveals his 'silent love' of the Catholic faith."

Dashka thought for a moment, nodding. "That," she said, "sounds like a very compelling thesis." She took a deep breath, and shook out her hair. She put on her glasses, and picked up her book.

"I very much look forward to your outline," she said, and read silently for the rest of the trip.

Chapter Twelve

Shakespeare's alleged poaching of deer from the park at Charlecote likely stemmed from more than a sudden craving for venison. Sir Thomas Lucy took advantage of his broad powers in the crackdown on Catholics to "enclose," or append to his estate, many lands that were once either private (Catholic) or public grazing lands. In her 1938 play The Wooing of Anne Hathaway, *playwright Grace Carlton suggests that for the Catholic youth of Stratford, deer poaching and other forms of trespass on Sir Thomas Lucy's lands were not just youthful pranks but overt acts of civil disobedience.*

As William Shakespeare spent himself and cried, "O true apothecary!" he experienced that momentary epiphany, that loss of self, that transportation to somewhere entirely else that often accompanies orgasm. Freedom. No care in the world. No responsibility. No past, no future, just satisfaction, release, ecstasy; oneness.

He and Rosaline were in a small meadow in the midst of Sir Thomas Lucy's grounds at Charlecote. Though it was called "the deer park," and there were deer to be found here, it was more properly a coney warren, and the rabbits who inhabited it were everywhere. There were, in fact, ten within William's eyeshot at the moment. Four of them were humping.

William had taken the mysterious box back to the house at Henley Street and secreted it in the bottom of the clothing trunk that he and Gilbert shared. He slept uneasily that night. He woke several times thinking he heard horsemen in the lane, or a knock on the door, or a scraping at the bedroom window; but it was just the wind. Once, he started up in bed thinking he saw the ghost of Thomas Cottom; but it was merely the moon casting a shadow of a tree branch on the bedroom wall.

In the grey morning light he had lain awake and wondered how he would fulfill the promise he'd made, to deliver the mysterious box to John Cottom in Lancashire. He couldn't, not until the end of the term. But as the day's Latin lessons crawled by he ground his teeth and thought more and more about the rank injustices to the Cottom family, and to his own.

At the end of the day, he had stealthily approached Davy Jones's house, and to his delight found Rosaline mulching its neglected rose garden. Even better, Davy Jones was, she said, already drunk and asleep. Using all the rhetorical tricks he could muster, William pleaded and cajoled her into a bold adventure. Starting out at sunset, they walked the four miles to Charlecote. Darkness had fallen when they approached a forlorn gate on the park's west side, guarded by a forlorn keeper's house on its left. They slipped quietly past the guardhouse and along the park's fence, which was made with vertical split-oak palings of different heights to confuse any deer considering a leap. It was meant to keep deer in rather than poachers out, and they soon found a low stave, scrambled over, and fucked madly, aroused by the sense of danger that they might get caught in the act by Thomas Lucy or his minions.

It was, for William, both a sexual conquest and a literal *fuck you and your deer park* to Lucy's authority.

Now, as William breathed heavily, Rosaline giggled beneath him. "Men may say strange things when they are spent, or so I am told. But what is this, of your apothecary?"

William covered the true association by kissing Rosaline gently on her flushed brow. "My apothecary? 'He who, with charms most strange and weeds too-pow'rful, human shapes did change!'"

"You know your Ovid well," Rosaline replied, then quoted back at him, "'O, give us way to slide into each other's arms! If such a bliss transcend our Fates, yet suffer us to kiss.' Hath your apothecary given you means to slide into me again?"

William kissed her again, then rolled off of her onto the grass. "A kiss must serve for now. 'Twould be a powerful weed indeed, so soon to change my shape to suit your pleasure. Though I be in the full flower of manhood, even a flower must fold, suck light and water, and rest ere it bloom again."

"Very pretty," Rosaline replied, and lay back, using William's breeches as a pillow. "Your love talk is like to gilding what is already gold."

"Nay," he said, running his finger along a wet streak that ran shimmering along Rosaline's thigh, "'tis more like to painting the lily white."

"A dainty picture to paint," said Rosaline as she pulled down her skirts, "with so large a brush."

William opened his mouth to reply, but nothing came. He smiled and shrugged.

"It seems at last that a woman has topped me."

She laughed and swung herself astride him.

"By repute many a woman has topped you. Or are you so Puritan as to not allow them so high a position?"

"No Puritan I," he said, no longer laughing, and rolled out from under her. They lay silent for a moment.

"William," said Rosaline suddenly, "I spoke not in jest when I said you should write. Even *Salmacis and Hermaphroditus*, extemporized though it was, shows Anthony Munday a bull's pizzle. You have the greater wit."

"But the less learning. I am too unschooled."

Rosaline leaned upon one elbow. "The stage need not be for men of learning only. Any man or woman, lettered or no, may see a play for a penny. You are lettered in the language of men and women, and what they say and do, and also in the tongue of love. The playwright's aim is to hold a mirror up to nature, is it not?"

"Mayhap, mayhap. But the road to London, to the theatre in Blackfriars, runs not straight from Stratford. One must first pay toll at Cambridge or Oxford."

"And where is that writ? You give yourself too little shrift of your skill and craft. Be not afeared to use what tools you are given," she said, grabbing playfully at William's crotch and pulling him toward her, "and use them while you may."

William was kissing her deeply when he heard a noise in the brush behind him, followed by a voice he knew.

"Ah, what an arse is here!"

William turned suddenly around to see Sir Thomas Lucy, on his horse.

"The naked arse, no less, of young William Shakespeare. Poaching deer in my park!"

William didn't bother to stand or reverence now. But he did pull on his breeches, and tried to riposte with the best weapon he had.

"'Poaching deer,' is it?" William replied. "That's a new one."

"William," whispered Rosaline urgently, but he was already caught out, and not inclined to give Lucy the smallest shred of satisfaction.

"'Hunting beaver,' I've heard," William continued. "'Laying in the short grass' is to the point."

"William!" Rosaline whispered, louder, as she twisted suddenly to look at something behind them. But William was focused on Sir Thomas.

"'Ploughing the untilled field,' befits the setting. 'Plucking forbidden fruit,' now that gets it across. But 'poaching deer'—"

William heard a thundering crack as something blunt and heavy hit him in the back of the head. As he fell he turned, and as blackness took him he caught a glimpse of Henry Rogers standing over him, holding the hilts of his sword like a club.

Chapter Thirteen

Accuse me thus: that I have scanted all
Wherein I should your great deserts repay,
Forgot upon your dearest love to call,
Whereto all bonds do tie me day by day;
That I have frequent been with unknown minds
And given to time your own dear-purchas'd right
That I have hoisted sail to all the winds
Which should transport me farthest from your sight.
Book both my wilfulness and errors down
And on just proof surmise accumulate;
Bring me within the level of your frown,
But shoot not at me in your wakened hate.

—Sonnet 117

The library jitney exited the freeway near the Berkeley Marina, and rolled up University Avenue toward the west end of the UC campus. Dashka finally put down her book.

"So," Willie asked. "What are you researching here?"

She shrugged, and shifted. "The War of the Roses. I'm working on my dissertation proposal."

Willie took a second to do the math on this. "Shouldn't it be approved already? I thought you'd already passed your exams."

"I did. And it was approved. But I . . . ran into a bump or two. I'm reworking it."

Willie jumped on this. "Aha, so *you*—"

"*I*," Dashka interrupted, clearly annoyed, "can still put the kibosh on your thesis—sexual favors or no."

Willie wisely changed the subject. "I'm staying up here for the weekend," he said as he put on his jacket and gathered up his backpack and the duffel. "So I won't see you on the way back."

Dashka looked at him without answering for a moment, seeming to consider. Then she put her book away in her black leather bag. "I'll be here for the next couple of days, too." She took out a pen and a small spiral notebook and scribbled. "My best friend from high school." She tore out the note and handed it to him. "Give me a call if you want. Or drop by."

Willie looked at it. It was an address in El Cerrito.

The van pulled into the circular drive at the top of University Avenue, and stopped under the giant oak that dominates Springer Gateway at the campus's western entrance. The driver opened the passenger door. The mustachioed man stepped out, followed by the mousy girl. Willie let Dashka go ahead of him.

As Willie passed the driver, he said, "I completely agree about Reagan. Thanks for the ride."

The driver grunted in response.

Willie emerged from the bus, and Dashka had turned back toward him and was puckering up to give him a peck on the cheek, when Willie saw Robin.

"Hey! Hi!" Willie said, and stepped forward, awkwardly ignoring Dashka and moving past her to hug a woman, his age, with wavy brown hair, a slightly crooked nose, not tall, but cute, with bright brown eyes.

She gave a short, comprehending look to Dashka. Then she gave a tight smile to Willie.

"Hi, honey. How was the trip?"

Part Two

POLITICS AND RELIGION

Chapter Fourteen

*Madman, thou errest: I say, there is no darkness but ignorance,
in which thou art more puzzled than the Egyptians in their fog.*

—Clown, *Twelfth Night*, IV.ii.42

As he walked onto the campus where his father had worked Willie's
whole life, the drug raid in Santa Cruz seemed like the distant past.
Today was Thursday, and he wouldn't be able to complete his delivery to
the Renaissance Faire until Saturday. He was grateful for the chance of
a couple of days in Berkeley, his hometown, to collect his thoughts, to
be himself.

"Thanks for meeting me," Willie said to Robin as they walked under the
redwoods and the giant eucalyptus grove along Strawberry Creek. Willie
liked this part of the walk; the trees formed a pleasant, transitional buffer
zone from Santa Cruz to Berkeley. "I thought I was surprising you."

"You told me on Monday you were coming. I thought *I'd* surprise *you*."

"I don't remember telling you."

"You were probably stoned."

They came out of the trees and under the shadow of the gigantic Life
Sciences Building, PHYSIOLOGY and BACTERIOLOGY looming over them
in towering neoclassical letters above a wide lawn. Willie felt a tug of pride
as he passed the familiar Department of Dramatic Art, nestled in a small
wood-shingle shack in a shady spot. Across a circular driveway, the mar-
quee of Durham Studio Theater advertised DOGG'S HAMLET / CAHOOT'S
MACBETH. They crossed the creek over a stone bridge, and a short flight of
steps brought them up to the wide cement expanse of Lower Sproul Plaza,
largely empty but for a few students, late to their nine o'clock classes,
watched from on high by the statue of a Golden Bear. Robin stopped at a
prominent bulletin board in front of the Bear's Lair, the campus pub. The

plywood was covered with notices of rooms to rent, bands playing clubs, political manifestos, plays opening.

Robin took a stack of flyers and a staple gun from her book bag. "Hold this," she said, handing Willie the flyers as she took one, and with a confident *ka-thwunk* of the staple gun, pinned it to the board.

RALLY FRIDAY!!!!
TIMOTHY LEARY
Speaks out against Carlton Turner, Ronald Reagan, and the
Fascist Tactics of the DEA
12:00 Noon
Upper Sproul Plaza
BRING SIGNS! BE HEARD!!!
This announcement brought to you by the committee to
F$¢K REAGAN!

"Who's Carlton Turner?" Willie asked.

Robin looked at him as if he were from another planet. "Reagan's drug czar since nineteen eighty-two?"

Willie hadn't followed politics, or much of anything, very closely during his years in Santa Cruz. "Right, right. And what's he doing now?"

Robin gave Willie a withering look. "Burr-other. It's true what they say about Santa Cruz, you really do have your head in the clouds. Have you heard of a little thing called the Anti-Drug Abuse Act?"

"Enlighten me."

As she moved around Lower Sproul Plaza, handing out and pasting up flyers, Robin told Willie about the Act: new legislation just signed by President Reagan that required mandatory prison sentences for first-time drug users. The only out: finking on other drug users. "I can see it now," she said. "Kids who get busted for crack turning in their parents because they have some hash in the underwear drawer."

"Oh, come on, that's not gonna happen," Willie said defensively, but he again had a vision of Todd at a metal desk under a single bare lightbulb.

"And the worst part is, there's a scale for the sentencing. Marijuana gets less jail time than crack. You know what that means?"

"More brothers in prison than suburban whites," said Willie, but his mind was busy trying to guess where on the sentencing scale giant psilocybin mushrooms fell.

"Yes. It's totally racist. Oh, and there was a vast budget increase for the Drug Enforcement Agency. They're using copters, planes, who knows, probably spy satellites, too, all over California." She looked at Willie seriously. "You and your friends should be careful."

Willie unconsciously shifted the weight of the duffel bag on his shoulder.

Robin continued, "So...we're going to try to take down Carlton Turner."

"With Timothy Leary? Is he the most credible opposition you could find?"

"He's more credible than Carlton Turner. In Berkeley at least. You know what Turner said last week? That marijuana—did you hear this?—marijuana causes both homosexuality *and* compromised immune systems ... and therefore, the AIDS crisis."

"No way."

"That's right," Robin said, "according to Reagan's top drug man, pot causes AIDS. Again...you should be careful."

Willie was beginning to feel distinctly uncomfortable. "I have been experiencing unusual cravings for butt-love recently."

"Leary's nuts, but Carlton Turner is *evil* and nuts."

"Maybe he's not evil," said Willie. "Maybe he's just a repressed, gay, self-loathing, alcoholic Republican."

Robin smiled cynically. "They always are."

She had finished papering Lower Sproul, and they trotted up the steps to Upper Sproul Plaza. For Willie, any vestigial feeling of the quiet, misty forests of Santa Cruz faded. The plaza was a giant petri dish of political life. Faculty, staff, and students of every age and description bustled to and from classes.

A short, dark woman in fatigues hawked copies of *The Daily Worker*. "The Soviet Union will outlast America! Read why here!"

A long-haired, spiral-eyed Jesus freak with a megaphone read from Revelation:

*"Sovereign Lord, holy and true, how long will it be before you judge
and avenge our blood on the inhabitants of the earth?"*

He continued his rant as Robin and Willie passed, but his brimstone
eyes bored in on Willie and screamed, *"Sinner!"*

Along the length of Sproul Plaza, leading toward Sather Gate, there
were tables arrayed end to end in the shade of two lines of pollarded trees.
There were tables for undergrad collegiate pursuits: the French Club, the
Geography Club, the Chess Club, and the Latin Club. There were tables
for ethnic associations, staffed by lonely, long-faced students offering
support for other lonely, long-faced students from Japan, the Philippines,
Taiwan, Africa, Palestine—the latter being the longest faces of all. There
were also tables for Jews for Jesus, Buddhists for Jesus, and Christians for
Buddha. The Democratic Party, the Communist Party, and the Green Party
were there. PETA, YMCA, NOW, and the ACLU were all represented.
There were tables for support groups for the transsexual, the transgen-
dered, and the transcendent. There were tables hawking hawkishness, and
tables hawking dovishness. Right to Life, Right to Death, Death to Gay
Rights, they were all here. And there were actually people checking out
the tables, too, picking up flyers, signing petitions, and talking earnestly to
the earnest kids sitting behind them.

Only one table was entirely forlorn, a single, melancholy, well-dressed,
clean-shaven young man sitting behind it: this was the Berkeley outpost of
the Log Cabin Republicans. The Gay Old Party was not a big demographic
in Berkeley.

And there were the crazy people. William the Polka-Dot Man lay in
front of Sather Gate at the campus's nineteenth-century entrance, wearing a white jumpsuit covered with large red dots and controlling the silent
machinery that prevented the Apocalypse. The Piano Man (not, thankfully, Billy Joel) played standards on a piano that appeared on Sproul each
morning from who knows where? The Bubble Lady blew soap bubbles
from a small green container and sold copies of her quite good books of
poetry. The Hate Man said clearly and viciously to Robin and Willie as
they passed, "I hate you," as he did to everyone, all day, every day. Then
there was the man who wandered around the plaza muttering nonstop in

some sort of high-level mathematical language, but who—either by choice or by curious lack of the self-promotional abilities possessed of the other Berkeley madmen- and madwomen-savants—had no snappy moniker: he was just Serge. Willie listened for a couple of seconds as he passed: "The imaginary number square root of negative one times Planck's constant divided by two pi…" Rumor had it that he was a former physics professor who took too much acid.

And then there were the performers. A solo guitarist played classical versions of Beatles songs. There was Stoney Burke, crazy or crazy like a fox, ranting a political comedy diatribe to a small audience. A juggler juggled a chain saw, a bowling ball, and an egg while his partner lay beneath him protecting his crotch to much laughter.

Robin was sticking a flyer to the side of the Piano Man's piano (by his silent, nodded permission) when Willie heard someone saying, "But soft, what wind through yonder lighter breaks?" Willie turned to the sound, and saw that on the steps of Sproul Hall, the very steps from which Mario Savio ignited the free speech movement in 1964, there were two young men, one freakishly tall, wearing tights, puffy shirts, and high-top sneakers, performing *Romeo and Juliet* to a craning crowd of two or three dozen students. He nudged Robin. "I'm gonna go check these guys out."

Robin nodded, uninterested. "Okay."

As he approached, Willie saw that the two men were actually three. One, wearing a bad wig and a dress, sat atop the shoulders of the third, whose head was cloistered under "her" skirt. "O Romeo, Romeo, wherefore art thou Romeo?…Romeo?" The handsome, bearded Romeo was busy hitting on a hot girl in the front row. "Up here, Romeo," said Juliet, then screaming with sudden hysteria, "on the *balcony*, you fucking moron!"

The crowd laughed.

"Dude," responded Romeo (after handing the cute girl his card), "you can't say 'fuck.' This is a facility of higher learning."

"No, it isn't, this is *Berkeley*." Another laugh. "I can say whatever I want to," Juliet continued. "The free speech movement started right here on these steps. *Joan Baez* sang here!"

"Joan Baez sucks!" said Romeo.

"Fuck you, Romeo," said Juliet.

The crowd, which had already doubled since Willie arrived, laughed uproariously. They were eating it up.

"Would you please say your next line!?" said Romeo.

Juliet crossed her arms petulantly. "I'm exercising my freedom of speech by *not* saying it."

"Just say it," Romeo pleaded.

A line from the scene suddenly popped into Willie's head. He couldn't resist, and called out, "O gentle Romeo, if thou dost love, pronounce it faithfully!"

The performers stopped, and turned to stare Willie down. The guy playing Romeo said, "Oh great, now we got a Shakespeare wannabe in the crowd." Laughter. Romeo continued to cut Willie, the heckler, down to size. "That's totally not the next line. You just skipped the whole balcony scene, genius."

From under Juliet's dress came the heavily muffled sound of the poor third actor. It sounded something like "That's fine with me!"

The crowd roared.

Juliet wiggled on his shoulders. "Quit it!" she said to the man under her dress. "Your beard scratches when you talk!"

The crowd roared again.

"Okay, Shakespeare," said Romeo to Willie, "give me the cue one more time."

"O gentle Romeo," said Willie, "if thou dost love, pronounce it faithfully!"

Then, acting to Juliet but pointing pointedly at Willie, Romeo said, "Lady, by yonder blessed virgin, I swear."

Willie smiled his most charming smile and said, "Fuck you, Romeo."

The crowd roared yet again.

"Okay, being funnier than us is not allowed," said Romeo.

The troupe moved on and rocketed through their shtick to a final tragic death tableau of Juliet splayed out on top of Romeo, dress hiked up to show most unladylike tighty-whities.

Willie laughed through the whole thing, and so did Robin. It had taken ten minutes, and they passed the hat afterward. It seemed like almost everyone put a buck or two in the hat, partly because the troupe cleverly spread out and surrounded the audience: no one could get away without making eye contact with one of them. Willie had only nine bucks in his pocket for the entire weekend, but he felt bad about screwing up their act.

As Willie dropped one-ninth of his life's savings in the hat, Romeo saw him. "Thanks. That was funny." Willie watched the flow of dollar bills—and a couple of fives, and at least one joint—wondering idly just how much dough these guys pulled in, in one show; and wondering, less idly, just how many millions of dollars Shakespeare made in the world, between plays, movies, books, tourism—he must be a billion-dollar industry. And the money was only the surface: what about the intellectual, moral, philosophical, poetic capital? Thinking about it made Willie feel small, and the prospect of his unwritten thesis seem huge.

Willie found Robin in the middle of the plaza. She tucked her remaining flyers and her BluStik back in her Copymat bag.

"Okay, I've done my bit for saving the world this morning. I've got some time before my next class, you want to get coffee or something? I'm kinda hungry."

It was a stunning day. Warm in the sun, cool in the shade. The preclass rush had quieted down a little. The Piano Man played "Moon River." Willie glanced over to the northeast, where Strawberry Creek ran through the campus, shrouded in live oak and sequoia, ivy trailing down its banks. The first time Willie had visited Robin in Berkeley, on a summer Sunday when the campus was quiet, they had picnicked by the creek and made out…Willie had gotten a hummer.

Now, he gestured with a nod toward the trees. "Maybe you could have a quick snack by the creek?" The second he said it, he panicked with the possibility that she might say yes—his dick, he realized too late, was still crusty with dried Dashka.

"Mister One-Track Mind," Robin said. "At this hour, I'd actually prefer coffee and a bagel to pure protein. Come on, I'll buy."

The couple headed out of Sproul Plaza toward Berkeley's south side. The light at Bancroft Way changed. As Robin stepped out into the traffic first, she reached back to take Willie by the hand, and guided him toward the bustling morning jostle on Telegraph Avenue.

Chapter Fifteen

*How might Shakespeare's famous punishment at the hand of the
most infamous pursuivant in Warwickshire have contributed to his
development as a playwright? His rich and complex treatment of
characters such as Richard III, Iago, and Edmund suggest an up-close
experience of the villainous type. And one need only revisit the grueling
blinding of Gloucester by Cornwall in* King Lear *to see that Shakespeare
had a visceral response to torture.*

William was shirtless, bound at the wrists to an iron ring bolted to a stone
wall. A whip lashed into the flesh of his back with a sickening crack. He
noticed with an odd detachment that part of the sound we associate with
the whip was simply the sound of flesh splitting open. He also noted that
this hurt, very much.

"Thrice more, Master Rogers," Sir Thomas Lucy said primly.

As the eighth, ninth, and tenth lashes ripped into William, he further
noted that his tolerance for the pain appeared to grow less with each
stroke. The first had been less painful than he had feared. The last three,
he was sweating with the effort of not screaming, and near to fainting.

He was in an outbuilding less than a hundred yards from the main
house at Charlecote: Sir Thomas Lucy's laundry room. Glancing around
to look for an escape, William saw copper pots for boiling clothes. It occurred to him that the pots were also large enough to boil a man. He saw
a tiled channel in the floor leading to a drain, and mused that blood might
flow through it just as easily as wash-water. On one side of the room was a
giant stone block suspended on a pulley over an iron plate. The device was
made to press Sir Thomas Lucy's shirts, but, William concluded, it would
be decidedly uncomfortable if applied to his chest.

Henry Rogers turned William around so he could face Sir Thomas Lucy.

Lucy wore no hat; his beard was still razor sharp, but the shock of red hair atop his head was wild and unkempt.

William breathed hard. "For what, my noble lord, am I punished thus?"

"For trespass, for poaching of deer, and for public lasciviousness with a maiden," said Lucy, who held in his hand a tightly rolled piece of paper.

William's head spun from the pain, and he felt words pouring out of him, his mouth overflowing like the banks of Avon in a flood.

"Begging your pardon, my lord," William said, "but no maiden she, as I was informed by none other than her apothecary good and true. Nor was our lasciviousness conducted in public, but privately in your coney warren. And if that be a crime, then arrest and whip your hares also, for they are guilty of my crime thrice or more daily, and of incest, buggery, and bestiality besides. I have ne'er poached my Lord Lucy's deer. As to the crime of trespass, I would plead guilty, were I before a judge."

Sir Thomas Lucy paced slowly back and forth in front of William, considering.

"Thou art a bold boy. Yet I would mark thy tongue. A wit as sharp as thine may be a weapon, and to assault thy betters with it, in these treacherous times, a capital offense."

"Am I like to be charged with using my tongue on a maid as well?"

"Vex me not with thy bawdy," Lucy snapped. "Thy mistemper'd tongue may be used as a weapon; but the selfsame blade might, mishandled, wound the wielder. Or, in other wise"—and here he smiled at William—"thy tongue may be used as salve: as a mongrel dog, wounded by the whips and scorns of its daily travail, will lick his wounds until they are no more, so might thou, with thy tongue's proper employ, heal thy family's festering canker."

"What mean you?"

"You know best," said Lucy, shrugging and softer now, "but surely your circumstances are not what they were in better days, when your father was bailiff?"

A thought raced through William's wrenched mind: *best not be too agreeable in this interrogation.* He let the flow of words continue unabated.

"The stages of a man's life are inconstant," William said. "Fortunes rise and fall like a sleeping man's breast: sometimes high and full, sometimes low and empty, but always to breathe again."

"Until breathing stops, and your man is dead."

William said nothing.

"It is possible, William," said Lucy, now William's best friend, "that the fortunes of the Shakespeares might rise again, if you but call upon your wit, and use your tongue as physic to this our clawed and bitten state. There is a cancer grows within it. Our Queen, God save Her Majesty, tries but to unify us, one nation under God's rule and the Queen's. But factions there are would have us forever cloven in twain, our loyalties split between Queen and Pope. This path leads only to ruin."

"No one may foresee the ends of all paths," William responded. "And in the end each man's journey leads only to his own conscience, which, in these times, must perforce be enclosed and fenced against trespass. Even as your coney warren, my lord," he added, and immediately regretted it.

Lucy stared at him.

"Spoken like an embittered papist."

William said nothing.

"Your punishment for trespass is paid," said Lucy, turning away. "Now I would ask of you questions that touch on matters of state. I pray you answer well and quickly, for Henry Rogers is an impatient man."

"I am no statesman, but a country schoolmaster and glover's son," said William.

"We are all statesmen in these times. What is a state but the sum of its men? And what is faith but those who profess it? I shall be blunt," Lucy said, and turned to look William in the eyes. "Are you a papist?"

"My faith is my own."

"Are...you...a papist?"

William didn't reply, because he didn't know the answer himself. He felt solidarity with the oppressed, and rage at the oppressors. But did he believe in an infallible Pope? Or even in God? He hadn't taken Communion from a Catholic priest in his living memory...would he if he could?

"By your silence," said Lucy at last, "I hold myself affirmed. Understand you, clever wit that you are, that while the Queen is its chief prelate, to be opposed to the Church of England is treason?"

"My Queen and I pray to the same God," said William. "I for her health and long life, and Her Majesty, I hope, for the health and long life of her subjects."

Sir Thomas Lucy looked at William Shakespeare, his eyes burning. "And for their loyalty, sirrah, for their loyalty."

Lucy unrolled the piece of paper in his hand. William could see, through its translucent skin, that it was a list of names.

"Knew you Thomas Cottom?"

"Nay," said William.

"What of his brother, John Cottom?"

"Master John Cottom taught me at the King's New School, along with much of the youth of Stratford."

"And so you knew his brother," Lucy said; a statement, not a question.

"Nay."

"This seems strange, to know the one and not the other."

"My Lord Lucy knows me, it seems," William replied, "and yet I vouchsafe he cannot name a one of my siblings."

"You have heard of Thomas Cottom, though, surely?"

"I have heard that he traveled to Rheims," William said.

"And thence?"

"I know not."

"A wit like you, no desire to guess?" Lucy mocked.

"To a nunnery?" William said, risking a joke.

Thomas Lucy smiled. "Ay, after a fashion: St. Peter's nunnery, wherein the Pope's whorish bishops prance and fawn at his feet."

William was caught up in the banter.

"'Twas ever the nature of toadies, to prance and fawn at their toadstool's feet—"

Without warning, Thomas Lucy slapped William hard across the face with the back of his gloved hand.

"Thou art an insolent boy. Thy responses please me not. Thou usest words both as a weapon and as a battlement. They keep at bay any true feelings in thy shallow heart; real feelings, such as pain. Therefore see to it that thou answerest in plain words, lest thou answerest in screams. Again: hast thou received aught from Thomas Cottom?"

"Nay, my lord," William lied.

"Come, sirrah, what letters hadst thou late from Rheims?"

"None." True enough. He had only the box, hidden amongst the spare hose and Sunday best in the house at Henley Street.

"And what confederacy hast thou with the traitors late landed in the kingdom?"

"None."

Lucy slapped William yet again, but this time he first whipped off his glove so that his ring, which bore the family seal of a dead-looking fish — a *luce*, William noted with the sudden detachment that came from pain — cut a red streak across his cheek.

William took a moment to recover. Again, he couldn't help using the only weapon he had. "Despite your tender ministrations, my lord, my answer is nay, neither documents nor letters have I received from the Continent, nor am I confederate with traitors."

Lucy regarded William closely, and then referred to his paper again. "What of Robert Debdale?"

"What of him?"

"Thou knowest him?"

"Nay."

"Knowest the name? Thinkest thou well ere offering thy answer."

William thought. So far Lucy had asked about all the protégés of Simon Hunt, his Catholic former schoolmaster. The New School had become, during his tenure, almost a prep school for the seminaries on the Continent. Lucy clearly thought that William might continue the tradition, despite the installation of Alexander Aspinall as Master. But William saw no harm in answering the question about Debdale truthfully. "Though I know him not, I knew of him once. He was, as I recall, also a student of the New School, some years older than me, and in the tutelage of Simon Hunt, with whom he traveled to the Continent."

"And thou hast had no contact with him since?"

"Nor never. He was seven or eight years my senior."

Lucy referred to his list one more time. "Knowest thou...Anne Hathaway?"

"No," William lied, and he didn't know why. Some lingering guilt, perhaps, or simply an approach by Lucy of too much intimacy —

Smack, again William was hit.

"Think again. 'Tis said thou hast bedded her."

"I have bedded many women. Two this day, if the woods of Arden and your coney warren may be accounted beds. I do not remember them all."

"Thou art a libertine."

"I am *liber*, and *eight*een, my lord. Perhaps you recall, the humors run toward sanguine at such an age."

"Anne Hathaway. Of Shottery. Thou recallest not."

William couldn't imagine what the connection between Simon Hunt, Robert Debdale, and his first lover could possibly be, but something in him recoiled at the thought of implicating her in the interrogation in any way.

"Nay."

"I do not see thee racking thy brain."

"I have no need, my lord."

"Then we shall rack it for thee."

He nodded to Henry Rogers, who removed the chain from the hook and yanked William roughly into the next chamber, where there was, indeed, a rack.

Rogers strapped William onto it. It smelled of sweat and fear. William said, his voice trembling despite his every effort, "Stretch me though you may, my mind will not stretch so far as to remember what I do not remember."

The rope, padded with linen so as not to leave any mark, tightened around his ankles and wrists.

Lucy nodded to Henry Rogers, and he pulled the roller at the top of the rack taut. William was stretched...not uncomfortably, but stretched. *This*, he thought, *is not so bad*.

"Then tell me of what thou dost remember. Tell me of thy mother, and her faith."

"My mother?"

"Thou rememberest her. Or didst thou fuck and then forget her, as well?" Sir Thomas Lucy asked calmly.

Sir Thomas Lucy himself gave a turn to the winch at the bottom of the rack. William heard a sickening pop as his left shoulder dislocated.

He screamed.

Chapter Sixteen

> *How like a jade he stood, tied to the tree,*
> *Servilely master'd with a leathern rein!*
> *But when he saw his love, his youth's fair fee,*
> *He held such petty bondage in disdain;*
> *Throwing the base thong from his bending crest,*
> *Enfranchising his mouth, his back, his breast.*

—*Venus and Adonis*, 391

Immobilized, Willie pulled ineffectually against the bonds at his wrists and ankles. He was spread-eagle, completely naked. Hot wax dripped onto his chest, and he flinched and shuddered.

Robin straddled him, and removed her bra.

Willie said, "Nice rack."

She lowered her body so her small, soft nipples were within an inch of Willie's lips.

"Have you been a good boy?"

"Yes."

"Then why aren't you in school?" Robin said, and dripped a little bit more wax on his chest. He flinched as it hit.

"Because, mistress, I take classes only on Mondays and Wednesdays, that I might attend thy court."

"Well answered," said Robin, and she leaned forward far enough for Willie to just barely brush her nipple with his tongue.

"Have you been doing your homework?"

Willie shifted, a little bit uncomfortably.

"Yes, mistress."

"Tell me about it."

"My thesis topic was approved."

Robin shifted off of him, and slipped out of her jeans and panties in one smooth move. She stood by the bed where Willie lay tied up. Robin had a student-cheap but comfortable apartment just off of College Avenue, a mile or so south of the campus. It was in a new building, and Robin had decorated it in a modern style: Jasper Johns and Andy Warhol prints framed in black lacquer on the walls; midcentury furniture finds from the local flea market; a wall covered with modular bookshelves featuring an entire college syllabus of Western Civilization, arranged approximately chronologically by subject from Hesiod's *Theogony* to *The Soviet Union Demystified: A Materialist Analysis.* Robin was a political science grad; she'd volunteered for Barbara Boxer's first congressional campaign four years ago and had spent a summer interning for her in D.C. Robin had been given a broken desk in a windowless office and told to look for abuses of taxpayer money in the name of something called the Project for Taxpayer Accountability. In fact, it was Robin who, in poring over the records of disbursements to government contractors, discovered the now legendary $436 paid by the Pentagon for a "unidirectional impact generator"—a $7 claw hammer. Of course someone else took the credit for the discovery, but Robin quickly developed a reputation as someone with a nose for underhanded goings-on. She was now doing social work, working on campus doing clerical work for the poli-sci department, studying for the GREs, and volunteering for the Boxer campaign. Check that...she was "now" naked and straddling Willie, just letting her pubes gently brush his erect (and hurriedly sponge-bathed, in Robin's bathroom) dick.

"Mmm. Did you show it to your senior advisor?" Robin cooed.

Willie's heart skipped. "What?"

"Your thesis. Did you show her the proposal?"

"Oh...yeah."

Robin picked up the candle by the bedside, and leaned back, holding the candle directly over Willie's balls. "What happened? Did she go for it?"

Willie had a feeling he'd better answer this reeeeally carefully.

"She wasn't into it, at first. But it's hard to tell with her. She doesn't give much away. Kinda cold."

"Really? She looked pretty hot to me." She tilted the candle, and let three drops of hot wax fall onto Willie's scrotum.

He flinched with a hiss of in-taken breath.

"In fact, she looked a little flushed," Robin continued. "Maybe she had a fever. Or maybe she just got out of bed or something." She let another drop of wax fall.

"AH! I...wouldn't know."

Robin shifted her position, allowing Willie to look at her from behind as she took his dick gently into her hand and gave it a stroke or two. She gave it a questioning look, as she might contemplate the purchase of a dress that she wasn't certain was quite her style. "So you're saying she didn't like it?"

Willie was silent, concentrating on the feeling in his loins. He heard and felt a sudden, painful snap in the most sensitive of all possible places. "OW!"

"Your thesis," Robin said, holstering the instrument of torture, her middle finger, while Willie watched. "She didn't like it?"

"She thinks it needs a little more."

"More? More what?"

"More research. A little deeper analysis."

"I think that's wise. You wouldn't want to get too far into a bad idea, don't you think?" She took him into her mouth; swallowed him whole twice.

"For sure."

"You'd hate to fuck up all the good work you've done in the department by letting your thesis get out of control, right?"

"Right." Right now, Willie would say or do whatever Robin asked, the feeling of dizziness running from his feet to the tips of his hair, acting like truth serum.

"Wherever your thesis is going to go, you want to be fully committed to it, right?"

"Right."

Robin turned again, and slowly, slowly lowered herself onto him. Breathlessly, she said, "Because your thesis sounds like it's going to be a very long...hard...job."

An hour later, they were both asleep in postcoital lassitude.

*　　*　　*

I'm on stage, playing Hamlet in the moonlight of the Quarry Amphitheater...but no, now it's the Greek Theater in Berkeley. The audience rustles, and they are not quiet like trees, but chanting, "Ham-let, Ham-let!" There are signs bobbing up and down, but I can make out only two:

WILLIE GREENBERG IS HAMLET!

WHEN PIGS FLY!

I say, "To be or not to be..." but I can't even hear myself through the chanting. Ophelia enters and the crowd goes silent.

"Good my lord, how does your honor for this many a day?"

"Are you honest?" I ask.

"My lord?"

"Are you fair?"

"What means your lordship?"

"That if you be honest and fair, your honesty should admit no discourse to your beauty."

"Could beauty, my lord, have better commerce than with honesty?"

She is an angry, jealous Ophelia, accusatory. And so I play a slippery Hamlet, words streaming out of my mouth in a torrent of mad bs.

"Ay," I say, "truly; for the power of beauty will sooner transform honesty from what it is to a bawd than the force of honesty can translate beauty into his likeness: this was sometime a paradox, but now the time gives it proof. I did love you once."

"Mayhap once, my lord, but never again."

This isn't the right line...and it isn't Dashka playing Ophelia. I realize too late that it's Robin, and her hand is in motion, smacking my left cheek. The audience hoots and cackles wildly, then suddenly cuts out like a bad laugh track.

I turn as the spotlight from the heavens comes up and illuminates the bed in the middle of the stage. There is a woman there, hidden by the headboard. I can feel it.

Polonius taps me on the shoulder. "The Queen would speak with you, and presently."

Caught between the compulsion to step forward and the urge to run, I can't move. My feet are like tree roots in the stage. I will myself to move,

to no avail. The restless audience murmurs. Whoever awaits on that bed,
I can't go to her. I'm petrified.

The phone next to the bed rang, and Willie woke with a weak scream.
Robin picked it up, still lying prone.

"Hello?...Oh, hi. Yeah, hang on."

Robin held out the phone.

"It's your stepmom."

"I'm not here," Willie said, and rolled over.

Chapter Seventeen

*It should be pointed out that Shakespeare was not entirely nor on
every page "modern." Whether it's statues coming suddenly to life (The
Winter's Tale), gods descending to arrange marriages (As You Like It), or
pirate ships escorting Hamlet around the North Sea, the Bard showed a
certain proclivity for the ancient device of deus ex machina.*

William did not fare well under torture. *That answers that question,* he
thought. After two turns of the rack, he begged Sir Thomas Lucy to stop.
He would tell Sir Thomas Lucy everything he wanted to know.

Sir Thomas Lucy said, "Tell me of Edward Arden and Mary, his wife."

"I have met them but once, and know little besides their names, not
even our exact relation," William replied, sweating and panting.

The answer seemed not to satisfy Lucy, who nodded to Henry Rogers.
Moving forward, Rogers leeringly poured hot wax onto William's ballocks,
and William screamed again. Henry Rogers grinned, and offered to cut
them off to alleviate the pain.

In a fountain of words, William told Lucy about his relatives on his
mother's, Mary Arden's, side. He told him that yes, his mother was certainly born Catholic, though he never saw her worship openly. He told him
about the time when he and the family were visiting his grandmother at
the stately brick house at Wilmcote, and he and his brother Gilbert were
playing hide-and-seek. He had ducked under his grandmother's bed, and
discovered a loose floorboard. Prying it open with a sense of discovery and
danger, he had found a carefully polished, gleaming silver crucifix and a set
of rosary beads, magical, alluring, and terrifying all at once. He'd slammed
the floorboard shut and run to hide in the washtub.

"Now," said Lucy, "tell me once more about Thomas Cottom." He nodded slightly to Henry Rogers, who gave the rack the tiniest turn.

But just as William finished his scream, and took a breath to tell Lucy about the locked box, there came a pounding at the door of the chamber. Lucy, annoyed, gestured to Henry Rogers; he, pissed off, left his work to answer it. The moment Henry Rogers unbarred the door and opened it, he stepped back and bowed deeply.

"My lord."

Sir Thomas Lucy also did his reverence, and stayed there as Sir Robert Dudley, Earl of Leicester, followed by three of his seconds, strode into the room. William recognized him from the day nine years ago at Kenilworth when Leicester had entertained the Queen and might have come to sword-play with Edward Arden but for the intercession of Lady Magdalen.

Leicester looked much older now, and he coughed.

He looked blankly at William. William suddenly forgot the pain in his shoulders and knees, the biting of the bonds at his wrists and ankles. He only felt how absurd he must look to Leicester, spread-eagle on the rack, his belly hair wet and curled with sweat and his ballocks dripping with comical little candle-drips of wax.

Leicester turned to leave, and as he passed Lucy, muttered, "Let him go."

Lucy stood upright in shock.

"My lord, this yeoman's brat is on the point of revealing secret papist enclaves amongst the nobility, in your own Warwickshire. I pray you let the inquisition play its course, and I shall deliver recusants and plotters that threaten the Queen's very life."

The Earl of Leicester stopped, and looked over his shoulder at William. His lower jaw worked back and forth for an instant. He breathed a short, sharp breath through his nose, like a caged bull. Then he coughed a long, racking cough. Before he was fully recovered from the fit, he choked out, "He is, as you say, but a yeoman's brat. I said let him go."

Then he was gone.

"Ay, my lord," said Lucy, with a bow to the already closed door.

William tried not to look too searchingly at Lucy. There were, he thought, a couple of ways this could go. Either Lucy would do what Leicester had told him to do; or he wouldn't.

Chapter Eighteen

Cassius from bondage will deliver Cassius:
Therein, ye gods, you make the weak most strong;
Therein, ye gods, you tyrants do defeat;
Nor stony tower, nor walls of beaten brass,
Nor airless dungeon, nor strong links of iron,
Can be retentive to the strength of spirit.

—Cassius, *Julius Caesar*, I.iii.90

Willie woke up on Friday morning only when Robin sat on the small of his back and thrust a cup of coffee in his face.

"Ambition, thy name is Willie. Get up, sleepyhead."

Willie groaned as Robin threw the covers off of him.

"Come on, I've been padding around being quiet for an hour."

He took the coffee and looked at the clock: 8:03.

"Jesus, why does Berkeley get up two hours before Santa Cruz? Is it a different time zone?"

Robin was loading up a large portfolio case with signs, flyers, and pamphlets. A bundle of sticks and posterboard waited by the door; a staple gun was slung in one of the loops of her olive green painter's pants. "It's not easy for a city, being on the cutting edge of political and social reform. Gotta start the day early." Robin took a sip from her own coffee, and put on a beret. Her hair was braided into two chestnut ropes that trailed across her collarbones. She wore black eye-shadow. All in all, Willie thought, she looked not unlike Patty Hearst in her manifestation as Tania. In pigtails. And sans the AK-47.

Willie and Robin had been dating since she was a junior and he was a senior as Berkeley undergrads. He'd wanted to apply to the Berkeley M.A. program in English, but learned from his father that the University of California had a unwritten policy not to accept graduate candidates from the same campus where they received their B.A. So he was exiled to Santa Cruz. He'd been taking the library jitney to Berkeley to visit Robin on weekends ever since.

"So are you going to see your parents this weekend?" Robin asked as she fed her cat, Mao—whom she referred to as the Chairman, or sometimes the Couchman, or sometimes, when he pooped in the corner next to the stereo, "You fucking piece of Commie shit."

"I don't know. My dad and I are kind of on the outs."

"What did your stepmom want last night?"

"What does she ever want? Attention. Her father's approval. A Bloody Mary."

"You should go see them," Robin said.

"There are a lot of things I should do. You know, by age twenty-six, Shakespeare had written six, maybe seven plays already?"

"So you've still got a year to catch up. Besides, people got old a lot younger then. Don't be so hard on yourself. I mean, you're very smart, but despite the soulful brown eyes, and despite the name...you're no William Shakespeare."

Willie felt his shoulders tense. He didn't want to start a fight before breakfast. He tried to laugh, but he failed. "What does *that* mean?"

"I didn't mean it that way. Don't worry, nobody else is William Shakespeare, either."

"You're saying I couldn't write a play?"

"Of course you could. You should." There was a heavy pause. "So, do you want to come to the rally?"

Willie considered. It was only Friday morning. He wouldn't be able to make his contacts at the Renaissance Faire until tomorrow. Besides hanging with Robin for the day, he only saw two other options: visiting his dad and stepmom, or going to the library to actually work on his paper.

"Sure," Willie said. He looked at the duffel bag, which sat on Robin's couch where he'd tossed it when he walked in yesterday. He considered taking it along with him now, but decided it was safer where it was.

.   .   .

If Sproul Plaza had been bustling the day before, it was a mob scene now. As Robin and Willie entered from Telegraph Avenue, there were already one or two of Robin's friends handing out flyers. The Piano Man was banging out "Lucy in the Sky with Diamonds." A sound crew was setting up microphones and a lectern on the top step outside of Sproul Hall.

Robin met a group of her friends under the shaded arcade of the student union building across the plaza, and after some coffee and genial Reagan-bashing, Robin whipped out her staple gun, and they got down to the work of nailing signs to signposts.

Willie looked at the signs that had already been scrawled out: PARAQUAT KILLS. JUST SAY NO TO TURNER. DEA: DRUG ENFORCEMENT ASSHOLES.

Willie found a big red Sharpie and a blank posterboard, and wrote:

MAKE LOVE ON DRUGS, NOT WAR.

He showed it to Robin. "How's this?"

She shook her head. "We're not trying to encourage drug use per se. How about MAKE WAR ON POVERTY, NOT DRUGS?"

"Not as clever."

"But more to the point."

"No, that's not to the point," said one of Robin's group, and held up a sign. "This is to the fucking point."

GIVE HINCKLEY ANOTHER SHOT.

The rest of the group groaned. Bill, the president of the Committee to F$¢K Reagan, snatched the sign away from the guy. "No way, Jeremy."

As Willie stuffed his own vetoed sign into a trash can, he checked Jeremy out. Stereotypical Berkeley radical. Long, kinky, dirty hair that hadn't seen a brush or comb in weeks. Pot-leaf t-shirt. Greasy jeans. And behind his wire-rim glasses, dull brown eyes that were swallowed by giant black pupils, even in the bright light of day. He was young; maybe twenty.

"I'm sorry, but I think Reagan's the fucking Antichrist," Jeremy said, continuing the argument as though it hadn't stopped.

"Yeah, well, if so, you're not going to be the one to take him out, right?" said Robin.

Angela, a pudgy dark-haired girl, didn't look up from the sign she was putting together, but said, "Excuse me, but I'm totally uncomfortable even *talking* about this. I don't mind protest, but anything that veers toward conspiracy to assassinate the President I prefer to avoid, okay?"

Jeremy grabbed his sign back from Bill.

"Exactly. You're all afraid Ray-gun's storm troopers are gonna come pounding on your door because of what you *say*, Angela. Speech is either free or it isn't. You can't have it both ways."

"You believe in absolute freedom of expression, too, Jeremy?" asked Robin.

"Absolutely."

Robin picked up the can of red paint next to Willie and threw the whole thing across Jeremy's sign, obliterating the slogan and splattering red paint over his greasy jeans and torn dime-store sneakers in the process.

Everyone was stunned for a moment.

"Solidarity, brother," said Robin, taking the staple gun away from him.

Willie laughed. "Doesn't freedom of speech end where your paint meets his jeans?"

"Yeah." Robin smiled at Willie. "So I'm a fascist. Protest me."

Everybody began to snicker, then to laugh.

Jeremy threw his sign aside. "Very funny. Fuck you, Robin."

This only made everyone laugh harder. Jeremy flushed red, threw his sign down, and stormed off onto the plaza.

Angela called out, "Jeremy, wait!"

"Let him go," Bill said. "I think he's tripping."

A half hour later, the rally began. Robin's group spread themselves around the plaza, which by 12:10 was packed with several hundred people, from fresh-faced undergrads to local radicals to strung-out druggies to curious tourists to faculty who had tripped with Leary in the old days. Willie stood next to a small, wiry, bearded guy with beady eyes who was holding up a sign while openly smoking a joint and yelling "Reagan sucks!" and "Don't blame me, I voted for Mondale!" at random intervals.

Willie glanced up at the guy's sign: it read MAKE LOVE ON DRUGS, NOT WAR. It was the sign Willie had abandoned.

A young woman from the Student Political Alliance stepped up to the microphone and the rally began in very earnest. She spoke about the growing AIDS crisis and how the fight against it was being ignored by the Reagan administration. She spoke of news that the administration had suppressed information that hypodermic needles could be cleaned by simply rinsing with bleach, a revelation that would have saved hundreds of lives in San Francisco alone, where AIDS was raging and needle-sharing among junkies and meth freaks was rampant. She spoke of how the War on Drugs was hypocrisy, because alcohol, tobacco, and now AIDS killed more people than smack, crack, pot, and all the other illegal drugs combined. She ended by declaring that the War on Drugs should be transformed into a war on the drug policies of the Reagan administration. Willie shrugged, nodded, and applauded. Not a brilliant turn of phrase, but it hit the nail on the head.

And then the girl at the mike introduced "a great American."

A salt-and-pepper-haired woman, short, dark, a little mannish, appeared on the Sproul steps. She slung a guitar strap over her shoulder to cheering and applause and stepped up to the microphone.

"Hi. I'm Joan Baez."

Amid the rapturous cheer, Willie turned to Robin.

"Can we go?" he asked.

"I should stay 'til the end. Why don't you go see your folks?"

Joan Baez or a visit with his stepmother. Tough call.

She launched into a tedious cover of "Shout," by Tears for Fears. Willie wasn't sure he could make it to the end. Those Shakespeare guys were right—she did suck. Something about her braying, humorless sincerity bugged the hell out of him. He wasn't sure he could make it to the end, but she finally stopped *Shout*-ing, and the crowd cheered again.

Then the earnest student activist—*Earnestine*, Willie dubbed her—stood up and introduced Dr. Timothy Leary.

The guy next to Willie went bonkers. He shrieked, "Tune In! Turn On! Drop Out!" over and over again in an entirely arrhythmic attempt to get a chant going. Willie looked around to see if anyone else was noticing the guy, and he saw one person, sitting on the far end of the Sproul steps, who seemed to be staring at him—or was he staring at Willie? Willie couldn't decide before the guy casually turned his eyes back to the podium. He looked familiar. Where had he seen him before? The mustache … then he remembered, it was the same guy who had been on the library jitney the previous day. The clerk. Had he recognized Willie, or just ignored him? *Probably he was just unfondly remembering the heavy breathing coming from the back seat*, Willie thought. Willie had a moment's panic that the guy would come up to him and Robin and mention something about the bus ride. He thought of the meltdown fight that would ensue between him and Robin, the long-day-into-night-into-early-morning deconstruction of the whole history of their on-again-off-again, open-closed, don't-ask-don't-tell relationship.

But then, he realized, it wouldn't matter much if the guy told her. Robin already seemed to know.

Dr. Timothy Leary stepped up to the podium, all electric gray hair and bright eyes. Willie had always thought of Leary as a crackpot, but his speech quickly had him hooked.

Throughout human history, Leary said, people from the ancient Greeks to Native Americans have used psychoactive drugs as a sacrament—which he defined as that which bridges the gap between the human and the divine—in their religious practice. Leary said he was not religious, but his scientist self saw, in the emergence of psychedelics as a force in Western culture, a turning point in human evolution.

The brain, he explained quickly, was a biological computer network of cells firing at five billion signals a second among thirty billion brain cells. Each cell can communicate with more than twenty-five hundred other cells; that makes for more possible synaptic connections in a single brain than there are molecules in the universe. Most of those cells, and the neural pathways between them, are unused. Where they *are* used, they tend, like ruts in a dirt road, to be the same routes traveled over and over again, like the one that tells us to walk to the refrigerator when we want a snack. "Imprinting," he called it.

But psychoactive drugs like LSD and psilocybin, which act on the higher levels of the nervous system, seem to break down existing imprints temporarily, allowing new ones to be created. In that open state of no imprints, of tabula rasa, it's common to experience ego loss: that moment of simultaneous wholeness, oneness, and nothingness that is the ultimate goal of all Eastern religions: enlightenment, the realization of Nirvana; the transcendence of space-time. The knowing of God.

Leary cited his triple-blind, monitored studies at Harvard. Seventy-three percent of a wide range of subjects found their LSD trips either very pleasant or "ecstatic." Ninety-five percent felt it was a life-changing experience for the better. Could even Jesus claim that kind of success rate?

But the Reagan administration doesn't want you to be able to have that positive, life-changing experience, Leary said. They're conservative, and conservatives by definition don't want your life to change. They like you just the way you are. Quietly working, paying taxes, keeping the hive running like good worker bees. Nothing wrong with that, Leary said to Willie's surprise, human society needs worker bees to keep the hive alive, and if everyone suddenly started re-imprinting their brain's programming, started writing poetry and music and painting mandalas, well, then, who would be left to mind the store? But in any organized society, he argued, there must also be the ten percent of smart people who design the widgets sold in the store. And there must also be the five percent or less of genuinely *creative* people who come up with ideas beyond widgets, ideas no one's ever thought of; the true geniuses who move civilization forward, the ones whose biological computers blaze enough new neural trails to paint the *Mona Lisa*, discover relativity, or invent television. And for them—and Leary looked out at the Sproul Plaza crowd, a few hundred of the smartest people in the country—well, just who the hell does Carlton Turner, the little worker bee, think he is, telling you what you should or should not ingest?

The crowd cheered wildly. The guy next to him screamed, "Make love on drugs, not war!" and Willie smiled with just a wee bit of pride. Maybe, he thought, just maybe, he was one of the ten percent, or even the five percent, and if he could just open those pathways and access the unused, unfired synapses in his brain, then perhaps he *could* write that paper, become something, somebody, the writer, poet, actor, playwright, the Renaissance man, the William Shakespeare he was meant to be. As the cheering began to die out, Willie began to chant: "Make love on drugs, not war! Make love on drugs, not war!" at first low and then more loudly, and others around him started chanting, too, until it spread through the crowd. He looked at

Robin; she was smiling at him but also shaking her head in mock disapproval. He shrugged, like the Grinch's dog, Max, when he finds himself riding, rather than pulling, the sleigh; and finally Robin joined in, too.

It was while the chanting was at its peak that Willie noticed Dashka coming down the steps from Sproul Hall and walking into the crowd. She took up a position at the edge of the throng. Willie was pretty sure she had glanced at him as she turned to watch Leary, but if so she didn't acknowledge him. In fact, she looked a little distracted. He might almost say shaken. Of course, he thought, she sees me with Robin. She'd definitely want to steer clear.

Then Willie noticed that just behind Dashka, a sandy-haired Berkeley campus police officer was staring directly at him.

He saw me start the chant.

Willie looked quickly away and stopped chanting. Topping the crowd, Dr. Timothy Leary launched into a diatribe against Reagan and the Drug Enforcement Agency and their tactics. He told everyone to be careful because with mandatory minimums and plea bargains only given to informants, you never know who's looking to fink on you. Your junkie cousin? Your alcoholic mother? A scared kid getting brainwashed by Nancy's Just Say No campaign?

And he warned against using the wrong drugs, the wrong way: alcohol, he said, acts on the animal, aggressive portion of the brain. Pot and hashish are "hedonic," great for sensory stimulation, food, sex, and music, but ultimately stupefying rather than enlightening. And even psychedelics, if taken in a negative environment, will produce negative results. There are, he said, two reasons to take drugs: to tune out, or to tune in. You must choose to tune in.

And then he made a big announcement, the commercial justification for appearing at the rally that day: a plug. He was going to debate the great issues of the day on an upcoming tour with Watergate coconspirator G. Gordon Liddy.

The crowd cocked its collective head like a confused spaniel.

After some smattered cheering and polite applause, someone off to their left, another lone voice, screamed, "Liddy's a fascist!" and then began to chant: "Death to the DEA! Death to the Pres! Death to the DEA! Death to the Pres!" Willie craned his neck to see: it was Jeremy. A lot of people, Willie included, were perplexed, not just by the poor scansion of the chant, but because they couldn't understand why a Berkeley radical would have a problem with a free press. But then, when the drug case next to Willie started chanting along—further mangling the rhythm of the rhythmless chant—everyone figured it out. Death to the *Pres*. Incitement to assassinate. Nobody else joined in.

Robin started toward Jeremy angrily, saying, "Jeremy, no—" but when she reached out toward him he knocked her arm away. She was caught off balance and fell to the pavement as the crowd stepped back. People started shouting, "Hey! Hey!" as Willie instinctively lunged at Jeremy, who was red-faced, eyes blazing black as he stood menacingly over Robin. "Leave me ALONE, Robin! Freedom of fucking SPEECH!"

Willie grabbed him and pulled him backward. Jeremy screamed in Willie's face, "Let me GO, asshole, your freedom ends at my fucking ARM!" Someone else said, "Okay, easy, easy!" and tried to grab Jeremy from behind; Jeremy spun on him with a flailing haymaker that caught the guy with an audible crack in the nose. He crumpled to the ground, blood gushing onto his face. Jeremy turned back toward Robin, but Willie pushed him away with a shove to the chest—then felt a strong, chubby hand closing around his own biceps. Willie struggled at first, but then saw that it was the sandy-haired cop. A second cop grabbed Jeremy, and led the two of them away. Willie looked over his shoulder to see Robin being helped to her feet by the crowd, her shocked face receding as she watched him go.

As Jeremy and Willie were led through the crowd, no one said anything. There were no outraged cries. Nobody pushed their noses up toward their forehead and began to oink. Only Jeremy complained, struggling and whining to the campus cop, "Ow, you're *hurting* me! That's police *brutality*, man!"

Willie and Jeremy were locked up in separate cells in a small private jail underneath Sproul Hall. At first Willie thought it would be kinda cool.

He'd be able to tell his grandkids that he had been arrested and dragged off to jail after a protest on the steps of Sproul Hall.

But then as the adrenaline wore off he began to wonder: would this arrest go on his permanent record? What kind of power did the campus police have? Would this be referred to the real police? What could they charge him with? The chant was surely protected by the First Amendment. He hadn't hurt anyone. But did the cops know that? They saw him shove Jeremy. What if they thought he'd been the one who broke the guy's nose? That would be assault. Then he thought about the duffel bag, back in Robin's apartment, filled with contraband. Is there any way they could find it? Do they routinely get search warrants for arrested campus radicals and their girlfriends to see if they're making Molotov cocktails in their student hovels? Or, even if he was released, what if between here and the Renaissance Faire he was arrested by the jackbooted storm troopers of Reagan's DEA? Would this bust count as some sort of first offense? *Fuck, what's the mandatory minimum for SECOND offenses?*

The incarceration was obviously having its intended effect on Willie.

But it was having an even greater effect on Jeremy.

Willie began to hear a low murmur from the holding cell next to his, a meandering melody anchored by the drumbeat footsteps of Jeremy pacing with increasing agitation.

After a few minutes the murmur became punctuated by fortissimo bursts of "shit!" "assholes!" and "fascists!" What was it Leary had said, about taking acid in a negative environment?

As the outbursts got louder and more frequent, the sandy-haired cop who had apprehended Willie walked past his cell to Jeremy's. Willie could hear the cop saying, "Okay, let's settle down, son. Be glad you're not in the city jail."

But Jeremy was freaking out.

"This isn't me, man! It is not *me*, I'm not expressing my*self* here. This is Robin's plan, all Robin's plan: do nothing and send me down the fucking river for it. You should've arrested her. Tell the city jail to arrest HER! She painted me, she grabbed me. Arrest her! Robin Rose, vice president of the Committee to Fuck Reagan, southwest corner of Webster and

Benvenue...arrest HER!!! Talk to HER about John Hinckley and shooting the President!"

"Settle down," the cop said. "Don't worry, we'll look into it."

Willie's stomach dropped to his feet.

They wouldn't. Jeremy was obviously frying on acid. But what if they did
look into it? If they just dropped by to talk to Robin?

His duffel bag was still sitting on the sofa.

Hi, is everything okay?

*Just wanted to talk to you about your friend Jeremy, and the rally this
morning.*

Sure. Would you like to come in?

Thank you, miss.

Just let me move this bag.

Was the zipper open? He pictured the bag gaping, the coffee can tum-
bling out, hitting the floor, and popping open, just like his backpack and
the hash pipe in front of Dashka. He pictured Robin's shock; he pictured
her in the city jail; he felt her anger, and her hatred.

For the first time, alone with time to think in his posh cell, he understood what the protest he'd been arrested for was all about. It was about
people whose only crime was eating a fungus that made you feel at one
with the universe, or smoking an herb that made for good sex—or merely
knowing someone who did, someone who maybe left a duffel bag on your
couch—and being thrown in jail. Not people like Jeremy, who actually
threatened or perpetrated violence; people who opposed violence, like
himself. Or like Robin. Again, he thought of her in jail. He thought of
Todd, and André, in jail. He thought of Jojo, and Dashka, all his friends
who got high, in jail. And then he thought of all the other friends who committed "crimes" regularly—buggery, sodomy, obscenity, consensual "statu-
tory rape." And it made him angry. What would it be next, religion? Could
they someday decide to chop off his own head in Sproul Plaza, for being
an agnostic? Yes, he decided. They could. And it pissed him off.

He thought again of Robin, in jail.

He had to get the duffel bag out of the apartment. Now. He couldn't tell
Robin, she'd rightfully be furious. He had to get out of this cell. And to do
that he'd have to swallow a gigantic lump of pride.

"Excuse me," Willie said to the cop who was now standing at a counter, filing paperwork as Jeremy continued to yammer senselessly. "Can I make my one phone call?"

The cop glanced over his shoulder, and went back to his work. "This isn't the movies. We'll let you go as soon as we've processed the paperwork."

"It's urgent. And it's just an on-campus call. To my dad." Then after a calculated pause, Willie added, oh-so-innocently, "He's a professor here?"

The cop looked over at Willie, weighing.

Ten minutes later, Alan Greenberg strode into the small police office, elbow patches blazing.

"Nice move, Willie. Very thoughtful."

Willie turned. "Thanks for coming, Dad."

"If this is some sort of revenge scenario—"

"It has nothing to do with the other day. It was an accident. I was trying to break up a fight."

"And yet it seems, once again, that you need my assistance."

Willie took a deep breath. He knew when he dialed the phone that this wouldn't be easy. "Yes, I do. But it's really not for me. There's something I have to do for Robin."

Alan considered for a moment, and then said, "I like Robin." He pushed his spectacles up on his nose and sighed. "One condition. I bail you out, you come visit me and your mother—"

Alan caught himself and recited Willie's correction along with him: *"She's not my mother."*

"I know, I know," Alan muttered. "But she'd love to see you."

"Okay, I'll come over. Today. Just give me an hour."

Alan nodded to the cop, who opened the cell door and let Willie out.

As he left, he heard Jeremy, ranting quietly to himself, "Death to the Pres! Death to the Pres!"

Willie never saw Jeremy again.

Chapter Nineteen

Nearly all playwrights are "political" on some level, and many are explicitly so. If Shakespeare grew up as part of a politically oppressed minority, it seems not unreasonable — although it is unfashionable under the academic tyranny that is New Criticism — to look for evidence that the experience influenced his work. If Shakespeare was raised as a dissident Catholic, this scholar feels compelled to ask: was he also, ab initio, a dissident Catholic writer?

William emerged from — or more exactly, was thrown out of — Charlecote in a daze, but in surprisingly little pain. He walked holding his shoulder, with a slight limp, bowlegged, and in absolute wonder at having been set free by no less than the Earl of Leicester himself.

It was early morning. Lucy had kept him imprisoned overnight. He had no idea where Rosaline might be. The last he had seen, Lucy's gamekeeper was escorting her firmly toward Charlecote's western gate. William limped away from the looming grey house and crossed the bridge over the river Dene that was a tributary of the Avon, but not without stopping first to wash and drink. He reached the gate and its two guards.

"Where is thy beaver skin, poacher?" one said as William passed, and the other laughed.

He turned right onto the main road and trudged on for another four long miles toward Stratford. The sky was overcast, the air wintry cold. The countryside was quiet but for the occasional squawk of a startled crow rising up from the grass as William passed.

After two hours, he reached the magnificent arched bridge built by Hugh Clopton that was and still is the eastern approach to Stratford-upon-Avon. He crossed it, passed by the open green space between the road and the Avon that served as a community archery range, and found himself looking up Bridge Street, with its row of houses down the middle.

William wanted to find Rosaline—to make sure she was still in one piece and unravished. A tall tankard of ale wouldn't hurt, either; William was parched. The town's two main inns flanked the entrance to Bridge Street: the Bear, on the left, was Catholic; the Swan, on the right, Protestant. William usually trod the middle road, up the hill to the Angel (Ralph Cawdrey, proprietor), where the only requisite belief was that Ralph's brew was actually drinkable.

Rosaline's cousin, Davy Jones, was Protestant, but William was disinclined to throw himself into enemy territory just now so he ducked into the Bear to ask if anyone had seen her or knew her whereabouts. There was a very small company gathered, it being late morning on a Saturday. At a table near the back he was surprised to see Arthur and George Cawdrey. There were two other figures, but William, coming in from the glare of the day, couldn't make out their faces in the darkened corner.

"How now, brothers Cawdrey?" William said. "Is your father's brew so ill that you must drink the competitor's brew betimes?"

They didn't reply, and seemed strangely grim-faced as William approached. "I seek Rosaline, the kinswoman of Davy Jones—"

As he came closer and his eyes adjusted to the dark, he suddenly recognized the face in the corner. "What ho…HA! Richard Field or I'm a dotard!" Richard Field stood up and they embraced. "With the dust of London still on his boots?" William continued.

"'Tis of the selfsame dust as that of Stratford, which is ever on yours," Field answered.

William and Richard Field were old friends and classmates, and their fathers friends and business associates before that. While several of the youth of Stratford had left the King's New School for Oxford or Cambridge, and a few had gone to the seminaries in Rheims, Douai, or Rome, young Richard Field had gone directly to London.

William slid onto a seat next to him. "You take your life into your hands, coming into a Catholic inn," William teased.

"Not in this Queen's reign, for the law is on my side," Field shot back.

Then more seriously, and low, "It is you who risk all, coming here. Even in darkened Catholic inns, there are spies."

"What spies here, if not the apprentice to a Puritan printer?" William said in jest, but George Cawdrey nodded toward a table by the front door, where sat a pale, thin fellow with a straggling red beard, talking to Thomas Barber, the Bear's proprietor. William didn't recognize him, and turned to his friends with a shrug.

George Cawdrey answered William's silent question. "'Tis Davy Jones's friend, the author of *The Death of Robin Hood*."

"Anthony Munday," said Arthur Cawdrey.

"I'faith? Marry, he must be wanting of ale indeed to bring his custom hither," William replied.

"Speak not too loudly, William," said Richard Field, low enough that Munday couldn't hear, "for his forked tongue, 'tis said, reaches even to Walsingham, and thence to the Queen herself."

William scoffed, and if anything he raised his voice. "What has Munday, that whoreson bombast-monger and splitter of infinitives, to do with Sir Francis Walsingham and his network of spies?"

Munday glanced at them, but then returned to his conversation with Barber.

"No rolling stone you, William," said Field quietly after a moment. "You gather too much moss and too little news here in Stratford. Walsingham uses players and playwrights both as informants. They're well-suited to the task, for they travel, they mix amongst all classes. The wealthy and powerful patronize them, drink with them, oft try to bed them. And where the promise of dalliance is offered, mayhap the lips will loosen, in hope that secrets given will be repaid with secret places offered. And amongst players are not just spies but also the spied upon, for they carry with them documents, parts, sides, and other such papers amongst which seditious tracts may be hid. And even in their lines, coded words and veiled references may be strewn. If a Caesar say, 'Let my Roman legions march on Gaul,' might it not be a popish call to arms against the Huguenots? The printed word may be a sharp and many-edged weapon, my friend.

"Which puts me in mind..." Field said. He opened a leather bag on the bench next to him and pulled out four new books, which he set in front of William. "For you, from the shop where I am apprenticed, and others roundabout."

William looked at the books.

"Plutarch's *Lives*...a new Ovid...*Orlando Furioso*, I have wished for this!"

"And the last volume of Holinshed, *The Chronicles of England, Scotland, and Ireland*," said Field. "Hot from the press, and best of the volumes yet, William. He does a passing fine rendering of the War of the Roses, right through the accession of Elizabeth." He pointed to a spot in the text as William flipped through it. "I particularly recommend the entry on Richard III."

They paused as a man descended from the rooms on the second story. His back was to them as he came down the stairs and took a table to himself, not far from Anthony Munday, but William nevertheless recognized him as Simon Pray, the strange horseman who'd given him the locked box from Thomas Cottom.

"And this?" William continued, holding up a volume entitled *The Palace of Pleasure*.

"A collection of stories, one a new translation of the old tale of 'Romeus and Giulietta' of which I know you to be fond. Dully told, I fear, but it is at least in English; I know you came back wounded from your battle with the French and Italian texts."

At the table by the front door, Anthony Munday's voice had begun to rise as the level of ale in his cup had lowered. He was jabbing a finger at Thomas Barber.

"I have said it in print and will say it here in popish Warwickshire, to any who may hear," and he raised his voice to fill the room, "the death of Thomas Cottom was the just punishment of a traitor to the state most foul." He looked about as if seeing who would respond and how, and his gaze rested particularly on the man who had come down moments before. There was a silence and a shuffling of feet as Munday took another draught from his mug. "As were the deaths of William Fillbie, Luke Kirbie, Ralph Sherwin, Edmund Campion, and all other wicked priests of the Jesuit seminaries past, present, or yet to come, for they are all traitors to Her Majesty."

George Cawdry whispered to the others at the table, "Are we to let this gauntlet fall untouched?"

"I have naught to say," said William.

"Ah, of course...*gentle William*," said George. "He has a sharp tongue for fellow players, and a sugared one for maids, but in matters of church and state, the greatest part of his valor is ever his discretion."

"Yet one may wonder at his discretion with maids, for judging by his face, they answer his sugared tongue with sharpened nails," chuckled Arthur. William touched his slashed cheek and looked toward Munday.

Munday drained his mug, and shrugged. "'Tis as I reckoned it. No Catholic will speak in defense of his evil faith; mayhap God, in punishment, has stricken dumb their tongues."

At last the horseman turned around. "'Tis said that Father Edmund Campion spoke most eloquently from the gallows," he said. Edmund Campion was one of the first, and certainly the most revered, of the recently martyred Catholic priests.

"'Tis said that the serpent spoke eloquently to make us all sinners," said Munday, turning to engage the horseman with a thin-lipped grin. "What of it? Campion died as a traitor deserves."

"Deserves?" said the horseman. "No man deserves drawing and quartering. 'Tis a punishment fit only for a demon, not a free Englishman of whatever faith."

"It is a punishment fit for a traitor," said Munday.

"Catholics be no traitors if they serve their Queen," said the horseman. "They ask only the liberty to pursue the truth of religion in open discourse. If the Queen fear but the truth, she is not half the prince I think her to be."

"Take care," said Munday. "Your words border on treason. Campion died a traitor to his church, his Queen, and his God. He groveled by the end."

"He did no such thing," said Richard Field. "I was there, and you lie."

There was a heavy silence. "You saw Campion die?" asked William.

"Ay. I was there."

All the faces in the pub that were within earshot turned to Richard Field.

"It was a miserable day, even for December. Cold and muddy with incessant rain the two days past. The tree at Tyburn is bigger than you might think, and is not—as I believed in my innocence—a tree at all, but a man-made structure topped by a triangle of three beams. Each might hang eight men at once; though that day there were but three. A scaffold, like unto a theater, towering over even the tree itself, stands to one side and others, smaller, roundabout. The scaffolds might hold a thousand or more, though there were many times that in the crowd that day.

"Campion arrived tied to a hurdle, having been drawn through the streets from the Tower. Already he was caked in mud, and covered in manure fresh from the horse that drew him, and he had been spat upon, and rotten lettuce and other refuse clung to his hair and brows, for he had been abused by many along the way. The crowd was exceeding restive and cried at Campion, 'Traitor! Papist!' or at each other, 'Sinner! Repent!' or 'Get you to Rome, if Romish you be!' and the like. There was a great press, but I stood low upon the scaffold with a clear view. The hangman cut Campion from his hurdle and assisted him to his feet. He looked half dead already, starved and limping. He'd been racked three times before his trial...."

Field paused, then said softly, "To which mockery I also bore witness. Upon the first day before his judges, when asked to raise his hand to swear an oath, he was unable, for the damage to his shoulder."

William felt a throb of pain in his own shoulder at the mention.

"Another prisoner standing nearby," Field continued, "taking pity, kissed his hand gently then raised it for him, so he might swear his truth before God.

"Three days his trial lasted, and though he was weak and racked they made him now debate the causes for which he had craved hearing. And yet they would not let him sit, nor gave him books nor paper nor pen with which to prepare or take notes. And though he could not for his injuries write, the Crown demanded any evidence he might present must be in writing.

"So the trial went, to its foregone conclusion.

"But on his last living day, at least, his shoulder was well enough that as he was taken from the hurdle and placed upon a cart, he was able to cross himself. The cart was rolled under the tripartite tree, the noose fitted to his neck, and he began to speak words of St. Paul, first in Latin then in English. But he was not allowed to continue, for one in the throng shouted at him to confess his treason.

"Campion said simply, 'I am a Catholic man, and a priest; in that faith have I lived hitherto, and in that faith I do intend to die; and if you esteem my religion treason, then of force I must grant unto you. As for any other treason, I never committed any; God is my judge.'

"He would have spoken more, but others who deemed their words of greater worth than those of the condemned would have their say."

Field turned to look at Munday with distaste.

"Anthony Munday it was who stood upon the scaffold, as trumpets sounded to silence the multitude, and he spoke for the Crown, reading from his *Discovery of Edmund Campion* a passage that he deemed worthy of the occasion of the man's martyrdom.

"He so assailed the life of Campion, and in such vicious prose, that the faithful to the Pope there attending began to hiss and curse, and Munday's response thereto was so splenetic and ill-mannered that even many who had come in joy to see Campion die joined the call, and Munday was shouted down, unable to continue."

Those listening turned to Anthony Munday at his table, but he remained impassive, allowing Field to finish.

"Finally Campion himself, pressed to beg the Queen's forgiveness, asked, 'Wherein have I offended her? In this I am innocent. This is my last speech; in this give me credit—I have and do pray for her.' He spoke most eloquently of his love for England and Elizabeth; swore that he never did aught nor intended aught to affright Her Majesty's power or sovereignty. He prayed the country would find the strength to encourage open discourse, to allow Catholics and reformers alike to worship in unencumbered peace. And finally, nearing tears, he beseeched any who, during his torment on the rack, he might have betrayed to forgive him his weakness. He meant to say more, but of his infirmity stumbled on his words, and taking advantage of the pause, the executioner began his office.

"First the horse was whipped and the cart lurched out from beneath him, and so Campion swung. Although he neither kicked nor struggled, he was quite alive, and his body of its own will gasped for air. It found some, but too little, and after several minutes, his face took on a purple hue, and his eyes began to bulge grotesquely from his head.

"The crowd gasped as one when despite his mortal state, his lips moved once again in prayer. Seeming angered to have his skill thus challenged, the executioner took this as his cue to lower the noose. Campion's feet barely touched the ground. The hangman with his knife quickly stripped from the priest—who was still alive but swooning—what rags were left about him, so that he was naked to the world. Then holding his knife aloft, he grabbed the poor priest's ballocks and his prick, full erect—which, a bystander noted to his wife, was a product of the asphyxiation—and with a single upward cut sliced the lot from the trunk.

"A profusion of blood gushed forth the gaping hole, and more dripped from the member itself as the hangman held it in front of Campion's bulging eyes. He tossed the gory manhood into a fire that stood nearby within Campion's gaze, and the sickly smell of burning flesh wafted over all the amazed mob, and some vomited with the sight and smell of it.

"But the deed was not yet full wrought, for Campion yet lived, and the executioner raised his knife aloft again and sliced ope the poor priest's belly, so that his entrails burst forth, and while he watched—though his sight, I thought, or hoped, seemed to be dimming now—the hangman drew out the entrails and fed them, still attached at the bodily end, into the fire, at which you could hear the choked cry of the priest's agony even through his noose. Quickly then the hangman pulled out the martyr's heart, which he held quickly aloft to beat twice in front of Campion's eyes ere they became fixed and it was clear his spirit had fled his body's torment.

"His heart went on the fire, and finally his stomach and lungs, and all was consumed while the hangman cut down the shell of Campion, and laid it upon a table. Trading his knife for axe, the executioner heaved a single mighty stroke, which cut off Campion's head as you might trim a hen for dinner, and then with many grievous blows cut the remnants into four, leaving a limb attached each to a quarter of the gory trunk.

"It was at the last but one of these blows that I felt, like the first hint of a hot rain, a single drop of blood upon my hand. A miracle it was to guide it there, for I would not have thought myself close enough to the spectacle to allow it, but there it was, the blood of a martyr upon my hand. And I beg salvation for my guilt in the affair, for by my standing by, and watching as it were a bearbaiting or game of bowls, I am complicit."

Richard Field raised his hand and regarded the back of it, turning it to catch the dim light fighting through the greasy front windows of the inn. As if his mind were quite far away, he said, "A spot of blood upon my hand, but a stain everlasting upon my soul." He rubbed the spot on his hand absently. "All the seas of Neptune will not wash it away, nor all the perfumes of Araby mask its stench."

After a moment he continued.

"There were two executions yet to be done that day, but I had seen enough for a lifetime. As I pushed my way out through the blood-lusting crowd, they pressed to take my place for a better view of the next display, for the hangman was pulling another priest from his hurdle. He couldn't stand on his own, and I heard the hangman brag that he had made the priest a foot longer by his racking. That was the last I heard."

Again they were silent. "God have mercy on their souls," said George Cawdrey, and drained his mug.

"And ours," added William.

They drank morosely for a moment. William had listened to the narrative thinking of the identical fate of Thomas Cottom. The emptiness in his own gut grew with the tale of Campion's disemboweling. "What nation have we become," he said to his companions, "where men of the cloth, of whatever cloth they be cut, are cut thus? We would not slaughter our farm animals with such dishonor, and yet a man, a priest, who gives his life to the service of God, is made to suffer such outrageous fortune."

Finally, Anthony Munday spoke. "Neither Campion nor Cottom nor any wicked Jesuit priest died for any service to God but rather for treason to the Queen, affirmed and proven in the Queen's court, and therefore true in the Kingdom of Heaven. Yet the horror of their deaths pales to the torments that await all such sinners in hell."

Richard Field turned red. "Then what more painful torments await Anthony Munday, who profits by the horror?" said Field.

"What mean you?" asked William.

Field gestured at Munday with disgust. "He sells pamphlets purporting to tell the tale of the demise of the Jesuit priests Campion, Cottom, and others beside. They are true in the particulars, mayhap, but like a painting drawn in ill light, are colored ill, in sickly hues that please only his spymaster, Walsingham."

"He should be answered," William said, anger finally rising within him and wrenching his ankles, knees, and shoulders that ached from his own brief encounter with the rack. "All these petty tyrants of small minds and smaller domains, these wardens of the inns and justices of the squares and constables of the church and magistrates of the bedroom—all these arbiters of righteousness, self-proclaimed, self-anointed, their logic turned upon itself like a snake swallowing its tail, all should be answered. They are devils, who would cast not just the first, but *every* stone, leaving naught behind of this earth but base mud and filth," William said, his thoughts getting ahead of his tongue.

In the darkened corner, the horseman also rose. "England may yet be exorcised of these devils and their minions and masters," he said. He came to the table where William and his friends were sitting. They waited, tense, to learn his intentions. The horseman knelt at Richard Field's side and picked up the hand upon which Campion's blood had been spilled. He bowed and kissed it, and his eyes burned black as he said in a whisper that was like the roar of blood in a vein, "*In nomine Patris, et Filii, et Spiritus Sancti. O Domine Iesu Christi, hanc manum puram ex sanguine hoc sanctissimo atque hunc virum malis manibus ex corpore expulsis ut vivat in pacem facere digneris!*" He stood and cried out in English, rasping from deep in his throat, "Out, daemon, OUT!" The light in the already dark room seemed to dim as the horseman's robes rose and rustled.

In the stunned silence that followed, the horseman looked about the room. He looked at Anthony Munday, who remained impassive, watching him carefully. The horseman pulled his hood over his head and turned to go, but then stopped and, turning back, leaned on the table and whispered urgently in William's ear: "You are in danger. By my weakness, we are all endangered, but you and your family the most."

William assumed he was talking about the contraband box from Thomas Cottom and glanced nervously at the spy, Munday, and then at his startled friends.

"I know not of what you speak."

The horseman's dark eyes clouded over as he nodded. "Ay, true enough." A corner of his mouth twitched an ironic smile. "Mayhap your ignorance will beget your joy, as your joy begat my sorrow. God forgive me, I have in my heart wished you dead many times this day."

William shook his head, angry and confused. "I? For what cause should I be so mortally wounded, even if only by the incorporeal arrows of a disturbed mind?"

"I have had my England taken from me, and I fear, my everlasting soul," said the horseman quietly. "But I would not have my heart ripped out even as Campion's was. I will not give her up now, not to thee nor anyone, mark me well."

The horseman turned and strode away, glaring at Anthony Munday and crossing himself as he went out the door.

Richard Field turned to William and said, "Know you what he was on about?"

"His fifth ale, I guess," William replied, bewildered.

"You know him not?" Field asked, confused.

William looked again toward Munday, who was busy chewing a cheese pie that Barber had brought. William lowered his voice to a level Munday wouldn't hear.

"We are strangers who have met. His name is Pray. He is clerk to a London lawyer."

"Clerk?" said George Cawdrey, also in a low voice. "I'faith, that was no clerk. He gives his true calling by his false name. Your Pray is a priest, William. 'Tis Robert Debdale of Shottery, one of the many who followed Simon Hunt to the seminaries. I know him from Rheims. An exorcist, 'tis said."

Anthony Munday had been pretending not to try to hear their hushed conversation, but now he finished his cheese pie and blinked heavily, like a lizard. "See," he said loudly, rising and reaching into his pouch, "to what ends our sovereign England might attain, if left to popish heretics? Exorcism of purported demons in public houses." Munday threw three coins clattering down on the table, then took from the back of his chair an oversize bag. He reached into it and pulled out two pamphlets, then walked over to put them gingerly on the table in front of Richard Field.

"I give you gratis these my true accounts of the deaths of these villains you would sanctify; consider them my reply to your most eloquent, if misguided, recounting of the death of the traitor Campion. Fare ye well." He bowed slightly to the group, and left with his head held high.

After they watched him go, the foursome craned their necks to read the cover of the top pamphlet:

A Brief Answer made unto two Seditious Pamphlets, the one printed in French, and the other in English, containing a defense of Edmund Campion and his Complices, their Most Horrible and Unnatural Treasons, against Her Majesty and the Realm. By A.M.

"One might hope the 'Brief Answer' briefer than the title," said George Cawdrey.

Richard Field flipped through the booklet.

"Munday has here taken several ballads made upon Campion's martyrdom that are sung in London, and answered them with his own hateful verse in the selfsame meter. Here...I know well the original of this one, it sings achingly of the very buildings and streets of London mourning Campion's death." Field sang in a halting voice:

"The Tower sayeth, the truth he did defend;
The Barre bears witness of his guiltless mind;
Tyburn doth tell he made a patient end;
On every gate his martyrdom we find.
In vain you wrote yet would obscure his name,
For heaven and earth will still record the same.

"This, when perverted and belched forth from Munday's poison pen, becomes:

"The Tower sayeth he Treason did defend;
The Barre bears witness of his guilty mind;
Tyburn doth tell he made a Traitor's end;
On every gate example we may find.
In vain they work to laude him with such fame,
For heaven and earth bears witness of his shame."

Field flipped another page or two. "He even claims that Campion was given 'books, as many as he could demand,' for his trial. Lies and deception!"

He threw the pamphlet down on the table. William picked up the second pamphlet and stared at it. It was, its cover proclaimed, an account of the execution of several priests, including Thomas Cottom.

William flipped through it: more of the same, railing against the traitorous priests and the Pope.

"This must needs be answered."

"William, be you Catholic or Protestant," Field said to his friend, "I know you to be a writer of great craft."

William turned to Field. "If I write it, will you print it?"

"I am but apprenticed to a printer, and a Puritan printer, too. Yet I shall, within a year, have my own press."

William flipped through the other pamphlet, shaking his head at Munday's god-awful balladry.

"A year. And yet these are injuries that crave immediate redress," William said. "I have neither the authority nor the learning to write of the death of Father Edmund Campion. And yet I might well and truly pen a ballad of the true tale of Sir Thomas Lucy."

Richard Field looked at William for a moment, then stood up and went to have a word with the proprietor. He disappeared briefly, then returned with a quill, a pot of ink, and five sheets of paper. He set the paper and ink down in front of William, then pulled out his own penknife and shaved the tip of the quill. Field dipped it and handed it to William. Then he reached into his purse, pulled out a single coin, and snapped it down on the table.

"Here is sixpence. I hereby commission, as the first fruit of your invention, a ballad upon Sir Thomas Lucy."

William thought for a moment, his pen poised above the paper. But nothing came to him. He picked up the sixpence and twiddled it absently in his left hand, noting as he did so that it had a gash across it, as if it had saved its bearer from the grievous blow of a blade. He noticed that the fleur-de-lis that were part of the Tudor device on its obverse were arranged identically to the luces in the Lucy coat of arms, though the flowers on this coin were smudged, and looked more like little ticks, or . . .

William suddenly remembered his brother Gilbert's pun. He began to scribble. He wrote quickly, and when he was done, he sang to an improvised tune:

> *"If 'lousy' is 'Lucy,' as some folk miscall it,*
> *Then Lucy is lousy, whatever befall it.*
> *He thinks himself great;*
> *Yet an ass in his state,*
> *We allow, by his ears, but with asses to mate.*
> *If Lucy is lousy, as some folk miscall it,*
> *Then sing lousy Lucy whatever befall it."*

His friends listened silently. They laughed at the opening pun; their smiles faded a bit as he went on. When he had done, they applauded.

Richard Field shrugged. "I'm sure you'll get better."

"Still," said George Cawdrey, who was by now rip-roaringly drunk, "'s fit to the purpose, wrapping the wolf Lucy in an ass's hide!"

"Will you print it, Richard, you bonny big dick, you?" said Arthur Cawdrey, who was also beginning to show signs of intoxication. In fact they were all well in their cups by now.

"I carry not presses in my saddlebags," Field answered. "And yet we may still disseminate."

"Ay! Copy it but three times, and we shall post it about the parish at the places we think most apt," said Arthur Cawdrey.

"We'll nail it to the very gate of Charlecote," said William, "and to every gate in town, just as Campion's head and quartered parts were hung upon the gates of London."

"Ay!" trumpeted George, "and we shall sing it to the maids in town to win their favor. The great ass's ears shall be filled to the brim with William's song!"

William took another piece of paper and began to copy the ballad.

The Cawdreys cheered. Richard Field looked thoughtful. Then George began to sing the ballad himself: "If 'lousy' is 'Lucy,' as...wait, how does it go?"

They sang it many times that day and into the night, as William dutifully made increasingly illegible copies.

Chapter Twenty

O mother, mother!
What have you done? Behold, the heavens do ope,
The gods look down, and this unnatural scene
They laugh at. O my mother, mother! O!
You have won a happy victory to Rome;
But, for your son—believe it, O, believe it—
Most dangerously you have with him prevail'd,
If not most mortal to him.

—*Coriolanus*, V.iii.182

Willie sat slouched in the overstuffed couch facing the picture window that looked out from the Oakland hills toward San Francisco Bay. It was late afternoon. Long shadows stretched across the bay, over the Berkeley Marina, across the flats of Berkeley and north Oakland, and up the foothills to where Willie sat. The sun was sliding behind Mount Tamalpais in Marin to the northwest, and as it did, the fog came cascading in over the coastal mountains.

As Willie watched, the Golden Gate Bridge, its single span effortless and graceful, a bold but earthy red, proclaiming its genius and its industry in every line, every cable, every girder, every head-sized rivet, was slowly swallowed up by the fog. Starting at its northern end, it simply floated away on a grey cloud into oblivion. The bridge gone, the fog rolled across the city, down the Presidio, and across North Beach. Coit Tower disappeared, then the downtown skyline, the Transamerica Pyramid, the Embarcadero, and one by one, the suspension towers of the Bay Bridge, then Treasure Island, Yerba Buena Island, and the ugly cantilevered girders of the bridge's Oakland side. In the space of two minutes, the flats of Berkeley and Oakland were invisible, too; finally the fog blew in wisps up the foothills, and streamed past the window where Willie sat, alone with Dr. Alan Greenberg and his second wife, Mizti.

"Wasn't that *pretty*?!" Mizti gushed. "Do you want another glass of wine, Willie?"

Willie shook his head.

"You sure?"

He shrugged, then held out the glass. Mizti poured, and as she did so she smiled a little too broadly. Tilting the bottle, her hand shook a little bit. She clanked the glass a little too hard with the bottle neck; Willie thought the goblet might crack, but it didn't. "Whoopsie! Sorry! Maybe you should have mine, too, ha-ha!"

Willie smiled a tight-lipped, utterly insincere smile. "Thanks, Mizti."

There was an uncomfortable silence. "How'd your errand for Robin go?" Alan asked.

"Fine."

The duffel bag sat safely between Willie's feet, tightly zipped.

Willie had run the mile from the campus to Robin's apartment building. The security gate at the front, which was always ajar, was of course locked, and he pressed her buzzer to no avail. She wasn't home. Willie didn't have a key, so he slunk around to the back of the building, scrambled awkwardly up a drainage pipe and onto Robin's second-floor balcony. He found himself praying to a god he didn't believe in that the sliding glass door was open. If it wasn't, he wasn't sure he could get down again. It was open. He retrieved the duffel and his backpack and left a note under the front door as if he'd slipped it in from the outside:

R, I'm okay. Jail was big fun. Going up to Dad's for the afternoon.
Back ASAHP. W.

The trinity of father, son, and stepmother sipped wine and watched the fog in silence. Finally Alan broke it. "So how's the thesis coming, son? If this is going to be the last quarter I pay tuition—"

"Don't worry, Dad. I told you, it'll get done."

Alan shrugged his narrow, tweedy shoulders and pushed his spectacles up on his nose. "Interesting use of the passive, Willie. It won't just *get done*. You actually have to write it."

Willie gave him a withering look, but no answer.

"So what's it about?" his father asked, and took a slug off a tumbler of single-malt Scotch.

"I'm still working out the details."

Alan laughed. "You haven't started, have you? Holy crap, Willie. This isn't a Ph.D.! It's a master's thesis. What is it, fifty pages?"

"Sixty."

"Sixty. It's been *two years*. Just write the damn thing. It's time to move on."

"It's not like I've just been sitting around the whole time. I worked last summer."

"You were waiting tables."

Willie felt Mizti's instinctive lunge at the first bit of conversation that didn't involve academia.

"There's nothing wrong with waiting tables, honey," she said to Alan. "He was making good money. More than I used to make."

Mizti had been working at an hourly hot tub rental place on University Avenue when Alan met her, not long after Willie's mother died. Willie thought it was too soon: *the funeral-baked meats did coldly furnish forth the marriage tables*, he had thought as he loaded up on pastrami and liverwurst at the Faculty Club reception.

Mizti had made a beautiful bride, of course. At five feet eight, 125, she was a little, but not too much, taller than Alan. There was some inevitable whispering and giggling at the wedding, along with a few deadly glares from Sheila's friends. While in the bathroom peeing, Willie had overheard a conversation in the hallway outside.

"She's certainly *statuesque*, isn't she?"

"If you're talking about the plaster between her ears, yes."

"What *does* she mean, spelling her name that way?"

"She changed the *s* to a *z* for the wedding. Alan says she thinks it looks more Jewish."

"A Judophile shiksa. Alan is finally living his own Woody Allen film."

"I'm thinking *Bananas*."

Snickers.

"More like *Everything You Wanted to Know About Sex*."

Laughter.

"I just hope the wedding night isn't *Love and Death*."

Guffaws.

"I think in her case it's *Take the Money and Run*." A couple of chortles, and several "ooohs."

Willie had emerged from the bathroom and smiled wanly into the vortex of embarrassed silence.

And yet, after the wedding, Mizti and Willie had gotten along fine. She was only seven years older than him. She still remembered what it was like to be sixteen, in high school, trying to get a date without a driver's license. When Alan would lock himself into his study at night, and Willie would come home late from a play rehearsal or a movie with his friends, he'd find Mizti watching *Dallas* or *Dynasty* or *Falcon Crest* and eating popcorn, and he might watch for a bit, especially if Heather Locklear was in a halter top or a silk robe.

At first Mizti would go upstairs at eleven every night, and he could hear her gently coaxing Alan to bed behind the study door, and Alan was coaxable.

But week by week and month by month Alan and Mizti's bedtime slowly got later and later, and sometimes Willie would come home to find Mizti asleep on the couch.

And then, one night in his senior year, he came home from a coffeehouse where he had been studying, trying to blend in with the UC students, and listening to a classical guitarist playing quietly in a corner. He had been distracted from his SAT studying—the guitarist was beautiful. Straight brown hair, big brown eyes; petite, a little boyish, but not too much...like a gymnast. And when she took a break, she had walked past him and smiled, and she had an irresistible crinkle around her eyes, not crow's feet of age but of impishness, and Willie had not been able to keep his eyes off her jeans as she ordered a coffee from the bar.

Taking the bus home, and then walking up the hill on a warm spring night, Willie had planned to steal a beer from the fridge and go to his room immediately to whack off to the image of the guitar girl. But when he stepped into the darkened kitchen, the refrigerator door was open, its light illuminating Mizti standing in front of it in a short silk robe, pouring into a glass from a half-empty bottle of Chardonnay. Willie started to back out of the room. But she heard him.

"Oh, hi, Willie," she had said, and as she turned her robe was a little bit too far open. She saw the line of his gaze and she pulled it closed again with a giggle. "Sorry."

She sounded a little bit drunk. "I'm having some wine. You wanna glass of wine?"

Willie said, "Oh, um, no thanks."

"Okay," she shrugged, and turned back to the fridge, bending over to put the bottle back on the lower shelf.

"Actually, sure, why not," Willie said.

Mizti turned and smiled, pulled out the bottle, grasped the cork, popped it, and filled a glass for Willie.

"Cheers," she said, and they clinked glasses.

They watched *Dynasty*, and Heather Locklear was in fact wearing an ultrashort silk robe. Mizti got up to refill her glass of wine one more time. She disappeared briefly upstairs, and when she came back a minute later and said, "Where did I put my wine?" a bit of smoke puffed from her lips. She took an inordinate amount of time to find the glass she'd left in plain sight in the kitchen.

Willie watched Mizti moving around the house, and at the sight of her nipples rippling underneath the silk, and the shape of her ass that while maybe not Heather Locklear's was still fine, really fine, his groin screamed at him. It asked no moral questions, so Willie did not answer them.

Finally *Dynasty* ended, and they talked. First just small talk, but then they talked about girls, and Willie's taste in girls, and Willie's utter lack of experience with girls. Willie had already had an erection for nearly an hour when Mizti exclaimed with wide-eyed, whispered wonder, "Ohmigod, you're a *virgin*!?"

It was all headed exactly where Willie dreaded and desperately hoped it would: to Mizti, on her knees on the Persian rug in the living room, her hair smelling of grass, giving Willie his very first blowjob.

But she had refused to fuck him.

"Trust me," she'd said, "it would probably mess with your head."

And now Willie sat in the fog atop the Oakland hills and sullenly sipped at a dark, leathery red wine.

"So try me," said Alan. "Sometimes just the process of saying something out loud helps clarify it in your mind. Tell me about it. It might help."

"What?" said Willie with rising panic.

Fuck, I haven't been listening. Tell him about…? He looked at Mizti, but she was smiling. His thesis, he was asking about his thesis.

"Well, what do you know about persecution of Catholics by Protestants in sixteenth-century England?" said Willie.

Alan Greenberg shrugged. "Not much. I can tell you about the exploration of identity in Robert Bolt's script of *A Man for All Seasons*, if you like."

"Do you know about all the executions?"

"Sure. It happened pretty much everywhere. On both sides. Burnings at the stake, the Inquisition, Huguenots, Bloody Mary."

Mizti perked up at "Bloody Mary," but seeing that it wasn't an offer, she refilled her wineglass and sank back into her chair.

"During Elizabeth's reign there were several Catholic plots to murder Elizabeth and put the other Mary—Mary, Queen of Scots—onto the throne," Alan concluded.

"Right," Willie said, although he didn't know about the plots, and hadn't realized until this instant that Mary, Queen of Scots, and Bloody Mary were two different people.

"So Shakespeare fits in how?" asked Alan.

Willie told him the tale of Sonnet 23, and Alan nodded, impressed.

"That's some clever scholarship."

"So my thesis is that Shakespeare was Catholic."

Alan kept looking at him, waiting. "I've heard that suggested before."

"You have?"

"I hate to slow you down on this, but I think you need more. One line in a fairly obscure sonnet isn't enough evidence to base a master's thesis on."

"Well, obviously I have more research to do," replied Willie, annoyed.

"Obviously. Are you spending some time at the library?"

"Yeah, I'm going to be there all night tonight," Willie lied.

Mizti had been shifting uncomfortably. "What about the man?" she asked.

Alan and Willie both looked at her as if artichokes had suddenly sprouted from her ears.

"What's that, sweetie?" asked Alan.

"Shakespeare the man? I mean, so he was being prosecuted by the Protestants—"

"Persecuted," corrected Alan.

"Whatever. It seems to me what's interesting is how that affected him personally. His family. His friends. And then how did it, you know, make Shakespeare Shakespeare? Maybe you could research that."

Willie looked at his dad. How to explain it to her?

Alan began. "Literary criticism and theory in the twentieth century tends to be entirely focused on the text, cupcake."

"It's true," Willie continued. "The biography, politics, and intention of the author—even his or her interpretation of his own writing—have been deemed irrelevant to interpreting or critiquing his or her work."

Mizti looked back and forth from Alan to Willie, stunned.

"Well, that's the stupidest thing I've ever heard. *I'd* be interested in hearing how the persecution of Christians—"

"Catholics," interrupted Alan.

"Catholics," Mizti corrected herself. "If that was going on when Shakespeare was a kid, just imagine how it must have fucked with his head. That kind of trauma in your family, at such a young age. What would that do to you? It must have had *some* impact on what made Shakespeare Shakespeare. I just think it's completely dumb that you can't talk about it."

Mizti sank back into her chair, sipped her wine, and looked out the window as the lights of Berkeley strove to burn through the fog.

There was another long silence.

"So you're sure you're okay for money?" Alan said to Willie at last.

"Yeah. I'll be fine. But I was wondering…could I borrow your car? I've got one more errand to run tomorrow."

Alan looked at Willie with vague disapproval. "Sure."

Chapter Twenty-one

If the Shakespeares were indeed oppressed Catholics, it's no surprise
that the earliest writing ever attributed to the Bard is a biting satirical
ballad punning on the name of Sir Thomas Lucy that was copied and
handed down through the generations in Warwickshire. But the mature
Shakespeare is known for his bantering, highly sexualized farce, his love
poetry, and his tragic family dramas, not for religious allegory or political
posturing. Perhaps this is because in the fall of 1582, Shakespeare's
own story took a plot twist worthy of one of his own convoluted
comedies...or, perhaps, one of his tragedies.

William Shakespeare, Richard Field, and George Cawdrey spent the night
at the Bear. Finally weary with copying "If 'Lousy' Is 'Lucy,'" William had
fallen asleep, head down on the table, pen in one hand, ale in the other.
He was the first to stir, and he instantly regretted it. His head throbbed; it
was infinitely more painful than his dully aching, racked shoulder.

He finished the stale, flat beer that was still death-gripped in his left
hand. He cleaned his pen. Then he poured himself another ale from the
tap. He drank it, and felt better. He woke Cawdrey and Field.

An hour later, Thomas Barber had come down from his rooms, served
a breakfast with more ale, and they were all well fortified against a cold
but dry November morning. William, George, and Richard emerged from
the pub and strode down the deserted street, three abreast: coat, cloak,
and cassock fluttered in the wind. Had slow motion existed, they'd have
been in it. Holstered in their belts were hammers; in one hand, nails; in
the other, copies of the first child of William Shakespeare's invention: a
bit of doggerel verse satirizing Sir Thomas Lucy. It was Sunday, and all the
Protestants in town were in Holy Trinity church. Most of the Catholics
were there, too. Those who weren't were shut in their homes, pretending

to be mad or in debt or both. At the High Cross, William, George, and Richard split up.

William had volunteered to return to the scene of his previous crime, to the very gate of Sir Thomas Lucy's great house at Charlecote. He retraced his steps down Bridge Street quietly, not wishing to call attention to himself. As he crossed Butt Close along the archery range, he saw a lone figure on the far southeast corner of the field, standing back to the river and shooting at a single target. The figure turned to look at him. *A woman*, William thought, and continued on toward the bridge. Three seconds later an arrow whistled past his ear and sank into the road three yards ahead of his big toe.

William jumped back, wheeled around toward the archer, and opened his mouth to call out some choice invective. But then he stopped. He plucked the arrow from the ground and walked across the dewy grass to where the archer stood. She fired another shaft, this time into the center of the target. *Thwunk*.

William extended the first, errant arrow to the archer. "You missed me."

"You lie, sirrah. I missed you not at all these eighteen hours," said Rosaline. She assessed the small cut on his face with a glance, then looked at the proffered bolt. She left it hanging in his hand and took another arrow from her quiver.

William watched her as she quietly fired two more arrows at the target. Each struck within two inches of the bull's-eye. There were four others, also grouped in an asymmetrical bunch around the target's center.

"Your shafts are exceeding well shot, Rosaline."

"And what of your shaft?" She fired another arrow into the heart of the target. "Where would you discharge it? It seems you use it for cruel sport, to pierce a bird and then leave it to die of its wounds. As this your practice grows to rumor and thence to repute, I foresee your shaft often there," she said with a sharp nod, "languishing in your hand."

"My shaft is my own concern. It is a man's care to keep it polished, trimmed, and sharpened, and to engage if battle be joined."

"As it is the care of a woman to keep her quiver full. But note that, if she cannot cut all her arrows from her favored trunk, she will go a-wandering; for i'faith there are many trees in a forest."

"Thus were women ever as inconstant in the filling of their quivers as they are in the quivering."

"And are men less inconstant?" she said, finally lowering her bow and turning on him. "What a manly name you have, William Shakespeare. Such a proclamation it is, of force and dominance. WILL, I AM! SHAKE SPEAR! But in some parts 'Shakespeare' is 'Shake-shaft,' is it not?"

"What's in a name? Rosaline may be Rosalind, and yet are both a rose, by any other—"

"Play not on my name; it's not as fit for sport as yours. 'Rosaline' has not such homespun wit as 'Will Shake-shaft,' who by a name will shake his shaft in the face of any maid with a bright eye and pretty locks."

Rosaline took the last arrow from her quiver and fitted it to her bow. "But then," she said as she sighted the target, "as ever when a shaft be loosed without skill or care," and suddenly she wheeled her aim up and to the right and let the arrow fly, over the target, to disappear in the wood across the river, "it is like to fly false, and be lost forever."

She lowered her bow and turned back to William. "Do I strike near the truth?" she asked, and her face was flushed and white with anger.

William had stood and taken it; he knew he deserved it. He was mesmerized by Rosaline's beauty and wit. He had encountered precious few who could take the jabs from his own tongue and then parry and riposte with such skill.

"You strike neither as near the mark as your surmise, nor as wide as your misspent dart," William said quietly. "Though it pardons not my faithlessness, know that after my evening's pastime with Sir Thomas Lucy—from which, and I thank you for your care in the matter, I was released with minimal injury—my first thought was for finding you. But matters of state o'erruled what should have been my initial care."

Rosaline softened, and touched his face gingerly. "I am glad to see you so little harmed. I hope there are no greater, hidden wounds?" William felt the sting of the lashes on his back, but said nothing. "Yet I wonder," Rosaline asked, "what matter of state trumped the nobility of your first intent?"

"The executions of priests of the Old Faith under the guise of protecting our Sovereign. I go forth today to strike a blow, be it small, for the right of our

Queen's faithful subjects to hold what private faith they will, without fear of torture or death." William held out the documents he held in his hand.

Rosaline took the papers and read the verse. "Lucy is lousy whatever befall it?" she asked. "In this, Ovid need not fear his reputation for poetry, nor Machiavelli for politic," she said.

"It is but a first blow," William mumbled. He felt her slipping away. She stood there in green skirts, Sunday-fine and matching her eyes, with a bodice the burnished gold of fall leaves, and red hair in braids about her shoulders. Two swans glided by on the river behind her, and he had a vision of her as a third, standing tall and proud on the bank of the Avon. The vision inspired him.

"The only legends here that need fear their regard are the swans of Avon, whose beauty is now surpassed by the swan on its bank," William said. "And as I am but a young man, tender in years, two short of even a score, I hope I may be forgiven for being young, and a man. But even so, I would not have your quiver empty, nor yearning for an errant shaft."

William took Rosaline's bow, and fitted the arrow to it. "The best way, if one bolt be lost, is by another to be found."

Standing next to her, he pulled back the bowstring, ignoring the screaming pain in his shoulder as he aimed at the target then wheeled high and to the right exactly as she had done, and let the arrow fly into the woods.

He set down the bow. "Let us follow the flight of the errant shaft, to see if it might once more find your quiver." He led Rosaline silently across the river and into the wood. William picked his way lightly amongst the trees, and as he helped Rosaline over one fallen trunk, he noticed again the fineness of her skin, the combination of delicacy and strength in her hand. Turning back to the forest, he stopped.

Buried in the trunk of an elm tree was the arrow William had shot. He looked up into the foliage. There, where the elm's branches intertwined with that of its neighbor, was Rosaline's arrow.

"What once was lost, now is found," said William.

He scrambled up into the tree and dropped down a moment later holding Rosaline's arrow. He plucked the second arrow from the elm trunk, and handed them both to Rosaline. "If this be not enough to make all well with your quiver, at the least it will not be barren."

She took the arrows back with a half smile. "A honeyed tongue with maids you have, indeed." She gestured to his papers. "Where falls your first blow for tolerance?"

"Upon the very gates of power."

"You will need someone to hold the nail to your hammer."

"Women were thus ever fixed on their nails, and men's hammers—"

"PLEASE!" interrupted Rosaline, raising a finger to his lips. "Stop."

He did.

"I would accompany you," Rosaline said.

"There is danger. Thomas Lucy and his seconds will look for those who begat this insolence."

"I care nothing for Thomas Lucy, and less for his seconds. Though they were not cruel to me, neither were they kind. And to all of Warwickshire, and the greater good, they are passing rude. I would assist you."

"But—"

"Deny me not," she said firmly.

He did not. They set out together, chatting and trading barbs nonstop for the four miles back to Charlecote.

They met no one on the road, but as they went over the rise past the centuries-old Loxley Church, they heard the sounds of a kyrie wafting from inside. The sun was still well short of noon when they reached the western gate to Charlecote. They briefly discussed whether to target this entrance or the finer gatehouse a mile farther on, an imposing new brick structure built as an ostentatious symbol of the pursuivant's power. William thought the new edifice more symbolic, but Rosaline won the debate over the extra two-mile walk, and the difficulty of driving a nail into brick.

They approached the wooden gate carefully. It was closed and locked. The two gatehouse guards who had bid William such unfond farewell were nowhere to be seen. William considered whether to hallo or not, and decided that anyone inside the gatehouse would surely hear the hammering in any case.

"Hallooo!" William hollered.

No answer but the squawk of one of the ever-present ravens.

"Send forth Master Lousy!"

Still no one answered.

"Tell him a young lover and poet will shake a shaft at him!"

Rosaline stifled a laugh.

William produced several nails from a pouch. He unholstered the hammer tucked into his belt beneath his cloak. William held up the verse. Rosaline placed a nail to it. William hammered it into the gatepost with three strokes.

It was one doggerel verse, hung on one gate in the middle of the backwater Warwickshire countryside. But at that moment William felt like the most powerful individual in the world.

An hour later, Rosaline and William returned to Stratford, retracing their steps across the Clopton Bridge and up Bridge Street toward the center of town. William was armed with two more copies of the verse. When no one was looking, he and Rosaline nailed one to the exterior wall of the Bear, then, emboldened, crossed the street to add one to the facade of the Swan.

As William nailed the last nail, Rosaline kissed his ear.

But then there was a touch less tender on his shoulder. A hand, not roughly, but firmly, grasped him and turned him around. Two stout men, farmers by their looks, towered over him. Each held a matchlock rifle. Behind them was a smaller man.

"William Shagspere?" growled the smaller of the two large men.

"Shakespeare, ay."

"Fulke Sandells is my name. This is my cousin, Master John Richardson."

"The names are not familiar to me," said William. "Men of Sir Thomas Lucy, I assume. I've no need of stretching again today."

The men looked at each other in confusion. "We know naught of Sir Thomas," Sandells said. "Friends and neighbors are we of a maid of Shottery of your past acquaintance. We hope you remember her most fondly and devoutly. Anne Hathaway is her name. And this is her brother, Master Bartholomew Hathaway."

The smaller man looked William appraisingly in the eye. "William Shaxper. We are here to inform you of Anne's impending nuptials, and most urgently request your attendance."

William looked first at the men, confused, then to Rosaline. He shrugged. "I remember Anne well enough, though I met her but twice or thrice while on my father's business in Shottery. But I know not to what family honor I have attained, to be thus summoned to her wedding."

The muscles in Bartholomew's jaw tensed. "It pains me that your remembrance of my sister is so slight; for hers of you is more weighty. She is three months with child, and her wedding day is to be yours as well."

The mark Thomas Lucy had made on William's right cheek healed quickly; the sting of the blow Rosaline struck to his left didn't fade for a long, long time.

Chapter Twenty-two

I am myself indifferent honest; but yet I could accuse me of such things that it were better my mother had not borne me: I am very proud, revengeful, ambitious, with more offenses at my beck than I have thoughts to put them in, imagination to give them shape, or time to act them in. What should such fellows as I do crawling between earth and heaven? We are arrant knaves, all; believe none of us.

—*Hamlet*, III.i.121

Willie was headed the wrong direction.

He was supposed to be going north, but he'd missed the right turn at the bottom of Tunnel Road and was now headed south. The wine hadn't helped him in finding his way; he was jittery, stressed out. He was always stressed after spending time with Alan and Mizti, but his stress was now doubled by the weight (though it was just over a pound) in the trunk of his father's Audi, and trebled by what he was about to tell Robin.

He finally navigated a meandering route to her street, found a parking space around the corner from her apartment, and sat behind the wheel. He wanted to smoke.

He got out of the car. It was going to be a chilly night in Berkeley, damp with the fog. He looked up and down the residential street. Empty, but for two students shuffling along with backpacks down the street away from him.

He got back in the car. The duffel filled with contraband was in the trunk, but he still had the last bit of Lebanese in his green backpack. He opened it, took out his pipe, loaded it, and looked up and down the street one more time...completely empty. He lit and smoked furtively, blowing smoke out of the cracked-open window. Immediately he felt the edge of his two hours with Alan and Mizti fade away, wafting up the street and dissipating over the hills like the fog. He took a second large hit...too large, as the smoke expanded beyond the bursting point in his lungs, and into his throat. He tried to hold it in, with one small cough, then two, but couldn't control it anymore, and the smoke reached up, yanked his uvula, and then exploded out of him in great racking coughs, filling the car with smoke. At the exact same instant he saw, coming across the street toward him and smiling, a friend of Robin's, one of the F$¢K Reagan gang, the black guy...

Tony...Tommie...Terry? Shit.

Still coughing, he reached over to stash the pipe in the glove box and open the passenger's side window to let some smoke out. By the time he turned, coughing and smiling, back to the driver's side window Tony/Tommie/Terry had passed by, without noticing him. Willie saw that he was listening to a Walkman, bopping his head and dorking out and singing "Walk This Way."

He dorked his way down the sidewalk, heading away from Robin's apartment. Willie hoped, for the poor brother's sake, that it was the Run DMC version of the song.

Willie figured he'd tempted fate enough, and he had a pretty good buzz on. He opened the car door, realized he'd left his backpack inside, retrieved it, and slid in through the always ajar security gate of Robin's building. Up two flights of stairs, navigating around several bicycles and an old used mattress in the hallway, he knocked and entered without waiting for an answer.

Robin was on the phone. She smiled and waved as Willie entered. "Willie's back. I'll call you later, okay?" She laughed. "I know. Yeah, okay. Bye." And she hung up the phone. "Darcy," she said, in reference to her neediest friend from high school. Willie didn't even want to know what bad-boy biker, what sidewalk artist, what itinerant, spitting punk rocker, had ruined Darcy's life this week, so he didn't ask.

Robin came over and kissed him lightly. "You want to go get some sushi or something? It's almost eight o'clock. I'm starving."

Eight o'clock. He ran some quick math in his head. He wanted to get to the Renaissance Faire before everybody crashed for the night. If he made his connection tonight instead of waiting until tomorrow, he'd have some cash beyond the eight bucks in his pocket.

"I'm kinda broke for sushi."

"I could make some pasta."

"Here's the thing," said Willie, and he leaned awkwardly against the table by the front door. Robin's lips went as tight as plastic wrap around a lemon.

"What's *the thing*?"

"I have to run an errand for my dad. Taking some stuff up to my aunt in Sebastopol."

Robin's brows furrowed. "What?!" Sebastopol was a two-hour drive. "What kind of *stuff*?"

I should've thought this out a little more.

"Some jewelry and old letters that he found cleaning out his mom's garage."

Better.

"They're in my dad's car," he added, gesturing toward the street to indicate he'd borrowed it and to keep her from asking to see the jewelry.

Willie had told Robin a little lie or two in their years "together." Of course their entire relationship was based on a big lie, but it was a lie of omission, a mutual agreement to look the other way. This felt different: a ploy; a subterfuge; a deception. It could blow up in his face a dozen different ways. Robin knew his dad and his aunt well. They were friends. She had their phone numbers. They had hers. But he made his lie, stuck to it, and comforted himself with the knowledge that he wasn't doing it to cheat on her. He was doing it because—the politics of victimless crimes and national drug enforcement aside—he simply couldn't stand the abject humiliation of having only eight dollars to his highfalutin name.

Robin was obviously a little ticked off. "Okay. Well, don't hurry back. I mean, drive safe." She went back to the couch, sat heavily, picked up a book, and started reading.

"I'll be back tomorrow. We can spend the rest of the weekend together."

She looked at him coldly. "Okay."

"I should be able to make the delivery to my aunt tonight." *King of the Fools...flag over his tent with a joker on it.* "And then I probably won't be able to get out of having breakfast with her in the morning." *Friar Law-*

rence. Everybody knows him. "You know, that diner she loves to go out to"—he hit "go out" slightly so that she wouldn't try to call at his aunt's because they'd be *out*—"I'll be back by noon. One at the latest. I promise. And"—and now he was making shit up left and right—"my dad promised to pay me a little bit for the delivery, too, so after I get the car back to him I should be a little more flush. I'll take you out to the Buttercup Bakery for brunch."

This obviously scored a point. Robin smiled at him, but still it was chilly. "Sounds nice."

"Okay." He walked to her and gave her a peck on the cheek, which she accepted. "Love you."

"Love you, too," Robin said, already looking at her book again.

"See you tomorrow. Love you," Willie said again feebly as he slunk out the door.

Willie stood outside the door in the hallway for a moment after it closed. He thought about going back inside, saying, "You know what, my aunt can wait, let's go get that sushi." But he really didn't have any money for sushi. He could go back in and say, "You know what, let's have that pasta," but that would seem like he'd decided he wanted her to cook for him. Shaking his head at his own spinelessness, he walked quietly and slowly down the stairs, back out into the fog, and stepped into the car.

Willie rammed the Audi into gear and peeled out of the parking place, scattering a flock of pigeons from the street. He raced around the block, down Haste Street (aptly named, he thought). He stopped at the corner of Shattuck and Center to grab a $1.50 slice of pizza and a Coke, then headed down University Avenue and onto Interstate 580 toward the Richmond/San Rafael Bridge and the Renaissance Faire.

Couldn't be more than an hour to Novato. I'll be there by ten. Plenty of time.

He wasn't on the freeway five minutes, and had just finished his slice, when he passed a sign announcing the next exit as CENTRAL AVENUE — EL CERRITO. He cocked his head. Then he frantically dug into his hip pocket, pulled out his wallet while driving, one eye on the road, and found the slip of paper. It said, in a bold script, Dashka, and there was a phone number, and then added as an afterthought:

c/o Kate Whitsett
5700 Central Ave #205
El Cerrito

Willie threw his head back against the headrest. He looked at his watch. He listened to the voice in his head, then the voice in his heart, and then the one in his loins. He wanted to think of Robin, he tried to think of Robin, but instead the image that came to his mind was Mizti, and the sweet smell of pot in her hair, and then of Dashka, not a picture image but a sense memory of touching between her legs for the first time—*oh my god*. He looked at the paper again; Kate Whitsett was intriguing as well.

He said "shit" aloud, and at the last possible second, swerved onto the Central Avenue off-ramp.

Chapter Twenty-three

*Aside from a tenuous alleged pun (hate away = Hathaway) in one
sonnet and a cursory mention in his will, the only knowledge we have
about the nature of the marriage of Anne and William is a single
line in a harried clerk's register. One can't help but wonder: was the
eighteen-year-old in love with the pregnant woman eight years his
senior? It seems unlikely.*

William's back hurt, his shoulder hurt, his knees hurt, his cheek hurt
where Rosaline had smacked him. And now his bottom hurt. His new
friends Sandells and Richardson had escorted him directly to Worcester
after only a brief stop in Stratford for William to pick up a bedroll.

Leaving his soon-to-be brother-in-law in Shottery, William had ridden
Bartholomew's swaybacked horse with its weather-hardened saddle. William
didn't ride much, and the fifty-mile round trip to Worcester was only
slightly less torturous to him than Sir Thomas Lucy's rack had been. He
passed the time by reading the translation of "Romeus and Giulietta" in the
book Richard Field had given him. It was dreadfully written, but featured
a couple of characters not in the versions of the story he knew: a "prat-
ing nurse" and a best friend and confidant for Romeus. And yet the one
character William always wondered about—the girl for whom lovelorn
Romeus pines before he meets Juliet—was still left unnamed.

William wondered if he himself was enacting Romeus: pining for his
lost Rosaline when his star-crossed doom was to marry someone he'd
barely met and then die.

They reached Worcester at nightfall, slept under a tree outside of town,
and on Monday morning walked into the cathedral at the heart of the
city. William paused to admire the crypt of King John in the chancel, but
was roughly nudged along by Richardson into the south aisle, where they

waited in a short queue and finally appeared before a bleary, watery-eyed clerk who took down the information for the marriage license.

"Names?"

"William Shakespeare and Anne Hathaway," said Richardson.

"Parish?"

"Stratford," said Richardson.

Sandells corrected him. "Nay, let it read Temple Grafton, for we are known to the priest there, and there was she baptized."

The clerk looked up, lids heavy with suspicion, and gazed at each of them in turn. William said nothing; if he was to be compelled to marry, he was happy to do so as far away from Stratford as possible. He watched as the bored clerk noted in his ledger that the marriage was to be "inter Wm Shaxpere et Anna Whateley de Temple Grafton." William was used to seeing Shakespeare spelled a dozen different ways: Shagspere, Shaxper, Shaksper, Shakespear, he'd seen 'em all. Some even insisted on making it Shakeshafte, or Shakestaff, which were more common names in those parts. When the clerk mistakenly entered Anne's name as Whateley instead of Hathaway, William said nothing, hoping that this might somehow make the marriage invalid.

Having taken the other information, the clerk gave a rote speech about the further particulars, indicating that the wedding might take place at any time after the crying of the banns.

Sandells and Richardson looked at each other like people who might never have attended a church. "Crying?" asked Richardson.

The harried registrar explained, "The matrimony must be announced in the parish church of both parties on three consecutive Sundays."

Sandells did a quick calculation on his fingers. "So the marriage may take place before Christmas—"

"No, no, no," the clerk interrupted. "No banns may be read from Advent Sunday, which this year falls on"—he consulted a calendar—"December second . . . until the thirteenth of January. The marriage may then take place in"—he counted the weeks—"February, at the earliest."

Sandells and Richardson exchanged glances. "Begging your pardon, good sir, but the bride will be waxing toward full by then. Is there no course by which we might hasten the solemnizing of the already consummated union?"

The clerk smirked. Then he handed Sandells a sheet of paper. "The marriage may proceed with but one reading of the banns thusly," he said. Richardson looked blankly at the piece of paper.

The clerk reached over, turned it right side up in Richardson's hands, and continued. "It states these requirements: that there appear no impediment by reason of precontract, consanguinity, or affinity; that no suit has begun concerning such impediment; that the groom should not solemnize the marriage without the consent of the bride's friends—clearly, already given in this case—and that the groom shall pay all costs if any legal action be brought against Bishop Whitgift and his officers for licensing the marriage. It requires a surety of forty pounds against such eventualities."

Richardson and Sandells exchanged another glance, and turned away to mutter to each other.

"Forty pounds?" said Richardson.

" 'Tis more than the worth of my farm and yours put together."

"Well, they can't take what we don't have."

Sandells looked at William. "If this marriage come not afore God as pretty and true as a ministering angel, in sooth, young lad, we'll cut your balls off and pay the surety with 'em, understood?"

William said nothing; he couldn't help but wonder what the sudden local fascination with his testicles was all about.

"Ay, we'll stand surety," said Sandells to the clerk.

The clerk signed and stamped things. "You must needs appear in the administrative court tomorrow to stand for the surety. I will then issue the license, but we will also need a statement from the parents of both parties affirming their consent. There is also," concluded the clerk with bureaucratic glee, "a small fee."

Sandells and Richardson looked darkly at William, who still, as he thought best, said absolutely nothing.

Chapter Twenty-four

The expense of spirit in a waste of shame
Is lust in action; and till action, lust
Is perjured, murderous, bloody, full of blame,
Savage, extreme, rude, cruel, not to trust,
Enjoy'd no sooner but despised, straight,
Past reason hunted and no sooner had,
Past reason hated as a swallowed bait...
Had, having and in quest to have, extreme
Before, a joy proposed; behind, a dream.

—Sonnet 129

It was too easy. The apartment building was two blocks off the freeway, across from a baseball diamond. Willie hung a right, parked, and thirty seconds later he was pressing the buzzer for #205—Whitsett. A female voice answered "Hello?" a little too loudly.

"Hi. My name's Willie. I'm looking for Dashka."

Music played in the background over the tinny speaker. "Dashka! It's a friend of yours. Willie. Should I let him in?" And then, after a pause: "Come on up." And the buzzer to the gate went off with a click.

He knocked at #205 and the door was opened by a girl in a terry-cloth bathrobe. Hair still wet from a shower. Pretty.... Blue eyes. Blonde. She looked kind of like... *kind of like the blonde from the Bangles.*

"Hi, I'm Kate. Come on in."

Behind her, Dashka emerged from the kitchen, holding a beer. "Hi, Willie. Glad you could drop by."

Kate shook out her hair as she turned back toward Dashka. "Your friend's cute."

Dashka pointed toward to the fridge. "Would you like a beer?"

"No, thanks, I can't stay long."

Dashka cocked her head, and Willie could practically hear her wondering, *Then what are you doing here?*

What am *I doing here?* Willie thought. "It turned out this place was right on the way to where I'm headed tonight, so I thought I'd say hi."

Kate held up a joint. "Do you have time for a smoke?"

Willie felt as though he had walked into something he didn't fully understand. But he rarely turned down weed. "Um...sure," he said, swinging his backpack onto the couch.

Willie pulled out a lighter from his pocket and lit the tightly rolled cigarette for Kate.

As she leaned over to catch the flame, Willie caught a scent of something in the air, blending with the sweet smell of the marijuana.

"Sour apple," Willie said.

"That's my shampoo," Kate said, impressed. She turned to Dashka. "I do like a man who can recognize a scent." She held out the joint for Dashka; Dashka's hands were full with a beer and an ashtray, and instead of taking it she sucked at it softly from Kate's fingers with lightly pursed lips. Kate passed it to Willie.

Her breath still held, Dashka said, "We were just deciding whether to go out or not."

Kate looked at Dashka, then at Willie. "I was trying to talk her into staying in. Sending out for Chinese food. Girls' night in. Pedicures, pajamas..."

Kate put her freshly showered feet in Dashka's lap, and wiggled her toes.

"But now," Kate continued, "there's a *boy* here."

"Don't worry, I really do have to go," Willie said.

But even as he said it, he had the feeling he wasn't going anywhere.

The next morning he had only jumbled recollections of the threesome. It was Kate who had kept the conversation flirty, nudging them toward it. Willie didn't object.

What normal, healthy, unmarried male would walk away from this?

The reality, while undeniably picturesque—there were several images he'd hang onto for a lifetime—was complex. Kate gave Willie a little attention at first, hand-jobbing and some perfunctory fellatio. When Dashka took over the job, Kate quickly rechoreographed the tableau, leaving Willie awkwardly to one side as she went hungrily down on Dashka. When Dashka returned the favor and Willie took her from behind at the same time, Kate held Dashka's lips pinned to her, so Dashka had been both distracted from Willie and completely blocking any view Willie might have had of the cunnilingual action. Willie felt detached, as if he were watching a pretty movie with an all-star cast and a stupid plot in which he was the badly miscast lead. Although he kept telling himself this was "allowed" in his relationship, he still felt shitty. He couldn't help thinking of Robin, and he also couldn't allow himself to think of what he was doing because he was trying to hold on to his orgasm. He tried to distract himself by focusing on a tattoo he now saw on Dashka's lower back: a pair of intertwining rosebushes, one white, one red, over a delicate script that read BY ANY OTHER NAME.

Finally Dashka's sex was too hot to handle and Willie finished inside her—though he pretended he hadn't so as not to seem selfish. He managed to stay hard, but by the time he found himself inside Kate, Dashka had gone to the bathroom, and Kate was asleep or pretending to be asleep; so he faked a second orgasm and then he, too, passed out.

I'm surrounded by five angry Ophelias. I summon up all the earnestness my acting skills can yield.

"I did love you once," I say. It sounds utterly hollow.

As one, the five Ophelias smile coquettishly back.

Then as one they begin to ululate wildly like witches, eyes blazing demonically. The sound swells, the pitch and volume so intense my head will surely split open, but they suddenly stop, turn to each other, and begin making out, grotesquely long tongues licking and probing until they melt into each other and finally dissolve into nothingness.

I'm left facing the bed illuminated by the spotlight from above.

Polonius taps me on the shoulder. "The Queen would speak with you, and presently."

This time, I know who is there. I'm Hamlet, and my next scene is with the Queen, my wanton mother. I step to the bedside, and the form beneath the dark sheets sits up.

It is not my mother.

It's Heather Locklear in a short, silk robe. She turns to me with a Mona Lisa smile, and silently raises her middle finger.

Willie woke with a splitting headache. He stumbled out of the beer bottle–strewn bedroom into the kitchen, where Dashka and Kate were having coffee and cigarettes. They looked ragged, too, and they weren't looking at him or at each other.

Kate was announcing plans for them to see a band that night, and pointedly didn't include Willie. Dashka responded monosyllabically: "Sure."

"Good morning," Willie said.

"There's breakfast," Dashka replied, with a nod toward the kitchen.

There was a pan filled with congealing grease on the stove, and on the counter, a half piece of shriveled, cold bacon on a plate between two stained paper towels: cold, used meat. He considered eating it, but the thought made him queasy.

He had a vision of the breakfast he had passed up: Robin sitting in the small of his back, handing him a cup of coffee, brunch at the Buttercup. He picked up the coffeepot. Dregs. Perfect. He poured himself a cup and drank it, black and bitter. He pulled a beer from the refrigerator and guzzled it to wash away the coffee and the headache. He gathered up his clothes, and with a mumbled promise to see Dashka back in Santa Cruz, he left.

Kate hadn't said a word to him, and Dashka hadn't said a word to Kate, her former "best friend from high school."

As he closed the door behind him, Willie caught one last glimpse of Kate giving Dashka an utterly hopeless glance.

In the elevator, lines from Sonnet 129 sprang into his mind, about lust:

Before, a joy proposed; behind, a dream.
All this the world well knows, yet none knows well
To shun the heaven that leads men to this hell.

A hell of his own creation.

Outside the apartment building there was a pay phone. He looked at his watch: 11:37. Robin would be waiting for him. He dialed her number. To his surprise, the answering machine clicked on. *In the shower*, he thought, relieved. He left a message: profuse apologies and something about his aunt needing a ride and help with her car that didn't make sense even to him. He promised that he would be back Sunday morning without fail. He would take her to Doidge's in San Francisco, the fussiest, most romantic brunch he could think of. More apologies; a lame, smoochy good-bye.

When Willie got back in the car he didn't start it but sat, staring straight ahead.

What the fuck, exactly, do you think you're doing?

He'd betrayed Robin three times in twenty-four hours. He'd been arrested. He was running drugs for the individual who, despite his immense likability, was arguably the biggest loser on the Santa Cruz campus. Arguably, as there was also the case of a certain would-be Shakespeare scholar, the son of a respected Berkeley film professor, who'd been putting off writing his master's thesis while doing little besides getting stoned and occasionally cheating on his girlfriend—who, incidentally, was funny, smart, sexy, and hadn't yet dumped him or, as far as he knew, slept with anyone else, despite their don't-ask-don't-tell understanding.

Willie put his head on the steering wheel and felt sorry for his sorry self. He sat up, and took a deep breath.

He would go back to Robin's. Take her out for brunch now. *With what money?* No, he had to deliver the drugs. He couldn't go back to Robin's as he was: no cash, no direction, no thesis, and no fucking clue of who or what William Shakespeare Greenberg was, let alone William Shakespeare of Stratford-upon-Avon.

He looked at his watch again. He would do it all. Right now. Today. Figure out his thesis before the library closed; deliver the mushroom tonight, or tomorrow morning at the latest; be back tomorrow.

Right.

He started the car, got back on the freeway, and headed back into Berkeley.

He found a parking space on a dead-end street on the north side of campus, took a single notebook from his backpack, then locked both it and the duffel in the trunk. He strode onto the campus and straight to the Doe Library in the shadow of the monolithic Campanile tower.

A quick consultation of the S drawer in the card catalog indicated that the works of Shakespeare and criticism thereof would be in the eight hundreds. He consulted a map, climbed the stairs to the third floor, and wandered through the stacks until he found a shelf marked 822.

Willie had never been much for libraries. He owned a well-worn hardcover set of the plays from 1913—his last birthday gift from his mother—and the *Riverside Shakespeare* that had been required reading for one of his undergraduate classes. The Department of Dramatic Art was bigger on lighting plots and scene shop than research, so every paper he'd written about Shakespeare as an undergrad had been done with no more secondary reading than the meager introductions in the dusty hardcover set and the *Riverside*'s voluminous footnotes, glosses, and appendixes. Even in the master's program at UCSC he'd gotten by more on style than substance. His whole "thesis," as it stood, and the whole of the "research" he'd done for it, consisted of getting very stoned late one night and flipping through the *Riverside*'s introduction, where, in the brief biography of Shakespeare, he had come upon the line, "Like all Elizabethans, he was—at least nominally—an Anglican whose forebears had been brought up in the Catholic confession."

Willie had been struck by the casual aside: "at least nominally." What did *that* mean? Willie had then flipped randomly to a spot in the book, and found the peculiar Sonnet 23.

O, let my books be then the eloquence
And dumb presagers of my speaking breast,
Who plead for love and look for recompense
More than that tongue that more hath more express'd.

He and Robin had just spent a late night watching *A Man for All Seasons*, the story of Sir Thomas More, on TV, and the line made sudden, stoned sense to him.

It was on the strength of that, and that alone, that he had pitched the thesis to Dashka Demitra two days later. That was his research: one sentence in an undergraduate text, one line in a poem, and the late movie on Channel 5.

But now he was here in the library, in the Shakespeare section, and he felt certain that with all these books he could prove that Shakespeare was a closet Catholic, a dissident, perhaps sending coded messages hidden in the speeches of his kings and courtiers. He browsed the books in the stacks.

This section seemed to be all compilations of the Works. Dozens of them. He walked down the aisle, continuing to scan. Not dozens...hundreds. He walked around the corner, to the next set of shelves. Here were biographies of Shakespeare by the dozens. There were also biographies written by the snobs who believed no commoner could write such exalted works: biographies of Francis Bacon as Shakespeare, Edward de Vere as Shakespeare, Christopher Marlowe as Shakespeare. There were biographies of the biographers. There were explications of the Histories as fiction, the Tragedies as fact, the Comedies as autobiography. He walked to the next stack...Shakespeare on stage, Shakespeare on film, Shakespeare on radio, Shakespeare in art. There were tomes on Shakespeare and feminism, Shakespeare and Jung, Shakespeare and Freud, Shakespeare and the melodrama of the Old West. There was, seemingly, no end to the takes on Shakespeare.

Willie felt panic rising in his chest. He had to come up with something new. Something brilliant. Something true. What if there was a book in here called *Shakespeare Was a Closet Catholic*? He'd be starting over.

Willie turned away from the criticism section. He hadn't seen any books about Shakespeare as a Catholic yet; if he didn't see it, he couldn't be accused of plagiarizing it. And Mizti was right: if Shakespeare was a Catholic, and Catholics were being executed left and right in his youth, it must have come out in the works themselves, right? *In the text.* Dashka had said it herself: "text, text, text." If there were references to Sir Thomas More, surely there would be other references to—Willie didn't really know much about Catholicism, but he was pretty sure he'd recognize them if he saw them. The Mass. Purgatory, that was a strictly Catholic thing. Rosaries. Crucifixes. The Trinity. Transubstantiation of bread and wine into the actual body and blood of Christ.

He went back to the section containing the works and stared at it blankly for a minute. He found himself gravitating to the smallest book on the shelf: *Shakespeare's Sonnets*. He figured he'd start where he'd begun. The sonnets were so personal. If faith and religion were driving Shakespeare the man, that's where they'd show up.

He pulled out the little book and stood in the stacks as he flipped through it, looking for references to God, or religion, or priests.

With increasing concern, he realized that there was very little God in these verses. There was love and beauty; there was passion, longing, betrayal, death, decay. There was a lot of sex. With "Will" a slang term for both "dick" and "cunt" in Shakespeare's day, Willie lingered over these lines:

Wilt thou, whose will is large and spacious,
Not once vouchsafe to hide my will in thine?

and these:

Make but my name thy love, and love that still,
And then thou lovest me, for my name is "Will."

Willie smiled at both the sexual punning and the idiocy of those who insisted the writer of Shakespeare's works was named Edward, Francis, or Christopher.

But there was precious little of God, or faith, or religion. He scanned the poems and made a rough count: the word "god" appeared three times...once in the phrase "little Love-god," i.e., Cupid; once in a colloquial "god forbid," and once in regard to the fair youth—clearly male—whom he calls "a god in love." In all instances, the word was uncapitalized. As he flipped through the pages, he saw "faith" a half-dozen times, all either in the colloquial "in faith," meaning "truly," or in reference to the faith—or the lack thereof—between two lovers.

In fact, the words that seemed to appear most often were "love"—probably hundreds of times—and, oddly, "Time." Time, almost always capitalized, as though it, not God, were something holy, to be feared and worshipped.

Devouring Time, Swift-footed Time, bloody tyrant Time, sluttish Time, never-resting Time, wasteful Time. Five sonnets at least were based on the conceit that the poet's verse was the one weapon that could defeat Time.

> *Not marble, nor the gilded monuments*
> *Of princes, shall outlive this powerful rhyme.*

What was it, Willie wondered, that had given the Bard such an obsession with Time ... and such certainty that his poetry would outlast it?

But that wasn't his thesis.

Shakespeare and Catholicism...

He closed the book and put it back. Perhaps the sonnets weren't the best place to start after all. He scanned along the shelves, and his eyes lit on a large, musty tome: *The First Folio of Shakespeare*. His heart foolishly skipped a beat. *It couldn't be an actual First Folio*—then he looked atop the spine: The Norton Facsimile.

He pulled it out and opened it. It was a photographic facsimile of the First Folio, dated 1968.

Cool.

He'd seen pages of the First Folio reproduced before—usually the table of contents listing all thirty-six of the plays attributed to Shakespeare at its publication—but this was different. The whole book, complete, typos and all, with the funny elongated s's that look like *f*'s and the Elizabethan spellings of "kisse," "dreame," "doo."

He took the book and found an empty cubicle. He opened it to the play he knew best, *The Tragedie of Hamlet, Prince of Denmarke.*

If he could find Catholic sympathies anywhere, he thought, he could find them in *Hamlet*. He scanned to the ghost scene...he remembered something about hell in there. He found it.

> *Gho.   I am thy Fathers Spirit,*
> *Doom'd for a certaine terme to walke the night;*
> *And for the day confin'd to fast in Fiers,*
> *Till the foule crimes done in my dayes of Nature*
> *Are burnt and purg'd away.*

Purgatory! *There it is*, Willie thought, as clear an indication of Shakespeare's theology as you could ask for. He took out his notebook and scribbled down the act and scene number of the speech. He flipped through the rest of the play, looking for more. What about the "To be, or not to be" soliloquy? All manner of meditation on the hereafter, there. He found it, Act Three, Scene One. Hamlet characterizes death:

To dye, to sleepe
No more.

Hm, thought Willie. *That doesn't sound Catholic. Or religious at all.* But in contemplating suicide, Hamlet develops further:

Who would Fardles beare
To grunt and sweat under a weary life,
But that the dread of something after death,
The undiscovered Countrey, from whose Borne
No Traveller returnes, puzels the will,
And makes us rather beare those illes we have,
Then Flye to others we know not of.

Willie could never remember what a fardel was, but no matter. Death was something from which "No Traveller returnes." What happened to the Rapture? The resurrection of the physical body? This was clearly not Catholicism; if anything it was a tremulous agnosticism.

He flipped to his favorite speech, where he was certain there was something about angels in heaven.

I have of late, but wherefore I know not, lost all my mirth, forgone all
custome of exercise; and indeed, it goes so heaverly with my disposition
that this goodly frame the Earth, seemes to me a sterrill Promontory;
this most excellent Canopy the Ayre, look you, this brave ore-hanging,
this Maiesticall Roofe, fretted with golden fire: why, it appeares no
other thing to mee, then a foule and pestilent congregation of vapours.
What a piece of worke is a man! how Noble in Reason? how infinite

*in faculty? in forme and moving how expresse and admirable? in
Action, how like an Angel? in apprehension, how like a God? the
beauty of the world, the Parragon of Animals; and yet to me, what
is this Quintessence of Dust? Man delights not me; no, nor Woman
neither; though by your smiling you seeme to say so.*

Willie closed the book and put his head down on the desk.

*This is no Catholic! He praises Man. MAN. He compares Man to a god.
Not to God, mind you, but "a god." Shakespeare was a pagan? No, that was
just poetry. He's a humanist and a cynical one at that. Man is the summit of
creation, and yet dust. It's nihilism. He sounds more like some confused, faithless, agnostic motherfucker like me than someone with a religious/political
axe to grind.*

Willie felt, at that precise moment, exactly like Hamlet: he had a
fucked-up family life like Hamlet; like Hamlet, he was charged with a task
that he seemingly lacked the emotional equipment to complete; and he
carried a packet of goods which, like Hamlet's death-sentence letter to the
King of England, was surely meant to deliver him to a rude ending.

*Maybe it's just Hamlet. He's only one character, in a particular state of
mind; maybe the nihilism is just a symptom of his depression, his melancholy.
Of course.*

He opened the book and flipped around looking for plays and speeches
that he recalled dealt with faith.

He spent all day sifting through the plays, and though he found Puritans
played as fools, he also found friars played as feeble; he found Shylock the
Jew at once base and profound. He found kingly but cocksure Catholics
like Henry V, and godly heathens like Pericles.

He came upon *The Life of King Henry the Eight.* Of course! Elizabeth's
father, Henry Tudor, had launched the Reformation in England. Surely
there . . .

He tore through the play. Henry VIII, the first Protestant King of England, came across as more Machiavellian than monstrous: determined
to keep England strong and his newborn dynasty healthy. Of Henry's two
wives in the play, the Catholic Catherine was noble and pious, forgiving
Henry even as he forsakes her. The Protestant Anne Boleyn was fickle at

first, but later exalted as "the goodliest woman that ever lay by man." Both, to Willie's dismay, were portrayed with humanity. Henry's dispute with the Pope, his divorce from Catherine, and his subsequent marriage to Anne Boleyn were portrayed as evils necessary to produce that flower of English royalty...

Elizabeth I.

If Shakespeare was a rebel, railing against an oppressive regime, he had an odd way of showing it.

He read the text all the way through; an entire Shakespeare play exactly *about* the moment that the Catholic/Protestant schism opened in England, and he found poetry and pathos, great pomp and small truths, but no codes, no hidden nods to the Pope, just, as in all his plays, human characters drawn with understanding and compassion.

None were more human than Cardinal Wolsey. The Archbishop of York and Henry's advisor was portrayed as crafty and corrupt, until his fall, after which he found self-awareness and a sort of redemption...and spoke of Sir Thomas More.

> *He's a Learned man. May he continue*
> *Long in his Highnesse favour, and do Iustice*
> *For Truths-sake, and his Conscience; that his bones,*
> *When he has run his course, and sleepes in Blessings,*
> *May have a Tombe of Orphants teares wept on him.*

Outright praise and honor for Sir Thomas More! Why, Willie thought, would Shakespeare bother to bury his admiration for More in a bit of syntactical code in a sonnet, then boldly praise him to the skies here?

It just didn't make sense.

I'm so fucked.

Willie left the Folio facsimile sitting on the cubicle desk. He took his notebook with its one, lonely note (*Hamlet*, I.v.9), walked back to his father's Audi, flung open the door, and threw himself into the driver's seat. He tore into his backpack and rummaged around to find his pipe.

Crap...did I leave it at Robin's?

No matter. He found a matchbook with a small roach—a couple of hits worth—tucked behind the matchsticks. Perfect. He had to drive, anyway. He smoked it and felt instantly better. He tossed the roach butt out the window, looked at his watch: 6:00. It would be getting dark soon; he should get to the Faire, and try to find his contact tonight.

Okay, he thought, maybe he was never meant to be a Shakespeare scholar, much less the next William Shakespeare.

He at least wouldn't fuck up at being a drug runner.

Willie had crossed the Richmond–San Rafael Bridge and was on a deserted transition road that ran past San Quentin State Prison when he saw the red and blue flashing light in his mirror, followed by a single *BRAWR* from a siren.

Chapter Twenty-five

In 1582, William Shakespeare entered adulthood juggling a pregnant
fiancée and a financially struggling family. Such an experience was
surely more influential in his development as an artist and human being
than whatever sect of Christianity he might have professed.

It was dark and pouring when William returned home, having walked the
mile from Shottery where he said an unfond farewell to Bartholomew
Hathaway's mare. Saddle-sore and soaking, he made his way grumbling
past the Shakespeare family dunghill, which was coursing with rivulets
from the rain.

Back in Worcester, Sandells and Richardson had made William—the
only one present who could write—forge the requisite permission documents for the wedding. Then they'd gone before the court and posted
the surety. The clerk got Anne Hathaway's name right the second time
around.

William Shakespeare was now duly licensed to be married.

When William straggled into the house, Gilbert was at the table declin-
ing *puella* on a wax tablet and John was half asleep on the best bed by
the fire, with Joan cuddled up next to him darning a pair of black hose.
"William's home!" she exclaimed, set aside her mending, and ran to embrace him. There came a soft shuffle of feet from upstairs, and Mary hid
her relief behind a sardonic smile as she asked, "And where has the young
master been these three nights past? Sowing the family seed?"

William stripped off his filthy, dripping clothes and stood warming
himself by the fire in nothing but his undershirt as the family watched.
"Mother, Father, I would speak with you in confidence."

"Gilbert, Joan, go to bed," said Mary gently.

"But Mother—" Joan protested.

"Ah! To bed hie thee. Edmund is already asleep, and bears watching."

"Ay, Mother," said Gilbert, and taking up his candle and tablet, nudged Joan as he passed. "Come on."

Joan trudged upstairs reluctantly after him, muttering, "Unto our resting place we go. To be stifled in the chamber, whose foul mouth no health-some air breathes in, to sleep, to dream, perchance to die..." and trailed away into silence upstairs.

"What is it, William?" said John. "You look as if you'd seen a ghost."

"That I have," said William. "The shade, forsooth, of mine own future."

Mary sat at the table, hands in her lap as William told the tale.

"Know you that I have been, of late, much free of my affections with the local maidenry."

"As young men are wont to be," said John from the corner, "and nothing wrong with that. Youth is like a sparrow, quick and ever-changing in its flight, and its beak in many flowers—"

"John," interrupted Mary, "let him speak." She turned back to William. "Naught good ever came of unbridled dalliance."

"You speak what I have learnt too late," said William.

Mary waited patiently, and William continued.

"There is a maid of Shottery who lives but a mile without Stratford. As I passed her house one day upon a walk, a path I frequented much this summer past, she hailed me from her garden. A corner of the garden fence had buckled, and she, trying to lift it back in place, had caught her skirts upon it. I helped the maid out of need, and she thanked me, then burst into unprovoked tears and sat heavily upon the cottage stair.

"'What cause,' said I, 'taps so deep a font of tears?'

"'Begging your pardon. I thank you for your aid,' said she. 'By my troth, I am much in need of aid in these dark days. My father died two months past, and I am unwed. My brother is master here, but he is oft abroad about his business, and I am left alone to act as mistress and master to house, garden, and field. I am no frail flower, and am used to the labor of a farm, but it is much to bear when compounded by my grief.'

"She dabbed her tears, and thanked me again for my pains, and went inside. She is not an old maid, not yet, though the first bloom of her youth is touched by the first light frost of winter.

"Thereafter I made it a point, upon my journeys near Shottery, to knock at the maid's door, and see that she were well, and enquire if there were posts to be lifted or holes to be patched. Upon my fourth such visit, I found her dressed as though for a fair, with flowers in her hair and a touch of paint upon her cheek, and she bade me enter for she had both a post to be lifted and a hole to be patched, she said.

"I was until that day chaste with the innocence of youth, but the maid, in her loneliness and her loss, sought comfort, and I gave it her. In return, she taught me much that day, and though I ne'er returned, from shame, I guess, or fear, a world of women, a feast of women, oped itself to mine eye."

"If I may put it in brief," said Mary, "you preyed upon the grief of her father's passing to win an old maid and lose your virginity, and then abandoned her."

William looked deeply into the fire for a long moment, then he spoke softly. "I know not who was the prey nor who the predator. Yet I have not abandoned her quite; for I left the most eternal part of me within her, and there it grows."

There was a long silence as his words sank in. Then Mary put her head in a trembling hand upon the table.

"Oh, fie," she whispered quietly to herself.

John stood up from his chair and his face flushed red. "What, you got a girl with CHILD!?! Od's teeth!" he yelled. Vessels in his nose swelled and burst as he towered over the half-naked William. "See you not our circumstance, how our house is filled and o'erfilled, our shop empty, and now you who are to be the might and muscle of my old age are to be tied afore your time to apron strings and swaddling cloth! By Jesu, though your name contains a Will, your will contains not your willy—"

"John," Mary interrupted. "Pay him no mind, William, he plays his part too well. Who is the maid?"

"Anne Hathaway, daughter of—"

"Daughter of Richard Hathaway," said John. "I know him well, we've done business! Oh, I can hear his rumbling at the Guild Hall now—"

"You don't go to the Guild Hall," said Mary.

"And you won't be hearing Master Hathaway's rumble anytime soon," said William. "He shuffled off the mortal coil this past July—leaving Anne a dowry."

John wheeled around. "How much, lad?"

"Six pounds, I am told."

"Bah!" said John, waving his hand in front of his face as if chasing away a gnat. "A farmer's dowry."

Mary asked William, "Does the maid wish to marry?"

"For her part, I know not. Her brother and two largest neighbors wish it, that is certain. They escorted me to Worcester to gain a license. It required a surety, for which they stood, and your signatures, which I perforce provided."

William fished the damp wedding certificate from his pouch and spread it out on the table. John turned away toward the fire; he couldn't read. Mary looked it over quickly, silently. "Well," Mary said, "it appears our oldest son is going to marry." She set the paper down and looked at William. "*Anne Shakespeare*," she said appraisingly. "You're going to be with her for a very long time." She shrugged then added, "I hope she was good."

Mary rose and headed back upstairs, and William heard the hushed bumpings of Gilbert and Joan retreating from their eavesdropping spots. William was left alone with his thoughts for a moment. What, he wondered, would life—an entire life—with Anne Hathaway as his wife be like? She had been good in bed, to be sure, and gentle with his awkwardness; though there was, later on, also a desperation and ravenousness in her that had taken him aback. But then it was his first time, and he would have been taken aback in any case. In the months since, he had become a connoisseur of the experience. His encounter with Rosaline was surely the gem of his collection. He doubted he could find one more precious. Yet he was also devastated to think the collection complete, the pursuit over.

"William, there is still hope." William started from his chair—he had forgotten his father was still in the room, and apparently reading his thoughts.

John continued in a low voice, "You need not be tied to the service of child rearing yet—ah, though it is a joy, son, a joy in your case," he added unconvincingly. "Do you, in sooth, desire to be both married and a father, three years before you are even come of age?"

"Would any man of wit and ambition wish it so?" answered William.

"Then remember, what man has planted by God's grace also may man uproot, and God provides the means to do so. If Anne Hathaway be of like mind, there be remedies. Speak to our apothecary good and true. See what hope Philip Rogers may offer; the cause which led the parties to this contract"—and here he held up the marriage certificate—"may yet be void." John winked at his son, squeezed his shoulder, and lumbered upstairs to bed.

Chapter Twenty-six

DOGBERRY: *You are thought here to be the most senseless and fit man for the constable of the watch; therefore bear you the lantern. This is your charge: you shall comprehend all vagrom men; you are to bid any man stand, in the prince's name.*

SECOND WATCHMAN: *How if a' will not stand?*

DOGBERRY: *Why, then, take no note of him, but let him go; and presently call the rest of the watch together and thank God you are rid of a knave.*

—*Much Ado About Nothing*, III.iii.22

Willie pulled the Audi carefully off the highway onto the shoulder, taking care to signal well in advance.

Stay calm. Everything is in the trunk. No way will they open the trunk, unless you really blow it. Stay calm.

As he heard the crunch of the CHP officer's boots approaching, he activated the driver's side window. Then he placed both hands atop the steering wheel. "Is there a problem, officer?"

This was a cliché, but he used it instinctively. It's a code, like saying whassup when passing a youth gang on the street, or howdy when entering a cowboy bar. It's a small act of submission, and if nothing else it tells the cop, it's cool, I know how this is supposed to go, I'm not insane on PCP, I'm not going to be trouble, please keep that gun in its holster.

The cop—OFFICER ANTHONY, his name tag proclaimed—bent down, took a quick glance around the car, looked Willie in the eye for a second, then stood erect.

"License and registration, please." *Good. We're still on the script.*

Willie handed over his license.

"It's my dad's car," he said to the cop. "Registration's probably in the glove box." Moving slowly, he leaned over, opened it, and— *SHIT! MY PIPE. SHIT! OH, SHIT. Don't panic. Stay cool.*

The pipe was sitting, visible to Willie but probably too deep inside for the cop to see, on top of the registration, the car's owner's manual, and a map. Pretending to look under the pile, Willie lifted up the entire contents of the glove box from the front edge so that the pipe slid all the way to the back, then "found" the registration slip on top and pulled it out, simultaneously nudging the map toward the back to cover the pipe.

Willie had quick hands.

"Here it is," he said, closing the glove box and handing the registration to the officer.

The cop said, "Please remain in the vehicle," and headed back to his car.

Willie breathed out a calming breath, but his mind raced. What was on his record? No warrants that he knew of. Parking tickets? Maybe. There was one he'd contested that he'd never heard anything more about. What if it had gone to warrant? Had his sudden disappearance from Santa Cruz aroused any suspicion? It shouldn't have. All his roommates and friends knew he often spent weekends in Berkeley—then, oh, well, fuck, he'd just been *arrested* that morning! By the Berkeley campus police. Do they share info with the CHP? What about the Drug Enforcement Agency? They must have some sort of central information-sharing database, right? Was he already in the computer? "William Shakespeare Greenberg, Berkeley radical, arrested at anti-DEA events. Known associate of Dr. Timothy Leary. Intellectual. Jew." What the hell was he *thinking*, attending a political rally in support of drug use when he was packing more than a pound of contraband? He thought of how conveniently close San Quentin was—he could see its dead yellow lights in his side-view mirror—and wondered without optimism how it would compare to the UC Berkeley Campus Police holding cell.

The cop returned. "Okay, Mr. Greenberg. You have a clean record, but I do detect what smells to me like marijuana either on your breath or in the car. Would you step out of the vehicle, please?"

With a sinking feeling in his stomach, Willie got out. "Stand hands on the roof, legs apart, please." Willie complied as the cop put his hands on his shoulder and knocked his legs apart with a firm kick. He made a quick pat-down search, then said, "Okay, just stand right over here, please." He guided Willie to a spot on the passenger side of the car, on the shoulder and out of the way of traffic. Willie noticed that the cop had a partner, still sitting in the passenger seat of the patrol car.

Willie watched with growing panic as Officer Anthony began a methodical search of the car. He opened the rear passenger door and searched the back seat; under the floor mat; deep in the seat itself. He felt the seat pocket on the back of the front seat. Then he closed the door and moved to the driver's side rear seat, repeating the motions. He closed the rear door and moved to the front. He checked under the steering wheel, under the seat, under the dashboard.

Fuck, this guy is fucking thorough!

From the squad car behind there was the cackle of police radio traffic as Officer Anthony checked the sun visors, the headliner. He opened the armrest console.

Then he leaned over from the driver's side and popped open the glove box.

I'm FUCKED! I'm fucking totally fucking fucked. No way does he not find the pipe. And once he finds the pipe, he'll search the trunk. Maybe he searches the trunk, anyway. Holy, holy crap.

Officer Anthony stopped, realizing that he didn't have a good angle to look into the glove box. He crawled back out the driver's side door, closed it, came around the front of the car, opened the front passenger door.

This is it. "Mandatory minimum sentences for first-time offenders."

Now the full meaning of it hit him in the solar plexus.

I'm going to jail. I wonder if I'll get raped? Of course I'll get raped. I deserve to get raped, for being such a fucking moron....

Officer Anthony reached toward the glove box. Willie heard a car door open. It was Officer Anthony's partner. He stood with one foot in the door, on the radio. With a nod of his head, he gestured that he needed to speak to Anthony.

Slightly annoyed, Officer Anthony climbed out of the Audi and walked past Willie. "Stay here."

Willie stood there trying to look innocent, with the door and glove box to his dad's car hanging open, the glove-box light illuminated, and Anthony talking in low tones with his partner about some call that had just come over the radio. After a few eternal seconds of consultation, Officer Anthony gave Willie's ID to his partner, along with a quick, clipped instruction.

Officer Anthony got into the CHP vehicle and picked up the radio while Officer Monday passed by Willie. As he did, he glanced at Willie's ID. He looked up, surprised. "William Shakespeare, huh? Written any masterpieces lately?" He laughed, then caught himself. "Sorry, I bet you get that all the time. I love Shakespeare." He leaned into the car, with its glove box still open.

A Shakespeare fan. Willie thought fast. *What quote, for a cop?*

"First thing, let's kill all the lawyers," Willie said.

The cop turned and grinned. "That's my favorite line. How'd you know?"

Of course it's your favorite, it's the one most often taken out of context.

But it had the right effect.

Officer Monday leaned into the car, still chuckling about all those murdered lawyers. He looked around casually. He closed the open glove box. As an afterthought, he searched under the passenger's seat cushion, pulled out a quarter and a dime. Then he closed the door and gave Willie the thirty-five cents.

"Your lucky day."

"Thanks."

There was a quick *BWAR* from the patrol car. Monday glanced over his shoulder.

"You know why we pulled you over, right?" said Monday, handing Willie back his ID. Willie shook his head.

"You were driving too slow. Usually means a stoner. Be careful out there, okay?" Monday said as he headed back to the patrol car.

Willie, flustered, said, "Okay, thanks. You, too."

"Good night, sweet prince," Officer Monday said as he got into the squad car and closed the door. Officer Anthony fired up the siren and roared out onto the highway, lights flashing. Somewhere out there was something more dangerous than a college kid doing forty-five mph on the freeway.

Willie got into his dad's car and drove—at exactly fifty-eight mph—toward the Renaissance Faire. In the sixteenth century, Willie hoped, everything would be less complicated.

Chapter Twenty-seven

What biographical influences set Shakespeare apart from not only all who came before him, but from contemporaries such as Munday and Marlowe? Samuel Taylor Coleridge, that writer of such opium-fueled Romantic poetry as Kubla Khan, *spoke famously of Shakespeare's "wonderful philosophic impartiality," his seeming ability to fully and without judgment inhabit the mind, body, and soul of princes and cutpurses, of heroes and traitors, even—one might argue* especially*—of women, and reveal their essential humanity. Whence came this peculiar ability of Shakespeare's to find oneness with "the other"?*

William had class to teach on Wednesday. His students seemed to sense something distrait in their normally sharp magister, and were quiet. Even class clown Richard Wheeler was glum, matching the grey, overcast sky, still heavy and drizzly from the previous day's rain.

After school, William went straight to Philip Rogers's shop. Nothing odd in that: it was on William's way home, and he often stopped in for a chat. But he still found himself looking around before he entered, to make sure there was no one he knew on the High Street. He saw only Hamlet Sadler, shuffling up toward Henley Street, taking no notice. William ducked into the shop.

He was hit by a hundred different scents at once. Myrrh, sulfur, mustard, rotting cod liver. Green earthenware jars lined the shelves. Boxes and bladders and skins were everywhere, filled with tinctures, salves, seeds, and decoctions. A stuffed alligator hung proudly over the rear door. And sitting at a cluttered table, wielding a tortoise shell as a paperweight, was Philip Rogers. Rogers looked at William as though he'd never seen him before. His eyes were black holes that seemed not even to reflect the flickering light cast by the single candle on the table.

He held in his hand a metallic pipe that looked of exotic origin. A thick smoke emanated from it, and from his mouth and nostrils.

William had never seen such a thing. "What devilry does our true apothecary conjure now? The eating of smoke and fire?"

"Ah, William," he said at last. "About to close up shop, I was. Merely tasting of a most exalted medicine, purchased direct from a sailor in the service of Sir Francis Drake himself. *Tobecka,* 'tis called, fresh from the New World, and inhaled to the lungs, as the primitives there teach, by burning to a smoke, thence to course through body, mind, and spirit. Only a few noblemen and sailors practice it. Forsooth, methinks they share not the knowledge with the masses for fear of losing their stores of the weed, it is that pleasurable."

And here he leaned forward and spoke conspiratorially, with what William thought a mad glint in the eye. "I have created my own recipe, mixing the weed with dried and crushed blossoms of our own local hemp, and yet a third leaf, very rare, from the southern climes of the New World and much beloved of the natives there. Together they produce a most immediate effect: a godlike energy suffused with a most peaceful calm—and a most stimulating numbing of the tongue. Will you try?"

He held out the pipe to William.

"Nay, though it sounds illuminating," said William. "I seek not drugs for myself, though to my benefit."

William explained the situation: a girl, nay a woman, with child, and was there a way to unmake what God and man hath made?

Philip Rogers considered, and took a long draw of smoke from the pipe into his lungs. "I have not the physic you seek," he said, "but there is one who, if the stars will have it so, may accomplish your desire. I will take you to her." He set down his pipe, snuffed out the candle, and took his cloak from a hook.

"What, now?" asked William, but Philip Rogers was already striding at an unusually brisk pace through the door.

William followed.

The cloud and drizzle had given way to a brisk wind, and ragged clouds were clearing. There was a waxing moon low in the sky as they hurried up High Street, passed the Shakespeare home in Henley Street, and continued on to the crossroads marked by the One Elm, dark against evening stars. They neither went straight on toward Henley-in-Arden nor right toward Clopton, but turned left, onto a narrow footpath that dove into the forest. After a half hour or so they came upon a clearing, and in the clearing was a single small cottage, surrounded by a sprawling but well-tended garden. A light burned in the window.

William knew the place. It was the home of Goody Hall, a widow, a midwife, and therefore by definition a witch. If Philip Rogers's shop was a crypt of dead herbs, desiccated by wind and heat, crushed by mortar and pestle, then Goody Hall's garden was their lush and living incarnation. Her garden was dense with deadly nightshade, mandrake and mugwort, pennyroyal and hemp, wormwood and hemlock.

When the door opened to Philip Rogers's signature knock—*bam bam bam bam... bam bam*—it revealed a woman so young and comely that William was taken aback. Surely, he thought, she is a crone, under some spell of unnatural youth. She smiled at seeing Philip.

"Philip Rogers, by the sun and moon! You are most welcome," then with a wink to William, "for ever does he bring me good commerce!" Introductions were made, and with water from a pitcher Goody Hall washed her hands that had been at work over a bubbling cauldron in the fire on the hearth. William sat and looked about. In contrast to Philip Rogers's apothecary shop, her house was tidy and inconspicuous. She put out a goodly amount of cheese, and took down three mugs and filled them with ale from a large pitcher. William took his mug and sniffed the contents.

She answered his momentary hesitation with a smile. "Strictly barley, hops, yeast, and water, I assure you. Now, what brings the glover's son and assistant schoolmaster to the witch's wood?" she said, and sat, taking a sip of ale and a bite of cheese.

William explained again his situation, and she asked before he had finished, "To the child's birth does the woman say ay or nay? For if she would say ay, then not by me will she be gainsaid. If nay, then why are two men here on her behalf, but not herself?"

William answered, "As the woman and I have not spoken since the news became known to me, I know not her disposition. Mayhap she has simply lured me to warm an empty bed, or, misled by my father's former station, to fill an empty purse. But I think not. There was, I think, a fire that burned true enough, but which has for a long autumn gone untended. Whether an ember still glows upon that hearth I know not. Of her desire or lack thereof to bear children, in sooth, I know not."

The witch smiled. "I see well how a maid might be seduced by your sugared words. Indeed, a cunning tongue may do much for a maid, both for good and for ill."

William shifted uncomfortably, unable to stop thinking that beneath this lithe young woman — she could not be more than Anne's age — was a gnarled old woman trying somehow to seduce him.

Almost as if she heard his thoughts, she continued, "But I am a witch, am I not, Philip? And witches, 'tis said, may see men as they are; and what I see before me is a truthful man."

She went to a shelf and took down a wooden box, and from the box pulled out a vial.

"Take then this vial. And if she be not imbalanced of the humours, or under other fit of madness, and if she well and truly — by all the saints and martyrs, and by God and Jesus and Mary and Joseph and Jove and Cupid and the Sun and Moon and Sky, and all the houses of all the heavens that now or ever rule her fate — wishes to end a life not yet begun, then and only then, this distilled liquor let her drink off. Mark you, the potion is most powerful when drunk at the stroke of midnight under a full moon, and if she will she should then remove her blouse and run thrice around the house where the child was got. And if it is meant to be, she shall swoon, and bleed, and the unborn remain so."

William took the small vial and put it in his pouch.

"That," said Goody Hall, sitting down again to her ale, "is ten shillings. But as you've made the journey to my cot, would you have aught else of me? I may augur your future in love or in commerce. I also cast spells and make other potions of love, for growing, healing, for increase of potency — "

"Love, growing, and potency I have in surfeit; power I desire not," said William, taking a small coin purse from his belt and opening it.

He gave her ten shillings.

She took it, and as their hands touched for an instant, she looked at

William intensely, then quizzically to Philip Rogers. She turned back to William, and her lips lifted at the corners. "I can also, if you will, show you the gateway to the spirit world, and beyond."

William wasn't expecting this. He shook his head. But there was something in her voice, and he found himself wondering just what she meant. *The spirit world.* He was surprised to hear himself ask, "Is it safe?"

The witch turned to Philip Rogers, and asked, "Is it safe?"

Rogers shrugged and leaned back in his chair. "Safe? Houses they say are safe, yet poor Richard Coombs was killed by a falling bedroom timber, was he not? So what is safe? Nothing."

William looked into the witch's eyes. They didn't scare him. Much. What did he have to lose, besides a life suddenly not his own?

"*Eamus,*" he said, and set his entire purse of coins on the table. "Let it be so."

For twenty minutes William watched as Goody Hall added ingredients to the brew in her pot. Herbs, a toad, a dried bat, several roots that William didn't recognize, and finally a handful of toadstools that would be *Psilocybe semilanceata* to later scientists. She walked over to the front door. There, lodged securely in a hook, was a broom. She pulled it from its place.

"Are you ready to fly?"

William said nothing as Goody Hall glided across the room to the cauldron. She spun the broom upside down as expertly as Little John might a quarterstaff. She raised the broomstick ceremonially over the cauldron, dipped the broomstick handle, and stirred the green, oily decoction. As she did she spoke an incantation, something in Welsh, which William knew bits of but not in this dialect.

As she chanted, Philip leaned over to William and whispered, "This is a great honor, William. Few are those pricked, who are chosen by a witch to share in the mysteries of the coven. Join at your peril, your pleasure, and your pain, but know that it does change you. You will not be what once you were."

"I wish not to be what I am now."

"Drop your breeches," Goody Hall said, and William did.

She took a bottle from a shelf and poured a generous amount of oil into her hands, then rubbed them quickly together to warm it. "Now drop to all fours and make like a stretching dog, palms outstretched as if in supplication, arse heavenward."

William obeyed, and she quickly and expertly spread the lubricant.

Goody Hall lifted the broomstick from the cauldron. "Prepare," she said, "to ride the broomstick to the place where witches meet."

"Try to be at your ease," said Philip Rogers. "It only hurts at first."

It did, but the lubricant did its job: the spongelike rectal tissue absorbed the witch's brew and sent it spinning through William's bloodstream, and his flesh began to tingle. After a few minutes, he watched with fascination as "Philip Rogers" melted and reformed itself endlessly, as "Goody Hall" transformed into the very crone he had imagined and then back into a girl, but not the same girl. First she was Rosaline, and she was naked and shining and tossing her curls and laughing. Then she melted again and re-formed as his mother, but it was his mother's head on Rosaline's shining body, and he hid his eyes at seeing her belly and her bush. Then she melted and came back as Anne Hathaway, soberly and hugely pregnant by a window, looking out at a grey misty day while knitting socks, four socks over and over again in a display of infinity that had William confused about exactly what he was seeing. Then finally she transformed one last time into his sister Joan, but it was Anne's hugely pregnant body, or so it seemed, and then she, too, melted away into nothing but a skeleton, and that blew away in a wind. The wind grew, until it blew away the table, and the cottage, and "Philip Rogers," and finally himself, and suddenly the wind was all around him and he was flying—or something that he thought must be him was flying, but it couldn't be him because his body had been blown away, had it not? He was a living ghost, a specter, a soul disembodied, as he soared over mountains, through clouds. He passed a tree-thicketed hilltop, and of his will, and yet not, he swooped around its far side, through the canopy of a forest and into a large clearing, where a coven of witches, naked, chanted as they stood and ground their nether lips against the broomsticks held between their legs like hobbyhorses, and they all as one stopped and looked up at his passing, and as he circled, they began at once to wildly ululate and raise and shake their brooms, and his spirit fled up again through the clouds, and then raced downward, through fog and mist, and when he emerged from the fog he was still flying, flying low, with the wind around him, but now it was a hot wind, and fast wind, a faster wind than he'd ever known, over a low hard path of some kind of stone, but stone such as he'd never seen, charcoal gray and smooth, and painted with eerily symmetrical lines, white and yellow, some continuous, some broken, and flashes like gems reflecting firelight spaced regularly in between so he couldn't help but count them, one, two, three, four—he got to twenty-five in moments, and they seemed to stretch off into infinity. And his mind's eye looked down to see his hands, his own hands and yet not, resting on a curve of shining leather—cheap leather, the shred of him that was still a glover's son noted—and lights and numbers that made no sense to him, a glowing half-clock dial with a hand pointing to a time that seemed to be 58; but he had the feeling he was in a room or a hutch of some sort, or maybe it was a metal cage, with windows, bright clear windows. Finally he thought he saw, outside the moving cage, the outlines of a village, nestled in a forest shadowed against the sky, a strangely bright sky.

The cage in which his spirit raced through the hot wind passed a large barn, and on the barn were written two words he had never seen together before: RENAISSANCE FAIRE.

Part Three

RENAISSANCE

One can imagine few places where the issues of politics, religion, family values, and sexual morality might come together in so compelling a fashion as they must have around the Shakespeare family hearth in the fall of 1582.

It was early. Predawn. William headed home, clutching in one hand the small bottle containing the witch's brew of drugs, brewed to force untimely from its womb his would-be child.

His bottom hurt even more than it had after the long ride to Worcester.

William didn't remember leaving Goody Hall's cottage in the woods, nor the return trip to Stratford. Philip Rogers had given him tea from the Spanish West Indies back at his shop; a restorative, he said. William felt sharp and clear in the front and center of his head but ragged around the edges as he padded softly and unsteadily through the half-light up to Henley Street and tried to slip, unnoticed, into the Shakespeare home. He was ravenously hungry, and tiptoed into the Great Hall to see what luck he might find in the pot. Mary emerged from the parlor looking fresh as a daisy and mightily peeved. "Good morrow, William. Thought you to slip in unnoticed, arriving home thus in the cock-light?"

William tried to smile naturally. "Ay, good my mother, for I wished not to wake you."

"Marry, I have been awake these many hours awaiting your return," she said, and gestured him into the parlor. "Come and sit. We must needs talk."

William followed her, trying to palm the bottle of potion into the folds of his sleeve.

William and Mary sat in hard leather chairs on either side of the fire.

His father, who was rarely awake at this hour, sat quietly in a dark corner on a stool. He looked as if he hadn't slept.

"William," Mary Shakespeare said, "you are our son. There is naught you could do on God's green earth to change that state nor to abate our love for you."

"Ay, Mum."

Mary nodded, and looked at her husband like she'd just given him a good thrashing, which she had. "Your father and I, though joined by bonds both spiritual and temporal, and surpassing strong, are not always in accord in all matters. Last night he recounted to me some small advice, cloaked in hints, which he imparted to you. Do you recall?"

William said nothing, but involuntarily fingered the bottle in his hand.

Mary waited patiently for a moment, then said, "You smell not unpleasantly of exotic herbs. Have you been to the apothecary, so early of a workday?"

"Ay, Mum, for a remedy to an affliction: I have of late, but wherefore I know not, been exceeding melancholy," said William.

"The cause is easily found out," Mary said. "You have had a life change thrust upon you, the surging tide of fate dashing the bark of youth and liberty most rudely upon the rocks of duty. Well might that lead to melancholy, even in the most splenetic of men."

"Ay, mayhap that is the case."

"William," said Mary, and her brow furrowed, "I oft have wished to have this talk with you—"

"If it is of country matters you wish to speak, of men and women and how they fit together, I have learnt much—"

"Nay, not that. It is of matters celestial, not bodily, I wish to discourse. I hope I have not waited too long, as I fear by your recent passion at the dinner table. If so, I beg your forgiveness."

William waited.

Mary took a breath. "You know well that my family is of the Church of Rome."

William snorted. "Indeed! I may hardly forget, as of a sudden there are many would have me stretched or hanged, burned or cut open for it. Though I marvel to hear it thus spoken of freely in our house, where faith has been like the bastard child in the room, neither speaking nor spoken of."

"Ay," said Mary. "Oft we bandy not that which touches us most deeply, nor do we for fear acknowledge the danger that lurks the nearest. We thought to inform you of much upon your coming of age, but now you are come to manhood before your time, 'tis time you knew all."

"What *all*?" asked William.

Mary picked up a poker and stoked the fire absently as she began to talk, the embers glowing orange at first then bursting into small blue flame. "The Ardens, you know, have been in Warwickshire since the time of William the Conqueror."

"Ay, so have I been told." William's father liked to brag about his wife's high lineage when he got drunk.

"And through all those generations, the Church of Rome and the glory of the Blessed Mother Mary, my namesake, and of the Father, and Son, and the Holy Spirit, have been our guides and our sanctuary." William shifted uncomfortably.

"Mayhap you remember it not," Mary continued, "but you were baptized in the Old Faith, and ere you could walk, heard Mass in the old rites. The troubles of London seemed far away in those days, and in Stratford we quietly worshipped as we had always done.

"But it was even during the year that John served as bailiff that the seeds of our downfall were sown. For Mary of Scotland allied with the northern Catholic earls, and they, thinking to place her on the throne, revolted. They were defeated, and the Crown's response was swift. Within that year the Earl of Leicester knighted Thomas Lucy to be his sword and hammer against papists in Warwickshire, and he set to with vigor."

Mary paused for a moment, and when she resumed her voice was thick.

"Father William Butcher, who baptized you at Holy Trinity, was replaced by a new vicar. The church's icons and images were defaced and its altar hauled down. Many Catholics who had grown wealthy were suddenly set upon by levies and taxes, fines and enclosures, and other impediments great and small. The unsanctioned trade in wool, in which your father and many others of the true faith prospered, was shut down.

"And then came the most grievous blow, dealt whence we least expected it. A papal bull excommunicated Elizabeth, and deemed her deposed and ripe for murder. O foolish impolitic! Meant to encourage a Catholic uprising, the bull achieved the contrary effect, for it forced every conscience to forsake either Virgin Queen or Holy Father. How should we do so? Why must we do so? Did not our Lord tell us to render unto Caesar that which is Caesar's? Why would the Pope join, perforce, the church and state that Our Lord would keep asunder?

"The next year, all the Crown's officers were made to swear an Oath of Supremacy to Elizabeth, as both Sovereign Queen and head of church. Many a proud English Catholic chose England over Rome."

Mary looked at John.

John leaned forward and there was a look in his eye William had rarely seen before. It was shrewd, and it was sharp.

"No doubt, my son, you think me mad. A dotard, mayhap, or a drunkard, or a fool, or all of these. No one fears fools and drunkards; they are left in peace to tend their families and rankle their friends and breathe their foul odors in the free air. So it has been with me. But . . ."

John Shakespeare looked from side to side mock-conspiratorially, as though there were spies in the very walls of the Shakespeare parlor, then whispered, "I am but mad north northwest. When the wind is southerly, I know a hawk from a handsaw." And he winked.

William shook his head, confused. "And what, pray you, means that?"

Mary answered, "Your father has played the part of the poor, mad old alderman, fallen on drink and hard times, to escape the swearing of oaths both damned and damning, that we might live in peace. And he plays his part well . . . too well at times," she said with an arch of her eyebrow toward John, before turning back to William. "But we are neither so poor nor in such hard times as we give out."

William was angry. "So what, then? Do you fawn and cower here, acting the cleaving of a chicken for eight as though it were a Saturnalia feast, only for the sake of Sir Thomas Lucy? What then of your family, and your faith? A faithless faith indeed, that believes not in itself, nor will stand for the right, but rather watches and weeps in silence while its priests are butchered i'the public square."

Mary Shakespeare's eyes flashed. "Fie, William! Are you yet so mean of understanding, despite all your wit!? To be silent when the soul cries out for justice is like a torture. Yet to be silent under torture may be accounted the bravest act of all, for it may protect your loved ones from a worse fate."

William went quiet, thinking of his own weakness on the rack.

Mary composed herself. "We are at war, William. Beneath the ribbons, the jeweled ruffs and sparkling diadems, and other festoonery of the summer of Elizabeth's reign, we are at war. A quiet war, of Englishman against Englishman. And we are much i'the minority. As were the very first Christians beneath the Roman yoke in ancient times, we are small and secret; yet also are we strong and true."

Now it was Mary's turn to lower her voice, and when she looked from side to side as though the walls held spies, she did it with all seriousness.

"There is resistance, William. Secretly, quietly, while keeping an inky Protestant cloak to the winds of the world, we fight back. Not just the Shakespeares, but my cousins the Ardens both at Wilmcote and Park Hall, and many other families beside—the Sadlers, Throckmortons, Hoghtons and Catesbys, the Barbers, Cawdreys, Cottoms, the Grevilles—too many to name—are of our cause, and together we do what we may to save our consciences and our souls at once."

"And what do you do?"

"What the oppress'd can do. We spy. We meet. We pull what frayed strings we hold, in this the tattered fabric of our cause."

"William," said John, "we know of your ill-treatment at Charlecote."

William was astonished; he had only been a guest in Sir Thomas Lucy's laundry for a matter of hours. "You...how? Whence?"

"Your maiden friend Rosaline went to the Bear for aid," his father replied. "A brave girl, that, for her family is of the new faith; for her even to be seen there was a danger."

William's stomach sank. Rosaline had saved him, and he had forgotten her.

"Did you not wonder wherefore you were delivered?" asked Mary.

William recovered and said slowly, "Ay, I marveled greatly at it. For I was set free by no less than Leicester himself."

Mary said, "There is a network of messengers, whereby we may get word back and forth to others of our cause within hours, when it would take a single man days to take the message."

"Few are there who have the ear of the Earl of Leicester," John continued, "and fewer still who might sway him to spare the rod to a Catholic. It was your mother's cousin, Viscountess Montague—a favorite of Elizabeth's despite her faith—who interceded with Leicester on your behalf."

William remembered Lady Magdalen, Viscountess Montague, well: the tall, stately woman who had diffused the near-swordplay between Leicester and Edward Arden at Kenilworth Castle in his youth, the day he had seen the Queen.

"I shall honor the Viscountess Montague ever hereafter," said William, amazed, and then turned his gaze on his mother. "As for my mother, and her family"—he found himself at a loss for words—"I have honored her ever."

"If you honor me in sooth," said Mary Arden Shakespeare, "then I would ask one boon of you."

"But name it."

"Be no longer my boy."

"Pardon?"

"Step forward now, William, and be a man."

"In what wise?"

"A man is judged by his fealty to family, faith, and country," said Mary. "Your family you may best serve by first having one. Anne Hathaway you have got with your child. Seek not, despite your father's counsel, to undo what God has done; seek not to murder your own with your apothecary's poisons. The child, if you will stay in this Catholic family and in this Catholic house, you will have, and a marriage sanctified."

William felt the walls of the house closing in on him, but he managed to speak. "Ay, Mum."

Mary nodded firmly. "Good. Our society, of defenders of the Old Faith, meets at regular intervals. These many years, when I have gone to visit my relations at Wilmcote, this was my true cause: to hear Mass and take both Communion and counsel. We are summoned to meet this Sunday— urgently, else your wedding plans would take precedence—at Park Hall. I shall make report of your mistreatment at Sir Lucy's hand, and—"

"I would escort you," William said.

Mary stopped. "But why?"

"For reasons threefold. One, for purposes of mine own: if there is a meeting of Catholics on the borders of Lancashire, I would seek any Cottoms who may attend, or who know their whereabouts, for I have remembrances of the school which I am bound to deliver unto John, my former master. Two, if I am now to take up the family's popish mantle, I would hear a Mass of the old rites, and mayhap take Communion. And last but not the least, I would not see my mother journey without her kin to see her kin."

Mary smiled. "I am usually wont to go with the Sadlers, our neighbors; but yours would be even more welcome company upon the road, and there are other shrines along the way, which I would have you see."

William stood and bowed deeply.

Mary stood and kissed William on the brow. "I have not been too weighty with you? I fear it; for though by all outward signs you are a man, yet methinks troubled times turn boys to men out of season."

Mary smiled, touched her son tenderly on the cheek, and rustled quietly up the stairs.

William looked at his father, who sat still upon his stool.

"Does this mean," said William carefully, "that in all these years, for the purpose of keeping out of church and the civic eye, that all your world was but a stage? That your baseness, your poverty, your love of drink, but a show?"

"Well," said John Shakespeare, "we are neither base nor poor, praise God and your mother's dowry. As for love of drink..." He shrugged, and began to laugh, low at first, then long and loudly, until William couldn't help but allow the whisper of a laugh along with him.

Chapter Twenty-nine

Knock, knock, knock! Who's there, i' the name of Beelzebub? Here's a
farmer, that hanged himself on the expectation of plenty: come in time;
have napkins enow about you; here you'll sweat for't. Knock, knock! Who's
there, in the other devil's name? Faith, here's an equivocator, that could
swear in both the scales against either scale; who committed treason enough
for God's sake, yet could not equivocate to heaven: O, come in, equivocator.

—Porter, *Macbeth*, II.iii.3

Willie winced as Alan Greenberg's Audi bottomed out with a metallic
crunch in a rut on the dirt road. That was all he needed now, to mess up
his dad's car—

"SLOW THE FUCK DOWN!" barked a voice with too much smoke
in it and as ear-rending as a band saw. Willie jumped; a half second later
he saw the ghostly apparition of an orange-vested parking lot attendant,
with stringy long hair down to his waist, a pocked face, dark sunglasses
even at night, and a gleaming walkie-talkie at his belt, float by his window.
"FIVE miles an hour!" the voice screamed again as the apparition faded in
the darkness of Willie's rearview mirror. Willie slowed down to five miles
an hour. He was barely moving.

One minute I'm going too slow, the next too fast. We as a society have a
very narrow window of acceptable behavior.

Willie stopped at a checkpoint and explained to a second, equally inimi-
cal and unclean security guard that he had passes waiting for him at the
gatehouse. A third guard growled at him to park "over there," in a long line
of cars in a cropped field of hay next to a barbed-wire fence.

Willie got out of the car and stretched his muscles after the long drive.
The sky was clear, and it was a warm night. He looked up at the stars, and
he thought of Orion's Schlong. It seemed less funny now. In the distance

he heard music, laughter, a drum beating. He took his backpack and the duffel from the trunk, and followed a sign that said PARTICIPANTS.

Approaching the performers' entrance to the Faire, he began to make out shapes in the darkness: fluttering ribbons on rough pine poles; wood frame fences swathed in burlap and guy-wired with thick rope; a Tudor-style gatehouse with a thatched roof and three windows, one of which was open. In a small courtyard in front of the gatehouse, people milled about in groups of three or four, sitting on hay bales, chatting and smoking. Although the Faire was long since closed for the day, several were in full Elizabethan costume: peasant dresses and bodices; pumpkin pants and flat caps; kilts and sporrans. A few were half costumed in baggy trousers or a skirt with a puffy shirt, an Elizabethan hat, or a cloak. Several were too cool for any of that after hours, and wore jeans and t-shirts, with a sweatshirt and perhaps a black leather motorcycle jacket against the night air. One of the fully costumed peasant girls played a reel on a recorder, while a straggly bearded middle-aged man in a kilt banged a rhythm on an Irish bodhran. A largish woman in wire-rimmed glasses sat alone on a hay bale smoking from a long-stemmed pipe. The whole place smelled not unpleasantly of mud, wet hay, tobacco, marijuana, bay laurel, and an occasional, earthier waft from the burlap-shrouded area marked PRIVIES.

Willie stepped up to the open window of the gatehouse. Inside there was a light, but he couldn't divine its source. A heavyset woman with thick spectacles regarded Willie warily.

"How might I help thee, good sir?"

"Um, I'm supposed to pick up some passes."

"Um, I'm s'posedta?" parroted the woman. "Best look to thy language, sirrah, it suiteth not this respectable shire." She had so many necklaces around her neck, of ivory and ceramic and rustic gold with inset gems, he couldn't absorb them all at once, not when she was speaking pseudo-Elizabethan at him. "Guild?" she asked.

"Excuse me?"

"What *guild* are you in? Please tell me you know."

Willie remembered his instructions from Todd. "Fools Guild." The woman looked at him like she had just sat on a grapefruit.

"Milady," Willie added lamely.

The woman shook her head, sighed loudly, opened up a recipe box, and flipped through a series of tabbed index cards. "Fools Guild. Figures. Ye fools should learn the local tongue. Name?"

"Greenberg."

She shuffled through the passes. "Willie?"

"That's me."

"Day pass, night pass, and camping pass. The full package." She eyed him suspiciously. "Thou knowest someone important, I trow?"

Willie thought of answering with an "i'faith" or an "ay, verily," but said nothing; speaking Elizabethan to a glorified and clearly power-tripping ticket taker just felt stupid.

"Can I see some ID?" the woman asked.

Willie produced his driver's license.

She squinted at it through thick glasses. "Santa Cruz."

"Yeah, UCSC."

The woman nodded. The answer seemed to satisfy her somehow.

"Who is thy guildmaster?"

"I don't know his name, I'm supposed to look for him inside. The King of the Fools."

"And you've never been here before?"

"Only as a visitor. Why, is there a problem?"

"Our entertainers are meant to be schooled in Elizabethan language, costumes, and customs."

Willie did a deep bow, leaning back on one foot and sweeping an imaginary hat off his head as he had when he'd played the Fool in a scene from *King Lear*. He sang along with the tune on the recorder behind him.

> *"He that hath and a little tiny wit—*
> *With hey, ho, the wind and the rain—*
> *Must make content with his fortunes fit,*
> *For the rain it raineth every day."*

The woman gave him a grudging nod. "Very well, Fool. Have you a costume?"

"Yes. Ay."

"Let's see it."

Willie rummaged into the duffel bag and pulled out the fool's costume, jingling and jangling. The woman looked at it distastefully. "Not a thing of beauty, but it's period."

She handed him his passes. "There you go."

"Any idea where I might find the King of Fools?"

The woman looked at him suspiciously once more. "No."

"Really? I was told everybody knows him."

"Then ask everybody," she said, and after one last, suspicious glance, looked away and made herself busy replacing the box of passes and shuffling some paperwork.

"Okay," said Willie sarcastically, "thanks, *milady.*"

As Willie stuffed his costume into his bag, a girl in a leather jacket with pink hair, a tangle of earrings in her pierced ears, and smoking a cigarette said, "If you're looking for the King of the Fools, his name's Jacob. You might try the coffeehouse. At the entrance to Witches' Wood. About four hundred yards inside, on the right. Just follow the scent of Turkish coffee."

"Thanks."

"No prob."

Willie headed toward the participants' entrance, showed his passes to the guard, and stepped through a burlap curtain into another, bizarro, universe.

Chapter Thirty

It is widely surmised that young Shakespeare witnessed performances by the touring theatrical companies that crisscrossed the English provinces. Each of these troupes was in the employ of powerful nobles who were well aware of their potential as propaganda organs, and all but the lightest comedies of the day carried political messages. Given the sociopolitical turmoil in his own life, one can imagine the young poet as both susceptible to and fascinated by the emotional and political power of the theater.

William finished out his week's work at the King's New School as inconspicuously as he could. He avoided the inns and Philip Rogers's apothecary shop, and overcame the occasional urge to visit Davy Jones's house and enquire after Rosaline. He neither saw nor spoke to any of his friends. He heard no word from his bride to be, and he sent none, though his parents were thick as thieves with the Hathaways. Mary had gotten word that Edward and Mary Arden planned to attend, and she pushed wedding plans forward with controlled panic.

After leaving the schoolhouse on Friday evening, William went home and fixed the broken cart wheel in the tanning yard, fed Lucy (the ass), then went inside and began to pack for the journey to Park Hall. William opened the trunk he shared with his brother, and took from under the bed linens at the bottom the mysterious box from Thomas Cottom. So much had happened since Robert Debdale had delivered it to him. It seemed heavier now, more sinister. The inlaid St. George's cross, a sign of the Old Faith, gleamed in the candlelight. He shook the box gently: a soft ruffle. Too light for gold. Rosaries, perhaps? The teeth or bones of a saint or martyr? Whatever it was, the last individual on earth but one to possess it had been executed, and the box and its precious contents smuggled away. He eyed the lock and briefly considered trying to break it, but then wrapped it carefully in a shawl and packed it with the rest of his gear.

While looking for a spare shirt, he came across Goody Hall's potion. What to do with it? He considered emptying it into the chamber pot, but it seemed such a waste. Ten shillings was ten shillings. He finally hid it in the bottom of the trunk where the box had lain hidden.

On Saturday, William and his mother set out from Stratford early, toward the northeast. At a tavern in the shadow of Warwick Castle, they shared a midday meal of meat pies, cheese, and ale. Then they turned northwest and rode for some hours, stopping for a late afternoon rest at Wroxhall Abbey—or what was left of it.

"What is this ruin?" William asked.

"Your grandfather on your father's side was baptized here," Mary answered with a pale smile. "I'm sorry you never met Richard Shakespeare. He was a kind man, much like your father, less many gallons of ale. His aunt Isabel was the prioress here, and his sister, your great-aunt Jane, was to succeed her. And in the village nearby lived Richard's brother William, your namesake."

William looked around at the ruined stones of the abbey, already trailing with creeping vines. "What happened here?" he asked, knowing the answer.

"The new faith came," said Mary, "and the abbey was thrown down."

They wandered amongst the stones. Mary took a rosary from her bosom and, after a look over her shoulder and a furtive genuflection, left it on the stones where the chapel's altar had once stood. Then she turned and mounted the cart.

They arrived at Park Hall after dark.

As they approached the gatehouse at the moat that surrounded the structure, a grim-looking pair of guards stepped out to bar their way with spears.

"I have no herald," said Mary, "and therefore humbly announce myself as Mary Arden Shakespeare, along with my son William Shakespeare, arrived in fealty to our Most Blessed Saint Mary and the one true church of our sweet Lord and Savior Jesus Christ."

One guard simply said "Ay, mum," and gestured to the other, who opened the gate.

As they crossed the moat and rolled up the carriageway, they passed a gardener standing by the path and leaning on a rake. Curiously, William noticed, there were no leaves to be seen anywhere about, nor trees to drop them. The approach to the great house had been entirely cleared of flora.

The ancient wooden house loomed in a tortured evening light. Park Hall was large, but time had not been kind to it. Only two windows were dimly lit with candles. The door to the great hall opened even as William and Mary walked up to it, and they were shown immediately by a young servant girl—a very pretty young servant girl, William noted, with corn-flower blue eyes, pillowy breasts, and a jest about her lips—to a guest room in the house's east wing, where they rested after the long journey from Stratford.

After an hour or so they were summoned to an evening meal in the house's great hall. There were perhaps twenty individuals. Many wore expensive clothes, gold rings, silver chains, and brooches. William felt positively Puritan—or was it simply poor?—in his travel-stained shirt, black doublet, and hose. Introductions were made, and William, who had a good head for poetry but not for names, immediately forgot most of them. There were many prominent families represented: Throckmortons, male and female, including Sir Thomas himself; two quiet and intense sisters, the daughters of Lord Vaux; Sir William Catesby, master of Coughton Court; Underhills from the south; a Richard Owen. There were also Smiths, lords of the manor of Shottery. William hoped they wouldn't ask him about their neighbors the Hathaways and the impending nuptials. There were also the Reynoldses of Stratford, along with several of their household that he recognized. Their presence made William feel less conspicuously out of his depth, for Master Reynolds was a yeoman, yet had he not honored William's own father when he was bailiff? And there was a haunted, smelly young man at the end of the table, who began drinking great draughts of wine the second he arrived and roundly insulted anyone who approached him. William asked his mother his name. "My cousin John Somerville, and best to stay well clear of him. A ha'penny short of a shilling, as they say."

At last Edward Arden entered, and bade his guests to table, and he went around greeting them one by one. When he stopped to greet Mary, he looked at William in amazement, and asked his age. "Eighteen, my lord," William responded. Edward Arden laughed. "My father used to say he wished there were no age between ten and twenty," he said, "for there is nothing in the between but getting wenches with child, wronging the ancientry, stealing, and fighting. I hope you prove him wrong. I bid you welcome, William." He clapped William on the shoulder, took his seat, and dinner began.

Conversation was small and hushed, murmured bits of gossip from London, of Elizabeth and her court. Growing impatient at the end of the table, John Somerville finally slammed down his cup.

"Enough of this small talk and prattle, the inconsequential whisperings of schoolgirls! Have there been any fresh roastings of Catholic cocks and guts this fortnight? Nay, the answer I know, for there are such feasts aplenty at Tyburn these days. Have they been avenged? Nay, answer that not, neither, for I see the lily-hued answers in every one of your pied faces. We dine only upon pheasants and capons tonight, and shall not taste revenge."

There was a silence. Robert Arden finally replied from the head of the table where he sat under a tapestry of the family crest that covered an entire wall. "Such stuff is not meet for table talk. We will have a full account of the state of our cause after our morning's assembly. Tonight, we celebrate our congregation with mirth. Eat apace, for there are players here to entertain you withal."

When the meal was finished, the company was led through the back of the house to a fountained courtyard. For once, William wished he wore a hat. It was a cold November evening, and despite the warmth from the many torches that lit the stage, he shivered in his inadequate cloak. Robert Arden announced that they would have the great pleasure of watching the Earl of Leicester's Men—"his players, not his pursuivants," Arden noted to a grim laugh—enact a play entitled *The Greek Maid*.

It was a tragedy, the tale of an innocent and devout maiden named Europa who was lured by Zeus, in the guise of bull, to take a ride upon him so that he might ravish her. It was immediately clear to everyone present that the tale was an allegory of innocent Catholics all across Europe being abused at the hands of a new and bestial incarnation of an old faith. And though William was cold, he watched, rapt. He knew the tale well from

Ovid, but the company of performers, Leicester's Men, were good. Very good.

The bull came to stamp in a meadow where the Phoenician maidens picnicked. Europa, the maiden, taken in by the beautiful, shining beast, approached it slowly in her flowing white robe, and tentatively caressed the bull's flanks. Frightened at first but then awed and seduced by the sonorous rumble of the bull's voice that emanated from behind a mask, she dared to touch a gleaming white horn—

A flash of gunpowder.

And when William's momentarily blinded eyes adjusted, he saw that the bull now carried the terrified Europa across the sea—via a water effect much as William had pictured for the fountain of Salmacis—to Crete,   . where, while tambours beat and viols sawed as though unstrung, the bull transformed with a whisk of a mask into wide-browed, almighty Zeus, who raped and then imprisoned the maiden.

Europa's final soliloquy, in her captivity, was heartrending:

"Pity me my fate, to be seduced by such a beast, so seeming-fair, so simple and so pure, without rich robes or jeweled scepters, with horns like a shining crescent moon, and yet to be at last betrayed. Cruel was the god that gored me, and left me to wither and die, thus a world away from kith and kin, in a forsaken tower of the Palace of Minos."

William's mother, sitting next to him, was crying.

His own tears he held back.

Chapter Thirty-one

Come now; what masques, what dances shall we have,
To wear away this long age of three hours
Between our after-supper and bed-time?
Where is our usual manager of mirth?
What revels are in hand? Is there no play,
To ease the anguish of a torturing hour?

—Theseus, *A Midsummer Night's Dream*, V.i.32

Willie had been to a Renaissance Faire, once, during the day, so he thought he was prepared for the temporal jolt that awaited him. He was ready for the jostling of genuine and well-researched Elizabethan elements—costumes, signage, and language, men with beards of formal cut, and women with voluminous whalebone-enhanced boobs—side by side with a retro sixties hippie culture of crystals and unicorns, herbal teas and drip-wax candles, all beneath an overlay of 1980s marketing sensibility: everything that was blatantly un-Elizabethan—generators, first aid outposts, pay phones—was swathed in burlap, but the ale-stands proudly advertised Dr. Pepper.

Willie was ready for all that.

But he'd never been to the Faire at night.

The temporal collision after dark was like that of a VW bus, a Harley, and a hay cart. Part geekfest, part campout, part house party, part orgy. As Willie entered, he saw a food booth directly across from the entrance crowded with half-costumed individuals lining up for a cheap dinner of pasta and garlic bread. To his left under a tattered burlap roof upheld with gnarled oak staves was a blacksmith's, complete with forge and anvil, filled with burly, hairy Scots. They all wore kilts, some wore tam-o'-shanters, some wore cloaks, some wore leather jackets. They all drank Michelob, and distorted Dire Straits blared from the blown-out speakers of a boom box on a hay bale. Unnoticed by the partying Picts, Willie passed along the dirt road toward the canopy of oak trees to his right.

He walked a little farther and, as promised, he caught a whiff of coffee and chai and cardamom, and a burst of music and laughter borne on the same breeze. He followed his nose to where the floor of the narrow valley rose up to meet the oak trees, and found a Middle Eastern coffeehouse, its signage all faux-Arabic script, with garden seating on hay bales around a stage under a small oak tree to one side. A dumbek drummer with long braided hair and a cigarette hanging from his mouth played alongside a twenty-something with a shaved head, a Gang of Four t-shirt, and knee-high, soft-leather boots, caressing out an Arabic melody on what looked like an Elizabethan lute yet sounded straight out of *Aladdin*. On the stage two belly dancers undulated, wearing sparkly Egyptian cotton skirts and t-shirts that said:

I'M WITH STUPID $\rightarrow$ and $\leftarrow$ I'M WITH STUPID

Willie stepped up to the coffeehouse counter. Behind it milled five or six women, all young and pretty, pouring hot water that seemed to come from nowhere into battered copper pots. A girl behind the counter smiled and came over to him. "Hi, there. What can I getcha?"

"Just coffee."

The girl smiled and came back a second later with a hot foam cup of what turned out to be very good java. "Do you want anything to eat?" she asked chirpily.

"No, thanks," Willie responded, stirring half-and-half into his cup. He was a little hungry, but the plate of food a customer was taking away was an entirely unappetizing pile of mush.

"Yeah, it's not very good," the girl offered. "I'm just so hungry. I totally forgot to have lunch, and I'm not really supposed to be working tonight, but I started, and now one of the other girls disappeared, so I should stay because it's really busy. Ugh."

It did seem busy behind the counter, but the girl seemed to show no urgency to return to serving customers. She was pretty in a classic-film style: black hair, brown eyes, lips made up with bright, deep red lipstick, that kind of perfect skin where she could've been an old fifteen or a young fifty.

"Hey," Willie said—anyone who liked to talk this much would as a matter of course know lots of people—"I'm looking for Jacob. Is he around?"

"Jacob, fool Jacob?" asked the girl-woman, but didn't wait for a response. "He was here a little while ago, but I think he's at the show. Why, do you need something? Because I have some mushrooms," she said helpfully.

"What show?" Willie asked.

"The night show, at the main stage."

"Which would be where?"

The girl-woman laughed. "You're *new* around here, aren't you? Come on, I'll take you."

"Oh...okay, thanks. That'd be great. What do I owe you for the coffee?"

"Didn't I take your money already?" She giggled. "I didn't, did I? I'm not very good at this." She giggled some more. "Hang on, I'll be right out." She disappeared, and Willie saw one of the other girls behind the counter shake her head as she watched the giggling girl-woman shuffle her way out a side door. She still hadn't collected Willie's money.

Nice gal, glad she doesn't work for me.

Willie's new friend—Rebecca, he learned—chattered their way up the canyon beyond the coffeehouse. It was pitch-black under the oak trees, and she produced a flashlight. Willie wished he'd been smart enough to bring his own. But as he watched, a raucous glow in the darkness of the dirt road ahead resolved itself into a gaggle of girls wearing a variety of colored, plastic glow sticks around their necks, singing an Irish neo-folk punk tune loudly and not entirely off-key. Trailing them was a little girl of no more than ten. She came running up to Willie with a big smudge of dirt on her cheek and a glowing blue fluorescent tube hanging from her necklace.

"You want some LSD on a stick?" she asked innocently.

"Sure," said Willie, caught a little off guard.

"Bend over," the little girl replied.

Willie did so and she fastened the necklace around his neck, stepped back to regard him for an instant, cocked her head. *"That's* pretty," she said, and skipped off to rejoin the wandering punk minstrels. Rebecca laughed, and said, "Welcome to Witches' Wood!" She led him into a space hidden behind a tarot-reader's booth that was draped with Indian fabrics and strewn with Moroccan pillows. As Rebecca rummaged for her jacket, Willie saw a tarot deck sitting on a table. He flipped over the top card, fully expecting it to be the Fool. It wasn't. He couldn't make it out at first in the dim light. He held his LSD on a stick up to it, and saw that it depicted a young man, contemplating the leaves bursting forth from a staff in his right hand.

"Page of Wands," Rebecca said, putting on her denim jacket. "I love that card. It's just, like, go! Be creative, be daring. Jump up and invent a new solution, on the spot! Trust your free will! I forget, did you say you wanted some shrooms?" She reached into an inside pocket and pulled out a small baggie with two small mushrooms in it. "Because I already took as many as I need. You can have these if you want 'em."

"Are they any good?"

"Oh, *yeah*, they are, I'm seeing God."

Willie took the mushrooms from the baggie and held them up. In the light cast by his luminescent necklace, they glowed blue.

He handed the baggie back. "No, thanks," he said. "I really need to make a delivery."

Willie and his new friend strolled back toward the center of the Faire, passing small groups carrying flashlights. Most booths were dark. There was a grungy-looking party going on at the archery range, all bleary eyes and Grateful Dead. Farther along, one of the ale stands had Bon Jovi blaring out an open side door, and Willie caught a glimpse of a bare breast peeking out from a puffy green dyed shirt as a girl raised an arm and a beer inside and screamed "Wooooo!" to *Slippery When Wet*.

"You want a beer?" asked Rebecca, nodding toward the ale stand.

"No, I'm good."

They passed one stage—the Inn Yard—dark now, though surrounded by a veritable food court of Elizabethan dining options: turkey legs, roast beef, cheese pies. Willie heard a loud wave of laughter coming from over the hill. They came around a bend in the valley, and he saw the main stage, forty feet wide, thirty feet deep, twenty feet high, festooned with flowers, ribbons and pennants fluttering in the evening breeze. A replica of Francis Drake's *Golden Hind* dominated one side. The stage was lit by the headlights of three idling long-bed pickup trucks parked around the perimeter of the rows of hay bales. There was an audience the size of which astounded Willie: four hundred perhaps. There were three guys performing some sort of broad comedy. As he got closer he recognized the guy in the dress. Tonight he was wearing not Elizabethan costume, but a fetching leopard-print miniskirt with pink, jeweled, plastic-rimmed sunglasses, a Marilyn Monroe wig, and giant breasts made of balloons. He was astride the bowsprit of the *Golden Hind*, riding it like a drunk girl on a rhinestone-cowboy bar bronco. And he seemed to be having an orgasm.

"No wonder they call it the *Golden Behind!*" he shrieked, his voice piercing through the crowd murmur and idling engines.

"Oh, yay!" said Rebecca, clapping her hands giddily like she had just been given a pony. "We got here in time for the Short Sharp Shakespeare show. Their night shows are the best. They always do something totally new."

The three guys in sneakers were nearing the end of an extended crowd-gathering introduction and launching into the main thrust of their performance.

"We now present for your late-night irritainment, the premiere of a work years in the making!"

The crowd cheered.

"A dramatization of our forthcoming seven-volume scholarly epic of Shakespearean studies..."

A rousing chorus of booos and scattered catcalls of "boring, boring!"

And then, with a devilish smile, one said, "Entitled..." and then the three belted out in unison, "*A Compendium of Drug Use in Shakespeare!*"

Wild cheers. Someone blew a horn, others beat on drums and shook tambourines or beat on their pewter cups. "You mean drug use backstage!" yelled a hairy, bearded man with a watermelon rind on his head. The heckle got a laugh, too.

The troupe momentarily ignored the watermelon-head. "We dedicate this performance to Ronald Reagan, Carlton Turner, and the entire Drug Enforcement Agency... who are sitting right over there. Thanks for coming!" Willie jerked his head hard toward where the troupe pointed, but it was of course a joke, addressed to a couple of Ren Faire security guards standing to one side with walkie-talkies. "Hi, guys," said one of the troupe to the guards. "Please arrest the heckler with the watermelon on his head."

The guards nodded and laughed along with the crowd. They were likely just as high as everyone else.

Covered by the laugh and seemingly from nowhere, like in a Warner Bros. cartoon, the threesome produced dirty, ragged cloaks, hunched over an imaginary pot, and launched into the witches' scene from *Macbeth*.

"Double, double toil and trouble," all three chanted in croaky voices, "Fire burn, and cauldron bubble."

Then one, witchlike, continued:

> *"Round about the cauldron go;*
> *In the poison'd entrails throw.*
> *Toad, that under cold stone*
> *Days and nights has thirty-one*
> *Swelter'd venom sleeping got,*
> *Boil thou first i' the charmed pot."*

And they all chanted in unison again, "Double, double toil and trouble; Fire burn, and cauldron bubble."

There was an uncomfortable pause.

Finally the bearded guy stage-whispered to the guy in the dress, "The toad, Pete. Throw it in!" And the guy in the dress produced a large rubber toad. He started to throw it in the pot, but first pulled it suddenly to his mouth and gave it a huge lick with what seemed a freakishly long tongue. The other two grabbed at the toad. After a brief scuffle, one snatched it up and gave it a wholly too-sensual French kiss before throwing it in the pot. Finally the bearded guy chanted with increasingly manic intensity:

> *"Scale of dragon, tooth of wolf,*
> *Witches' mummy, maw and gulf*
> *Of the ravin'd salt-sea shark,*
> *Root of hemlock digg'd i' the dark,*
> *Liver of blaspheming Jew,*

Gall of goat, and slips of yew
Silver'd in the moon's eclipse,
Nose of Turk and Tartar's lips,
Finger of birth-strangled babe
Ditch-deliver'd—"

"Dude. DUDE! Chill out," interrupted one.

"That is some sick shit, man," said the other.

"Birth-strangled babe? And what was that about Jews and liver? That is such a stereotype."

And they continued on in that vein, moving quickly to other Shakespearean scenes of poisoning, drinking, and imbibing of potions. Gertrude got hilariously, rippingly drunk watching Hamlet and Laertes trying to prick each other with blades dipped in LSD. In a gay porn takeoff, Phuck squeezed the juice of a concupiscence-inducing flower into the eyes of a foursome of Greek lovers, a fairy, and a guy named Bottom, in a Shakespearean donkey show.

"Wanna get high? Take it in the eye!
Wanna have a blast? Do it with an ass!"

Finally a befuddled, lecherous friar who only had eyes for Romeo's "Golden Behind" gave Juliet a sackful of sleeping pills accompanied by a string of tasteless Marilyn Monroe jokes. Romeo discovered Juliet face-down on a bathroom floor and wailed over her death, ignoring her cartoony snore (ZZZZAAAWP—*wee-weeweewee*...ZZZZAAAWP—*weeweewee-weewee*). Inconsolable, Romeo bought some goods from a passing drug dealer—who assured him "It's killer shit"—guzzled it, and promptly died on top of Juliet, his last breath a comically choked whisper:

"O true apothecary! Thy drugs are quick!"

Chapter Thirty-two

*How could Shakespeare, if he was an oppressed Catholic, be so
essentially apolitical in his drama? As any touring actor knows, audience
sensibilities can vary widely from town to town: one night an audience
of urban intellectuals, the next a beer-swilling, blue-collar crowd. At
some point, Shakespeare the young dramatist seems to have learned that
tailoring the play to the playgoer is simply good business. Perhaps it is
that very dexterity that helped his drama, first among his contemporaries,
to transcend politics and reveal a universal compassion and humanity.*

The play was done. The musicians were playing a dance and the mood
had lightened. There was ale and William stood next to the tap, drinking
and feeling out of place. Mary was across the courtyard, talking with her
Arden relations. A young man came up to the tap next to William. He
looked familiar.

"Is there aught left for a thirsty player?"

"Ay, ay," William said, and stepped aside from the tap for the boy, whom
he now recognized. "Fie, a pox upon me for my sight. Europa! Well done,
well done! Your source I know well, yet ne'er have I seen the story upon
the stage. Surpassing fair," said William, and raised his cup.

"Thank you, my lord," said the lad, bowing. "Richard Burbage, at your
service."

"To a lord your service may be, but not to me, for I am none," William
replied.

"May not service also be unto a lady? For so I am told."

"Marry, and some might say 'tis the best service, though all here would
put God first, I fear. But pray you, sirrah, do you call me a lady?"

"I know not what else to call you, for I know not your name."

William told him and they poured another ale together.

"How comes it," William asked, "that Leicester's Men play thus with unbated swords in the matter of the Old Faith, when your patron the Earl wields a mace for the new?"

The young man shrugged. "These are matters for greater minds than mine. You might ask my father." He nodded to the older man now approaching the tap: the player who had enacted Zeus and the Bull behind their masks. His clothes were neat but of an older style, and ragged around the edges. He wore a leather codpiece. "Father, this is William Shakespeare. My father, James Burbage. William here has a query—"

"I heard, Richard." He gave William a glance while he poured his beer. "Our patron Leicester is of the new faith, to be sure. In his company of players, there are many faiths: those who profess the new faith, those who openly profess the Old Faith, those who profess the new but practice the Old, and the lion's share who are wanton sinners and have only the faith that they shall burn in hell for it. I myself am in some two of those categories."

James Burbage turned and raised his cup, drained it, reloaded, and continued, "We may play wanton with many commandments, but to a man we obey the first commandment of the theater: Know Thy Audience. It is not difficult, in a Protestant house, for us to but move this wink here and that nod there, and of a sudden our Catholic screed becomes a Puritan parable of Zeus as Pope, raping innocent, devout Europe—and Elizabeth most personally—via his *Papal Bull*."

"So you are troubled not by the crimes against our Catholic priests? Betrayal, injustice, hangings, beheadings?" William asked.

"This is the stuff our plays are made on. Without such suffering, we would have neither art nor commerce," Burbage said.

"You cannot be so faithless, and so cruel."

Burbage shifted. He lifted his codpiece. He scratched underneath it. Finally he said, "I'm old enough to remember, lad, that there were all those crimes of man against man under our last Sovereign—Bloody Mary, as some call her—and burnings beside. Many more died for their faith in her five years' reign than in Elizabeth's twenty-five. No faith, it seems, owns the market on butchery. Our butchery, at least, is but playacting. We show men as they are, as they were, as they could be. We are a glass, wherein men look and learn, mayhap, something of themselves. For performing that office, we need beg no forgiveness."

"And yet," said William, "you perform here, amongst this particular company, with seeming passion."

"*Seeming* is our trade. And there's profit in it, too. There is insatiable hunger in England for theater. In London especially. A man may make a pretty penny upon the stage, if he will but commit to London nine months a year."

"And besides," said young Richard Burbage, "who would not play with passion, who wishes to be a player? 'Tis the best of all possible worlds, to act, and dress up, and travel the country. We've just come from Coventry, and play Shrewsbury next."

William was silent for a moment. The pretty servant girl came up to the tap, carrying a tray of empty mugs. "Pray you pardon, my lord," she said.

William turned to look at the elder Burbage—but Burbage was looking at William.

"Master Shakespeare," the girl clarified.

William turned, surprised. His father was Master Shakespeare. Yet he liked being called "my lord" by a curtsying girl with pillowy breasts. "Ay?" William said.

"My lord Arden has summoned you to a council, my lord."

"Me?"

"Ay, my lord. This way."

William looked at Mary, who had watched the exchange from nearby. She nodded to him with a proud smile.

Chapter Thirty-three

The best actors in the world, either for tragedy,
comedy, history, pastoral, pastoral-comical,
historical-pastoral, tragical-historical, tragical-
comical-historical-pastoral, scene individable, or
poem unlimited; Seneca cannot be too heavy, nor
Plautus too light. For the law of writ and the
liberty, these are the only men.

—Polonius, *Hamlet*, II.ii.396

After the play, Rebecca wanted to go talk to Pete, the guy in the dress. But Willie wasn't comfortable with other people's backstages. He never waited to meet guys in bands or actors in shows or—well, once he waited to meet an actress in a show, but he was trying to stay focused. "I should really find Jacob."

"If he's here, he'll be backstage. Come on," Rebecca said, and took Willie by the hand. They made their way through the hay bales as horns and noisemakers razzed about them. Short Sharp Shakespeare had been followed by a men's vocal group singing lusty versions of already bawdy songs while wearing fishnet hose and G-strings.

"*My man John put his thing that was long*
Into my maid Mary's thing that was hairy…"

With a nod and a casual "hey" to the security guard, Rebecca strode past a sign saying Actors Only, and through a burlap curtain. Backstage, the costumes were a blur of color and freakiness. Willie had a vague impression of Zeffirelli's *Romeo and Juliet* meeting a John Waters movie.

Rebecca walked up to Pete, who sat on a hay bale, taking off his miniskirt.

"Hi, handsome!" Rebecca said, and ran toward him. "Great show! *What* a great show. Ohmigod, drugs in Shakespeare, where did you get *that* idea!? I was dying! This is my friend Willie, he's looking for Jacob, have you seen Jacob?"

"Um, thanks...hi...no, no, I haven't," Pete replied, trying to catch up with Rebecca's flurry of questions. "He was here, but I think he went to actors' camp."

Willie remembered Todd's instructions: *He has a joker flag flying over his tent.* "And which way would that be?"

"That way..." said Pete vaguely, then did a double take at Willie. "Do I know you?"

"I was your heckler in Berkeley yesterday. *Fuck you, Romeo.*"

"Right, right! That was really funny. How's it going? How'd you like the show?"

"Hysterical. Especially the digs at Reagan. I thought you missed a couple of obvious drug references, though."

"Really? Like what?" Pete asked, genuinely curious.

Willie shrugged. "I thought for sure you were going to do a gag of Cleopatra getting off on the asp poisoning." Willie mimed holding a wriggling snake in front of himself and shrilled out in a piercing falsetto, "Come, thou mortal wretch! With thy sharp teeth this knot intrinsicate of life at once untie! Where art thou, death?" He mimed putting the snake to his nipple, and faked a breathless orgasm, "Come hither, come, come, COME!" and finally made with his lips a credible sound effect of a balloon bursting and a breast deflating. He gestured to Pete's balloon breasts. "Wouldn't be too hard to put a pin in a rubber snake and pop one of those babies."

Pete looked Willie up and down. "You an actor?"

"Not professionally. I've done some Shakespeare."

"Hunh."

"So," said Rebecca to Willie—she was clearly bored of the Shakespeare chat—"if you go out to the main road, back the way we came, but when you see the security guard on the right, you go up the hill. Actors' camp is at the top."

Willie's time with Rebecca was apparently done. She was sitting on the hay bale next to Pete while he undressed, and it didn't look like she was leaving.

Feeling suddenly like a third wheel, Willie said, "Okay, thanks. Nice meeting you. See you around."

"Okay, bye," said Rebecca sweetly enough, but she was already making goo-goo eyes at Pete.

"See ya," said Pete.

Actors, Willie thought. He followed Rebecca's directions, out the burlap curtain and past the singing troupe.

> *"Beneath the spreading chestnut tree*
> *The Village Idiot sat,*
> *Amusing himself by abusing himself*
> *And catching it in his hat..."*

Willie heard the cheers and the shouted choruses fade as he walked around the corner. He saw a group of actors headed up the hill and fell in behind them. He showed his paperwork to a security guard, who examined it closely and looked suspiciously at Willie's street clothes and small bag. Willie felt his heart race.

"You staying in camp?" he said.

"Yeah."

"Already got a site? It's crowded tonight, because of the night show."

"I'm hoping there's a girl waiting for me in her tent," Willie lied. Then he added, for credibility, "Rebecca."

The guard smiled slightly at the name. "If you can get her to stop talking, maybe you'll get lucky," he said, and let him pass.

Chapter Thirty-four

Shakespeare's plays are filled with cautionary tales of conspiracy, rebellion, and usurpation. From Hotspur to Macbeth to Brutus to the restive gangs of Romeo's Verona, murderous or intemperate youths drive many a plot. Shakespeare certainly had ample models for such characters among the Catholic conspirators of his day.

The pretty servant girl led William up a narrow stair into a high turret of the house. There, a ladder descended from the ceiling and William climbed through a hole that opened out into a hidden chamber, set up as a council room. Already there were a dozen or so of the company from downstairs assembled about the table, talking in low tones. William sat down, feeling more out of place than ever. After a few minutes Edward Arden rose, and the room quieted.

He led the room in the Lord's Prayer, and then spoke. "Good gentles all, friends and family of the one true faith, I bid you welcome to Park Hall. We have congregated in what should be joy and peace and to celebrate the sacrament, yet there are worldly matters which demand our attention.

"When last we met, a year past, there was great promise. Fathers Edmund Campion and Robert Persons were here, spreading hope and resolve that we might practice our faith, quietly if neither in secret nor in glory. And now are those two excellent men martyred, along with Thomas Cottom and many more beside, and Tyburn's noose closes ever more tightly about us.

"Also, we have of late heard a rumor which, if true, bodes well for Elizabeth's spinner of webs, the spymaster Walsingham, yet most ill for our cause: Robert Debdale, 'tis said, has been set free from the Tower of London."

There were murmurs around the table, and faces looked grave. Master Smith of Shottery asked the same question that was on William's mind.

"Should we not rejoice that our friend and neighbor has been set free? This will not be ill news to the Debdales, nor the Hathaways, Paces, and Richardsons of our village."

"In his freedom, we may rejoice," Arden replied. "Yet I fear the price he paid to gain it. Others such as Campion have watched their own entrails burned rather than speak the names of those who preach the Old Faith, and the names of those who harbor them. We may hope that Debdale also kept faith, and that his release was gained in some other wise. But we must double our discretion—"

He was interrupted by a loud laugh from John Somerville. "What, shall we dig deeper holes in which to cower?! Weave darker cloaks in which to shroud our womanish tears of melancholy? Fie on discretion! Let us *act*!"

"What would you have us do, John Somerville?" said Edward Arden.

"What ought to have been done the instant the whore Anne Boleyn's daughter Bess first drew blood upon our priests: cut her throat i'the very church she has with blood defiled."

There was a silence, and an uncomfortable shifting.

Edward Arden bristled. "You speak treason, sir, and foolishness beside. You would have us murder an anointed prince, and to the enmity of her spymasters and torturers add that of all England? The sky of Warwickshire would blacken with the smoke of those burned in the reprisals."

"Only if we merely pray, and wait to be burned. Let *us* rather do the burning, to save ourselves and our faith."

"If we resort to burnings, we have already lost our faith," said Robert Arden.

"Then it is lost; that gone, I will have no more of losing friends, and neighbors, and countrymen." He stood up, tipping over his chair. He pulled from his breeches a matchlock gun. No one moved.

"By God, if you, my good and noble lords, will not act, then I shall!"

Arden lowered his voice, keeping it steady. "John," he said, "ever have I tried to love you as my daughter does, but firearms are not welcome in my council. Get you hence. Go."

Somerville waved the gun around wildly. "I go, nuncle, I go—to London, this very night, where I swear upon my grave I will go up to the Court and shoot the Queen through with this pistol!" Clumsily, he lowered himself out of the turret, his bloodshot eyes, wild hair, and finally his gun vanishing through the hole in the floor.

There was a scuffle below as another voice said, "Ho, there, look to, look to!" A moment later another face rose into the turret, one that changed William's expression from fear to joy in an instant.

It was his old schoolmaster, John Cottom.

He looked about at the assemblage, then glanced back down the hole. "I see I missed the good part," he said. "Forgive my lateness." He picked up Somerville's chair and set it right. As he sat, he saw William, and smiled.

"*Salve, Iuliemus. Quomodo Linguam Latinam agis?*"

"*Male, magister, male,*" replied William quietly.

Robert Arden closed the meeting with a prayer for Somerville, and a final warning. "Hide your rosaries, your crucifixes, and your practice of love's true rites. And beware Robert Debdale! And so, good night until we meet again for the morning's Mass."

As the company slowly dispersed, John Cottom spoke with William, asking after certain students of the New School and families of Stratford. He had relocated back to Lancashire, where, he said, "'Pope' is not a four-lettered word, for now at least."

"Magister," said William, "I have been most grievously saddened by your brother's murder."

Cottom nodded.

William continued in a low voice, "I have in my chamber a remembrance I would deliver unto you, if you will."

"And I would have it gladly," said Cottom, surprised. "But I first must needs speak with Master Arden, and I am weary from late travel. Stay you for tomorrow's Mass?"

"Ay," said William.

"Then if it please you, we may meet thereafter?"

"Ay, magister," William said.

"It is good to see you, William," said Cottom with a smile. He went to talk to Robert Arden, and William and Mary went to bed after the long, long day. Although he couldn't remember being more tired, William slept a fitful sleep.

Chapter Thirty-five

The wise man's folly is anatomiz'd
Even by the squand'ring glances of the fool.
Invest me in my motley; give me leave
To speak my mind, and I will through and through
Cleanse the foul body of th' infected world,
If they will patiently receive my medicine.

—Jaques, *As You Like It*, II.vii.56

Willie climbed a narrow, winding path up a surprisingly steep hill through silhouetted oak trees. It was late; midnight, Willie guessed. He passed a plywood building and heard the sound of running water and giggling. A couple wearing nothing but towels and carrying shampoo walked toward the ramshackle hutch. Showers. Judging by the commingled laughter and hooting, communal showers.

Beyond them, on either side of a path along the ridgeline, there were dozens of campsites under the trees. Some were elaborate parachute tents, lit with Coleman lanterns and festooned with ribbons; some were one-man pup tents; some had no tents at all, just pads and sleeping bags laid out on the ground. Small groups of revelers clustered around the larger tents, talking, drinking, laughing, smoking.

At the far end of the camp, Willie saw a large white tent with a single colorful flag flying over it: a playing-card joker, in the exact same pose as a Tarot-deck Fool, stepping fearlessly and fatefully off a cliff and out into the void. The fool's costume, he noted, looked much like the one he carried in his bag.

Willie approached the tent. There were camp chairs and a lantern set out in front. A bottle of single-malt Scotch, an ashtray, and several beer bottles were scattered about. Laughter and hushed voices came from the tent.

"Hello?" Willie called toward the tent. No one seemed to have heard. The giggling inside continued. "Hello?!" Willie called louder.

"Hello!" came a female voice in response that was somehow simultaneously annoyed and amused.

"Sorry, I'm looking for Jacob."

"Who wants him?" said a male voice.

"My name's Willie. I'm a friend of Todd's. From Santa Cruz."

There was a pause.

A moment later a head popped out of the tent's door flap: a slender, smiling face, with a pointed nose, eyes lined with crow's-feet, wire-rimmed spectacles, and a long, braided beard with small flowers woven into the braids.

"Hello," Jacob said. "Welcome to paradise!" More giggles from the tent behind him—more than one person. "Pull up a chair, my friend, I'll be right out."

Willie sat, and after a minute Jacob emerged wearing drawstring cotton pants and a Ren Faire t-shirt. "May I offer you a libation?" he asked as he sat.

"Sure, thanks."

Jacob found the least grimy shot glass available and filled it with Scotch. "William, was it?"

"Willie."

"Willie. How's Todd?"

"Oh, if you know him you know how he is."

"You go to school with him?"

"I suppose," said Willie, "though somehow I never think of him as actually going to school—"

Jacob threw his head back and laughed, a long, hearty laugh. "In faith, good sir, in faith! A scholar! What are you studying?"

"Literature. Shakespeare."

"Shakespeare!? Ah! Soft butt! What wind from yonder widow breaks, I am the yeast, and Juliet is the bun!" He grinned.

He's totally nuts.

Willie reached for his bag. "So, can we—"

Jacob stopped him. "Ah-ah-ah...not yet. Let's just chat a little. I like to get to know my transactors before transacting transactions."

"Okay," said Willie, leaning back into the camp chair.

"So tell me, o scholar, how many long, numbing years have you spent in the mouse-maze of academia?"

"I'm working on my master's thesis."

"What is it?"

"What's what?"

"Your thesis. What are you trying to *say*?"

"Oh, well..." Willie didn't know what his thesis was anymore. But for lack of any other idea, he said, "Basically, that Shakespeare was a Catholic. You see —"

Jacob threw his head back and laughed. "Bullshit!"

"What — why?"

Jacob shook his head emphatically. "Shakespeare wasn't *Catholic*. He was a *humanist*! In case you hadn't heard, there was this whole *Renaissance* thing that happened around his time?"

Willie started to protest, but Jacob continued, "Oh, sure, he might have *claimed* to be a Catholic, he might have *claimed* to be a Protestant, he might have *claimed* to be a respected married man, but we know what he was *really* doing, don't we, he was fucking and drinking and getting high on big, juicy Warwickshire *mushrooms*, wasn't he? If he's a Catholic, *I'm* a Catholic, and I actually *am* a Catholic, but I'm *not*. I mean, *nobody's* a Catholic, really, are they, especially *Catholics*. Nor *should* they be!" And he threw his head back and laughed even harder than ever. "BEND OVER, COUNTRYMEN, LEND ME YOUR BEERS!" he boomed in full voice. "My apologies, but iamb what iamb! Ha! Another libation, sir?"

Willie, stunned to silence, held out his glass. Jacob just grinned at him.

Finally, Willie spoke to break the impasse. "So...is...King of the Fools, is that a full-time thing?"

"Oh, no, it's strictly an extracurricular activity. A *super-extra*-curricular activity, a *macro-super-extra*-curricular activity, as it were." Another laugh. "Oh, no, my real, real, fake job is much more interesting: chess."

"Excuse me?"

"Chess. You know, little black and white men and horsies running around a checkerboard? I'm a professional chess player. In fact, I have a tournament tomorrow, I should REALLY get some sleep soon." He still smiled broadly, positively beaming at Willie.

"Well, okay then," said Willie as he discreetly pulled the duffel bag toward him.

"WAIT! One more thing, Willie the Shakes. Any *real* Shakespeare scholar should be able to quote a bit o' the Bard. Recite for me, forthwith and posthaste, some lines from *Hamlet. S'il vous plait.*"

"Really?"

"Please," said Jacob, and his smile, though it didn't leave, was a little tight around the edges.

No problem there: Willie had had the lines floating in his head for several minutes:

> "...*since brevity is the soul of wit,*
> *And tediousness the limbs and outward flourishes,*
> *I will be brief: your noble son is mad:*
> *Mad call I it; for, to define true madness,*
> *What is't but to be nothing else but mad?...*
> *That he is mad, 'tis true: 'tis true 'tis pity;*
> *And pity 'tis 'tis true: a foolish figure.*"

"Ha!" said Jacob. "The action suited to the word, and the word suited to the action! Well done. You are a gentleman and a scholar, Willie the Shakes."

Jacob pulled his chair over, much closer to Willie, and said, more quietly but still smiling, "I had to make sure you were who you said you were.

> "...*for we are at the stake,*
> *And bay'd about with many enemies;*
> *And some that smile have in their hearts, I fear,*
> *Millions of mischiefs.*

"From *Julius Caesar*," continued Jacob. "You'd do well to keep an eye out, Willie the Shakes. Rumor is, there are DEA agents here, at the Faire, undercover, this weekend. And you know what they say about rumors: always true. So, if you have any more deliveries to make"—and here he launched into his best Elmer Fudd impersonation—"be vewwy, vewwy careful!" And he threw his head back once again, and laughed, then drained his Scotch, stood, and went to the tent. He opened the flap and motioned Willie inside.

"Now, why don't you come into my office, *young, fresh Willie?*" He said the last three words a little too loudly toward the flap of the tent. Willie entered, and when his eyes adjusted to the light, he could see that the tent was larger than it seemed from the outside. It was filled with people, maybe seven or eight, men and women, all naked and engaged in a stunning variety of sex acts. Some looked at Willie and giggled, most continued about their business. Willie set down his duffel bag, and pulled out the fool's hat to get at Jacob's pot and his mushrooms. When Jacob saw the hat, he laughed, snatched it away gently and crowed:

"As I do live by food, I met a fool...
A worthy fool! Motley's the only wear."

Willie handed Jacob his dope; Jacob handed Willie a roll of hundred-dollar bills and his hat. Willie put the money away.

One of the orgy girls, quirkily pretty with short, bright red hair, crooked teeth, and pierced nipples, looked up from the noisy blowjob she was giving. "Your friend's cute, Jacob. Does he have a place to stay tonight?"

"Well, I don't know," said Jacob with exaggerated innocence. "*Do* you have a place to stay tonight, young, fresh Willie?"

Willie shrugged and said, "Here's a night pities neither wise man nor fool." Then he sang:

"He that has a house to put's head in has a good
*   head-piece.*
The cod-piece that will house
Before the head has any,
The head and he shall louse;
So beggars marry many."

Jacob laughed again. "What the fuck does *that* mean, fool?"

In response, Willie took off his shirt. Two of the orgy girls, and one of the orgy men, looked at him approvingly. Willie smiled. "It means, thanks for the place to crash." He rolled the shirt into a wad, tucked it into the darkest corner of the tent, laid his head down on it, and quickly fell asleep to the lullaby of gentle moanings and slurpings.

Chapter Thirty-six

If the youthful Shakespeare was, as we have conjectured, surrounded by Catholic rebels—and was possibly at some stage a rebel himself—one can't help but wonder what event or series of events caused him to turn the other cheek, to become the philosophically impartial "Gentle Will" of legend, whose works so exalted peace, order, and humility.

Mary and William woke to the sound of church bells. William rose, used the chamber pot, and looked out the small window of their room. It overlooked the courtyard where the players had played, now stone-cold in the dim morning light. The sky was ransacked with grey clouds on gray clouds. William couldn't tell if the sun had risen or not. A murder of crows circled slowly up beyond the house's western wing.

There was a knock at their door, and the pretty servant girl led them with a candle down a corridor to the great hall, gathering other guests as she went. The entire company from the night before, plus a few late arrivals, were soon assembled.

After a few moments, Robert Arden moved toward the back of the hall. "Come now," he said, and extended his hands in supplication, "all ye faithful and beloved of our Lord and Savior, sweet Jesus, come ye and see ye and hear ye that to which our Sovereign, or those who serve her, would have you remain blind and deaf."

Two servants pulled aside the large tapestry of the Arden family crest to reveal a wood-paneled wall. Another servant removed a single board from the paneling, behind which there was a single iron ring. Robert seized the ring and turned it once to the right then pushed, opening a door to a hidden corridor.

"Behold, you Lucys and Leicesters and Sir Francis Walsinghams! Here is naught but my wine cellar!" Everyone smiled grimly. Robert took a torch and led the way into the corridor. It soon ended in a flight of stairs, down which the company filed. At the bottom, William found himself in a wine cellar indeed, a small room with earthen walls and lined on three sides from the floor to the low ceiling with bottles of Rhenish and claret, sack and malmsey.

Today the wine cellar was not a wine cellar only, but also a chapel. The room was draped in tapestries depicting the Passion, and atop a low platform under a tapestry of St. George stood a simple table altar and a small ambry to hold the wine and wafers. Standing at the altar, wearing a priest's robes, was a pale man with a mop of dark hair. William recognized him from somewhere...he had seen him, just recently. Was he at the evening meal? Robert Arden approached him, and when the priest turned in greeting William saw that he held a staff, a deacon's crosier, at a certain angle, as if he were holding a rake—yes. It was the gardener. He genuflected, blessing the congregation. William's mother crossed herself and knelt quickly with the others, and William belatedly did likewise.

The Mass began. William had been to enough Protestant services at Holy Trinity Church that he could recite the rites backward. Although John never attended, Mary took the children nearly every Sunday. William himself had stopped going a year or so ago, begging other work to be done. But he hadn't been to a Catholic Mass in his memory. He only knew that it was reviled amongst the practitioners of the new faith as wicked, idolatrous, debauched. He wasn't quite sure what to expect. Virgin sacrifice perhaps.

The service was the same.

Really, almost exactly, the same as the Anglican Mass William knew.

The priest sprinkled holy water. He sang a psalm in a beautiful tenor. It was Psalm 46, and though William was lost in the voice and didn't follow all of even the simple church Latin, he noticed *turbabitur*, "shake," and also something about the breaking of spears, or was it arms? William rubbed his shoulder. The psalm sang of nations at war and kingdoms falling. It sang of God and refuge.

As the service progressed, William stood at the moments he was used to standing, knelt when he was used to kneeling. He joined in singing the Alleluia, and his voice rang out louder than he expected it to in the small space.

He noticed a few tiny—*tiny*—differences in the service, a word here and a word there, a prayer moved here, an extra saint mentioned there.

No virgins were sacrificed.

The reading of the Gospel was from Luke, and it was one of his favorites:

> *"I say unto you which hear,*
> *Love your enemies, do good to them which hate you,*
> *Bless them that curse you, and pray for them which despitefully use you.*
> *And unto him that smiteth thee on the one cheek offer also the other;*
>   *and him that taketh away thy cloak forbid not to take thy coat also."*

William rose and opened his arms to heaven and said *"Et cum spiritu tuo"* on cue, and then at last it was the time for the Eucharist, and the priest of the Old Faith mixed water and wine just as the priest of the new faith at Holy Trinity mixed water and wine, and he recited the same words of Jesus at the Last Supper:

> *"This is my body, which is given for you. Do this for a commemoration*
> *of me.... This is the chalice, the new testament in my blood, which*
> *shall be shed for you...."*

The priest placed the bread in the wine and then...then he lifted the cup over his head.

That was different.

In the new faith, this raising of the cup over the head, the adoration of the Eucharist, was deemed idolatrous. It elevated the wine and the bread—relics, things—over the spirit of Christ. It might as well be a golden calf. Or a sacrificial virgin.

The priest lowered the cup. It had been raised for all of five seconds.

William sat in wonder and amazement that this, *this* was the foul service of the Church of Rome, for which priests were whipped, starved, racked, beheaded, hanged, and drawn and quartered. In the face of the pale priest he saw a vision of a millennium of priests and deacons, bishops and arch-bishops and popes: he saw the whole of bloody Christendom backward in time: from Gregory XIII who set off riots by changing the calendar with a word; to Pius V who excommunicated Elizabeth; to Urban II who began the Crusades; to Stephen VII, who exhumed his decomposing predecessor, dressed him in papal vestments, then tried and executed him; all the way back to Clement, to Peter, to Jesus himself. He saw all the hangings, dismemberments, and burnings, and all the countless smaller, inglorious deaths—with no crowds chanting or cheering or jeering, on battlefields and in sieges, from small wounds and pricks of the bowel, from dysentery, starvation, and shock—that had been wrought in the name of Him who had preached meekness, mercy, and unconditional love of thy enemy.

William wept.

Now the congregation moved to take Communion. One by one they stepped forward and knelt and put out their tongues and waited for the priest to slip forgiveness, everlasting life, and oneness with Father, Son, and Holy Ghost on their tongues.

William hesitated. He had been baptized; he could take Communion without fear of damnation. Mary held out her hand to him. In a second he thought: *I can turn my back on the Church and deny the Eucharist; but must I then turn my back on the Word, and the words of Jesus—and what words, what perfect, beautiful words—"this is my blood of the new testament, which shall be shed for many unto remission of sins."*

As he shuffled forward in the queue, William didn't know what he would do. Even as he knelt in front of the priest, he thought he might refuse to open his mouth, and yet here he was, kneeling—

But the priest withdrew the wafer. William looked up, thinking the priest had divined his innermost thoughts. But the priest wasn't looking at him. He was looking beyond him, to the secret door. There was a sudden clamor and commotion on the stairs outside the hidden chapel, and the door burst open. It was the pretty servant girl. "My lord!" she blurted breathlessly.

The congregation turned to look at her, annoyed. There was a "sshh" or two.

"There are men crossing the lawn, my lord! Sir Thomas Lucy's men, I'm told, and they are armed."

Robert Arden moved quickly. "We must dissemble!"

There was a rush of activity. Some began to move the altar. The priest hurriedly took a wooden box from the ambry, tucked it under his arm, and turned, but he stepped sideways on the platform's edge. He fell awkwardly, and William, the closest to him, instinctively reached out and caught him. "*Benedicite*," the priest muttered, but when he tried to put weight on his right foot, he grunted in pain. Another man came to help William.

"Master Owen...my foot is lame, I fear," the priest winced to the man.

"Come, to the priest hole. Quickly now." Nicholas Owen took one of the priest's arms on his shoulder, and William took the other. Owen led them to the far side of the wine cellar, past the servant girl, who hurriedly poured from a bottle of wine into cups that Robert Arden distributed to the anxious congregation.

Owen stopped in front of a tall wine rack, left the priest in William's arms, and to William's confusion, took down a bottle of wine himself. But he wasn't drinking under stress. He reached behind the rack where the bottle had been, there was a faint *click*, and the rack swung silently on well-oiled hinges out from the wall.

'Tis a pretty rack, William thought.

Where the rack had been, Owen lifted a floorboard that was also cleverly fitted with hidden hinges. Beneath it, there was a small space with a chair, a table, some food, and a pitcher of ale.

"Help him down," said Owen, and William squeezed down the hole into the hiding space, supporting the priest as Owen lowered him. A moment later, the vestments, sacred vessels, the ambry, and finally the altar itself, deftly folded up on hinges, were passed to William. But before he could clamber back out, there was a scuffle on the stairs outside, and Owen put a finger to his lips then quickly closed the floorboard and the trick wine rack, shutting William and the priest into utter darkness.

There was a bumping and scuffling above them. He could hear the muffled voice of Robert Arden. "For what cause, good sir, are we thus disturbed at our leisure?"

"Prattle not on with your lies, my Lord Arden," said a sneering voice that William recognized instantly as that of Sir Thomas Lucy. "In the small hours of the night we arrested a member of your household, John Somerville, who was drunkenly shouting in the streets of Banbury that he had a pistol and planned to shoot the Queen through the head with it. We have been informed by this traitor that a popish Mass is to be held here upon this day, which under the law of the land is treason. And here we find, in a hidden church, a congregation of pretty papists indeed."

"This room be neither hidden nor a church, my lord," responded Arden. "It is but my wine cellar, the delights of which I am sharing with a few close and trusted guests of my household. We were of late discussing the merits of this sixty-four claret, which, though I fear past its prime, displays yet an earthy sweetness and puts me in mind of dark, ripe cherries. Will you taste?"

"Search the room," said Sir Thomas Lucy.

William and the priest, side by side in the dark, did not move. There were scufflings and knockings, soundings and tappings, as Lucy and his men tried desperately to find the priest-hide ingeniously constructed by Nicholas Owen, who had built many holes, hovels, chambers, and garrets in Catholic noble houses all over England, behind chimneys, in columns, between walls, under floors, in ceilings, wainscoting, benches, and book-shelves, and no two alike, the better to confound the pursuivants.

And confound them they did. Though footsteps trod not two feet from William's head, the floorboard didn't open. As the trembling priest took William by the hand and squeezed it, William's fingers brushed across the box that the priest clutched tightly in his hand.

The box. It was nearly the same size and shape, William thought, as the box back in their chamber. *A box with a St. George's cross on it. A remembrance from Thomas Cottom. Delivered by Robert Debdale.*

William heard Thomas Lucy speak again. "Master Rogers, take them all to the great hall, and determine their names and parishes. You, Master Belch, take a party to search the rest of the house." Overhead, a cacophony of footsteps moved away into the house. After a moment, William squeezed the priest's hand and moved, slowly, toward the hinged floorboard. He could feel, in the dark, the priest silently imploring him not to move, to be quiet. William put an ear to the floorboard. He heard nothing in the room above, only a distant bump from somewhere far away in the house.

William considered. To emerge was to endanger the priest, and thus the entire company. To leave the box untended...who knew? It all depended on what was inside. Soil from the Holy Land? Ashes, the relics of a burned priest of France? A list of names of priests in England?

He would have to take the risk, to protect one and all: the priest, the box, family, and faith.

Disengaging silently from the priest's grasping hand, he felt around above his head for a release mechanism. He found it, and after a quiet *click*, he could feel rather than hear the rack swing open. He nudged the hinged floorboard upward, slowly, slowly. Without looking back at the priest he emerged into the now empty wine cellar, and closed the floorboard and rack.

He heard muffled voices. He went silently up the stairs, carefully opened the hidden door, and peeked around the tapestry into the great hall. Henry Rogers and Sir Thomas Lucy were interrogating the company seated about the table. Mary Shakespeare sat calmly at one end, hands folded in front of her, answering the questions of Sir Thomas Lucy. "I do but visit my cousins Arden...as I do once a year in love and fealty."

"And know you aught of this, Mistress Shakespeare?" Lucy held out to her a crumpled piece of paper. "Thy brat is oft seen prowling in my park, and this was nailed to my gate hard upon his last, uninvited sojourn there." Even from across the room, William recognized the writing on the paper as his own hand: If 'lousy' is 'Lucy,' as some folk miscall it...

Mary took the paper, scanned it, and handed it back calmly. "Neither for scruple nor for art would my son write so ill a verse."

William found himself straining forward to hear his mother—and nearly cried out when two other of Lucy's men passed by within a foot of his nose, coming from the west wing of the house. They stepped around the table to present their information to Thomas Lucy, and because of the angle of the table Lucy and all his men were, for the moment, turned at least partly away from the tapestry. Mary, at the far end of the table, was facing William.

William took his opportunity. He poked his head a bit farther out, and Mary saw him. He made a motion with his eyes toward the east wing of the house.

Mary's gaze glanced over him without stopping, and she gave a barely perceptible nod, then looked up at Lucy. "Why must my lord persecute thus the Shakespeares?" She stood, and with growing agitation, her voice rising and her hands now trembling, said, "You take our honor, our livelihood, our very lands! You fine and surety us into poverty!! Our children may neither eat nor be educated, marry, it is too much!!!" And with that she rolled her eyes back in her head and went limp, as though fainting.

Lucy and his men lurched forward to catch her, and in their confusion William slipped out from behind the tapestry, along the wall, and back down the hall toward his and Mary's room in the house's as yet unsearched east wing. He slipped past the entrance to the rear courtyard garden, up the stairs, and into the room where he and Mary had slept.

He found the box where he'd left it, undisturbed. He picked it up and looked around for a hiding place. There was none. The box was too large, and the room too spare, to imagine hiding it here. He would have to make it back to the priest-hide. But now he heard the sound of footsteps coming down the hall toward him. Lucy's men were beginning to search the east wing. He heard tables being overturned. He was trapped. He looked out the small window onto the courtyard below.

William had an idea. He picked up the chamber pot in the corner. It was unemptied. He moved to the chamber door and listened for the approaching search party. When, as best as he could guess from the commotion, they had reached the door to the rear courtyard at the bottom of the stairs, he stepped across the room and flung the entire pot out the window onto the pavement below. It shattered to pieces. He stepped back into shadow and watched, heart pounding, as Lucy's men emerged into the courtyard in response to the sound. They looked at the broken crockery, then up and about wildly. One ran back inside and after a few seconds—during which William whispered to himself "please, please, please"—reemerged with Lucy and Rogers in tow. They looked at the shattered pot, and around the empty courtyard, and up toward the hall's many windows. William took up the box again, turned for the door—and gasped to see a figure watching from the doorway: the pretty servant girl.

He looked at her helplessly, but she glanced at him, then at the box, then moved quickly toward the window, and as she did she plumped her breasts up revealingly in her bodice.

"Go!" she whispered.

As William ran out the door, he heard the girl yell down to the courtyard below, "I pray you pardon good my lords, my buttery fingers were unapt to my morning's chore..." She was still talking, and Lucy's men were gawking up toward her pillowy breasts, as William glided down the stairs and past the open courtyard door.

He slipped back into the great hall and Mary, now sitting calmly in her chair again, watched him noiselessly as he ducked behind the tapestry and back down into the cellar and the priest-hide. The priest again took William's hand, and held it in silence for another two hours until the sounds of Lucy's men in the house had died away and Nicholas Owen opened the hidden floorboard.

William, still clutching the box, helped the priest out of the hole. As the pretty servant girl tended to the priest's sprained ankle, wrapping it expertly in strips of fabric torn from her skirts, William bowed to her.

"I prithee, most excellent and resourceful maid...what is thy name? For I would ever recall it as a badge of wit and beauty in equal measure."

She looked at William and smiled. "My mother calls me many things, sir: shrewish and cursed, amongst other epithets less endearing. But my friends do call me Kate."

The priest spoke to Robert Arden, gesturing to William. "My lord, is this young man known to you?"

Arden smiled a deep breath like a proud uncle. "This is my cousin William Shakespeare, son of Alderman John Shakespeare, of Stratford."

"He is a stout lad. Bless you, my son," the priest said with a benediction.

John Cottom gently took William aside, trying not to stare at the box under his arm. "William...if you are done saving priests from the rack and I know not what else, would you now deliver me the remembrance you bespoke?"

William and John Cottom found an empty room. Cottom righted a table that had been overturned in the ransacking, and William set down the locked mahogany box. "It was delivered to the New School in Stratford—by Robert Debdale, though at the time I knew him not," said William.

Cottom looked at it, and reached out to touch the inlaid cross. Tears welled up in his eyes. He crossed himself. "From my brother, Thomas," he said, softly. "Thank you. I thank you most heartily."

"I fear there is no key," William said.

"But there is," said John Cottom; and he drew a key from a chain around his neck. "This was ever how my brother sent icons and relics from Rome. Key and lockbox, by separate paths. I received the key, but never until now the box. The key have I kept, as a memorial."

William watched as Cottom inserted the key and clicked the lock open. He lifted the hinged lid. On top there was a handwritten note. Cottom picked it up. "It is in Latin," he said. "I shall translate," he added, managing despite his grief a rueful smile and a knowing look to William, his former remedial Latin pupil.

"My most dear brother John," he read, "I send these in hopes that the blessings they confer will spread throughout England and buffet our cause. They are of great holiness and power, for they have been blessed by the Holy Father himself. In faith that you will see them well bestowed, in the name of the Father, the Son, and the Holy Ghost, and the Blessed Virgin Mary, your loving brother, Thomas."

Under the note was a piece of fine velvet. John Cottom peeked beneath it, then looked at William. "This remembrance you bring unto me shall be the salvation of many of the faithful." He pulled back the velvet to show William the box's contents: many stacks of thin, square crackers.

Communion wafers blessed by the Pope.

Cottom thought for a moment. "Methinks I know where these might best be used. Know you the church at Temple Grafton?"

"Ay. It is the very church where I am to be married, in one week's time, to Anne Hathaway of Shottery."

"I'faith!? I gladly hear of it. I thought you yet young and random in your affections, but you shall find marriage a comfort in troubled times. So, you will know the priest there, Father John Frith?"

"I know him yet by reputation only. A dotard, they say, who wastes his days in the healing of birds."

"He is not so dotard as he puts on," said Cottom. "Some priests hide in holes; he hides behind age and seeming madness. It is but an antic disposition he puts on to put off the pursuivants. In sooth, he is a great bulwark of the Old Faith, and many go to him for the old rites."

Cottom folded the cloth back up, returned the note to its place, and locked the box. "You would do me a great favor if you would act the messenger one last time, and deliver this unto Father Frith, with my good wishes." And he handed William the box.

William looked at the offered sacraments. He was no longer certain that the way of dissent, of spreading the Old Faith or any faith, was his path. But it was his mentor, John Cottom, whose wit and grace glimmered even now through his profound grief, who was asking.

"Ay," William sighed, "for my teacher and master, and in recompense for my failure, despite all his efforts, in the higher learning of Latin, I will do so," he said, and took the box and key.

As they rode out from Park Hall late that morning, Mary and William passed James Burbage's troupe, loading their props and costumes onto a wagon. "Fare thee well, William Shaksper!" said Richard Burbage. "If ever you wish to become a player, seek us out. You would make a fine spear-carrier!" William waved.

Mary looked thoughtful for a moment. "Master Burbage ... do you perchance play at weddings?"

James Burbage stepped forward. "Ay, my lady, and births and funerals, too; even conceptions, if it be your pleasure."

William protested. "Mother, make not my wedding more of a spectacle—"

But the mother of the groom wasn't listening.

She continued to Burbage, "A comedy perhaps, of a young man who stumbles unwitting into wedlock, but makes the best of it."

"In fact, we have lodged amongst our trunks and sides an Italian tale of two star-crossed lovers. As writ, 'tis tragedy, but we might freely adapt it to a more festive conclusion, and produce a merry nuptial entertainment."

Mary jumped off the cart and huddled with Burbage, discussing scheduling and payment.

Chapter Thirty-seven

The grey-eyed morn smiles on the frowning night,
Chequering the eastern clouds with streaks of light,
And flecked darkness like a drunkard reels
From forth day's path and Titan's fiery wheels:
Now, ere the sun advance his burning eye,
The day to cheer and night's dank dew to dry,
I must up-fill this osier cage of ours
With baleful weeds and precious-juiced flowers.
The earth that's nature's mother is her tomb;
What is her burying grave that is her womb,
And from her womb children of divers kind
We sucking on her natural bosom find.

—Friar Lawrence, *Romeo and Juliet*, II.iii.1

There were no Ophelias in the dream this time.

"My lord, the Queen would speak with you, and presently."

I move slowly toward the woman lying on the illuminated bed.

It must be Mizti.

"Hamlet, thou hast thy father much offended."

It isn't Mizti.

Her hair is loose around her head, and lovely, a blazing nebula of stars against the dark sheets, a Van Gogh nightscape.

I sit on the bed beside her.

"Hi, Mom."

"William..." she says, laying a hand on my arm. "Given the choice, to be or not to be...always choose to be."

I know what she is going to say next: it is everything. It echoes in my
head every day of my life.

"Be who you are," she begins, but she is having difficulty speaking,
"Be...be..." and now she's drowned out by horns that blare from above,
blending with the spotlight from the stars: the hunting horn of Orion in
the heavens. The light grows blindingly bright....

And Willie awoke. The blaring horns came from the valley below along
with pipes, drums, the sounds of a booming orator, and a cheering crowd
punctuated by tambourines and bells. Sir Francis Drake was entertaining
the crowd waiting for the Faire's front gates to open. Willie was the last
one left in the tent. He panicked as he tore into his duffel bag, certain he'd
been duped and ripped off...but no, the money and the coffee can holding the giant mushroom were undisturbed.

He crawled blearily out of the tent. Jacob was now in a full fool's costume, battening down the empty camp for the day. "Good morning, Willie
the Shakes! I'm late, it's been a pleasure, there's still some coffee in the
pot." Willie poured it gladly into a ceramic mug on the table.

As Jacob hefted a large leather bag, Willie said, "I need to find the guy
they call Friar Lawrence. You have any idea where he might be?"

"In fact, I do, I do!" Jacob took off his spectacles and cleaned them. "He
says Mass every morning at the End of the World. You can still catch him
there, if you hurry. Faire thee well, fool!" As Jacob disappeared into the
forest and down the hill, he called over his shoulder, "And be on guard for
spies! Spies of the enemy!"

Willie downed his coffee, wondering what the Mass at the End of the
World must be like, then rinsed out the cup. He ducked back into the tent,
changed into his own fool's costume, and went jingling away down the hill,
with the duffel bag and the precious mushroom slung over his shoulder.

Willie presented his passes at the gate. The guard looked dubiously
at his wrinkled fool's getup, but let him pass. The Faire was a bustle of
activity: vendors putting out their wares, rumbling watering trucks spraying down the dirt in the main roadway to keep the dust down, haggard
actors, jugglers, and musicians slumped on hay bales, sipping coffee and

eating eggs and home fries to dull their collective hangover. Willie caught a whiff of bacon from the booth serving breakfast, and stopped. He was starving; he'd had no food since last night's slice of pizza. But he had to find Friar Lawrence. As he hesitated, a small parade went by: a dozen or so youngsters ringing bells and waving banners and staffs led by yet another bespectacled, chubby woman, and singing in time to a drumbeat:

"Awake, awake!
the day doth break,
Good craftsmen open your stalls.
Come greet the light,
Shake off the night,
The Faire is open to all."

No time for breakfast. Willie asked a young passing fishmonger, who was missing a front tooth, where the End of the World was.

"Marry, the very end of the Faire, my lord," she said in the curious accent that all Faire-speakers seemed to have learned. "In yonder vale," and she pointed out the direction.

Willie trotted through the Faire toward its far end, scanning back and forth for anyone dressed in friar's robes. He couldn't believe how far back the Faire wound into the oak-lined canyon. He passed one stage, then a second and a third, and dozens of booths selling dragons and candles and boots and blank books and earrings and a thousand other blurred items that didn't quite register as he ran by.

When he got to the "End of the World"—a small stage in a clearing where the Faire ended in a cul-de-sac of shady, overhanging oaks—he learned from a nearby jeweler that the Mass had just ended, and Friar Lawrence had gone off down a secret backstage path—"the freeway"—that wound along the side of the canyon behind the booths for the length of the Faire. For the moment, the stage at the End of the World was empty. There was no audience on the two dozen or so hay bales; no customers had made it back this far yet. Willie sat under the tree in his fool's costume. It was a beautiful morning, crisp and clear. Oak branches waved gently over his head. He took out his pipe, which he had reclaimed from the Audi's glove box and still had a pinch of Lebanese in it, and stealthily took a single hit.

Pleasantly buzzed, he decided to walk slowly back along the main road toward the front of the Faire, certain he'd spot Friar Lawrence. But thanks to the hash, he got easily distracted along the way. He stopped at a numismatist's booth; there was a complete set of Elizabethan coinage, and he asked to see the sixpence. It was dated 1578. Shakespeare was alive that year. He would have been fourteen. It was possible, Willie thought, that Shakespeare himself once held this coin. ELIZABETH REGINA it said on it, and other Latin he couldn't make out. The obverse had a dent across it...the remnant, perhaps of some barroom brawl. He looked at the price tag. It was cheaper than he expected. On an impulse, he bought it and put it in his pocket.

He browsed jewelry, looking idly for something for Robin, but nothing seemed her style; it was all dragons and crystals and fairies. He browsed the stall filled with nothing but blank books, but they made him think of all the work he hadn't done on his thesis. He tripped out on the melting colors at a booth filled with grotesquely dripping candles of enormous size and uncertain shape. He was trying to decide whether what he was looking at was a clipper ship or a spider's web, when he heard a female voice behind him.

"Willie?"

Willie tensed. Who would know him here? He thought of the gigantic mushroom still in his bag. Even without the pound of pot and the smaller stash of shrooms, it was still enough to be a felony. He turned, and for a second he didn't recognize the girl.

Shit...could this be an undercover agent? If so, she's the opposite of inconspicuous, she is just, yow! Some sort of Asian blend—

She had been smiling in a peculiar way, but suddenly she looked pissed off. "*Don't* tell me you don't know who I am?"

And then he recognized her. From the Faire near L.A. He remembered her kiss, her skirts hiked up, the *caelestissime strictus cunnus caelorum*, but her name...

"Hi. Hey! HEY!"

"It's Anne," she said with a withering look.

"Yeah, I know."

She looked like she didn't believe him.

"How's it going?" Willie added quickly.

"Fine," she said, "fine."

"Sorry, I didn't recognize you at first. You look a little different. Did you change your hair?"

She looked like she was about to storm off, but then she took a deep breath and forced a smile, making an effort. "Yeah. Yeah, I changed my hair. Nice costume. Looks like you're here to party."

"Oh, yeah, a little bit. Actually, I'm looking for someone. Do you know Friar Lawrence?"

She looked at him funny. "Um...yeah. He's right there." She gestured toward the next booth down the road. In front of it was a tubby man dressed in brown monk's robes, holding a meat pie aloft, and calling in a practiced, rich, resonant hawker's voice, "Get your savory meeeat pii—iieess! The most heavenly filling in heaven, hell, or on eaaaarrrrth!..."

Willie recognized the friar's voice, but couldn't place it. A cowl hid his face.

Willie turned back to Anne. He didn't want to be rude to her, but he was suddenly dying to get the deal done and get out. "Duh! Thanks, Anne, thanks. I'm sorry, but I've gotta go talk to him. It was good seeing you again—"

"Hang on, wait," Anne snapped, stopping Willie. Then she hesitated. "Look, I—I was going to try to find you, but I didn't know how. I didn't change my hair. I gained some weight. I got pregnant."

Willie was already stoned. Now he went numb. "Yeeaaahhh...?"

"I got pregnant with *you*."

Willie was stunned to silence for a moment. Then, regretting it even as he said it: "Are you sure it was me?"

If her earlier look was withering, this one was positively infernal. "Yes. I'm sure."

A voice pierced through the general noise and Willie's haze, coming from the ale stand.

"Mistress Anne Whateley, we have need of thy tapping arm!"

Anne turned and looked back at her, yelling, "I come anon, milady!" then turned back to Willie.

"I have to go back to work. I'm in a parade a little later, but otherwise, if you want to talk, I'll be at this ale stand 'til five."

Willie still didn't know what to say. He just nodded.

Anne shook her head, short, sharp movements of utter annoyance. "Okay, *bye.*"

Willie watched her go. He was so flummoxed that when he looked away, vaguely in the direction of Friar Lawrence, he barely registered that the face of the pasty-hawking priest who now turned toward him, wrapped in the monk's cowl, was one he knew.

Friar Lawrence saw Willie instantly. "Willie Greenberg! Hail and well met!"

"Friar Lawrence" was Dr. Clarence Welsh, professor of literature at UC Santa Cruz—the very man who held Willie's academic career in his hand like a slowly congealing meat pie.

Chapter Thirty-eight

*It's a truism that nothing changes one quite so much as the sudden
responsibility of marriage and parenthood. That Shakespeare faced both
in 1582 — that he would now be expected to be a provider of food for
the table and moral guidance for the family — would surely have marked
a turning point in the young poet's life.*

The week following the secret Mass at Park Hall was taken up entirely
with preparations for the wedding. William came home from the school
one day to find that John, Gilbert, and Joan — with assistance from Ralph
and George Cawdrey, Richard Field, and Richard Tyler — had cleaned up
the backyard in preparation for his bride's arrival. Mary spent the last several days with cousins at Temple Grafton, overseeing preparations for the
postwedding feast at the local inn yard.

Two nights before the wedding, William hitched up Lucy (the ass) to
the family cart. On the way out of town he picked up Ralph Cawdrey,
and together they rode to Charlecote. William had a bow and arrow, and
this time, with a single shot, he really and truly did poach a deer from Sir
Thomas Lucy's park. He and Ralph loaded it onto the cart and took it back
to Stratford: it would be the main course at William's wedding feast.

When he got home late that night, William expertly skinned the deer
and left the hide to dry in the now neatly arranged backyard. He went
quietly upstairs — and heard sobbing coming from behind Joanie's door. It
was nearly midnight.

He found her sitting miserably on her bed, tears streaming down her
face. William sat down next to her.

"How now, Joan?" he whispered, so as not to wake Gilbert asleep across
the small room. "What grief so hoary could come to one so tender and
young?"

"So young," she said, "and yet so whorey indeed. William…"

She broke into great heaving sobs, between which she choked out, "I am…quick…quick with … with child."

William was so stunned, he said nothing for a minute while Joan cried. When he recovered himself, he stammered, "Joanie…you are but *thirteen*. Who…?" She gave him the most miserable of looks, and William understood and asked no more, because he knew with a brother's intuition the answer: bonny young Spencer Lucy.

"Wish you then to be with child, and to marry?"

Joan shook her head, sobbing.

Of course she wouldn't. More than anything in the world, more even than her brother whom she idolized, she loved her father. *We'll have no talk of a union of Shakespeares and Lucys at my table. A plague on their house!*

And yet it wasn't merely that.

"He was so cruel to me, when I told him. He berated me, and I fear would have beaten me, but I ran—" She broke down sobbing again. "I would not, I would NOT marry him, nor have his child!"

"Fear not, nor weep no more," William said, and he went to the boys' room and the trunk where he had hidden the potion from Goody Hall. He returned and showed it to Joan. "This distilled liquor drink thou off, and by God's grace presently shall your affliction melt as snow beneath a summer's sun."

Joan snatched the bottle and would have drunk it right away. But William stayed her hand and led her quietly outside the house. The moon was just short of full. *Close enough*, thought William, *for neither is she waxed full*. He made her take off her blouse, and then drink the potion, and finally run three times around the house, as Goody Hall had instructed. When they returned to the bedroom, William put a blanket around her.

"We need never speak of this, but let it be a lesson to us both," William said, "hereafter not to dally unless we would our dalliance last a lifetime."

Joan nodded silently. William embraced her, and she continued sobbing until finally she fell asleep. When both woke in the morning, there was blood in Joan's bed.

William washed the bedding in one of the vats of solution in the tanning yard.

Chapter Thirty-nine

I will, as 'twere a brother of your order,
Visit both prince and people: therefore, I prithee,
Supply me with the habit and instruct me
How I may formally in person bear me
Like a true friar. More reasons for this action
At our more leisure shall I render you.

—Duke Vincentio, *Measure for Measure*, I.iii.44

A troupe performed commedia dell'arte on a small stage in front of a curtained gypsy wagon that acted as both backstage and dressing room. A lovelorn Isabella with long blonde braids sang a song about a large prop fish.

"He's got little fishy eyes,
and little fishy lips!
He's got little fishy fins
On his little fishy hips!"

In the back row of hay bales in the theater—only half full, as it was still early in the day—Willie and Clarence Welsh sat, unnoticed.

"So, Mr. Greenberg," said Welsh, "how goes your thesis? Will we have the pleasure of reading it this year?"

"Yes, sir. I hope so."

"As do I. As does the provost, and apparently, your esteemed father. Do we have a topic?"

"Yeah," said Willie evasively. "Dashka signed off on it. I have it written down, but I'm not ready to describe it verbally—"

"Try," said Welsh. "It's an excellent exercise, and perhaps I could help focus it."

Willie hesitated. "I don't think—"

"I insist," Welsh said firmly.

Hopelessly, Willie took a deep breath and said, "Well... it's based on the idea that Shakespeare was Catholic." He gave Professor Welsh the pitch, and his explication of Sonnet 23. Welsh listened carefully, urging Willie on, while at the same time he pulled from his pouch rolling papers and a small baggie of pot and deftly rolled a joint.

When Willie had finished, Clarence Welsh asked, "You haven't done too much research on this yet, have you?" And to Willie's amazement, he lit the joint.

Willie looked around nervously. It seemed everyone else nearby was fixed on the stage, laughing at the story of the girl and her fish. "I've done some. I mean, I still have more to do." Clarence Welsh passed the joint to Willie. Willie felt odd, getting high so casually with his professor, but he took a hit, just to be polite, and passed it back. *Wow. That is good. And strong. Really strong. Sledgehammer strong.*

"Because you know," Welsh continued, "the theory that Shakespeare was Catholic has been around quite a while."

Willie felt his heart sink. The smoke had expanded in his lungs, and he tried to hold it but failed, coughing. "Really?" he managed to choke out.

"Davies, in the seventeenth century, famously said Shakespeare died a papist. And it seems that you haven't yet stumbled across a book published just last year: *Shakespeare: The Lost Years*, by E. A. J. Honigmann. Or an older work entitled *The Shakespeares and the Old Faith*. Both make the same case."

"Um... no." The pot was creeping into Willie's brain. *Really strong.*

"Professor Honigmann posits the theory that Shakespeare was part of a very large Catholic network in Warwickshire and Lancashire that included his mother, Mary Arden."

"Really?" said Willie miserably.

"He further posits," said Welsh, "that Shakespeare's schoolmaster, John Cottom, likely secured young Shakespeare a post as an assistant schoolmaster in the home of a prominent Catholic family in Lancashire. This seems to me unlikely, as Shakespeare must have been in Stratford to impregnate Anne Hathaway at the time Honigmann cites, but he nevertheless presents some quite compelling arguments. If the subject interests you, you might wish to read it."

"Dashka," said Willie, the word and thoughts coming with more difficulty now, "said that every biography she'd read said he was Protestant."

"Ms. Demitra," said Welsh, "despite her talents and charms, and they are many"—he paused to take another hit—"is neither an historian nor a biographer. She is a literature student, and has had it drilled into her—once too often, perhaps—to focus strictly on the text."

"So it wouldn't be a new idea, my thesis."

"Master's theses rarely are," said Welsh.

Willie felt empty and useless. He would never finish the paper. He wasn't cut out for academia. He would go back to Berkeley, get a job in a coffeehouse or a bookstore. Maybe his dad could swing him a job on campus. He'd get an apartment. Robin would probably dump his useless ass.

Welsh seemed to sense Willie's despair. "But it's quite clever of you to have parsed that line in Sonnet Twenty-three, and come up with that thesis without having read the pertinent literature," Welsh said. "That shows promise. Tell me, aside from a possible reference to Sir Thomas More, do you see other evidence of latent Catholicism in Shakespeare's drawing of characters? That sort of moral certainty and rigid dogma?"

"Actually, no. Not at all."

"Nor do I. What do you find most compelling about Shakespeare?"

"I don't know," said Willie. He felt stoned, and a little vague, but he tried to put his deepest feelings about Shakespeare into words. "I suppose . . . the timelessness of the characters. The diversity. They're so recognizable, even to a modern reader. It's almost as if he was the very first writer to think like a modern human being."

"Ah. I concur. Shakespeare, in some sense, helped create the modern man, didn't he, his influence is that pervasive. He held the mirror up to nature, but he also created that mirror: so the image he created is the very one we hold ourselves up to. It's almost like a time-travel paradox, isn't it?"

Willie didn't follow this one. *He must be as stoned as I am.*

"So," Welsh continued, "you've just proposed a fine thesis topic: Shakespeare as the first modern playwright. Not biographically, perhaps, but as revealed in his works. How does he display a modern sensibility in his drawing of characters? His portrayal of women? His cultural and social diversity? That, I would be interested in. And of course, you might explore the possibility that if, as you suggest, he was part of an oppressed Catholic underclass, he might well have been shaped by firsthand experience of an oppressive regime that mingles politics and religion...much as we are oppressed by certain forces that would make our path to enlightenment a crime, eh?" said Welsh with a wink. "Speaking of which, I believe you are carrying something for me?"

"Here?" said Willie. The crowd in the theater had grown. On stage, the Pope appeared, deus ex machina–like, to annul the girl-with-a-fish's marriage to her evil landlord.

"I wouldn't worry," Welsh said, and held up the sleeve of his friar's robe. "Who would suspect a goodly Catholic priest of crimes against the state?" He laughed.

Willie opened his duffel and removed the coffee can. He set it on the ground, hidden between the rows of hay bales, and carefully removed the mushroom from the can.

And as he handed the giant fungus gently to Welsh, and touched it one more time, a synapse opened by Clarence Welsh's killer pot fired, and Willie saw it all in a flash. The mushroom was a modern sacrament. The forces that hounded Shakespeare and his family were like Reagan's DEA agents. Ronald Reagan was Queen Elizabeth—no, *Nancy Reagan* was Queen Elizabeth. *Just say no to Catholicism.* Carlton Turner would be Elizabeth's spymaster; what was his name? But then who were the bad guys...the ones out there hanging, drawing, quartering, and beheading in Nancy's name?

Willie looked around in a paranoid panic, and at that very instant, two figures entered the shady outdoor amphitheater.

One was a pale nobleman in austere, Puritan black garb, with a shock of red hair and an arrowhead beard honed to a razor's point. He looked entirely familiar, though Willie had never seen him before.

Next to him was a man wearing a dark cape, with long black hair, a dark mustache, and dark, burning eyes. Perhaps because he was as stoned now as he was then, Willie suddenly remembered where he had seen him first: he was there the night they found the mushroom. Dashka's friend from high school. He was on the library jitney bus, arguing Reagan's side against the bus driver. He was at the rally on Sproul Plaza. And now he was here, and he was scanning the theater. He caught Willie's gaze, and nudged the black-garbed Puritan next to him.

Willie glanced at Welsh. He was admiring the mushroom openly. Willie pictured Professor Clarence Welsh, at a metal table under a bare lightbulb. The Puritan and the mustachioed man were moving toward them. Willie grabbed and shouldered his duffel and backpack, snatched the mushroom back from Welsh, and took off running the other direction, toward the woods, without looking back. He heard Welsh, behind him.

"Willie! Wait...!"

But he was already in the forest, trees flashing by. He came on a path that headed away along the side of the canyon to his left in the direction of the center of the Faire. *The Freeway.* Two surprised jugglers saw him sprinting toward them at full speed and ducked out of the way.

Willie looked over his shoulder: there was no one else behind him, but he couldn't see far through the forest. The mushroom was still in his hand. He couldn't toss it aside; he didn't know much about drug dealing but he knew you don't leave evidence lying around. He couldn't hide it. He couldn't flush it. He couldn't keep it. So as he ran, he did the only thing he could do.

He ate it.

All thirty-two grams.

Enough, he heard Todd saying, *to get ten people ridiculously high.*

He saw an opening back into the Faire, two women passing through a flap of burlap below him. Beyond it he heard bells ringing and drums beating. He stashed his duffel and backpack neatly next to the entrance, as though they belonged there, and stepped through the burlap curtain into the Faire. Yet another parade was passing by; some sort of a mock wedding procession. At the head of it was Anne, wearing flowers in her hair. He ducked into the middle of the parade, trying to look like he fit in. And even as he did so, the psilocybin—which between his empty stomach, his adrenaline rush, and the massive size of the dose, had activated almost instantly—began to spark a million new connections in his brain.

Chapter Forty

*Whatever the nature of his engagement and marriage to Anne Hathaway,
in Shakespeare's works weddings are, with few exceptions, symbols of
unity, fruition, and abundance. Nearly every comedy ends with at least
one; several end with two; A Midsummer Night's Dream ends with
three. The sanctity of the wedding ceremony and its ability to bridge the
human and the divine (as when the god Hymen descends to perform
the quadruple wedding that ends As You Like It) became a hallmark of
Shakespeare's drama.*

The night before the wedding, John Shakespeare took William down to
the Bear for a night out. He bought round after round of ale, and about
the time his eyes were starting to glaze over, he gave his son his take on
marriage.

"My son," he said, his speech slurred and a comical wisp of hair listing
off his head like a ship's mast in a tempest, "when I wed your mother I did
it for the ducats, I freely say that now. I had naught, and she had a dowry,
and a family, and I thought someday to make us gentlemen, me and you
and Gilbert, and all the Shakespeares ever after."

He drained his mug. "And in that I failed. Yet Mary has ever been true,
and tended me when I need tending, a blessed saint. Your wife comes with
but little dowry, and yet it is not naught, for six pounds thirteen shillings
fourpence is ten marks. And ten marks is ten marks." He laughed at some
inside joke.

"But the Hathaways are a good and respected family, and if naught else
your bed will never be cold, and there's a comfort. And if once you thought
Anne fair and comely enough to bed, mayhap your bed will be warm indeed, and there's a greater comfort. And if respect and ardor grow to love,
well, there's the greatest comfort of all."

John stood on the table, nearly falling twice as he toasted William. "Come ye one and all to my son his wedding tomorrow, and see what comes to pass when a young Willy doth Shake his spear to a comely Anne who hath a way twixt the sheets!" And there was laughter and toasting all around.

Sunday, December 9, was an unusually clear day, and warm for Stratford in December, which is to say, not warm. The sun shone wanly in a clear sky, and the air was chill but not bitter. William and his family, along with his friends and neighbors, set out toward Temple Grafton in a caravan, stopping first at Anne's house in Shottery on the way. A wagon decorated with flowers and ribbons waited outside her house, but Anne was not yet finished with her couture. As William had yet to have his interview with the priest who would perform the service, it was decided that William and John should ride ahead, and the remainder of the party would follow.

Father and son arrived at the small church atop the hill in shady Temple Grafton in the late morning, and John took William to the rectory to meet Father John Frith. John Shakespeare made a brief introduction and left William, holding the box of blessed wafers, sitting at the rectory desk. The room smelled of bird droppings and fresh wood shavings. There were birdcages tucked in every corner, and a constant cacophony of squawking, chirping, and trilling.

"If you will pardon, I must tend to my patients while we speak," John Frith said. He picked up three small, soft leather bags of different colors. "I must fill up their cages with baleful weeds and precious-juiced flowers. Great, my son, is the powerful grace that lies in herbs, plants, stones, and their true qualities!"

Father John Frith was old. He had a failing white beard, braided and stained at the sides of his mouth with unidentifiable yellow dribbles. He shuffled about the cluttered room, administering medicines from the three different bags. The contents of one he gave the birds as food; one contained an herb that he rubbed under their wings; one held a sort of paste that he applied to wounds as a salve.

As he made his rounds, he gave William a rote prenuptial speech that said in many more words the same thing his father had told him the night before. But then Frith turned to William, his eyes bright as he peered over wire-rimmed spectacles.

"I am told you are baptized and confirmed in the Old Faith, is this true?"

"Yes, Father."

"Good," he said, turning back to his birds. "I solemnize weddings in both faiths, times being what they are. But my heart is only with the old rites."

William set the box of wafers down on the desk, and removed its cloth covering. "In respect of which," William said, "I commend this to you. It comes from Rome, by way of John Cottom of Lancashire, and Thomas, his brother."

Frith cocked his head at the box, and William handed him the key. Frith set down his medicines, took the key, and silently and deliberately unlocked the box. He read the note from Thomas Cottom, and crossed himself. Then he peeked under the cloth inside and smiled. He peered at William.

"Thank you, my son, for your pains in the delivery. I have no coin for your labors, but you shall receive spiritual recompense." He held up a wafer. "With this wafer blessing your wedding Communion, you shall have a rite wherein God himself lights the aisle, and angels sing i'the choir."

He replaced the wafer, closed the box, and picked up one of the many jars on the desk. "The sacrament of marriage," he continued, ministering its contents to a turtledove in the corner who stood perched on one leg, its other wrapped in a bandage, "is to me the holiest of holies, for it is at once the most human and the most divine—as is Christ, both human and divine."

He gestured up at a simple cross on the wall, which in the new style bore no ravaged body, but was a symbol only. "Those who practice the new rites forget this. They would make Him wholly divine. What of that? What means His suffering on the Cross, if His body be absent from it? What means His sacrifice, if Christ feel no human pain in the offering of it? When He was pricked, did He not bleed? If He were tickled, did He not laugh? I hope that you will feel in today's sacrament the union of the human and divine, for the bond between man and woman is both. Neither one part nor the other is diminished by the sharing, but each truly, fully, and wholly one. Remember also: when you share this holy bread that by the greatest of all mysteries becomes the very body of our Lord, that it is truly His body; and that by taking it you share Communion not with Christ only, nor just with your wife only, but with all humanity, all Creation, past, present, and future.

"It is," he concluded, tapping the box with a smile, "most powerful medicine."

William suddenly felt the urge to bare his soul to the gentle old priest.

"I confess, Father, I have of late been melancholy in thinking on what our faith has wrought. How comes it that even those who commune with Christ so oft break His very precepts by killing in His name?"

"To be human is to sin," the old priest shrugged. "'Twas ever thus, and yet we do what we can. We thank sweet Jesus for dying for our sins; we pray; we confess; and we take Communion to remember why we do so. And in that, surely, there is no harm."

He set down his bag of bird medicine. "There. I have given you all the little wisdom my great years have gathered."

He came to stand over William. "*Benedicite*," he said, and kissed William on the forehead. "Now go forth and be married."

William walked out of the rectory and into the cool air. From down the lane leading to the church came the sound of a lute and drum. The bridal procession.

He hadn't seen Anne Hathaway since he'd lost his virginity to her three months before. She was riding on the wagon, her brother Bartholomew driving. Bartholomew checked the old mare in front of the church, and helped Anne down. She wore a green gown, accented with purple and black, under a midnight blue cloak. She held a bouquet of muted fall flowers in her hand: Michaelmas daisies, primrose, and sweet rosemary. She looked handsome, William thought, in the smart but sober way he remembered her. The flowers and ribbons in her hair softened her a bit. And he knew that under the sobriety there was mischief, and softness of another order.

She kept her eyes downcast in modesty as the musicians played her down the aisle. And when she joined William at the altar, she gave him only the briefest searching look before she cast down her eyes again. In that moment, he felt a chill. He saw something eternal in her eyes. He had forgotten how blue they were: the deep blue of a lake at twilight.

And they were set off by her black hair…black, he thought, like the shining black of a raven.

For the second time in a week, William listened to the full Catholic Mass. There was again singing of psalms, prayers, and readings. The last of these John Frith had chosen from the Gospels:

> *"From the beginning of the creation God made them male and female. For this cause shall a man leave his father and mother, and cleave to his wife; And they twain shall be one flesh: so then they are no more twain, but one flesh. What therefore God hath joined together, let not man put asunder."*

William was thinking of this — of oneness — as he spoke his marriage vows, and heard Anne speak hers. As they exchanged rings, he wondered whether it was love or duty that would bring them together as one flesh. He didn't really know what that meant, to be of one flesh with another, though he had felt something of it under the influence of the witch's brew, in dreams, or at the moment of orgasm, perhaps—

He looked out upon the congregation, and caught sight of a silhouetted figure standing in the vestibule at the back of the church. This time he recognized her from a distance, just before she turned and walked out: Rosaline.

It was time for Communion. John Frith took out the box of wafers William had given him and mixed the wine and water. He took up the Eucharist. Anne and William knelt. The priest held out a wafer to Anne. She leaned forward slightly, and with her tongue, slipped it into her mouth.

And then, for the second time, William confronted the body of Christ. This time, he took the dose.

Will was bewildered. He walked along in the wedding parade, and did his best to dance and sing with the rest of the party, but he felt like he was going out of his mind. The enormity of the sacrament he'd taken, creeping through his blood like a bacchic vine, sending out tendrils to the outer edges of his very being, made him feel like something or someone else. The surroundings swirled around him dizzyingly, a confused, disorienting palate of colored burlap and ribbon; the smells were outrageous, the most elegant perfumes and scents of strange spices and exotic foods punctuated with the overpowering stench of raw sewage and unimaginable body odor.

Will rubbed his eyes; was this Temple Grafton or a country fair?

Will tried to steady himself and to recognize the faces around him. There were Father John and Mother Mary; there was Jacob; there was a woman with a bizarre pointed hat; there ahead of him was Dashka—what was she doing here? He passed a black-clad Puritan holding a Bible and screaming, "Papist sinners repent!" and a woman wearing no dress but hose, blue and so tight you could make out the shape of cunt lips underneath.

The wedding procession arrived at the Inn Yard. At one end, under the trees, was a stage where a quartet sang ribald verses. The songs he knew well, or thought he did; he couldn't understand the words, because the singers sang in an accent that was strange, strange! The perimeter of the yard was ringed by tables offering forth every manner of feasting-foods: that savory smoke must be the venison he'd poached, but there were also turkey legs, a giant meat pie in the shape of a peacock complete with a tail of delicate sugar, surrounded by small paper trays filled with potato chips. On a table was a stack of small, sweet wedding cakes the size of mini-pizzas baked as gifts by the wedding guests, and awaiting the traditional kiss over them, the first kiss between the bride and groom.

Flowing from the taps were ale, beer, and wines; and also lemonade and warm Dr. Pepper, served by a variety of wenches with teeth shockingly rotten and shockingly perfect, with skin dark as an Ethiope or pale as ice, ravaged by pox so festering that it nearly made him sick, or sculpted and painted into a vision of a beauty that surely surpassed that of Cleopatra or Helen of Troy.

Overwhelmed, he leaned against the ale stand, and looked around the crowd...there were many people here, some he recognized, many he didn't. Of course, the greater part of two villages would be here for the wedding, Shottery and Berkeley, the last weekend of the Faire and free venison courtesy of the Shakespeares.

Where is Anne?

On the small stage set for the entertainment of the Inn Yard, the singers finished and the players bounded out on stage, wearing just undershirts and hose of uncanny color and fit. After much shenanigans, they announced, "My lords and ladies, we now intend to perform for you the most mirthful tragedy of *Romeus and Juliet!*"

As they launched into a breakneck version of their prologue, Will stood astounded. He knew this story well, and yet didn't know it at all, and yet he felt he should. He knew the source: it was the very same tale of Romeus and Juliet he admired. There were pieces of the story he didn't recognize, additions or improvisations on the original; and yet the characters were so human. He knew the players, or some of them: was that Pete, in the dress, or Richard Burbage? The performance was so bold, so presentational, so entirely for the benefit of the groundlings; and yet also there were moments when the players spoke to each other as they might in the street, small and real, their gestures temperate, smooth, and gentle. He felt like all the other plays he had seen might as well have been performed by town criers or teenage drama classes for their amateurism. And yet, though he knew the tale to be a tragedy, it was witty, filled with pratfalls and slapstick.

There were also brazen jokes at the expense of Lord Burghley, Ronald Reagan, Queen Elizabeth, the Earl of Leicester, Walsingham, and Madonna.

When Romeo, for so he was called, came forth to lament his lost love, his friend and confidant named her "Rosaline." Rosaline. *A Rose by any other name*, he thought. Where had he heard that before? He remembered, or thought he remembered, the image of a red and white rose entwined, in the small of a woman's back. . . .

Will's head reeled. Time melted. He was watching, all at once, his past, his present, and his future. And then space began to melt, first the scene on stage, then the crowd around him, laughing and talking, all seemed to dissolve like the wax candle he had seen this morning, into a blur of color. The ground around him began to melt, and then his legs. He staggered away from the ale stand; he had to get out of the crowded Inn Yard, he needed to lie down, or something. He stumbled past a man in a t-shirt, with a hole where his left eye should be and a t-shirt that read I Visited the Tower of London and All I Got Was This Stupid T-shirt. He saw a sign marked Pryvat, and stepped through the flap of burlap beneath it.

The world was spinning, but what he saw inside was more confusing than anything he'd seen yet; it was a woman.

She had deep blue eyes and shining, raven-black hair. Anne Hathaway. Or was it Dashka?

And she was on her knees, deeply kissing, with cloven lips, the naked blade of another man.

The man with long black hair, a mustache, and eyes that burned like dark fire.

Immediately on seeing Will, the mustachioed man turned, hiked up his trousers, and called, "He is HERE!"

The woman saw Will, and put a trembling hand to her forehead.

Will's shock and nausea turned to desperation. He turned and sprinted back out into the Inn Yard. On all sides, men in black doublets, some lettered DEA on the back, and bearing matchlocks, swords, and AK-47s appeared, surrounding the assembled party. Within seconds, they quietly apprehended many. The Puritan with the red hair and arrowhead beard took a smiling, bespectacled man by the arm: *the priest, or the fool, or both, and an innocent regardless*, Will thought as his mind spun. He lunged forward and pulled a light sword from the scabbard of another agent in black, who had half a finger missing from his right hand and his knee in the back of a prostrate vagabond. Will knocked the surprised agent hard on the head with the sword's hilt and felt a surprising surge of satisfaction as he fell unconscious. Then Will turned and swatted the red-bearded Puritan on the behind with the broad of the blade. Furious, the Puritan let go of the bespectacled priest, who immediately ran off into the forest. The Puritan advanced toward Will, brandishing a weapon. Will might have run him through with his sword, but then he saw a tankard filled with lemonade on the hay bale next to him. He swept up the cup and threw the contents into the Puritan's face. While the Puritan yelled, momentarily blinded, Will dropped the sword, dove in between the hay bales, and belly-crawled through the audience toward the stage.

Through the confusion, the theater troupe on stage had kept playing their comedy: the show went on, and no one in the front rows of the audience noticed that anything was going on behind them. Will arrived at the side of the stage and stood stealthily, scanning quickly for the mustachioed man and the Puritan. He saw them both searching the crowd.

There was no escape he could see: agents in black were at every exit. He looked up on the stage. Romeo and Juliet had just met and fallen in love. Juliet told Romeo as he tried to steal a kiss, "No means *no!*" Juliet climbed on another man's shoulders to do the balcony scene. As she did, she farted audibly. A muffled voice came from the human balcony, "Juliet, you farted in my face!" and the hidden actor produced an impossibly tiny tinderbox and lit it with a flick of his thumb and waved it, and the groundlings gasped and laughed. Juliet called out, "Romeo, my Romeo!" and Will knew that in a moment a Romeo would enter and say, "But soft, what wind through yonder lighter breaks?" But in that instant, Will knew there was another scene, a soliloquy, before Romeo entered, and he knew what it was, and he knew that he knew it; he looked down at his clothes. Had he really worn Quiney's old codpiece today?! He checked his pouch: there was Field's dented sixpence. He felt his hat: cuckold's horns. Painfully prophetic, to be sure, but fit to the present need. He knew he'd blow the punch line to the fart joke, but it was a matter of life or death; he hoped they'd forgive him. In the instant before Romeo entered, Will leaped up on the stage and started speaking:

"Nay, I'll conjure too.
Romeo! humours! madman! passion! lover!
Appear thou in the likeness of a sigh:
I conjure thee by Rosaline's bright eyes,
By her high forehead and her scarlet lip,
By her fine foot, straight leg and quivering thigh
And the domains that there adjacent lie,
That in thy likeness thou appear to us!"

He became Mercutio: he quivered his thighs; he jingled the bells on his costume; he accented "domains" with a lewd thrust of his hips; and he threw Romeo his new entrance cue, "appear to us!" Romeo entered with a bemused look. Will crossed past him toward the curtained escape whence he'd come, and as he did he whispered, "I will explain myself anon." He exited toward the back of the stage, glancing over his shoulder toward the audience. As Romeo soldiered on, "But soft, what light through yonder window breaks?" and Juliet replied "Romeo, Romeo, wherefore art thou Romeo," he saw the mustachioed man and the Puritan, still scanning the audience, but ignoring the fools capering on the stage. Will pushed through the curtain, and finding himself backstage amid a jumble of props and wigs, he jumped into an empty costume trunk, pulled the lid closed, and stayed there until nightfall.

Chapter Forty-three

Canst thou not minister to a mind diseas'd,
Pluck from the memory a rooted sorrow,
Raze out the written troubles of the brain
And with some sweet oblivious antidote
Cleanse the stuff'd bosom of that perilous stuff
Which weighs upon the heart?

— *Macbeth*, V.iii.40

There is no documented case of a fatal overdose of psilocybin mushrooms. Unlike many fungi, they're not actually poison; about the worst that's likely to befall you physically from eating them—assuming you resist any temptation to fly off a tall building or stop a speeding train with your outstretched hand—is an upset tummy. There's also no documentation of permanent psychic damage from psilocybin. You get high; you trip; it could be fun and silly, could be intense and scary, but whatever happens, after four or five hours the high drifts away and you're yourself again.

Or, sometimes, an updated, rebooted version of yourself.

Willie spent five hours in the costume trunk. The sounds of crowd noise, Faire parades, drug busts, and Romeo and Juliet bumping about in their comical death throes turned into colors. The black, musty closeness of the trunk turned into a hum. The hum and the color became one and melted into endless geometric patterns that turned into mandalas on his eyelids. Then his eyelids melted, and then his eyes did, too, and he saw nothing and everything in dazzling light. The hum grew so loud he thought his ears would burst. And then suddenly the light became a single beam that lit a bed. On the bed was a shape...a familiar shape...his mother's hair, loose about her face, a starburst. Shades of gold pulsated in an aura around it. Her lips moved.

She said: "Given the choice to be or not to be, always choose to be." She took his arm gently, and he could feel the light enveloping him. "Be who you are. Be...be..." and she was having difficulty speaking, but then she took a last strained breath. *"Be my Will Shakespeare."* And then she smiled weakly and died.

The hum of the light and the darkness burst back upon him at once and exploded into a million million shards. He was simultaneously the hum, the light, the darkness, the destruction, and the birth of it all. He was no longer himself. He was no one. He was everyone.

He was Shakespeare. Will Shakespeare.

When the lid to the costume trunk opened, Willie had been coming down for long enough that he was reasonably confident it wasn't the lid of his own coffin. Short Sharp Shakespeare's props and costumes mistress shrieked as though it were, but she calmed down surprisingly quickly when Willie said:

"Hi."

"Hi," she responded, without missing a beat. "Lemme guess...Jack?"

As Willie looked up out of the box, Pete, the guy in the dress, leaned over and peered in.

"Oh, hey! We were wondering where you went." He helped Willie out of the trunk. "You know you kinda fucked up our fart joke, right?"

Willie winced as his limbs uncurled like Saran wrap. "I know, and I truly apologize. I hope the addition of a few lines of Mercutio to *Romeo and Juliet* wasn't too far out of line."

"No," said Pete, "not at all. Actually, we might keep it." Then, after a short pause, he asked lightly, "Hey, you want to join a comedy Shakespeare troupe?"

Willie didn't answer right away. He just nodded for a few moments, thinking. Finally he asked, "Was it but my idle fancy...or was there a DEA raid during *Romeo and Juliet*?"

Pete nodded in disbelief. "Yeah. There was."

Willie thought for another moment. Then he said, "I like the political material in your show. If I joined, could we do even more?"

Pete nodded back. "Abso-fucking-lutely."

When Willie came back out into the Faire, it was the end of the day. Everyone was tired and dirty, drunk and happy. A wind had kicked up. The dust of the day blew through the canyon and caught the golden afternoon light filtering through the oak trees. Willie asked a passing girl—dressed inexplicably as a vampire—the time. "Five o'clock," she said. He went straight to the ale stand, where Anne should just be getting off of work. As he approached, she emerged from the workers' entrance.

She smiled at seeing him, and spoke to him in character. "How now, good sir?"

"God ye good den, Anne Whateley, tap mistress of the Inn Yard Tavern," Willie responded, and the Faire-speak came easily to him.

"I thought mayhap I'd ne'er see thee again," Anne said.

Willie nodded thoughtfully. "Marry, I feared me the selfsame thing. And yet, here I am." He bowed to her, sweeping the foolish cuckold's coxcomb from his head with a jingle.

They both watched as a woman, obviously a Faire patron, walked by in a pointy, peaked princess hat with silk flowing from the top.

Anne laughed. "How out of period is *that*?"

"Anne," said Willie. He took a deep breath, and he looked steadily into her eyes. "I want to do the right thing."

Anne cocked her head. "What do you mean?"

"Only if you want to. Entirely your call. But if you do...if you want a father—unworthy me—around in any way...I'm saying, we could get married."

Anne stood for a moment, stunned. When a sound finally came, it was an involuntary laugh. She quickly covered her mouth with her hand. "Oh, oh, I'm so sorry, I didn't mean to laugh, but...ohmigod, that's so sweet. But...Willie..."

She put her hand on his arm gently. "I had an abortion last month. This isn't the fucking Middle Ages, thank God."

"Oh," Willie stammered, "I—I'm sorry. Okay—"

"I'm sorry, I would've talked about it with you but I didn't know where to find you—"

"I'm sorry, I should have—"

Anne stopped him. "No. That's okay. Thanks. I mean, *thank you*, Willie."

"My name is Will," Willie said, surprised to hear himself say so. "I'm going by Will, now."

"Okay," she chirped, then nodded up the hill toward actors' camp. "Hey, I'm filthy. I was going to go grab a shower. You wanna join me, Will?"

Willie remembered the giggles coming from the shower the night before. He felt the familiar call from his groin.

"Tempting," said Willie. "But, no, thanks. I should get back to Berkeley before it gets too late."

Anne pouted, mock-miserably. "Boo."

"It's nothing personal," Willie said. "But as long as we're not walking down the aisle anytime soon, I believe I have some issues to work out about women. I haven't dealt with my mother's death well," Willie said, and he couldn't quite believe that he was speaking honestly and openly about it. "So I've been trying to be something she said, instead of what she meant."

Anne was staring at him blankly. "And more prosaically," Willie continued—he hadn't even told this to Robin before—"my stepmom hit on me when I was sixteen."

"Wow," said Anne again, overwhelmed. But then she recovered. "Well, who can blame her? You were probably cute when you were sixteen."

They chatted a little more, and hugged and said awkward good-byes, and finally Anne said, "One last thing: if you ever find yourself in this situation again, 'Are you sure it was me?' is the exact wrong thing to say."

Willie went to where he'd left his backpack and duffel just before the mushroom hit; they sat undisturbed on their hay bale. He found a privy, wet and smelly after a day's use. To his senses, still heightened and sensitized from the mushrooms, it was almost unbearable. He held his breath, and changed out of his borrowed fool's costume, trying to keep from getting urine on either it or his jeans and t-shirt. He was tired, but determined to get back to Berkeley that night. He wanted to talk to Robin. He had so much to explain, and to apologize for.

There was nasty weekend traffic on US 101 through San Rafael, and an accident on I-80 headed into Berkeley. By the time he found a parking space on Webster Street it had been dark for a couple of hours. He saw faint light flickering in Robin's second-story window. The security gate was ajar. He ran up the stairs to her apartment. The door was unlocked. He opened it and went in.

Bill, the president of the Committee to F$¢K Reagan, said, "Oh, shit," and quickly rolled off of Robin onto the couch.

Robin pulled a skimpy dress over her naked lap with one hand, and put a trembling hand to her forehead. "Get out. You were supposed to be back *yesterday!*"

Willie stood silent as his stomach dropped to the floor. Then, his voice quavering but controlled, he said, "I'm sorry I lied."

Robin helplessly shook her head, a look of utter confusion and rage on her face as tears welled in her brown eyes. "Get OUT!!!!"

He turned, walked out, and closed the door. As he stumbled down the stairs, the stinging in his own eyes resolved into tears, just as though he had been slapped in the face.

Chapter Forty-four

*Adherents of literary New Criticism are quick to separate the works
of the Bard from the historical Shakespeare and his political, social,
and personal context. But Shakespeare's genius as a storyteller must
be at least partly attributable to his very real-life experiences. Why,
for example, dissociate the adulterous sexuality, the pain, the longing,
and the homoeroticism of "the poet" in the sonnets from Shakespeare's
known or deduced real-life experiences with an older woman, a dark
lady, and a fair youth? The examination of the events and emotions
that made Shakespeare Shakespeare not only illuminates his work, but
it illuminates ourselves; and that, surely, is the ultimate goal of both
literature and literary criticism.*

William opened the costume trunk and carefully removed the pieces for his
role as the cuckolded husband in *The May Girl*. The scent of musty fabric
brought back the day, six months earlier, when he had hidden in the very
same trunk and, with the assistance of the Burbages, escaped Sir Thomas
Lucy's raid on his wedding and left Stratford—he thought forever.

But now the Earl of Leicester's men found themselves again in Stratford-
upon-Avon. They were engaged to perform at the town's Whitsunday pageant. And William was with them. It was a stunning spring morning, with
the scent of dewy grass, primroses, and daffodils in the air and fluff from
the first dandelions floating across an electric blue sky. There was a quiet
shuffling in the tiring-house as the players prepared to go on. William
listened with half an ear to another group on stage: Davy Jones was mangling his way through the dire and dour arhythms of Anthony Munday's
The Death of Robin Hood. William noted with a smile that at least Arthur
Cawdrey's jolly Friar Tuck seemed to be getting a few good laughs.

Richard Burbage, lugging a basketful of props, elbowed William as he passed. "Taught you not your townsmen, during your days as a country schoolmaster, how to manage a line of verse?"

William smiled ruefully, "There is only so much to be done of a Whit-sunday, with the verse of a witless Munday."

Burbage laughed, "Ay, I hate Mundays."

As William turned his attention back to his costume, he saw a hesitant, drawn face peeking through the curtain at the back of the tiring-house. It was his wife, Anne.

"William?"

William had been dreading this moment. He had built a fort against its coming. Keeping his attention on the costume piece in his hand—which, he noted with embarrassment, was a pair of cuckold's horns—he said, "What ho, Mistress Shakespeare. How fares Henley Street? How does the dunghill grow?"

She ignored his long-planned barb, for she had long planned to let it pass.

"William, I beseech you, may we speak?"

William set down the horns and picked up his costume cloak, shaking out a wrinkle. He didn't respond.

Anne persisted. "I would have you meet your daughter." She pulled aside the curtain to reveal a newborn infant in swaddling clothes, waving its arms and spitting.

William came out from the tiring-house, and he looked at his newborn daughter, and then at Anne, and then at his daughter, and then at Anne. It was the twenty-ninth of May. His daughter had been baptized on the twenty-sixth. The fact that the corporation of Stratford-upon-Avon had booked the Earl of Leicester's Men to perform at its Whitsunday pageant was entirely coincidental.

"Her name is Susanna," said Anne.

"A Puritan name," said William.

"Verily," she said. "I would not have the one fruit of our barren bed be pluck'd untimely. But what's in a name?"

William tried but failed to look away from his baby girl, whose entire left hand was in her mouth. "What of my father, and my mother, and my kin, and my mother's kin?"

"Your mother, well enough. Though she hates your absence, the money you send adds warmth to her hearth. Your father, in slow decline; yet those days when he is himself, he is himself. Today he farted in church, where Mary had dragged him unwilling. I think she will not do so again. Gilbert and Joan are well, though Joan is subdued these past months."

William tried to cover the gigantic tug at his heart at the mention of Joan.

"As for your mother's kin..." Anne continued, but then she stopped.

"My mother's kin?"

"Edward Arden's gardener, Hugh Hall"—and she lowered her voice—"or Father Hugh Hall as all about know him, is arrested. Between his capture and that of John Somerville...it bodes not well for Master Arden. There is hope his wife, Mary, at least, may be spared the gallows."

William felt a gaping hole open in his chest, at the thought of wise Edward Arden and the kindly gardener-priest, cut open and quartered. He didn't let himself even think of beautiful Mary on the tree at Tyburn.

"William," said Anne, "I must, for mine own content, expound to you my thoughts and deeds upon the day of our wedding."

"What would you have me know," said William, "that I did not see in all its swollen fullness? The very taste of Debdale's seed?"

Anne bounced the baby in her arms and looked out over the archery range on the Avon's banks. On stage, the players finished declaiming Munday, and William felt a flash of hatred.

"I loved Robert Debdale," Anne said. "And had for years, ere you came to my bed. Robert was ever on fire for the Catholic cause. He burned—not so hot as John Somerville, yet he burned—to see all in Shottery worship as they would, for it was ever a Catholic town. He saw the evil that approached when no one else did, and went to Rheims, to be strong for us both...for my family...for the family we planned. In sooth, I loved him...and so long I waited, while he studied abroad...until I could bear it no longer. And there were you, in the flower of youth and quoting Ovid...ay me."

She stopped for a moment, and brushed back a tear and a laugh. On stage, Davy Jones's troupe had finished, and James Burbage belted out a prologue to *The May Girl*, and introduced its dumb show.

Anne collected herself. "I loved Robert Debdale, William, and was bitter beyond measure when I found that in his absence, and in my weakness, I had become quick with your child. He wept all the night he returned, all night and most of the next day. But it was less for my weakness, which he forgave me instantly, than for his own: for he had broken under torture. Yet all he spoke under duress, he did because he thought to save both himself and me, and thus secure our future. So, he spoke of the Ardens, and the Shakespeares, for he remembered your father from his days as bailiff, and knew him to be recusant."

"O damned treachery! What weakness and sinful pride—"

"Ay, with time's keen sight we may call it so. But who knows, what one will say when put to't upon the rack?"

William thought of his own weakness at Charlecote, and fell silent.

"They set him free," she continued, "but only on the promise of future betrayals. And when he found I was to marry, to William of the Shakespeare-Ardens—William Shakespeare whom, I gather, he suspected of trespass and incitement to uprising and many other things beside—and in a Catholic rite, with many of the Old Faith there assembled—"

"I know how this tale ends," William interrupted. "All comedies end with a wedding; my wedding ended with a tragedy."

"I know not what to say, but if this will mend: I am most truly sorry."

"What of your true lover now?" William asked. "What of Robert Debdale?"

Anne shrugged, pale and cold as a tower. "Gone again. Arrested, I fear; if not yet, then soon. He was only let free long enough to lead the hunt to the Ardens—to our wedding," Anne said, and she began to cry. William comforted her, and took Susanna when she, too, began to cry.

After a minute, Anne gathered herself. "William ... I know you love Ovid. So against this day, I too have learnt lines, though not of my own composing, and which my tongue hath no skill to deliver. I will say them but from my heart, if you will hear them?"

"I will hear them with the same organ whence they are offered."

Anne looked as though she was about to begin, but then she laughed through her tears, "I am sore afraid, for you are a player, and a poet."

"And the father of thy child, and I am told, too gentle when giving direction. I will not berate your performance. Speak, and but suit the feeling to the word."

Anne took a breath, and soberly she said:

> *"There Baucis and Philemon liv'd, and there*
> *Had liv'd long marry'd, and a happy pair:*
> *Now old in love, though little was their store,*
> *Inur'd to want, their poverty they bore,*
> *Nor aim'd at wealth, professing to be poor.*
> *For master, or for servant here to call,*
> *Was all alike, where only two were all.*
> *Command was none, where equal love was paid,*
> *Or rather both commanded, both obey'd."*

Anne looked at William without irony or rancor, and William looked back.

At that moment Susanna gurgled, a deep-throated gurgle of the type only infants and hanged men can muster.

"Would you raise her in the Old Faith?" William asked.

Anne replied, "I would have *us* raise her in the Old Faith."

William reached out tentatively and stroked the infant's cheek as gently as he could with the back of one finger, and even that seemed rough and rude. "Were I to raise her in a faith, it would be a new faith indeed," William said, half to himself. "Anne, I have seen things. Things I do not yet in full measure understand. But I will not raise a child, yours, mine, or ours, in a faith that preaches love to its own but murder unto others; and so, it seems, do all faiths."

Anne smiled faintly. "What faith, then, would you have your child learn?"

William thought for a long, long, time, and he stroked Susanna's cheek, and she didn't cry.

"I would teach her," he began, "faith that her world will be better than ours, and in this life, not the afterlife. I would teach her that there will come a time when she might herself ascend the stage as a player without shame. A day when doctrine is debated, but not a cause for murder. A day when there is no subject so sacred or serious that it may not bring laughter. A day when races of east, west, north, and south vie not, but live and work together, and yet may jest upon each other, for laughter's sake, and without offense. A day when bubbling, fruity drinks with hints of plum and anise are served from seeming bottomless taps. A day when physic is given not only to heal the sick, but to enlighten the quick.

"And," he said, picking up his giggling daughter, Susanna, and flicking a finger at her nose, "a day when plays by Will Shakespeare of Stratford-upon-Avon are played still, and all know them, and scholars study them, and writers expound upon their themes: a legacy and an intimation of immortality that might outlast even thee, my daughter."

He held Susanna up and kissed her.

"She looks like you," Anne said.

"Nay, she is too fair," William replied. "I see your face in hers."

On stage, *The May Girl* had begun in earnest. There came a call from the tiring-house.

"Will!" said Richard Burbage, and a moment later he leaned out from the tiring-house curtain wearing long lashes and a dress. "Your time is come! To the point, to the point!"

"I needs must go," said William.

"I know it well. And yet though you go for a time, may you not also stay where three generations of your family reside—stay in spirit, if not in body?"

"What you propose...it would not be a simple life."

Anne managed a pained smile. The darkness in the depth of her deep blue eyes was that of Robert Debdale. "What life is?"

"There is a woman of the Queen's court with whom I am in love; hopelessly, I fear. And there is a youth—" William said. But then he shook his head. "But of that I dare not speak. In short, I will be much of the year in London, where my weakness finds many temptations, both dark and fair, to further weakness."

Anne thought for a moment. "For the sake of our child, and your mother and father of whom I have become most fond, and in respect of your wandering craft, I would condescend to keep warm your second-best bed. But not the third. There, I draw a line."

William laughed softly. "Your honesty pierces sharp as Cupid's arrows."

"Will! Your cue!" came a frantic call from the tiring-house.

As William leapt up the stairs and donned his cloak, he said, "We leave for the Continent in a fortnight, for a three-month tour. Will you believe me when I say I shall think on't?"

"Ay," said Anne. "I take you at your word."

Will made his entrance as the cuckolded husband...just a fraction of a second late.

Chapter Forty-five

I cannot blame thee for my love thou usest;
But yet be blam'd, if thou thyself deceivest
By wilful taste of what thyself refusest.
I do forgive thy robb'ry, gentle thief,
Although thou steal thee all my poverty;
And yet, love knows, it is a greater grief
To bear love's wrong than hate's known injury.
　　Lascivious grace, in whom all ill well shows,
　　Kill me with spites; yet we must not be foes.

—Sonnet 40

It was two weeks before the end of the spring quarter at UC Santa Cruz when Willie knocked on Clarence Welsh's office door, and entered.

Sitting at Welsh's desk was Dashka.

"Come on in," she said, without making eye contact. She riffled through a stack of papers on Welsh's desk, pulled out a bound manuscript, and leaned forward in the chair to hand it to Willie.

Squee.

Willie looked at the cover of the paper. Scrawled in red Sharpie across the top in Clarence Welsh's hurried hand was:

"Never was such a sudden scholar made!"
Excellent. See me re: possible publication.

"Congratulations," said Dashka. "You're a master of arts."

Willie continued to stare at the paper for a moment, without any of the joy or triumph he'd expected to feel. It all seemed so academic.

He nodded, flipping though Welsh's page notes, which were mostly of the "good" and "well put" variety. He had written "quote here?" in a couple of places early on, but then stopped.

"Both the professor and I really liked it. A historical explication of Shakespeare as the first modern playwright. And I loved the citation from *Gilligan's Island*. Ballsy. But it worked."

"Thanks."

"The section about Hamlet's family dynamic was awesome. And where on earth did you get the idea to use Anthony Munday's *Robin Hood* as a counterpoint to Shakespeare's genius?"

Willie couldn't remember whether it was something he had researched or whether it came to him in a costume trunk. "I honestly don't recall."

"Well, you really got inside Shakespeare's head. Good job. It got me thinking, maybe I should do more of a historical take for my dissertation. *The War of the Roses: History, By Any Other Name*."

"Sounds good," he said, without looking at her, and headed for the door. "Good luck."

Her voice stopped him. "Willie, wait."

Willie turned and looked straight into the depths of her eyes. "I'm going by Will these days."

She said, "I'm really, really sorry if I hurt you."

"Okay," said Willie.

"I wanted to explain what happened."

"Okay."

"Robbie—he's the guy you saw me with at the Faire...we're not together. We never were."

"This makes me *very* curious how you define 'together.' If a blowjob isn't 'together,' fine, but what about sex in the back seat of a bus? Is that 'together,' or—"

"Stop it. Come on, you and I had been involved for, what, like, three days?"

"Long enough for you to somehow rat me out to the DEA."

"Oh my god...Willie...Will...that wasn't me. Robbie was already informing on your friend Todd."

Willie shook his head. "What?"

"I hadn't seen him for three years until that night in the pastures. We dated when I was in high school. He was older, and I was...well, he had all the power. And when I saw him, he still did. Like an addiction, you know? Five years clean and then one fix, bam. You know how it can be, you don't always do the smartest thing...in relationships."

She shook her head, as if shaking a spider out of her hair. "Ugh! Anyway, the next night, the night before the jitney ride, he called me. At first, he was all cagey about what he was up to. He said he was working in 'law enforcement,' but he wouldn't say what. He asked if I wanted to go to the Ren Faire with him that Saturday, because something cool and big that he was involved with was going down. I like the Faire. And I had no idea you were going to be there. You didn't tell me you were going."

"That still doesn't explain why you were fucking me in the back seat of the bus while he was sitting in the front."

"He told me he was 'casing' someone. Said I shouldn't acknowledge him. I should have figured it out. Later, at the rally, it occurred to me he *might* be a narc, but before that...I don't know, I was all messed up over him, I had a crush on you, it was all just...well, it was very intense. But you've got to believe me, I didn't know he was following you. It didn't even occur to me that you were selling drugs. I thought he was following the bus driver!"

Willie thought about it for a minute. The details fit together.

"So...where's your friend now?"

"I have no idea. We went out once, but he's turned into a Reaganite fuckhead. He kept calling, but I told him to fuck off months ago."

Dashka put a hand on Willie's arm. "I am so, so, sorry."

Willie was still angry, and hurt, and he knew he had no right to be because he had been at least as hurtful: to Robin, to Dashka, to Anne. He looked out the window, past the stacks of the *Journal of Shakespearean Studies*, at the redwoods and a flash of the Pacific gleaming in the afternoon sun of Monterey Bay. It was a perfect spring Wednesday—if one followed the Gregorian calendar decreed by Pope Gregory in the fall of 1582. In Protestant, Elizabethan Stratford, it would have been Whitsunday.

Willie took a deep breath, and let it go. He looked at Dashka. And this time he saw that she was not just a hot chick, but smart, vulnerable, sad, and, he thought, a little bit tired.

Willie shrugged. "To be fair, I did have a girlfriend that I didn't tell you about."

"Hey...yeah!" she said, mock perplexed. "What was up with that?"

"That was me being a total fuckup."

Dashka laughed. "At least you were a sensitive, intelligent fuckup. There are men out there who are a lot worse."

"But presume not that I am the thing I was, for God doth know, so shall the world perceive, that I have turn'd away my former self."

"*Henry the Fourth, Part Two*," Dashka cited. "So...what's done is done?"

"Ay, Lady Macbeth," Willie cited her back. "What's done is done."

Dashka nodded toward the paper in Willie's hand. "So, what next? Ph.D.?"

Willie laughed. "Oh, no. Dad wears the tweed in the family."

"What're you going to do?"

"I'm already doing it. There's this comedy troupe—Shakespeare, mostly, with a subversive political twist. They're touring Europe, and one of them can't go. They asked me to join."

"Not Short Sharp Shakespeare?"

"You know them?"

"They're hysterical. That's terrific! What a great experience. You'll finally get to whip out all those speeches you memorized." Then Dashka asked too casually, "And what about your girlfriend in Berkeley? Are you still with her?"

Willie wasn't quite sure how to answer this. He had sent Robin at least a dozen letters in the past six months. He'd gotten one pained reply.

"I'm working on it."

"You want to be with her?"

"There's a lot of water under that bridge. But I don't know if it's enough to put out the fire. Maybe we'll forgive and forget...or maybe just conclude."

Dashka shrugged. "As for you forgiving her, you managed it okay with me just now. And if she needs to forgive you..." She flashed her mischievous smile. "Just quote some Shakespeare for her. And if that doesn't work, you can quote the Bard to me, anytime."

"Okay." Willie laughed. "But just so you know, I'm going to be extremely cautious about getting high with you and your friends again."

Willie walked out, but then poked his head back in the door. "Hey, how's the professor doing?"

"He's okay. He's going to serve three days on weekends over the summer. The university's being cool. He'll teach in the fall."

"Good," Willie said. André was free, too, but Todd, despite Willie's substantial contribution to his legal fund, hadn't been so lucky. He would be out in two years.

"Good?" Dashka said. "I can't believe he went to jail for some pot."

"It could be worse," said Willie, thinking of Edmund Campion. "At least we don't live in the fucking Middle Ages."

Will sat at a corner table in a seedy bar with the rest of the troupe before the last show of the tour, in Verona. As the others drank and laughed and cursed about the minutiae of the afternoon's performance, he twiddled his lucky sixpence in one hand and scribbled on a sheet of paper with the other.

"What's that?" asked one.

"Next year's income, I hope," said another.

"Poetry," said Will.

"An Ode to My Willy," said the first again with a snicker.

Will shook his head. "Not comedy. A sonnet," he said. Then softly to himself, "For the woman I love."

The company laughed and hooted. "Which one?" they said in unison, and then laughed more, that they had said it in unison.

Will smiled thoughtfully. He finished writing the last line. "You tell me," he said, and read the poem aloud:

"Where idle weed and thorny rose do seek
To suck a common provender of light,
The creeping weed, unwholesome in his reek,
Will spread, and stunt the well-trimm'd bush's height.
Apothecaries then will physic give:
Sweet potions urge the rose's sap to rise,
Its buds to bloom, and verdancy revive,
While sudden poison seals the weed's demise.
Yet some gard'ners are in nature's craft so bold
To fire the weed, increasing rose's beauty

By coaxing growth anew from cinders cold.
I would, for my rose, thus express love's duty.
   My sorry leaves I'll burn; the ash of me
   Will feed the soil, that I might grow in thee."

The events I've described as having taken place in 1582 are a pastiche of fact, legend, and surmise. My main goal was to tell a ripping yarn, but I also wanted, as much as possible, to make the Bard's story at least historically *plausible* in its larger points, and not contradict the historical record. At this I surely failed; like Willie Greenberg, I am no scholar. But there are also a few points where I knowingly tweaked the facts, and I want to confess those here.

Although Warwickshire legend does tell that young Shakespeare was whipped for poaching deer in Thomas Lucy's park, there is no suggestion that he was ever racked there. I doubt that Lucy kept a torture chamber in his laundry room, but he was certainly a rabid anti-Catholic who profited from being on the mightier side of the day's culture wars. Thankfully, Lucys of a gentler variety now reside at Charlecote. One can, for a few quid donated to the National Trust, still visit their laundry room and imagine the weight of Sir Thomas's great shirt-press applied to one's very own chest.

I've borrowed a detail or two from Thomas Cottom's execution and transposed them to the account of Edmund Campion's. These are minor, having mostly to do with Anthony Munday's (equally unsavory) roles at the two events.

William Shakespeare and Anne Hathaway applied for their marriage license on Saturday, November 27, not the following Monday as I've described.

Most egregiously, the story anticipates the arrests of John Somerville, Edward Arden, his wife, Mary, and the hidden priest Hugh Hall. These actually took place in late 1583, a year after the marriage of William and Anne. I hope this will be forgiven in a tale that depends upon the bending of time for its effect. Placing the arrest of the Ardens at William's wedding was a fiction I simply couldn't resist. The end result, at any rate, was the same: Edward Arden was hanged, drawn, and quartered on December 20,

1583. His nephew John Somerville, scheduled to meet the same fate on the same day, was found the night before, mysteriously hanged in his cell. Father Hugh Hall—who testified against Arden—was set free. So was Mary Arden.

I should also mention that while the physical world of northern California in the 1980s is real—Willie's on-campus housing, Robin's apartment, and the spot (now marked with a monument to free speech) where Willie took in the rally on Sproul Plaza can be found almost as easily as the Shakespeares' house in Henley Street—the events that take place there, and the characters who inhabit it (even those with recognizable names) are fictional. This is certainly the case with my placing the Renaissance Faire at Black Point so late in the year as October—that happened only once that I recall, due to rain, and it was not in 1986.

Interview with Jess Winfield

1. What was your inspiration to write this novel with dual timelines and dual protagonists?

I've always wanted to tell a tale revolving around Shakespeare's life in 1582, a year that was extraordinary in both his biography and in the ongoing negotiation between politics and religion in Western culture. At the same time, I wanted to portray Shakespeare as a living, breathing, sensual, and all-too-human young man, rather than the pedestal-bound bust he's become in our cultural consciousness. It occurred to me that creating a more contemporary doppelgänger for the Bard could create an entry point that even the biggest Bardophobe could get a handle on. I also found that the dual timelines allowed me to portray, through the protagonists' differing options and choices, both how far Western civilization has come in four hundred years—and how much further it has still to go.

2. You went to Santa Cruz and Berkeley and joined a three-man Shakespeare troupe just like Willie Greenberg, so he's your alter ego, right? Was your relationship with your stepmother as . . . um . . . intimate as you portray Willie and Mizti's in chapter twenty?

Willie is not nearly as autobiographical as some readers have assumed—and my dear stepmom, were she still alive, would be truly shocked by your second question! Willie and I share memories of some of the same places and types of characters, but there are many, many differences in our pathology. Willie is the only child of a widowed Berkeley professor. I was one of three children raised by a single mom, a freelance writer in Southern California. Willie grew up in Berkeley and then did graduate study at UC Santa Cruz. I passed through UCSC as a freshman, then attended Berkeley, but I was never a graduate student anywhere. I did spend quite a bit of time on that library jitney, but sadly, I never had sex on it. It's funny, no one ever asks if the character of *William* is in any way autobiographical. Yet he and Willie face many of the same universal issues that I wanted to explore. How does one move past a dysfunctional childhood, mend or move on from broken relationships, get out of a crappy job/school/house, and make something meaningful out of life?

3. *Was it difficult coming up with parallels for the two stories?*

If anything, I had to resist the temptation to flood the narrative with too-clever mirrorings. At first I spent a lot of time trying to make the two stories exactly parallel, but then I realized that there was little point in telling the same story twice. That breakthrough allowed the two plots to develop as their own dictates demanded . . . as long as they intersected at the points where they had to intersect. The bigger problem was dealing with the two narratives textually. Because of the back-and-forth chapter structure, if I wanted to move, delete, split, or combine chapters in one timeline, it meant I had to move, delete, split, or combine chapters in the other one as well, often against my will (no pun intended). I hope I've smoothed out the resulting seams so that the reader doesn't see them; but even the inattentive may notice one fairly obvious cheat in the back-and-forth construction.

4. *Were you worried that one timeline would be more compelling than the other? That people might skip one set of chapters in favor of the other?*

Constantly. Willie Greenberg has a lot to measure up to as a coprotagonist with William Shakespeare. But that's part of what the story's about: before any of us can become a Shakespeare, we have to overcome convictions of our own inadequacy; and it helps to have a role model. At eighteen, Shakespeare didn't know who he would become; neither does Willie at twenty-six. I think of them as approximately equal in emotional development, with William perhaps a bit ahead. He is at least working to help support his family. But what I didn't expect was that readers would cut Shakespeare so much slack simply *because* he was Shakespeare. For example, more than one reviewer noted that Willie uses quotes from Shakespeare to seduce women. But no one seemed to have a problem with William using Ovid for the same nefarious purposes. My hope is that readers will take Willie and William on equal footing; after all, Willie may actually become the next Bard.

5. *What is your writing process? Do you outline? Do you write every day? Did you write the story in a linear fashion, or focus on one timeline before tackling the other one?*

My writing process varies depending on the project I'm working on. Once I had the idea to do the dual timeline structure for this book, I spent a couple of months just doing research. Then one night I was (pardon the overshare, but it's true) standing at the urinal during intermission of a Beethoven concert when the first three paragraphs of the book flashed through my mind. You never know where inspiration will strike. I began writing pages the next day. I completed the first chapter of each timeline to see if it was any fun. I showed them to a few people, who encouraged me to continue. I then set aside the two chapters and spent months outlining and researching the rest of the story. When I went back to writing the narrative, I did so in linear fashion, switching from one timeline to the other just as the reader does. I think this was wise, as it kept me from getting bored with either of the two characters. And no, in contravention of all the Rules of Writing Fiction, I don't write every day. I write when I have something to say or have a deadline, whichever comes first.

6. *You lived in California in the 1980s, so that was probably easier to write than the chapters set in 1582. What research did you do for the Elizabethan chapters?*

I actually researched both stories fairly extensively. Although I did live in Santa Cruz and Berkeley in the 1980s, I was there a half-decade earlier than Willie. So I had to do plenty of checking up on 1986: what songs were on the radio, what books and theories were in academic vogue, what were the dates of battles in the War on Drugs, and the like. I also went back to Santa Cruz, visiting the cow pastures below Cowell College with my very tolerant wife in the wee hours of a chilly October morning, to make sure that Willie could see the stars I said he could see in chapter three. I did a lot of research about political and religious developments of the sixteenth century, research that yielded great characters like Anthony Munday, John Somerville, and Robert Debdale. But it was the feet-on-the-ground, on-site research that was the most edifying.

Two examples: when I went to Sproul Plaza to fact-check for the scene where Willie is arrested at the rally, I already had in my mind's eye an idea of where he was standing. I went to that spot, and found myself standing on something bumpy. I looked down and was delighted to see the monument to free speech mentioned in the Afterword . . . it had been installed there since my own time at Berkeley. I also prowled around the Bard's haunts in and around Stratford-upon-Avon for a week or so. Rather than hiring a car, I rented a bicycle, trying to get a feel for what the distances would be like when covered on foot or by donkey cart. I cycled from Stratford to Charlecote, where I was thrilled to find Thomas Lucy's laundry room—I had originally set the scene of William on the rack in a generic outbuilding, but the laundry room provided a much richer array of implements of torture. But my favorite bit of research was strictly, geekily, literary. When I wrote the scene of William improvising a pageant of *Salmacis and Hermaphroditus*, I had three texts side by side on my desk: the original Latin (like Willie and William before him, I have "little Latin"), a modern translation, and the 1567 English translation by Arthur Golding that Shakespeare would likely have been familiar with. I tried to create a text approximating what Shakespeare might have extemporized: mostly the Golding version, but with a few twists of phrase from the Latin that might have stuck in his head . . . and a phrase or two where he thought both might be improved upon. Yes, I'm afraid that's my idea of a good time.

7. *How did you approach the challenge of creating dialogue for the Elizabethan characters—especially William Shakespeare himself? Was that daunting?*

Yes! I nearly didn't make it past the first line of Shakespeare's dialogue. But then I remembered, he's not Shakespeare yet, just a kid with a literary bent stuck in a meaningless job, and I've been there. That took some of the pressure off. The dialogue in the William chapters I wrote to sound approximately, but not authentically, Elizabethan. I didn't want to scare off readers who have difficulty with Shakespearean language. I dropped the "est"s and "eth"s on second- and third-person present verbs, and changed the Elizabethan "thee"s and "thou"s to "you"s almost universally—only using the familiar second person when a character is denigrating someone of a lower class (as in Thomas Lucy's interrogation of William—although he switches back to a more obsequious "you" when he's playing "good cop"). That helpeth readability a lot, believest thou me! But otherwise, I tried to use strictly Elizabethan vocabulary. I would search the *Complete Works* for any word I thought questionable, to see if Shakespeare had used it. Despite all my care, an attentive reader did catch me using one word that wasn't coined until the eighteenth century: "dramaturgy."

8. *The characters, especially the Renaissance Faire types (such as Jacob, the King of the Fools), seem so real. Are they based on real people?*

Unlike Willie, who is an outsider, I spent quite a bit of time working at Renaissance Faires, so there are a few select characters there who appear more or less "as themselves." I, for example, make a cameo as a member of the "Short Sharp Shakespeare" troupe . . . I'm the "balcony," the one with my head up Juliet's dress. But most of them are composites. The King of the Fools and the Fools Guild are both real, but Jacob is a combination of various Kings I've known over the years—they elect a new one every year. I should say that no King, to my knowledge, has been either a drug dealer or a chess champion.

9. *Were any characters in the story inspired by characters in Shakespeare's plays?*

There are echoes of various Shakespeare characters in both timelines. I often thought of Willie as starting out as Hamlet (hence his recurring dream) but saving himself from a tragic ending, and maturing into more of a Prince Hal. I imagined the blustery John Shakespeare as the Bard's inspiration for Falstaff (witness the False-staff reference in chapter ten). Identifying the robed, drug-dispensing academic Clarence Welsh with the robed, drug-dispensing Friar Laurence was of course intentional. Willie's father and stepmother, with their o'er-hasty marriage, are a sort of mirror image of Claudius and Gertrude in *Hamlet*—though I confess they also owe a bit to Bill S. Preston's dad and stepmom in *Bill and Ted's Excellent Adventure*. And one of my favorite characters, poor little Joanie Shakespeare, grew out of nowhere to become a Goth version of Juliet. That came about when I noticed that in the crucial year of 1582, she, like Juliet in the play, was a very vulnerable thirteen-year-old: too young to be married, and certainly too young to be having babies.

10. Why did you have the scene of Campion's execution related by a third party (Richard Field) rather than have William witness it firsthand?

From a strictly technical standpoint, I would have had to contrive a reason to get William to London, which would have been awkward. Alternatively, I could have had an execution take place in Stratford's own Market Square, as they likely did, but I wanted to give the impression of the troubles of distant London slowly creeping toward isolated, provincial, and largely idyllic Warwickshire. And in the end, I'm very pleased with the secondhand account coming from Richard Field. There is a layer of pathos added to an emotionally disturbing story by having a messenger recount it. It's a technique that was used often in Greek drama—Oedipus blinding himself, Medea's poisonings, and Antigone's suicide all take place offstage—and I figured if it was good enough for Aeschylus and Sophocles, it's good enough for me. It worked so well, in fact, that I'm using the device more extensively in my next novel.

11. You had two other careers before you became a novelist. How did your experiences in the Reduced Shakespeare Company and at Disney TV Animation help or hinder you in writing this novel?

Aside from forcing me to gain an improv-quick familiarity with the *Complete Works*, performing my own written material on stage helped develop my sense of comic timing, and especially of an audience's attention span. I learned to keep things moving (maybe you've noticed my chapters are quite short!).

As a screenwriter at Disney, I was a wordsmith working in the most visual of mediums: animation. An animation script is intended to help storyboard artists *see* what's in your head. So I was continually pushing my writing to be more visual . . . a good thing in a novel. And of course, writing a few dozen half-hour scripts was great for practicing the writing of dialogue. Especially applicable to this novel was the work I did on a cartoon version of *A Midsummer Night's Dream*, starring Mickey and Minnie Mouse and Donald and Daisy Duck as the four lovers and Goofy as Puck. I tried to use Shakespearean dialogue wherever possible, and it helped me to develop the pseudo-Elizabethan (but, I hope, still-accessible) style I used in *My Name Is Will*.

12. You mention in the Afterword that you "egregiously" tweaked the historical record for the ending. At what point do you decide to veer from historicity for the sake of storytelling? And do you feel that doing so diminishes the novel in any way?

I was perhaps a little hard on myself in the Afterword. I claimed not to be a scholar, but I feel confident in my knowledge of the comings and goings of various priests, nobles, Shakespeares, and theater troupes in and around Stratford in 1582. I'm proud of the fact that I knowingly made only three changes, and only one large one. The first, regarding the day on which William Shakespeare and Anne Hathaway were granted their wedding license, was done to avoid having characters sit around for a week between the Sunday of William and Rosaline's act of civil disobedience at Lucy's gate (it had to be a Sunday; William's absence from his job would have been noted on any other day) and William's being dragged by the ear to Worcester. The second, my combining small details of Edmund Campion's and Thomas Cottom's executions, was to me worthwhile in order to fully realize the nasty character of Anthony Munday. And my "egregious" change, moving John Somerville's madness and Edward Arden's subsequent arrest forward by a year, to coincide with the Shakespeare's wedding, was essential. It was the ending the story demanded, and I vividly remember my thrill the day the plot point came to me. When strict historicity works as storytelling, that's fine and fun. But this is a novel—fiction, not history—and the success of the story on its own terms must be paramount.

13. The story seems to promote drug use. Do you condone the use of illegal drugs?

No. But neither do I condemn it. As the crusty jitney bus driver suggests, people get high, always have, always will, so legislating against it seems like a waste of time and potential tax dollars. Of course there are dangers to irresponsible drug use. Willie is stupid for getting stoned enough that it affects his driving in chapter twenty-four, and he's very lucky he doesn't end up in prison for it. The political firebrand Jeremy isn't so fortunate. But as the fictionalized Timothy Leary points out, the use of drugs, whether legal or illegal, in proper dosages and in controlled environments, can have lasting beneficial effects. And I think William made the right choice in giving his little sister his contraband vial. My stance is that drug use is as morally and ethically neutral as watching television or eating; all three can be detrimental to the individual mind and body and costly to society at large if done injudiciously.

14. We never actually see William write any of the plays that are credited to him in your book. Do you have a stand on the "Authorship Question"?

I don't stand on it; I jump up and down and scream bloody murder on it. There is in my mind no serious "question" regarding the authorship of the vast majority of Shakespeare's works. There is simply no hard evidence that anyone else wrote his plays. For a longer analysis of this, you can visit my Web site at www.jesswinfield.com and check my blog entry on the subject. Here, I'll just say that all arguments positing a different author or authors—Bacon, DeVere, Marlowe, whoever—begin with the proposition that Shakespeare couldn't have written the works attributed to him because he was an undereducated glover's boy from the country—a proposition rooted in intellectual class prejudice in its most insidious form. I know, there are some Great Minds (Freud, Einstein, Orson Welles, Derek Jacobi) who believe that someone besides the "Stratford boy" must have written the canon. I think those great minds should have stuck to psychoanalysis, physics, filmmaking, and acting, respectively, rather than positing which social castes can or cannot produce great dramatists. *My Name Is Will* suggests that everyone has an inner Shakespeare, and that a youth shaped by political and economic oppression, misspent in taverns among working people, "fighting, wronging the ancientry, and getting wenches with child" is more likely to bring forth a great artist than upper-class privilege and a university degree.

15. What's your favorite part about being a writer?

I love it when the narrative surprises me: when I get teary-eyed or laugh out loud at something that unexpectedly appears on the page; when characters take on a life of their own. Rosaline, for example, proved to be a most unruly creation. I conceived her to be merely one in a string of sexual conquests for William. She'd have none of it. When William was on his way back to Charlecote to nail up his satirical verse on Lucy's gate, I was as surprised as he was when that archer next to the river fired an arrow in his path, and it turned out to be Rosaline, rightfully pissed off at having been abandoned. The same is true for Dashka, who turned from evil temptress in Willie's relationship with Robin into a much more sympathetic character; whereas Robin, whom I originally imagined making an honest, responsible, politically aware man of Willie, well . . . I don't know if she's worthy of him.

16. The state of both Willie and Robin's relationship and William's marriage are left unresolved at the end of the book. And you mentioned your "next novel." Will it be a sequel to My Name Is Will?

I always envisioned *My Name Is Will* as the first part of a trilogy (that's my Tolkien fandom coming through). Part one would cover Willie and William as young men coming of age in their small towns and end with their heading off on theatrical adventure. Part two would show them at the height of their careers, men of the world. Part three would deal with their more reflective return home. But at the moment I'm working on another story altogether. It doesn't involve Shakespeare at all, though it does deal with his greatest contemporary: Cervantes. Keep an eye on www.jesswinfield.com for further details.

Discussion Questions

1. The narrator notes that "Will" has several different meanings. Which of those meanings are at work in the title of the book? How do each of the two protagonists relate to their name, and how does their attitude toward it change over the course of the story?

2. The "contemporary" narrative is actually set in 1986 rather than the present. How have sexual mores and the relationship between politics and religion changed since then? Has the United States become more or less like the book's portrayal of Elizabethan England? How might the story have changed if the contemporary story had been set in 2008 or 2009?

3. The two timelines in the story intersect in four places. Where are they? To what extent do the two stories merge in chapters forty-one and forty-two? How do the intersections affect Willie and William? What does each learn from the experience?

4. Aside from Willie and William, are there any characters in one timeline that have parallels or near-parallels in the other?

5. *My Name Is Will* has been optioned for a film adaptation. If you were casting a movie of this book, would you have the same actor play both Willie and William? Are there any other roles you'd double-cast?

6. The Fool is a recurring symbol in both Shakespeare's plays and in this book. What does it mean to be a Fool? Which characters in this book

seem Foolish to you, and to what extent are their Foolish choices rewarded or punished?

7. The relationships of Willie and William to their parents is a prominent element in the story. How do the advice, nurturing, and support (or lack thereof) that each protagonist receives from his family affect their development as young men?

8. How do you think Willie's journey through the different settings of UC Santa Cruz, Berkeley, and the Renaissance Faire reflects Willie's emotional and intellectual journey?

9. As the subtitle suggests, there is a lot of sex in the story. Do you find it gratuitous, or do you feel it supports the book's themes of self-discovery and interconnectedness? In what way do the passages about hermaphroditism—from the performance of *Salmacis and Hermaphroditus* to the digression about banana slugs—advance those themes? What about the Dashka-Willie-Kate threesome?

10. *Webster's* defines "hero" as "a man of distinguished courage or ability, admired for his brave deeds and noble qualities." It defines an "antihero" as "a protagonist who lacks the attributes that make a heroic figure, as nobility of mind and spirit, a life or attitude marked by action or purpose." Would you call Willie a hero or an antihero? What about William? Which of their actions or attitudes would you cite to defend your assessment?

11. The character of Willie seems to reach a low point in chapter twenty-four, when he wakes up after the threesome and enumerates the mistakes he's made so far. At that point he resolves to "Do it all. Right now. Today." How well does he succeed in his plan of action? Are there indications of change in his character from this point forward, or is he just the same old Willie?

12. Some readers have noted that the stakes in William's story are higher than in Willie's story. Willie certainly wouldn't have been hanged,

drawn, and quartered if that cop had found his pipe in chapter twenty-six. What do you think this says about the two different times in which the story takes place?

13. There are a number of quirky relationships in the story, from Robin and Willie's "don't ask, don't tell" arrangement to Mary and John's sharp-tongued ribbing of each other, to the odd couple of Alan and Mizti, to the marriage of convenience that Anne Hathaway offers William at the end. Do you think any of the relationships are successful or have a hope of lasting? Which ones, and why?

14. The novel ends somewhat ambiguously. Where and when do you think the final chapter takes place? Who do you think wrote the "Shakespearean" sonnet at the end? And to whom do you think it's written? Which, if any, of the women in the novel do you think Willie ends up with? What about William?

Acknowledgments

First I must thank Alexandra Sokoloff, Franz Metcalf, and Elaine Sokoloff for helping to nurture this story at every step from conception to completion. Only they know how much of their light illuminates my pages, and I am eternally and humbly grateful.

I am among the luckiest writers alive to have an agent as exemplary as the delightful Ellen Levine, an editor as smart and dedicated as Cary Goldstein, and a publisher as fresh and focused as Jonathan Karp and Twelve Books. I fancy myself a man of letters, but so many letters herein would have been wrong without the editorial prowess of Mari Okuda and Christine Valentine. I also fancy myself a man of Photoshop; for that, I hope Anne Twomey and Twelve's art department will forgive me.

The list of those kind or foolish enough to read parts or all of the early drafts is too long to list here, but some gave advice and/or encouragement above and beyond the call of friendship. For this I especially thank John Wray, as well as Kent Elofson, Dawn Rose, David Rose, Danica Lisiewicz, Nicole Roberts, Claire Martin, Rover, Shannon Wade, Nick Revell, Laura McLean, Douglas Pease, Thomas Scoville, Karen Dionne and backspace.org, Jeff Kleinman, Douglas Purgason, the Weissman family, Ob Askin, Jim Kelly, Nancy Gunn, and Erin Wallen. I'm indebted to my Reduced Shakespeare Company mates Adam Long and Daniel Singer for the spirit if not the details of the fictional Short Sharp Shakespeare; to Claire Asquith for the tantalizing explication of Sonnet 23 in her book *Shadowplay*; to Dr. Charles Mitchell of Loyola University for information about Elizabethan hangings; to Don Ashman for his assistance with my rusty Latin; and to Roxanne Hamilton, Jennifer Nickerson, Susi Nicholson, and the housing offices and graduate students of the University of California, Santa Cruz, for not having me arrested as I prowled their campus researching locations. Also thanks to Kevin Patterson, Mark Sellin, Dan McLaughlin, and

Jon DeCles for their assistance and contributions regarding various things Renaissance Faire.

Finally, I thank my wife, Sa. Everything they say about novelists and their obsessive late-night sneakings to the computer, scribblings in bed, and story-problem-related mood swings is true. Enduring them requires almost superhuman resources of love and patience, which she has in spades. Not only that, she read the book, and liked it.

As a founding member of the Reduced Shakespeare Company, JESS WINFIELD cocreated the full-length show *The Complete Works of William Shakespeare (abridged)*, which premiered at the Edinburgh Festival Fringe in 1987 and became an international sensation, leading to multiple world tours and engagements. After leaving the "other" RSC, Winfield spent ten years writing and producing award-winning cartoons for the Walt Disney Company. He left Disney three years ago to write this, his first novel. He lives in Los Angeles with his wife.

ABOUT TWELVE

TWELVE was established in August 2005 with the objective of publishing no more than one book per month. We strive to publish the singular book, by authors who have a unique perspective and compelling authority. Works that explain our culture, that illuminate, inspire, provoke, and entertain. We seek to establish communities of conversation surrounding our books. Talented authors deserve attention not only from publishers but from readers as well. To sell the book is only the beginning of our mission. To build avid audiences or readers who are enriched by these works—that is our ultimate purpose.

For more information about forthcoming TWELVE books, please go to www.TwelveBooks.com